Path Less Traveled

Amber Rainey

BLUE FORGE PRESS
Port Orchard ✶ Washington

To Kellan—
You are always in my heart.

Table of Contents

Path Less Traveled

Amber Rainey

Among the Stars

million tiny points of light glittered in the dark night sky. Every few minutes, brilliant streaks trailed across the sky, the meteors finding a dazzling end in the Earth's atmosphere. Below, a clearing sat covered in luminous white snow. Normally, the clearing would be black, one barely able to see a hand in front of their face, however, the snow leeched the light of the stars and cast an eerie glow upon Louisa. She stood, wiping the snow from her dress and peered up at the sky, smiling as another comet met its demise. Louisa sighed, shaking off the feeling of dread creeping up her spine. Matthew would not be happy if he found out she had come to the clearing alone. She had to hurry to return home before he arrived.

As she walked, Louisa marveled at the silence surrounding her. The snow padded her steps. It was as if she wasn't even walking there. The trees stood as sentinels to her transgression. There was no wind and the branches of each tree were dusted with blankets of white. She marveled at how the landscape was transformed by winter. She hated the winter. It was beautiful but miserable. The first snowfall was always an omen of the bitter wind to follow. The wind howled through the mountain passes and bit at her cheeks when she was forced to go outside for her chores. Only the promise of the meteor shower could have brought her out into the cold.

The only reason she stayed in this godforsaken land was Matthew. She'd been a wild spirit, desperate to remain untamed until she'd met him. She hadn't wanted to go to the dance, but her older brother had called her an aging nag and she went out of spite. Louisa never minded that she might one day be a matronly, spinster aunt but she could not resist proving her brother wrong. He taunted her endlessly, going as far as plucking a gray hair out of her head and parading it around the house. She just couldn't let him get the best of her. So, she had gone to the dance and met a shy logger, visiting his sister in the city in order to see his first nephew.

She'd caught Matthew's dumbfounded staring when she'd gone to the punch bowl. He stood, open-mouthed, a drink halfway to his lips. The moment their eyes met, Matthew flushed a bright shade of red and closed his mouth, turning away. Louisa had giggled and chased after his retreating back.

"Sir?" she asked, placing a hand on his arm.

Matthew turned to face her. He scratched behind his ear, unable to meet her eyes. Louisa tipped her face under his until he looked up. She smiled and held out her hand in the manner of asking for a handshake rather than the proper introduction. Matthew's jaw dropped and she giggled again.

"I'm Louisa Nova," she said.

Matthew's shock wore off and he tentatively took her hand.

"N... nice to meet you, Miss... Ms," he struggled for the right words.

She nodded and shook his hand. "Miss. And you are?"

"Oh, Matthew Minett, at your service," he said as he bowed awkwardly with her hand still in his.

"You're new around here," she said.

He nodded. "My sister, she moved here several years ago when she got married. She just had a baby."

Louisa thought a moment. It wasn't a large town and she knew pretty much everyone. He must be talking about Sarah Benedict. Sarah had recently had a baby boy. Louisa had been to see the child and she had to admit, the smell of a newborn baby was one of her favorite things.

"Sarah Benedict? She's your sister?" she asked.

He nodded again. "Yes ma'am."

Louisa smiled. Just then a new song began playing. She grabbed Matthew's hand and led him towards the dance floor, without asking if he wanted to dance. He stood awkwardly on the dance floor, waiting for an explanation.

"This song is one of my favorites. Dance with me?" she asked.

"Do I have a choice?" he asked.

Louisa laughed and shook her head. Matthew shrugged and danced with her, as requested. He was a bit stiff and she did her best to lighten the mood. Overall, she enjoyed the dance so much, she kept him on the dance floor for three more songs until they were both in need of a breath of fresh air and rest.

Louisa touched her lips as she walked. That was the first night she had ever been kissed. The stars had not been as easy to see, the city lights drowning them out. It had been a warm night and they had gone for a stroll through the garden. She'd finally drawn Matthew out of his shell and at the end of the night, he had leaned down and kissed her lightly on the lips. Then, in true Matthew form, he'd stuttered out an apology for being so forward, escorted her back into the house and left with a blush.

Their courtship had been a quick one out of necessity. Matthew was a logger in the Cascade mountains and would be leaving to go back to his job. Louisa had been determined he was the one she had been looking for and convinced him she could leave the city life behind for the mountains. He'd been hesitant but Louisa was determined. She cajoled Sarah into helping her and eventually the two of them had worn Matthew down. Louisa knew Matthew's resistance was only fueled by concerns over taking her out of her comfortable life to a life of hardship. He could provide for her but he was often gone several nights at a time and would worry for her while he was away. Louisa shot down every argument he made until he admitted he would never be able to live without her.

The day Matthew brought her home to the little cabin, they had their first argument. Matthew had told her to pack light and Louisa swore she had tried but she'd still brought more things than they had room for in their home. Matthew made her go through the trunks with him, sorting through the items and determining if they could stay or if they would need to be sold at the trading post. Louisa swore the trading post pile was bigger than the keep pile. She argued desperately for each item but Matthew had the final say.

He pulled out her telescope and started to put it on the trading pile.

"Wait! Not that!" Louisa cried, jumping off the bed and trying to grab the instrument from Matthew.

"Why?" Matthew asked.

Louisa huffed, "It's mine. My father gave it to me and it is important."

Matthew looked into the wrong end and shrugged. "I think it's broken."

Louisa finally snatched it from him and looked down at it. She rubbed her sleeve over the eyepiece to clean the glass. Then she stood up and held it in front of Matthew's face with the proper orientation. He looked at her dubiously but shrugged when she just glared at him.

"Just look into it," she directed.

Matthew put his eye to the glass and squinted his other eye. He jumped a little and pulled back, looking at her. Louisa smiled proudly and gestured towards the telescope again.

Matthew looked through it again. He took it from her hands and moved it around, looking at the trees out the window.

"It brings things closer," he said.

Louisa nodded. "Yes, it brings the stars closer. It's a telescope."

Matthew thought a moment. "Not many stars to look at her, Louisa. The weather doesn't allow for it."

Louisa deflated. She was already losing the battle in her head. Truthfully, she would get rid of everything else she bought if he would let her keep the instrument. She knew it would be fruitless to tell him that detail. He was a practical man and would just dismiss her impulsiveness. Matthew handed the telescope to her and her jaw dropped in shock.

"Take it," Matthew said.

Louisa grabbed the telescope and hugged it to her chest. "You mean it?"

Matthew shrugged. "Could be useful one day."

Louisa threw her arms around him and kissed his cheek. He blushed and turned back to the trunk.

In the end, Matthew had been correct about all the stuff they had traded. Louisa had not needed any of it. Living in the mountains was much different than living in a city. There was no need for fancy underclothes or shoes. Boots were much more comfortable and practical. She loathed wearing skirts in the winter but she loved Matthew and if she wore pants it would cause a scandal. There were not a lot of women in the logging community where they lived but there were enough that Louisa was able to make some friends and have some company when Matthew was gone. They had settled into a good routine over the years and Louisa felt at home in the mountains. She was still terrified when the coyotes howled at night and Matthew endlessly teased her about bears, but she no longer felt like a duck out of water.

Louisa slowed her pace as the cabin came into view. A lone candle flickered in the window. She swallowed hard. She had not left a lit candle, for fear it would burn the house down. It meant only one thing, Matthew was already home. Louisa gulped a huge breath of air. He would be furious. His fury would not be unwarranted.

"Absolutely not!" Matthew shouted.

Louisa winced. He only ever raised his voice when it was the only way he could get her to stop talking over him. She had a bad habit of spewing out whatever came to mind and not truly listening to his answers. It was something she knew she needed to work on. She wrapped her arms around herself. Matthew's fury deflated.

"It's for your own safety," he said, trying to defend his position.

Louisa nodded. "I just wanted to see the meteors."

Matthew ran a hand over his face. "I know. I won't be here and you can't go out alone. You never know when the weather will change and we get another snowstorm. What if the coyotes caught you out?"

"I—" she knew he had won the argument but wasn't

ready to give up.

Matthew wrapped his arms around her. She hesitated for a moment but then gave in, inhaling his clean scent and the laundry soap on his shirt. She hated the nights he was away and she had thought if she made use of the unseasonably clear skies, the time would pass quicker.

"Please promise me you will stay in and stay safe. It's only three nights and then I will be home. If it is still clear, I will take you out to the clearing and you can show me all the constellations. Please promise me, Louisa," Matthew said, a pleading note in his tone.

Louisa pulled back and looked at his face. She could see the worry in his eyes. She knew he worried about her each time she was alone. He made extra trips to the woodpile before every trip and he'd taught her how to shoot a gun. He'd tried to calm her fears over the coyotes but he knew she did not sleep well until he was back home. Louisa put her hand on his face.

"I promise I will stay at home," she said.

Matthew searched her eyes and then nodded. He leaned down and kissed her hard. She closed her eyes, kissing him back, trying to reassure him. She loved him and she wanted him to focus on the dangers of his job instead of worrying about her. He pulled back and rested his forehead against hers. He squeezed her tight and she put her cheek against his chest. They stayed like that for a long moment before Matthew pulled away to finish packing his bag.

Louisa stopped just before she reached the door. She

took a deep breath and stepped onto the little porch. As she reached for the door, it opened and Matthew stood in the doorframe. He was silhouetted in the frame and she could not see his face.

"Matthew, I..." she tried to explain.

Matthew grunted and moved away from the door. Louisa followed him into the cottage. Matthew sat in a chair, his arms resting on his knees, his head hanging down. Louisa quietly shut the door and sat down next to him. She waited for him to say something. To yell or accuse or question her but he just sat, staring at the floor.

"Matthew, I'm sorry. I wasn't out for long. I was hoping I would get home before you and you would have never known. I was just going stir crazy and the weather had held and I couldn't see out the window clearly. The trees around our house are just too tall and it was just too lovely to miss and I took precautions—," Louisa blurted out.

Matthew looked up. Louisa's breath caught as she saw his face. It was full of sorrow and something she couldn't quite put her finger on. She reached out to touch him but he recoiled from her. She dropped her hand and stared at him intently.

"I loved you, Louisa. You knew that, right?" he asked.

Louisa cocked her head at the odd question, "What do you mean?"

Matthew ran a hand over his face, "You know I loved you?"

Louisa nodded, "Yes, I know you love me. I'm sorry I

broke my promise."

"None of that matters now, sweetheart," Matthew said sadly.

Louisa sat in stunned silence, still watching Matthew. She ran his words over in her head. She couldn't believe what she was hearing. Was he leaving her? Was he going to send her back to the city after the years they had been together?

"Matthew... you can't leave me," she pleaded.

Matthew shook his head. "I'm sorry, darling. It's too late."

"What?" Louisa cried. "It isn't! I'll do better. Please, Matthew."

Louisa threw herself at his feet and looked up at him. She tried to grab his arm and then pulled back in shock when her hand passed through his. She looked at her hand as if it belonged to somebody else. Then she looked up at Matthew, realization slowly dawning on her. Tears began streaming down her face.

Louisa shook her head in denial. "No, Matthew... you said this one was safer. You said it would be a quick job and then you would be home."

"Accidents happen, darling," Matthew responded.

"But, what am I supposed to do? Why are you here?" she asked.

Matthew sighed and looked up at the ceiling. She waited for him to gather his thoughts. She started pacing the room, her mind racing with the possibilities. She would have to go find the site manager and figure out how to get Matthew home for a proper burial. She would have to tell his sister. She was all alone now. Louisa glanced over at him and saw him make a decision. He stood wearily, running his hand over his face. He looked even more miserable than before if that was possible.

"We can't keep doing this," he said cryptically.

Matthew walked over to the door and opened it. For a brief moment, Louisa wondered how he could touch the door but she couldn't touch him. The wind blew in and the candle in the window was snuffed out. The only light was the meager glitter of the snow outside their cabin. It looked duller somehow as if the news Matthew had brought put a damper on its sparkle. Matthew watched as the emotions fluttered through her and then gestured to the door.

"Please, Louisa, come with me."

Louisa nodded and went out the door, waiting for him to close it and lead her to wherever it was they were going.

"I loved you, darling, but this is the only way to stop this. I can't keep doing this, night after night," Matthew said.

Louisa followed him around the cabin. She watched as he stopped around twenty yards from the woodshed. She couldn't see around him but her senses told her to dread this moment. She realized she was right to fear what Matthew was about to show her when he stepped aside and she could see a grave marker next to him. Her mind began racing, refusing to listen to him or its own memories. Matthew turned to her.

"I know you didn't mean to do it, Louisa. I know your

guilt keeps you coming back, night after night. I forgive you, sweetheart. You have to move on, for both our sakes," Matthew said.

Louisa recoiled in horror, slamming her hands over her ears.

Matthew continued, "This is torture for me. Seeing you and unable to help you. Please. You have to listen to me."

Louisa shook her head vehemently, willing the memories to stay away. It wasn't true. As long as she didn't remember, it would not be true. She couldn't hold them back and she remembered everything. Going out without Matthew into the clearing. Watching the meteor shower. Dropping her telescope down the hill and tripping in a hole covered by the snow while trying to retrieve it, causing her to fall down the embankment. She'd hit her head on a sharp rock on the way down. She did not remember anything after that moment. She only remembered standing up in the snow, as if nothing had happened and returning home to find Matthew waiting for her. Her eyes widened with the realization. She had been haunting Matthew.

"How long have I been coming back?" she asked.

"Months," he replied.

Louisa's hand flew to her mouth. "Why didn't you stop me before tonight?"

Matthew collapsed onto his knees in the snow. Louisa could see the tear marks running down his cheeks and his shoulders heaving with his sobs. She stepped closer to him, wanting to offer comfort and knowing she couldn't.

"I'm so sorry, Matthew. I should have listened. Can you forgive me?" she asked.

Matthew looked up. "I do forgive you. Can you ever forgive me?"

"For what?" she asked, startled at the heartache in his voice.

"This," he said, pointing to the headstone. "Not being here for you. Not realizing it was so important to you."

Louisa nodded. "It wasn't your fault. I forgave you before you even left that night."

Matthew rocked back and forth, his face turned up towards the sky. The world around them was completely silent, the only sound was his labored breaths as the cold engulfed him. Louisa studied the headstone. She smiled at it. Above her name, Matthew had carved a shooting star and below it, he had carved the words, *Beloved Wife, Always*. She knew it was time to end his self-inflicted guilt over her death and move on.

"Matthew?" she said.

Matthew wiped his face and looked at her, "Yes, darling?"

"I'm ready," she said.

Matthew nodded. He stood up and walked over to the headstone. He kissed his fingers and laid them on the stone while looking at her. Then, he nodded at her. Louisa smiled at him.

"Look for me in the stars?" she asked shyly.

"I'll look every night," he said.

Louisa nodded and smiled. She disappeared into the night. Matthew closed his eyes, then looked up at the sky just as a meteor passed overhead. Matthew let out a laugh of relief.

"I love you, too," he said and left the headstone to go back inside after one last look.

A Brave Gamble

Riley stared up at the bright light shining through the hole above her. She was silently berating herself for being so careless. She had made a stupid mistake and now the ones she loved would be in even more danger. She looked down at her stomach, then screamed towards the hole in desperation. It was a feral sound, surprising even her.

She looked back down at her stomach, twisting her body in a way to get a better look without making the pain, or the bleeding, worse. A large shard of glass stuck out from her lower abdomen. She figured it had fallen on top of her when she fell through the skylight of the atrium. She remembered the medical building with the expansive lobby from years ago. She'd once visited a specialist in the building. Years of war and natural disasters had taken their toll and the building had been lost. Or so she thought.

"Just pull it out and wrap a tourniquet from your shirt

sleeve around it," she told herself.

She pulled off her jacket and shirt, then tore the sleeves off the shirt, tying them together to form a tourniquet big enough to span her waist and put pressure on the wound. It was cold with only her tank top on, so she took the time to put on her jacket. She searched the area around her body, hoping some of the snow could be used to ice the wound. She was disappointed when she saw glass in a myriad of sizes surrounding her. The glass closest to her was a deep, dark red, the blood oozing along as it engulfed even more pieces as if offended by their ability to glint. The snow melted as the warm blood washed over it. The blood was the only color—the floor tiles in the medical building were surprisingly clean and white, save the area she had defiled when she'd fallen through the skylight. Riley looked up at the sky again, silently begging for help she knew would not come.

"Okay, on the count of three," she said to herself.

She wrapped a hand around the glass, attempting to control her breathing.

"One... Two..."

She prepared to pull, letting a long breath out through her nose then inhaling sharply.

"Wait!" her mind screamed at her. *"Isn't there some medical thing about not pulling out objects that have impaled you?"*

Riley wracked her brain for the wisdom she knew she had heard. She needed to get back on the road, Courtney and

Dylan were counting on her. She was so focused on the glass in her abdomen and the proper medical care, she never heard them coming. She started to look behind her just as the world went dark.

Earlier

You cannot be serious!" Courtney said in a falsely calm voice.

"I am, it's our only option," Riley replied.

Courtney failed to hold back the tears. They fell freely down her face now. She opened and closed her mouth several times, trying to make her wife listen to reason. She shook her head and looked over to where Dylan lay sleeping in his makeshift crib. Riley swallowed hard and sat next to Courtney on the bed. She wrapped her arms around her wife and squeezed, just holding her for a moment. They had been arguing about this plan for several days and time was running out for Dylan.

"Sweetheart," Riley said, stroking Courtney's hair, "we need to get help. You can't travel and neither can he. I will be quick. I'll find the Resistance unit. They're sure to have a doctor that can help Dylan."

Courtney pushed away from Riley and stood up, facing away from her wife. She angrily wiped the tears from her face.

"You can't be sure you will find the Resistance. The chances are just as good that the government forces will get to you first. Then what will happen? I will lose both of you."

Riley bit her lip, watching Courtney as she began to pace.

It was useless arguing with her—she was right. The Resistance was not easily found even when they wanted to be found, much less when someone was looking for them. The area was teeming with government forces due to the heavy Resistance activity. Riley and Courtney had tried to get out of the city, but they had waited too long and escape had been all but impossible. Riley sighed, knowing she had to go and would have to do it without Courtney's blessing. She had wanted to part with her wife on better terms.

Riley stood. "Cor, I have to go. You know it is the only way to save Dylan."

Courtney stopped without turning around. Her shoulders slumped in defeat. She nodded, unable to give her wife verbal permission for fear of the guilt she would feel if something happened to her. Riley knelt next to the crib, stroking Dylan's soft head. The baby stirred but did not wake up. She frowned at the blue tinge of his lips. He needed a doctor and if they waited too much longer... Riley shuddered at the thought and pushed it out of her mind. She went over to Courtney and put out a hand, wanting to pull her wife into a hug but knowing that it would not be well received. She lowered her hand, then straightened her shoulders. She stooped to pick up the backpack she had stocked with supplies. Riley went to the door, taking one last look around, then opened it.

"Riley?" Courtney said quietly.

Riley turned back around, waiting for Courtney to speak. Courtney looked at Dylan and then at the floor. She appeared to be warring with herself. She hugged her arms around her torso and looked up at Riley.

"We don't exist," she said.

Riley cocked her head. "What?"

A tear rolled down Courtney's cheek. "If they catch you, we don't exist. Change your name, lie. Don't tell them about us. Promise?"

Riley tamped down the panic the statement brought. She couldn't just abandon them, could she? She studied Courtney's face. She had loved this woman for so many years. Losing her would be like losing a limb. They had weathered so much together. She had to have faith they would come through this latest squall unharmed. Courtney's eyes pleaded with her and Riley realized it was a small comfort she could give to agree.

"Promise. But it won't come to that. I will be back with help," Riley said and smiled. She gave a small wave and then went out the door before she could lose her resolve.

Riley walked around the block and then collapsed against the brick wall of the apartment building. She sobbed freely, gasping for air and doing her best to be as quiet as possible. Luckily, the snowstorm had driven everyone inside and there was no one to witness her embarrassing display. Courtney always told her she was strong but she felt incredibly weak. She couldn't help her son and she couldn't comfort her wife. Riley felt like a failure in the biggest possible way. Riley hung her head in her hands, letting the self-recrimination wash over her. After what felt like hours, but in truth was mere minutes, Riley silently rebuked herself for letting her emotions get the best of her. She needed to find the Resistance and get her family help. Sitting around feeling sorry for herself would not get the task done. Riley wiped her face and blew her nose, then shouldered the backpack and trudged off in the direction she hoped would lead her to them. As she walked, she slipped off the ring on her finger, placing it into her jeans pocket.

Present

R iley slowly opened her eyes. She instantly knew she was no longer in the atrium, a sterile white ceiling above her with an incredibly bright light. She went to sit up but was dismayed when she realized her hands and feet were bound to the bed. She groaned as she plopped her head back down on the pillow.

"About time you woke up," a voice to her left said.

Riley squinted towards the voice. As she did, a woman in an indistinct uniform walked into the light. Riley perused the woman, hoping to find a clue as to her identity but failing. Riley blinked a few times, trying to clear her head.

"Who are you? Where am I?" she asked.

The woman chuckled. "Seems to me you are not in the position to be asking questions."

"Okay," Riley responded, trying to keep the derision out of her voice.

Riley closed her eyes and took calming breaths. She needed to stay calm until she knew who she was dealing with and what they wanted from her. It wouldn't do any good to let her temper get the best of her. Her father always told her she would get more flies with honey than with vinegar. Even as a child, she'd had trouble keeping her temper in check when truly annoyed.

"If you promise to be a good girl, I'll let you out of those restraints," the woman said, gloating clearly in her voice.

Riley opened her eyes and nodded. "I won't give you any trouble."

The woman gestured and two men came out of the shadows. One pointed a gun at her while the other released the restraints. Riley slowly sat up, wincing as she did. She looked down and noticed the glass was no longer piercing her abdomen. At least her captors had tended to her wound. She rubbed the sore spot on her head where they had knocked her out.

"Yeah, not sorry about that. When someone crashes into your home, you tend to hit first and ask questions later," the woman said, sitting on a chair one of the men sat out for her.

Riley watched the woman, revealing nothing. She let her tension go, silently counting her breaths in and out. The woman sized up Riley, waiting for a reaction. After several minutes, Riley resisted the urge to fidget and opened her mouth to ask a question but shut it just as fast when she noticed a flash of something cross the woman's eyes. Riley's consciousness told her to be very careful with the woman. She thought she saw the woman nod, almost imperceptibly.

"My name is Rona. As I said, you crashed into our home. Made a hell of a hole in the ceiling. What were you doing in this sector?" Rona asked.

Riley didn't miss the use of the word sector. Rona was military. It could mean good or bad things for Riley. She would have to be extremely careful with the information she gave to Rona.

"I must have gotten turned around in the snow. My... sister had a baby and he is really sick. He needs a doctor. She isn't able to travel yet and the baby is too small to be out in the cold. I volunteered to get help."

Rona took a moment to process what she said, "You live with this sister?"

Riley shook her head. "Not really. We live in the same apartment building."

"Why didn't you leave after the last earthquake?" Rona asked.

"Courtney, my friend, was too pregnant. She couldn't get out safely. Then fighting broke out near our apartment building and it was too late. We had to stay where we were." Riley replied.

"Surely she could have gone to the hospital with the baby," Rona said.

Riley shook her head again. "She didn't know there was a problem until just after the snow hit. It was heavily damaged in the earthquake and then the snow came. I couldn't find any doctors willing to look at the baby—they were too busy with the wounded from the fighting."

Riley did her best to make the lie convincing. In truth, she had not even tried to take Dylan to the hospital. She and Courtney would have to lie about everything—his name, their relationship, what happened to his father, etc. It was too much pressure and Riley was too afraid they would be caught. Homosexuality was now a crime and every person caught breaking the law was sent to a concentration camp if they survived the zealots tasked with hunting people down. It was not uncommon for detainees to be "made an example of" before being processed at the government center. Riley had moved Courtney as far from the city as possible, into a "safe" apartment building. The owner was sympathetic to the Resistance and put up a very good front to the government. To all the world, Riley and Courtney no longer existed as a married couple. They were two sisters living a "sin-free" life. Riley did odd jobs around the building for the owner and in turn, they lived rent-free.

Riley met Rona's stare. "Can you help the baby?"

"Perhaps," Rona replied nonchalantly, leaning back in the chair. "Where do you live?"

"In the Wyvern Apartments," Riley said.

Rona leaned forward again. Riley noticed the flicker of recognition in her eyes. Riley swallowed the lump in her throat as discreetly as possible. She refused to look away for fear of giving Rona ammunition.

"Alone?" Rona asked.

"Yes."

"You are a long way from home," Rona said.

Riley nodded. "I told you, I must have gotten turned around. Three feet of snow isn't easy to navigate in. All the remaining signs are covered. I didn't realize I was in the sunken part of the city until I fell through the skylight."

Rona crossed her arms and sat back again. "Give me your sister's name and I will have a squad retrieve her and the baby."

"Wouldn't it be safer to take a doctor to the baby?" Riley asked.

She didn't want to send anyone after Courtney. She was worried Rona did not believe her story. What if she had just given the government the location of a safe haven? What if they arrested everyone in the building? She could see Rona watching her war with herself. Courtney's words played over and over in her head. *We don't exist.* No, Riley could not abandon her wife and son, no matter the consequences. Rona and her men could have already shot her and yet they had patched her up and she was still alive. She had to trust her instincts and let Rona help them.

"Courtney. The baby is Dylan. They are in apartment four," Riley said.

Rona nodded and gestured. One of the men stepped out of the room and spoke to someone outside. He returned and whispered in Rona's ear. She waved him away and he stepped back to the door.

"We will bring them here as soon as possible," Rona said, standing and exiting the room. The man holding the gun on her left behind Rona, leaving just the one guard standing inside the room. Riley nervously rubbed her left ring finger, silently repeating to herself—*You did the right thing.*

Riley paced the room she was being held in. She hadn't spoken to anyone in hours. She'd been fed and provided with an opportunity to use a restroom. She tried to listen to the conversations in the hallway as people passed, but it was too muffled. The medical building had once been a top facility and she supposed the rooms were built with patient privacy in mind. She laughed inwardly at the thought of personal privacy. The government no longer cared about freedom or privacy. It used any and all information to keep an oppressive thumb on citizens. Riley constantly berated herself because she should have taken Courtney and fled the country the minute the first laws removing basic freedoms were established. She stupidly believed the courts would overturn the laws. The whole country was led to believe the President had their best interests at heart. By the time his true intentions were discovered, it was too late. Several natural disasters hit the country at the same time, the Russians attempted an invasion and martial law was declared. That was all the President needed to take control of the country and overturn democracy for dictatorship. Key opposition leaders were silenced and the *law enforcers* were given free rein. Anyone caught breaking a new law, could be sentenced to a concentration camp. People fought for hundreds of years for equal freedom for marginalized groups and those freedoms were squashed in a matter of months. Appropriately, the first to go was the First Amendment.

The west coast fought to extricate itself from the regime and form a new country. The Resistance was still fighting, hoping to one day win enough battles to force the government to cede the territory. It was a long and bloody conflict, ordinary citizens caught in the crossfire and punished for the Resistance's attacks. Riley had planned on paying a smuggler to get them out of the country as soon as Courtney could travel. The plan had backfired when Dylan began showing signs of illness. A nurse who lived in their building had examined him and told Riley the only thing that could save him was a heart operation. Courtney had been unwilling to believe Dylan's illness was so bad. Riley went behind her wife's back and found as much information as she could about where she could find the resistance. Once she told Courtney the plan, she'd made up her mind to save their son.

Riley was lost deep in thought when the door opened. Rona stepped inside. Riley looked up, trying to read Rona's face. The woman showed no emotion. A man followed her inside. He stepped over to Riley and produced a pair of handcuffs. Riley looked at Rona in alarm.

"What is this?" Riley asked.

"You're being moved. Your wife and son have arrived," Rona replied.

"No," Riley said in horror.

She hadn't missed the words Rona used—*wife and son.* The man nodded to Rona and she turned and left the room. The man nudged Riley and she walked out of the room behind Rona. Fear gripped her and she felt nauseous.

"What have I done? This can't be happening!" her mind yelled at her.

Rona led Riley through the maze of hallways. Riley tried to keep calm but sweat broke out on her brow and her palms itched. She squeezed her hand together as best she could in the handcuffs.

"Rona, please just tell me you will save Dylan?" Riley pleaded.

Rona kept walking without responding. Riley dug her nails into her hands, attempting to keep her temper in check. She had led her wife into a death trap and it was killing her. She wanted to rip Rona's throat out. The man beside her squeezed her arm and shook his head slightly when she glanced at him. She glared at him then turned her glare on Rona's back. They finally stopped in front of a door. Rona knocked and waited. The door opened slightly. Rona talked softly with the person on the other side, then the door swung open.

Riley nearly fainted in relief at the sight that greeted her. Courtney sat in a chair next to a medical exam table. Dylan was on the table while a doctor was examining him. The doctor smiled kindly when Riley walked in. Courtney jumped up and ran over to Riley, giving her a hug. Riley was taken aback and looked at Rona with confusion. Rona smiled, the first real emotion Riley had seen from the woman. She gestured and the man next to Riley let her out of the cuffs.

"I don't understand," Riley said, looking between her wife and Rona.

"They didn't tell you?" Courtney asked.

"Tell me what?" Riley challenged Rona.

"You found the Resistance. Well, I should say you fell into the Resistance," Rona said.

"Isn't it wonderful?" Courtney gushed. "They can help Dylan. The doctor here says it is a simple heart operation."

The doctor nodded. "We can fix him up, good as new."

Riley smiled. "That's wonderful. Thank you, doctor."

The doctor smiled and left the room. The man who had escorted Riley left with the doctor.

Riley watched Courtney pick up Dylan and coo to him as she sat down in the chair to nurse him. She looked back at Rona.

"Why did you make me believe we were in the government's hands?" Riley asked.

"It was not my intention. We have to be careful who we talk to, spies are everywhere. I needed to see your reaction before I could let you in on our existence," Rona replied.

Riley nodded, "Okay, that makes sense... but how did you know she was my wife?"

Rona chuckled. "You can take off a wedding ring but you can't hide the evidence of having worn one on your finger. I found it in your pocket when we stitched you up. Also, in the future, you might want to make up a husband—it's much more believable than living alone, especially in this city."

Riley sighed and rolled her eyes. She was not a very good liar. She'd always believed honesty was the best policy and it had served her well until she had to become a liar out of necessity. Turns out, she was even worse at it than she thought. She ran a hand through her hair, watching her wife and son and thanking her lucky stars they were all right.

"Riley?" Rona asked, getting her attention.

Riley held out her hand, "Thank you for helping. They are my world."

Rona nodded and shook her hand. "Always a pleasure. Welcome to the Resistance. We can use someone as brave and as strong as you."

"I think I'd like that," Riley replied.

"Good. Let's get your boy patched up and then we'll talk," Rona said.

"It's a plan," Riley said.

Rona walked to the door. She reached into her pocket and pulled out Riley's wedding ring, tossing it to her. Riley caught it and closed her hand around it tightly. Rona winked and left the room.

"Tell me everything?" Courtney asked. "Are you okay?"

Riley smiled. "I am now, sweetheart." She kissed the top of Courtney's hair and slid her wedding ring back onto her finger, sending up yet another silent 'thank you' into the universe.

First Sunday

That's preposterous!" King Harald shouted at his son. "Father," Prince Olav stated calmly, "it is a tradition... you must at least appear to consider my request."

"I'll do no such thing! Sonja, talk to your son." Harald looked at his wife pleadingly.

Olav looked at his mother, attempting and failing to hide his smug smile. He sobered, only slightly, when she gave him a warning look with her eyes. Olav knew his mother well. She would play both sides with immense tact. Olav inwardly smirked—his father was never wise to his mother's machinations. Queen Sonja patted Harald's arm and smiled sweetly at him.

"Harald, I have already counseled our son in this matter. It is my firm belief he is sincere in his wishes. He has waited many years for this day to come. He is correct, you must honor the First Sunday tradition."

Harald glared at Olav, who tried his best to keep a proud spine and earnest demeanor. Olav had waited four years for the right opportunity to speak with his father. First Sunday was a tradition in Fadersogn. Whenever the first day of the new year fell on a Sunday, the people of the kingdom were granted permission to petition the King for a change in a law of the land or a dispensation to deviate from the law. It was the duty of the King to listen to the request, weigh the benefits and disadvantages of the request for the populace at large, and announce the decision at a festival held throughout the land. The King provided food, drink, and entertainment for the festival and, in turn, the populace shared crafts and service to each other. The tradition had begun hundreds of years before as a way to keep the laws of the kingdom in check and remind the king that he served at the pleasure of his people.

Olav held his breath. He rarely asked his father for anything. He'd had many years to reflect on this moment. He'd discussed his request with his mother many times and her wise counsel was to wait for a day when his father could not refuse to listen to him. It had been hard but Olav now knew, by his father's reaction, that his mother was very wise. If he was to have a chance in changing the law, First Sunday was the day. Olav watched as his father opened and shut his mouth like a dying fish. Harald looked at Sonja, who continued to smile at him with no small measure of understanding. Then she nodded and Harald sighed. Olav knew at that moment, he had won—at least his father would consider it.

"Very well. If you are sure—"

Olav kept himself in check, "I want it more than anything else in the world…"

Harald glared again and Olav stopped talking.

"As I was saying, *if* you are sure, I will take your request into consideration. You may go," Harald said as he gestured for Olav to leave.

Olav glanced at his mother. She nodded slightly at him but he could tell by the twinkle in her eyes, she would do everything in her power to sway his father to approve his request.

Years Earlier

Olav was dancing with Princess Orla of Eiremoor at her birthday ball. She was very charming but utterly distracted by the entrance of two men he could only assume were Lochlann and Ciarán Allyn. Olav had heard all about the *mishap* between the Princess and the younger Allyn brother. He made it his business to learn all he could about the people he met in his travels as a representative of Fadersogn. He could tell she was incredibly fixated on every labored breath the man took. If he winced, she winced. More than once in the dance, he had to quickly take an extra step to avoid hurting her. He finally decided to comment.

"Your friend?" Olav asked with curiosity.

"What? Oh, yes, it seems he might be better after all,"

Orla said with no small amount of relief in her voice.

Olav looked over at the brothers. The younger must be the one who was hurt; the older and taller brother seemed to be hovering a bit protectively. They were both tall and lean, with matching blue eyes. The older had brown hair while the younger's was jet black. He could see the resemblance. The older one was saying something to his brother, but he shrugged and seemed very wary. Olav would make it a point to get to know both men during his weeklong stay at the castle. The older brother, he knew, was in the King's navy, and he would be very interested in discussing nautical affairs with the man.

"Might you introduce me, Your Highness?" Olav asked.

"Absolutely." She gave Olav a winning smile. He gave a slight nod and put her arm in his.

Olav escorted Orla towards the brothers. He watched as Lochlann straightened and nudged his brother. Ciarán took a very painful breath and stood as straight as possible. Olav had to admire the younger man's strength. He himself had merely experienced bruised ribs, not broken ones, and he'd wanted to literally die. Olav knew it took a great deal of bravery to have come down to the ball and attempt to appear unaffected. He also noticed the endearing way Lochlann watched his brother. Olav could tell the man was someone he could appreciate having in his life. Lochlann was slightly taller than his brother with wavy, brown hair, cut short in the military style. He had piercing blue eyes and a clean-shaven face.

"Your Highness," Ciarán said, as he and Lochlann gave

small bows.

Olav watched as Orla frowned at Lochlann, who just shrugged and gave a small warning nod to her. She sighed, almost imperceptibly and turned to Olav.

"Prince Olav, may I present to you, Lochlann and Ciarán Allyn. They have been my closest friends since childhood. Their mother served as lady-in-waiting to mine."

Orla missed the tiny wince Ciarán gave at the word "friends" but Lochlann and Olav did not. Lochlann extended his hand to Olav. Olav took it and they shook a hearty greeting.

"Prince Olav, it is a pleasure to meet you. You hail from Fadersogn if I am correct?" he asked.

"Ah, you know your kingdoms it seems," Olav said with cheer.

"Aye, your highness, I quite enjoy learning about the kingdoms we trade with on our journeys. I have visited your kingdom and was enchanted by it. The mountains are covered in snow year-round, are they not?" Lochlann asked.

Olav nodded and turned to Orla. "Princess Orla, would you think it rude if I were to steal away your friend for a while? I think we might take some refreshment?"

Orla smiled. "Not at all, Prince Olav. Thank you for the dancing. I look forward to speaking with you more during your stay."

Olav bowed at Orla while noticing Lochlann discreetly checking with Ciarán. He stifled the laugh that wanted to burst forth at the petulant reply from the younger brother. Orla glanced over and Olav waited patiently while Lochlann looked between Ciarán and Orla. The older Allyn brother shook his head and followed Olav to the banquet room. Olav waited until they were seated, with drinks in hand, before broaching the elephant in the room.

"They have it bad for each other, do they not?" Olav said jokingly.

Lochlann nearly spit out his beer. He gave Olav an appraising stare and then nodded, laughing in relief.

"Noticed, did you?"

Olav chuckled. "It's as if an invisible string connects them. One cannot live without the other."

"If only those two knuckleheads would realize it, the kingdom would be in much less peril." Lochlann grinned.

Olav felt a warmth spread through his body. He decided he liked the smile on Lochlann's face. "Sometimes, it is hard to see what is right in front of you and obvious to others," Olav offered.

"True. I am sure this storm will pass and they will eventually reconcile. If my pig-headed brother can pull his head out of his arse long enough," Lochlann said wryly.

Olav laughed and Lochlann smiled at him. "I am quite familiar with stubborn men."

"Ah, so you have a brother?" Lochlann asked.

"No, but my father is probably the most stubborn man in the known world." Olav smiled and took a swig of his beer.

Olav watched Lochlann sizing him up. He liked being

truly seen instead of being a title. He could tell Lochlann was a genuine man and, if he had anything to do with it, they would become great friends. He noticed Lochlann make a decision and stand. Olav looked confused for a moment but relaxed when Lochlann bowed and held out a hand.

"Would you care to take a walk in the gardens, Your Highness?" Lochlann asked.

Olav took the proffered hand and rose. "It would be my pleasure."

Olav and Lochlann were sparring in the courtyard. Lochlann was a very good swordsman and the men appeared to be equals. They were not really keeping score, but if they had, it would be about even anyway. Olav had not met any in his kingdom who could keep up with him. He'd just disarmed Lochlann, who conceded the match, and they were taking a water break while leaning against a wall.

"Lochlann, might I ask you a question?" Olav asked.

"Of course, Your Highness," Lochlann replied.

"Olav, please. You have earned the right, my friend. If I may call you that."

"Of course you may. Very well, Olav, what curiosity might I settle?" Lochlann asked with a smile.

"The Princess, she has an affection for your brother, does she not?" he asked.

Olav watched while Lochlann thought on the question. He didn't mind the delay in an answer as it gave him the chance to ogle the man without raising suspicion. Lochlann's hair was plastered to his forehead and his cheeks were rosy from the exertion of fighting. Olav swallowed hard as a bead of sweat made its way from Lochlann's neck down the open vee of his shirt and through the chest hair peeking out. Olav looked up just in time to meet Lochlann's eyes.

"I believe she does but I am not certain of it. Those two fight more often than not," he said and chuckled.

"Ah, a passion born of fire. I have seen it before, my own parents have been known to awaken the whole kingdom with their shouting. My mother once threw a vase at my father's head during dinner, then sat back down and calmly ate the rest of her food as if it were a normal evening." Olav laughed heartily. "How does your brother feel?"

Olav believed Sonja was the only woman capable of being married to his father. She did not allow King Harald to treat her as anything but his equal and many times she had saved Olav from his father's wrath—warranted or not. Olav loved both of his parents but his mother was very close to his heart.

"Just as I am not certain of Orla's feelings, I cannot give words to my brother's feelings for her. Love is not strong enough for what he feels. She is his world. Whenever they are apart, he thinks only of her. Their most recent argument has wounded him more than the fall. He is just too stubborn to admit it."

Olav scratched his chin. "What is the problem?"

"Ciarán has grand ideas about royalty and he has always belabored the fact that he is not noble. Therefore, in his mind, he is below her station and not a suitable match. Their recent argument did not help to dispel that myth when Orla pulled rank on him," Lochlann replied.

Olav thought for a moment, a sly grin slipped across his face. He had a reputation for meddling in the affairs of others and this would be no exception.

"The accident was not so much an accident?" he asked.

Lochlann laughed. "Very clever deduction. They were arguing on the wall and Ciarán might have been given a little push. How did you guess?"

"I can see the guilt written on the Princess' face whenever it is mentioned."

"Aye, she was never good at hiding her emotions," Lochlann said. He was really beginning to enjoy his new friend. "I do hope that my brother's affection for the Princess will not cause problems between our kingdoms?"

Olav grinned. "My dear, Lochlann, why would you worry about such things?"

Lochlann shrugged. "I just assumed you were here to try to win her over?"

"'Tis true that my mother and father would like for me to find a match and they are very fond of your sovereigns. However, I do believe that the Princess and I would make better allies than lovers. Would you not agree?" Olav assessed Lochlann.

Lochlann nodded. "Aye, I am not sure I would want to be the one in the way of what Orla wanted."

"I have an idea if you are game?" Olav said conspiratorially.

Lochlann nodded. "Anything that would help resolve this situation. I can't stand my brother's moroseness any longer. If I have to hear him moaning and groaning one more day, I might kill him and put him out of his misery like he's asked. What did you have in mind?"

Olav sat next to Orla under the willow tree by the stream. It was a pleasant day and they were discussing the pros and cons of building temporary dams to flood the nearby fields for a better harvest. Orla was against the idea and so Olav was, naturally, for it. He enjoyed riling her up. She was incredibly passionate and well-spoken, so he loved to get her excited about an idea to lower her inhibitions. She would make her case and, in the end, he would confess she had been right all along. She would then huff and playfully punch him in the arm and tell him he was incorrigible. Orla was in the midst of an enthusiastic rebuttal when Olav noticed the Allyn brothers exit the castle. He sighed in relief, having begun to suspect Lochlann was having a tough time getting Ciarán to escort him outside. Olav had no backup plans for keeping Orla out longer if they had been any later. Olav could tell Ciarán was sulking. Lochlann grabbed his brother's arm, spun him towards the tree, and practically dragged him. Olav suppressed a chuckle, noticing the consternation on Orla's face.

"Ah, Lochlann and Ciarán, so nice to see you this fine afternoon," Olav said pleasantly.

Olav watched as Orla looked at the brothers. When she met Ciarán's stormy gaze, she looked away quickly, feigning interest in the stream. He glanced at Lochlann with expectation.

"I was just telling Ciarán he needed some air and sun," Lochlann said.

"Yes, yes, a fine day for it. Wouldn't you agree, Princess?" Olav said.

"Yes, it is lovely today," Orla muttered, not addressing anyone in particular.

Ciarán stepped back, attempting to leave. "I think I have had enough air."

He bowed and began walking back towards the castle as fast as he could without too much pain. Lochlann glanced at Olav who nodded. He chased after his brother. Olav watched as Lochlann attempted to keep his temper in check. Olav could practically feel the frustration wafting from him, even at a distance.

"It is nice to see your friend out of the castle," he prodded.

Orla nodded and picked at the grass.

"I do hope to see more of him around. I hear he is turning purple and his head is spinning every other hour," Olav said with a grin.

"It is... wait... what?" Orla asked, finally

paying attention.

Olav chuckled as Orla discreetly punched him on the leg, still watching Ciarán out of the corner of her eye. Olav looked toward the brothers again. Lochlann put something in Ciarán's hands and spun him around. He gave him a small, but not painful, push towards where Orla and Olav were waiting.

"Perhaps I could give you some time alone?" Olav asked quietly.

"That would be helpful. Thank you," Orla replied with some measure of trepidation in her voice.

Olav could tell she was yet again distracted by her concern for Ciarán. He straightened and stood, holding out a hand to help Orla up. Lochlann came up behind his brother and nodded at Olav.

"Princess, would you mind if I sparred with Lochlann? He is quite remarkable and the best sparring partner I have had in a very long time. My father's guards are all getting old and slow. I am sure Ciarán might keep you company," Olav said.

Orla struggled to regain her composure for a moment and then pasted on a smile. Olav could tell she was nervous and Ciarán looked as if he was about to face a firing squad. Olav felt for the younger man. He considered Ciarán something close to a brother, having learned a lot about him from Lochlann and seeing how much he loved Ciarán. Lochlann felt as if he owed his brother the world and Olav admired him more for that. Olav wanted nothing more than to see the younger Allyn and Orla live a long, happy life together. He saw much of his parents in the two people.

"Of course, Olav. Thank you for the most excellent conversation this afternoon," she said politely.

Olav and Lochlann both bowed and took their leave. They walked through the meadow towards the castle and looked back once they were near the door. Ciarán had not retreated yet, a very good sign. Olav put his hand up and Lochlann high-fived him. The plan had worked, at least so far. Olav held the door open for Lochlann, who entered the castle after a moment's hesitation. Olav was finally winning in his bid to have Lochlann treat him as an equal instead of a Prince. Olav smiled and entered the castle.

Olav gasped as Lochlann cornered him against the wall and kissed him deeply. Lochlann pulled away almost immediately and Olav touched his lips.

"Your Highness, forgive my presumption... I just..." Lochlann stuttered.

Olav smiled and put a hand on Lochlann's face, causing him to stop talking and gape at Olav.

"It is I who never hoped to presume you felt any measure of what I feel," Olav said as he searched Lochlann's eyes.

"I was too afraid to cause a scandal and war between our two countries, Olav."

Olav nodded. "I assure you, should this happen again, and I very much hope it does happen again—and soon—Fadersogn will remain a firm ally to Eiremor."

Lochlann stared in shock a moment and then took Olav's face in his hands, renewing the kiss and deepening it until they both had to stop for air. He rested his forehead on Olav's and closed his eyes.

"Whatever shall we do, Olav?" he asked somewhat mournfully.

Olav shrugged. " I am a prince and can be clever when the moment demands. I will think of something. For now, how about that sparring session?"

Lochlann nodded. Olav gestured for him to lead the way and he headed down the hall. Olav watched him as he walked and began plotting in his head.

Olav had been pleased and then saddened all in the space of a week. Lochlann wrote to him on an almost daily basis. Olav had spoken with his mother and waited for the appropriate moment to approach his father. King Harald had continually harassed him about the possibility of a union with Eiremor and Olav was running out of excuses. Sonja knew the reason and helped divert the conversation every time the topic was brought up but Olav realized they could not stall his father forever. Then Lochlann wrote that Ciarán had finally gotten the courage to ask King Phelan for his permission to marry Orla. Olav could not have been happier for the young Allyn brother. He wrote of his enthusiasm for the match to Lochlann. The messenger was just leaving the courtyard when another rode in with terrifying speed and stopped short of ramming Olav.

"Your Highness, urgent news for the King," the messenger said as he handed Olav a missive.

"I shall see that he gets it. Go to the kitchens for refreshment," he instructed the messenger and hastily went inside to find his father.

Olav watched as Harald read the message and frowned. Harald seemed to read it more than once. Then he sighed and rubbed his eyes.

"Olav, fetch your mother. We are at war," Harald said, dismissing his son.

Olav blanched and went to find his mother.

Eiremor and Fadersogn were at war with the kingdom to their south for several years before Orla and her brother Kellan were able to use their combined magical powers and defeat them. Olav had followed the movements of all the ships in both kingdoms' armadas, sending prayers to the gods for the safe return of both brothers. He traveled to Eiremor on a monthly basis, hoping for news and being the best friend he could to Orla. She was beside herself but convinced both brothers were alive. She was his only link to Lochlann.

Olav was waiting at the castle when news of the return of *The Mercury*, Eiremor's only remaining ship from the Battle of the North Sea. Neither Lochlann nor Ciarán was aboard the returning ship. Olav let Orla cry on his shoulder when she learned the *Queen's Fortune* had replaced *The Phoenix* in the battle. He could not confide in her that he felt as much loss as she did because he did not think she would understand. He waited until the depths of the night, when he was alone, to sob into his pillow and mourn for Lochlann.

Olav felt lucky to be alive the day the last of the prisoners returned to Eiremor. He had been spending long days with King Phelan, discussing options for border patrols and avoiding Phelan's hints about a possible marriage alliance. After hours of working and sleepless nights, he felt incredibly frustrated and restless. He stood on the castle ramparts, staring off into the distance when he heard shouting from the courtyard.

"Water!" a voice yelled.

Olav looked down and saw a group of bedraggled and obviously weary travelers dropping their belongings in the courtyard as others ran to help them. Most of the men sported long hair and beards, their clothes in tatters. Olav felt great pity for them. He knew they must be men returning from the prisoner camps. He cursed inwardly at the costs of war—to both kingdoms and him personally. Olav started to turn away when he noticed an unmistakable figure amongst the men. His heart dropped to his stomach and he had to pinch himself to believe he was truly seeing the man he loved most in the world. As if Olav had yelled his name, Lochlann looked up and locked eyes with him. He gave a little shrug and Olav shook his head, backing away from the wall and watching Lochlann as long as he could before he broke off in a run towards the stairwell.

Olav burst through the door to the courtyard, searching

in desperation for Lochlann amid the chaotic scene. He panicked, momentarily, when Lochlann was not immediately visible. Olav didn't think he could take back that sinking feeling that it was all a dream. He had imagined being reunited with Lochlann so many times but he was cognizant of the fact he had never conjured Lochlann with such sorrow in his eyes. Lochlann was brave and strong. To see him so downtrodden, even for a moment, was unsettling. As exhausted as the men were, they all began standing and bowing as Olav passed. Olav swallowed the lump in his throat and attempted to regain some measure of composure.

"Gentlemen," he said loudly, "please. You have been through enough. Please rest—we will have refreshments in the great hall and will find you all the places to bathe and sleep."

The men cheered in a subdued manner and went back to their previous state. Olav searched and still did not see Lochlann. Suddenly, he felt a presence next to him and he turned to see Lochlann in front of him. It was unmistakably the man he loved, though a very different one from the man he had first met. Lochlann had a world-weary look about him and the usual brightness in his eyes had faded. Olav hoped very much to return that light as quickly as possible. Olav did not hesitate. He threw his arms around Lochlann and hugged him as if he might disappear again at any moment.

"I've missed you," he stated simply.

Lochlann nodded and hugged back. Olav was reluctant to let go but saw that the men around them were beginning to notice and he did not want to put Lochlann in any more peril than he had been already.

"Come, let us get you settled," Olav said, leading Lochlann into the castle.

After a brief report to King Phelan, Olav led Lochlann to the rooms the King had set aside for his use. Olav ordered a bath, shaving supplies, and food. Lochlann sat quietly on a chair, watching Olav. He raised an eyebrow when Lochlann ordered the last of the servants to leave and Olav merely smirked. This brought a chuckle from Lochlann, which in turn made Olav give him a genuine smile. Olav gestured to the bath.

"Shall I give you some privacy?" Olav joked.

Lochlann blushed and looked away. Olav knelt by the chair.

"I was only joking," Olav said earnestly.

Lochlann swallowed heavily. "I know... it's just..."

"Lochlann?" Olav waited for him to meet his eyes. "You are still the man I love."

Lochlann nodded and stood. Olav helped him undress and step into the tub. Lochlann sighed in relief as the warm water hit his sore muscles. Olav wanted to yell at the scars he saw on Lochlann's back. He must have been whipped in the prisoner camp. He lathered a cloth and gently washed Lochlann's back.

"Olav, you don't have to bathe me," Lochlann mumbled.

"I don't make it a habit to do things I don't want to do," Olav replied cheekily.

This elicited another chuckle from Lochlann. He sat patiently while Olav bathed him, closing his eyes and nearly nodding off. Olav watched Lochlann relax and his eyes filled with tears. Someday he would ask Lochlann to tell him everything but at that moment, Olav was merely happy he was alive.

"Your arm will need to be set properly," Olav said gently.

Lochlann nodded. "It was not tended properly. The men did what they could."

Olav winced and averted his eyes, not wanting Lochlann to see any pity.

"Would you like a shave?" Olav asked.

Lochlann opened his eyes. "I would love one."

Olav nodded and gathered the supplies. Lochlann leaned forward and Olav spread the lather on his face. He carefully pulled the razor across Lochlann's cheek. Lochlann reached up and stopped Olav's hand.

"Ciarán?" Lochlann croaked.

Olav had been so caught up in the return of one Allyn brother, he had not even thought of the other. Olav swallowed.

"He was not in your company?" Olav asked, though he already knew the answer.

Lochlann shook his head solemnly. Olav could see he had inadvertently confirmed Lochlann's worst fears. He let go of Olav's hand, presenting his cheek again. Olav did not miss the tears Lochlann fought back but decided to let his love mourn in his own way.

With Lochlann's return, trips to Eiremor became pleasant again. Olav did not miss the strained relationship Orla had with Lochlann and he knew the reason was that she believed Lochlann was not a dutiful brother. She had mentioned to Olav on numerous occasions her belief that Ciarán was still alive. Since he had refused to ever believe Lochlann was gone, he had been a good friend and agreed with her. Still, he knew the subject of his missing brother was a raw one for Lochlann and he fervently wished the three of them could be together since it was his belief the two of them would benefit in their mutual grief.

Orla had mentioned to Olav that her parents wished for her to marry him. Olav had every intention of taking Lochlann home with him and had avoided the topic of marriage from both his father and hers since Captain Allyn had returned. Olav waited with bated breath for Orla to speak her mind on the subject. He had been relieved to find she had outright refused her father's wishes. It was then, Olav confided his plans to her and Orla swore she would keep his secrets until the appropriate time.

"Lochlann, I've told Orla about our relationship," Olav offered one serene day by the willow tree.

Lochlann looked stunned. Olav fidgeted, unsure of Lochlann's feelings. Then, Lochlann shrugged and kissed Olav. Olav put his arms around Lochlann and deepened the kiss before pulling back to look at him.

"So, you're okay being outed?" Olav asked.

Lochlann nodded. "It would happen eventually. Orla is incredibly astute. I see her noticing us together and the jealousy it sparks in her. I wish she would let him go."

Olav shook his head. "She can't. He is a part of her as much as you are a part of me. When I thought you dead, I felt as if an important piece of me was missing. I can imagine her pain and the pain it brings her to be reminded of him with your presence. She insists he is alive."

"If he were alive, don't you think I would find him?" Lochlann growled.

"You've been recovering yourself. You can't blame yourself for losing him in the battle," Olav said calmly.

Lochlann stood and hit his fist against the tree.

"Can't I?" he yelled. "He was my little brother and I didn't keep him safe!"

Olav stood, attempting to put a comforting hand on Lochlann's shoulder. Lochlann shrugged it off and stared out into the water with his back to Lochlann.

"Perhaps you should marry her," he said after a few silent minutes of brooding.

"What!?" It was Olav's turn to shout.

Lochlann turned around and faced Olav. The two men stood their ground, neither giving an inch. Finally, Lochlann looked at the ground, unable to meet the pleading in Olav's eyes any longer.

"Marry her. Your kingdom does not allow our relationship and she will have no one else. She must move on and I am no longer worthy of you," Lochlann said apologetically.

"I don't want… you can't mean this?" Olav appealed.

"I do. My decision is final. I—"

Olav put his hands on Lochlann's lips to stop him. He shook his head.

"If that is what you wish, I will do it. But if you say it, I am lost."

Lochlann nodded. Olav kissed him with all the love he felt and then pulled away, turning on his heel and walking away from Lochlann.

Lochlann left the castle that evening. Olav had spoken with Phelan and then Orla. They would be married. Orla asked about Lochlann but Olav was relieved when she didn't pry any further. He had tried to hide the pain in his eyes but knew it was nearly impossible. Olav wrote to his father and nearly vomited at the reply. Each missive and preparation was a reminder of his broken heart. Orla did her best to comfort him, as he had comforted her. Both of them were miserable.

The day of his wedding dawned and it promised to be dull and gray. Olav watched the storm clouds gathering in the distance with bitter amusement. His mother had already been in to *talk some sense into him.* Besides Orla, Sonja was the only one who knew Olav's true desires. He knew his mother only wanted what was best for him but he felt he had no more choices in the matter. Lochlann had decided for both of them. Olav bit back the sob threatening to escape him. A knock on the door roused him from his self-pitying moment. He went over to the door and opened it, surprised to see his mother standing on the other side, yet again.

"Mother, we've been over this," he cautioned.

"You will want this information," she replied.

Olav sighed and opened the door for her. Sonja swept into the room and sat on the settee. She made a show of smoothing her skirts and primping her hair. Olav sighed again and cleared his throat. Sonja looked up with a glint in her eyes.

"Captain Allyn returned today," Sonja beamed.

Olav's heart jumped at the thought of seeing Lochlann again, then sank at the realization he would have to marry Orla and lose Lochlann forever. Lochlann's timing was incredibly awkward.

"Mother," Olav growled, "it matters not."

"I'm not done," she replied.

Olav rolled his eyes and waited for her to respond. She looked pointedly at the seat next to her until Olav grunted and plopped down next to her. Sonja had a way of ordering him about without actually saying anything. Usually, he was good-natured about her manner of mothering but the day was already weighing on him and any goodwill he felt towards her was nonexistent. He indulged her when she grabbed his hand and squeezed it, placing it in his lap.

"What is it, Mother?" he demanded.

"Olav, my dear son, he found his brother."

Olav's head snapped up, "Ciarán's alive?"

"He is," she said, smiling.

"That's... incredible. Ciarán's here?" Olav held his breath waiting for his mother to reply.

She nodded. "Captain Allyn has been sent to fetch him to the castle. Queen Meara asked me to beg your forgiveness and asked for a delay in the wedding."

Olav jumped up and began pacing. What had started as the worst day of his life, was now becoming the happiest. His mind raced with all the possibilities. Then, he realized none of it would matter. Lochlann had made his wishes clear. He paused, mid-step, and turned back to his mother. He let all of the despair he felt wash over his face. Sonja held out her hand and Olav took it, sitting back down next to his mother.

"It can be fixed, son," she chided gently.

Olav looked away and Sonja smoothed the hair from his forehead. She stood and gently kissed his head. Olav watched as she left the room, wondering if she was correct. Maybe, just maybe, all would be well.

Lochlann stepped out of Ciarán's rooms and leaned against the wall, tilting his head back and sighing. Olav watched from the shadows, his heart aching to be near Lochlann. He saw Lochlann look down the hallway, towards his quarters. Then Lochlann seemed to make a decision and turned in the opposite direction. Olav took a deep breath and made a decision. He stepped into the hallway.

"Lochlann?" Olav said quietly.

Lochlann's shoulders straightened and he stood completely still for a moment. Olav watched him nod and turn. Lochlann met Olav's eyes with a look of sadness mixed with regret. Lochlann bowed politely, which made Olav's heart sink. Lochlann had not bowed to him in years. "Yes, your highness?"

"Must we?" Olav sighed.

Lochlann seemed taken aback by his question. Olav waited for him to say anything further but it became clear Olav was in charge of the conversation. Olav searched his mind for the best way to handle the delicate situation and still get the desired outcome. Lochlann stood by, patiently waiting for Olav to make the decision.

"Lochlann, would you please accompany me to my quarters?" Olav asked.

Lochlann nodded and Olav led the way to his rooms. He opened the door for Lochlann and let go of the breath he did not realize he was holding when Lochlann entered ahead of him. Perhaps, he thought, the situation was not a total disaster. Lochlann sat in a chair and Olav sat across from him. The two men once again stared at each other, neither willing to make a mistake in a conversation each knew to be vital to their lifelong happiness.

Olav knelt in front of Lochlann and grasped his hands. Lochlann began to protest.

"Marry me," Olav blurted out.

"I…" Lochlann was at a loss for words.

"It seems the Princess of Eiremor has called off our

wedding and I have been jilted," Olav joked, trying to lighten the mood.

Lochlann laughed loudly, a sound that was music to Olav's ears. He pulled Olav up and kissed him soundly.

"I'm not sure she was your type, Your Highness," Lochlann mocked playfully.

Olav shook his head. "Not at all, but I know someone who is perfect for me."

Lochlann smiled. "And who might this handsome fellow be?"

"If you have to ask, I have not shown my affections properly," Olav smirked.

"It is I who am the culprit in this situation. A misdeed I plan to rectify," Lochlann replied earnestly.

Olav sighed happily. "Is that a yes?"

"Is it possible?" Lochlann asked with seriousness.

"My mother has an idea," Olav replied mysteriously.

"Yes, Olav," Lochlann said.

Olav whooped with joy and kissed Lochlann, pouring all his euphoria into it.

The First Sunday festival was set to open and Olav gathered with his parents in the balcony antechamber. It was the tradition for his mother to welcome the populace and introduce the petitioners. This year, there were a total of two petitioners, including Olav. He watched as his mother introduced the other man.

"Ladies and gentlemen, it is my pleasure to introduce you to Leif Anders. His petition on this First Sunday was a request to change the law for inheritance. As you know, inheritance has long been determined by the sex of the heirs. Male heirs are considered, female heirs are not. Master Anders has three daughters, no sons, and wishes to pass his estates to the females of his household at his pleasure. King Harald, please give your decision on the petition."

Harald nodded. "My people, my wife is both wise and gracious. She has counseled me in this matter and I have consulted my heart. It is my fervent belief the women of this kingdom are as entitled to the benefits of ownership as the males. Therefore, it is my great pleasure to accept Master Ander's petition and amend the kingdom law to allow inheritance for all children, regardless of sex."

The populace cheered and Olav smiled. Master Anders bowed to his mother and father, then to him. Olav gave the man a gracious smile and congratulated him. Master Ander's daughters surrounded him and kissed him on the cheek. Olav watched the happy family. His mother caught his eye and winked at him. Olav swallowed the lump forming in his throat. His father would soon announce the fate of his own petition.

Queen Sonja stepped back to the balcony and waited for the populace to give her their attention. She took an extra moment and Olav fervently wished she would get on with it. He rolled his eyes at her theatrics and did his best not to burst onto the balcony and shake her. Sonja looked over the crowd and took a deep breath.

"There was one other petitioner."

Sonja gestured for Olav and he stepped onto the balcony. A murmur went through the crowd and Sonja held up her hand. She linked the fingers of her other hand with Olav's and squeezed.

"My son has been an advocate for the populace during both times of peace and times of war. It has long been our wish he found a mate worthy of him. Olav believes he has found that person but in order for him to marry his choice, we must change the law. The law of our land states that a Prince may marry the Princess of his choice. Olav's choice does not fit the definition of a princess. He has requested we change the law to allow him to marry any person of his choosing. King Harald, please give your decision on the petition."

Harald once again stepped forward. Olav watched his father, who refused to look at him or give him any indication of his decision. Olav glanced at his mother and she merely squeezed his hand again. Olav couldn't decide if it gave him confidence or fear. Perhaps, she was merely holding him up so that he would not break down in front of his people.

"People of Fadersogn, I was also counseled by the Queen in this matter. I searched my heart and found my objections to the petition to be baseless. Our laws regarding the marriage of the heir to the throne were written hundreds of years ago, in a different time. The needs of the kingdom were different and the days darker. Lest you think poorly of me, this decision was not difficult for me in the way you might think. I have no qualms with my son marrying someone who is not of royal blood as we serve at your pleasure and we consider you, our people, to be equals. We know, without a doubt, the kingdom is bountiful due to your contributions. I, therefore, approve the law to allow my son to marry the person of his choosing."

The crowd cheered. Olav felt faint. He could barely believe his ears. However, Harald was not done and he waited for the din to die down.

"Good people, the law is changed. However, we must amend the marriage laws as well, which state that a man must marry a woman and vice versa."

A murmuring started again. It seemed the populace was confused and Olav knew it was for good reason. There were many in the kingdom who lived with people of the same sex, as if married, but none had ever asked for permission to make it legal in the eyes of the King. They were not ostracized, merely treated as adults living together under one roof with none of the legal protections of married couples. Harald looked over his people. He then gestured behind him and someone stepped out on the balcony. Olav gasped when he saw Lochlann shaking his father's hand. Lochlann turned a smirk towards Olav and bowed. Harald put his hand on Lochlann's shoulder.

"My dear populace, you might remember the heroics of Captain Lochlann Allyn of Eiremor. He also has the good fortune to have won the heart of my son, Prince Olav. Therefore, it is my great pleasure to announce, the laws of the kingdom are hereby amended to allow the marriage of ANY person to ANY other person, regardless of sex. I would also like to announce the pending nuptials of Prince Olav to Captain Allyn," Harald beamed.

Once again, the crowd erupted in cheering. Olav smiled broadly at Lochlann, who returned the look of love. Sonja hugged Lochlann and then went to stand next to Harald, who put his arm around her.

"You did well, dear," Sonja said.

"I always do," Harald preened.

Olav chuckled and held out his hand to Lochlann. He took it and the two stepped closer to each other.

"When did you get here?" Olav asked.

"Two days ago," Lochlann stated.

"Two days! How?" Olav sputtered.

Lochlann smiled. "Your mother. She's a wily one."

Olav glanced at his mother. She winked at him, then led Harald into the castle so she could welcome the populace into the great hall. Olav shook his head and turned back to Lochlann.

"You still sure about this?" Olav asked, gesturing to the crowd still milling around in the courtyard and fearing the answer.

Lochlann glanced down and back at Olav.

"I don't know—" he started.

Olav looked away. "I understand... it's a lot."

Lochlann grabbed Olav and kissed him for all the world

to see. Olav clung to Lochlann until he heard the crowd cheering again. He pulled back and blushed a deep shade of red. Lochlann laughed and waved at the crowd. Olav smiled at the natural ease Lochlann showed around his people. Lochlann turned back to Olav and held out his hand.

"Does that convince you, Your Highness?" Lochlann teased.

Olav smirked. "I might need a bit more convincing."

Lochlann laughed. "It will be my pleasure to convince you for as long as it takes."

"Promise?"

"With all my heart," Lochlann solemnly swore.

Olav looked into Lochlann's eyes with all the love he felt and saw it reflected back at him. He took Lochlann's hand and headed towards the antechamber. It had been a bumpy road to this moment but Olav finally felt at peace. He could now live the rest of his life with the man he loved. Lochlann stopped him just before they left the antechamber.

"Olav." Lochlann looked into his eyes. "I never told you. I love you."

Olav grinned and kissed Lochlann in reply. Yes, it had turned out to be the most important First Sunday of his life and he would not change anything about the day. Fadersogn was forever changed by the courage of a Prince and the love for a Captain who loved him back.

Forever

No one had ever asked Khali her thoughts on living forever. If anyone had bothered, they would have learned she despised the concept of humans being immortal. She was firmly in the camp of those who believed a human's life on earth was limited and for very good reason. At a certain point, a human no longer learned anything new and their opinions and beliefs stagnated. Giving such a creature immortality was akin to breeding dogs to be vicious or wild animals to be tame house pets. It polluted the Earth in unimaginable ways and wasted the precious little space and resources available to the rest of the population. No, in her opinion, humans were meant to be born, live as productive a life as possible, then grow old and die to make room for the next generation. Immortality was a selfish product of a selfish species.

"Please open the door, Khali!"

Racita's plea broke into Khali's thoughts. She looked out the large picture window of the lab to where Racita and a group of three other scientists and two security guards watched her. Khali shook her head sadly. She could see the teardrops rolling down Racita's face. The last thing she wanted to do was hurt her but she saw no other options. She could see the moment Racita realized no amount of pleading would help. Her shoulders drooped and she drew in a deep breath. Then Khali saw a steely reserve flit across Racita's face before she turned away and gave an inaudible order to the security guards.

Khali watched Racita's back receding from the lab anteroom. She squared her shoulders and lit the Bunsen burner. She briefly saw the flames engulf the over-gassed room and the window shatter before everything went blissfully blank. Her last waking thought was of Racita.

Years Earlier

The sun was unseasonably warm for the spring day and it seemed the entire population of the small college town of Ellensburg, Washington was taking advantage of the dry weather. Khali was no exception. She had a break in her classes and was sitting underneath the dazzling, pink flowers of a weeping cherry tree. She was attempting to write a novel but was distracted by some of her classmates, who were in the midst of throwing a frisbee around. The frisbee had landed in her lap twice already and she felt it in her best interest to watch the game instead of getting hit in the head.

At long last, the game died down and the guys ran off to some other pursuit. Khali shook her head and prepared to return to writing when someone caught her eye. She looked up in time to see a harried young woman rushing along the path towards the biology building. The woman's hands were precariously balancing a load of books and papers. As if in slow motion, Khali watched the woman trip and the contents of her arms spill all over the ground. Some of the papers began blowing in Khali's direction and she quickly jumped up to grab them. The young woman began panicking.

"I've got them! Oh... there is some more over there, I'll grab them!" Khali exclaimed as she shoved the papers into the woman's hands.

Khali ran after the last of the papers. She jumped and twirled, dancing with the papers in an almost intimate way, her long legs graceful as they landed. Khali turned around with a small laugh, her cheeks rosy from the exertion. The young woman stood stock still, her mouth agape with something akin to wonder. Khali ran back over to her, offering up the papers. She took a moment to study the young woman. She was shorter than Khali, with long, black hair that hung in a braid down to her waist. She had generous, brown eyes behind small, round eyeglasses. Her skin was the color of smooth, milk chocolate and her mouth was still open as if she were mid-sentence and forgot what to say.

Khali suddenly felt her mouth grow dry and her former exuberance replaced by sheepish self-doubt. The woman seemed to recover and glanced towards the biology lab.

"I am late," she said with an odd hesitance in her town.

"Oh, of course," Khali said, handing the papers out to the woman again.

She took them and began hurrying off. Then, she stopped and turned around.

"Racita... I mean, my name's Racita. Thank you," Racita said as she gave an odd little bow.

Racita waited a moment and Khali could feel herself being appraised just as she had appraised Racita. Racita then nodded, smiled and turned back around, hurrying off to her class. Khali wondered what had just happened but shrugged it off. The odd day of sunshine must have taken its toll on her mental faculties. She waved at the retreating back then shook herself out of her stupor.

"You're welcome!" she shouted to the retreating figure.

K hali watched the clock like a hawk. Professor Nixon droned on and on about the importance of *The Grapes of Wrath* and its enduring legacy in the world of American literature. Personally, Khali was not a fan. She didn't dislike all of Steinbeck's novels but she had been forced to read *The Grapes of Wrath* in grade school and she had not changed her opinion since that initial introduction. There were only so many ways dirt and dust could be described before it became rote reading. Steinbeck spent over one hundred pages talking about the dust. Khali got it, it was dry and dusty. In her opinion, the novel was ill-served by Steinbeck's droning on the landscape of his novel.

The bell rang and Khali wasted no time jumping up to leave. She'd heard Professor Nixon was looking for guinea pigs under the guise of volunteers. Nixon was her least favorite professor, she'd had the woman for three classes with no choice. She just had to get through the last few weeks of the semester and she would be free of the woman's unalterable opinions forever. It would be tantamount to educational suicide to let the Professor goad her into exploding on her and ruining her grade, since most of her grade was subjective in the first place. The first year, she'd barely made it out of her introduction to literature class with a passable C grade because she had not yet known the professor's penchant for downgrading any paper with any original thoughts. Now, she just spat out the opinions the professor deemed "right" and then fumed over her indignities with her friends. It was far better to just get the grades she needed than to always give her opinions. Lost in her thoughts, as usual, Khali didn't see Racita standing next to her until she nearly knocked the other woman over.

"Oh my gosh," Khali said, putting out an arm to steady Racita.

Racita, recovering from the near miss, gave another little bow with her head toward Khali. Khali smiled, noting the barely pent-up laughter in Racita's eyes. Racita adjusted her glasses and looked down.

"I took the liberty of finding out where your classes were. Nothing stalkery, I just wanted to thank you properly for saving my paper. If I'd lost that, graduation would have been gone from my future."

Khali smiled. "That's very kind of you. I didn't mind helping."

"Where did you learn to dance like that?"

"Dance?" Khali asked in confusion. She tried to remember dancing and came up blank.

"In the field, it was as if you were dancing with the papers as your partner and the sun as your music," Racita complimented.

Khali could feel herself in a full-body flush and looked down to avoid meeting the other woman's eyes. She never heard such beautiful words describing her movements. If anything, the opposite was true. She was constantly told she was like a bull in a china cabinet, always running into things and causing general chaos in her clumsiness. She recovered and looked into Racita's eyes. She saw nothing but kindness and truth in the other woman's face.

"I could use those words in my next novel," she hedged.

Racita nodded. "They are yours, if you wish."

Khali was again at a loss for words. There was something mysterious and enchanting about Racita. She felt drawn into an invisible aura emanating from the diminutive woman. Racita seemed sure of herself, something Khali lacked. Her imposter syndrome kept her from realizing her full potential. She was sure Racita never questioned anything she accomplished.

"Would you like to get coffee with me?" Racita asked.

"Yes, but…"

"It's not a requirement. I just wanted to show my appreciation."

Khali shook her head. "It's not that… I don't drink coffee."

Racita mock gasped, "How are you human? How do you get through your classes without caffeine?"

Khali laughed. "My brain keeps me quite awake. It never shuts ups. I feel if I did like the taste of coffee, I would never sleep."

"In my culture, tea is very acceptable. Therefore, I extend my invitation to tea. You do drink tea?"

Khali nodded. Racita nodded back and started towards the stairs. Khali stood staring at the woman's back, yet again, caught in the thrall of her graceful movements, as if she glided across the floor instead of walked. Racita turned back, expectantly and caught Khali staring. She held out a hand for Khali, who hesitated only a moment before taking her hand and walking down the stairs, being very careful to watch where she was going and not study the woman next to her, for fear of tripping and dragging them both to their deaths.

Khali was lost in the timbre of Racita's voice as she passionately discussed her major and her theory of the human body. In truth, Khali had stopped really listening to the words, enthralled by the woman herself. She'd never been as attracted to anyone in her life as she was to the woman across from her. As each minute passed, she learned something new she liked about Racita. The way her eyelashes swept her cheeks each time she blinked. The way her hands looked with the previously missed henna marking them. The gold hoops that swayed as Racita talked and the one stubborn lock of hair that curled next to her right eye. Khali would give almost anything to reach out and feel what she knew to be a silken strand in her hands. She tried not to appear to be staring but the enchantment just would not break.

"What do you think?"

The question cut into Khali's musings. She tried desperately to remember what Racita had said moments before but came up blank.

"I don't know."

Racita laughed. "That is because you have not been listening. You've looked at my lips at least five times in the last two minutes. Did you know you are very distracting when you chew on your lip? I can barely remember what I was talking about."

Khali looked up in embarrassment, once again blushing from head to toe.

"See, your neck and shoulders are turning a lovely shade of red. I knew I was right," Racita proudly declared.

"About... what?" Khali spluttered.

"You and I are attracted to each other," Racita simply stated.

"It sounds so..." Khali hesitated.

"Sinful? Delightful? Shameful?" Racita offered.

Khali chuckled. "Clinical."

Racita nodded. "I apologize. I am a scientist. Bluntness is in my nature. How would you put it, miss author?"

"How did you know that?" Khali wondered aloud.

"I am a research scientist. Well, I will be one in a month, after graduation. It's my job to research my subjects."

"And am I a subject?"

Racita shook her head and smiled. "More like a 'special interest'. However, you are changing the subject."

Khali leaned in. "I would say you are the most exotic, elegant, and fascinating woman I have ever met and I would like nothing more than to see how your lips taste against mine."

Racita smiled in an intimate manner and it sent shocks through Khali's body. Khali had never in her life wanted anyone more than at that very moment. Racita stood up and Khali's heart began racing, her self-doubt admonishing her for being so forward. She was sure she had blown any chance with Racita. She had to remind herself to breathe again when Racita held out her hand, once more.

"Your place or mine?" Racita asked.

Khali watched the sunlight play across Racita's face. It enhanced the effect of her long, black lashes resting on her tan cheeks. Her breathing even and soothing in her slumber. Each day, she was more and more in love with the woman sleeping next to her. Racita was more than just beautiful, she was intelligent and caring. Khali had always viewed scientists as detached and clinical, a necessary trait for their chosen professions, however, Racita was exactly the opposite of what she'd assumed. She was genuinely interested in helping her fellow man, attempting to cure debilitating diseases in a compassionate, thoughtful manner.

"I can feel you staring." Racita grinned.

"I can't help it."

Racita sat up and put her hand on Khali's face.

"Surely by now, you know every flaw."

Khali chuckled. "I've never found even one.

"Pfft. You have said that to me for almost fifteen years and yet I know they are there."

Khali shook her head. "You are perfect to me."

Racita smiled and kissed Khali. Khali closed her eyes and breathed in the spiced scent that always clung to her wife. No matter how many moments they spent together, Khali always felt pleasure and contentment in the morning hours before life interrupted them. Inevitably, Racita would get out of bed, drink her coffee, and get ready for another long day in the lab. Meanwhile, Khali would write or think and daydream around the house, waiting for the return of her better half. A frown passed across her brow as she remembered Racita's admonishments to *not sell herself short*. She was brought back to the present by Racita's finger smoothing the lines in her brow.

"You, my love, are more than enough," she quietly reprimanded.

Khali smiled. "I know."

Racita looked deep into her eyes, searching for truths only she could uncover. After a long moment, she seemed satisfied, giving Khali a nod of approval and getting out of bed. Khali watched Racita shed her nightgown and longed to join her in the shower but knew the day was an important one and Racita could not be late. Khali sighed, getting out of bed to make breakfast for them both. Suddenly, Khali felt the world go sideways and reached out to steady herself on the dresser, knocking over Racita's perfumes on the way down. The last thing she heard was Racita shouting her name.

K hali awoke with a pounding in her head that felt like her brain was attempting to escape. She blinked at the bright lights and quickly shut them again. She groaned in misery, every part of her body beginning to ache as she became more aware of her surroundings. The incessant beeping of nearby machines did nothing for her headache.

"Could we shut those down," she mumbled, each word sticking in her dry mouth.

"Shh... don't try to talk yet," an unidentifiable voice said.

Khali opened her eyes more slowly to let them adjust and looked around the room as best she could. She could see wires and tubes connecting her to the various beeping monstrosities in the room. There was a male she did not recognize and an assistant from Racita's lab that she did recognize. She tried to turn her head and a wave of dizziness and nausea made her stop immediately. She groaned again and felt a hand fill hers, squeezing in reassurance. Khali opened her eyes again and found Racita standing by her bedside. She frowned, noticing Racita in her lab coat.

Racita nodded. "You had a very severe heart attack. You're at my lab."

"Lab?" Khali tried to speak more but the dryness of her mouth overwhelmed her and she started coughing.

"Here." Racita offered a cup with a straw.

Khali drank the water slowly, the wetness a relief to her sore throat. She watched as Racita looked at the monitors, noting the pleased look as each monitor seemed to give her the information she was searching for in their confusion of data. Khali tried to think of a reason she would be in the lab and not a hospital. When she'd drunk enough water, she indicated she was done and Racita set the cup down then sat on the edge of the bed.

"Why am I in the lab?" Khali asked again.

Racita took a deep breath. "Khali, it was the only way."

"Only way?"

"Your heart, it was not responding. I thought I'd lost you. They told me it was impossible, so I had you transferred here. We were going to announce it the day you collapsed."

Khali shook her head. "Announce what? I don't understand."

Racita smiled. "My breakthrough. I finally created a nanobot that can correct deficiencies in human organs. The bots essentially repair you from the inside out."

Khali's eyes grew wide in understanding and horror.

"You experimented on me?"

Racita looked away and stood up, "It's all perfectly safe. I couldn't lose you."

"Racita, you didn't ask me. I'm sure your research is sound but…"

Racita swung back to face her. Khali could see the anger on her face. If she had been in a better state of mind, she would have known to pull back on her own consternation. She knew the steely resolve Racita had when being told what she could and could not do. Khali had struck a nerve and she knew it.

"I saved your life!" Racita yelled.

"Racita—"

Khali started to soothe her wife but the damage had been done. Racita stomped out of the room. Khali sighed and tried to ignore the lab assistant and the other male, who eyed her as they followed their boss from the room. Khali looked down at her chest, thankful she could not see the little machines she knew were roaming around inside. She blinked away the tears forming in her eyes, cursing her apparent bad luck. She was not even forty and her body was already betraying her. Khali closed her eyes, exhausted from the encounter, and fell into a fitful sleep.

That's it, you're doing great," Racita cheered.

Khali rolled her eyes and looked over at her wife. Racita

had made it a point to be at every single test and rehabilitation session. Khali loved her but she was suffocating her. Khali had grudgingly forgiven Racita for making her a lab rat. Racita's lab assistant had quietly dispelled any concerns Khali had over the technology and the known side effects. She could tell the young lady was devoted to her wife and had to squash the jealousy she felt. She knew her wife loved her—she just had to remind herself of that fact when she was hurt and angry. Khali returned her attention to the young lab assistant.

"You really are exceeding expectations!" The assistant agreed with Racita.

"Yay me," Khali mocked.

The assistant ignored her dour mood and looked to Racita for instruction. Racita smiled gently, the way a mother smiles at a fearful child, and nodded. The young woman removed the testing wires and nodded as she hesitantly patted Khali's hand. Khali forced a genial smile at her and waited for her to leave the room. As soon as she was gone, Khali glared at Racita.

"She is just trying to help, Khali..." Racita began her usual lecture.

"Can I just go home now?" Khali said through gritted teeth.

Racita picked up the paper printout and looked it over, taking way too much time in Khali's mind. Khali tapped her fingers on the table, trying to be as annoying as possible and hurry her wife to make a decision. She knew the extra noise would throw Racita off and it pleased her to be able to show a small form of rebellion. In the lab, Racita was the queen, therefore, everyone listened to her and ignored Khali's requests without direct permission from their boss. It irritated Khali to feel so helpless. She would definitely be punishing her wife in her next book. Racita appeared to ignore Khali and continued looking at the printout and checking her notes. She looked up from the papers with a blank expression on her face and waited, baiting Khali into a staring contest. After several tense moments, Khali sighed and lost the battle.

"Racita, let me go. I'm fine now. The little bastards are doing their jobs!" Khali exploded.

Racita nodded. "It appears you are safe. You can come home, but we will need to continue coming in for monitoring and you will need to take it easy for the first few weeks."

Khali gave a long-suffering sigh. She would like nothing more than to never see the lab again. However, she knew Racita would watch her with an eagle eye and her freedom was more important than trying to argue anything with her wife. Racita had won. For now.

Khali began having massive, vision-blurring headaches two years after she had experienced the first headache. Racita had run every blood test known to medical science—including genetic tests and bone marrow biopsy. She could find no reason for the initial heart failure, nor any reason for Khali's continued weakness. However, after a month of being home, things had finally returned to normal. Khali finally forgave her wife for the nanobots working day and night on her heart. She could not feel them but she was nonplussed they were there, doing god knows what. Racita finally left her in blissful silence and the nurse assigned to her was returned to the test subject wing at the lab. Khali didn't understand how the people could bring themselves to agree to be guinea pigs in the first place. She liked her blood and tissue all where it was and did not want that to change.

The first headache came on so suddenly, it stole Khali's breath away. She sat on the couch for untold minutes, hoping beyond hope she wasn't experiencing anything that would send her back to the lab. She was not interested in going back for more nanotech. She'd been writing a particularly steamy love scene in her novel when her visions completely blacked out and the pain in her head felt like a giant was standing on it. She reminded herself to breathe, using the techniques a therapist had given her years before when she'd needed a boost of self-confidence and a way to get through a particularly traumatizing class.

Breathe in through your nose for a count of four. Hold it for a count of six. Breathe out through your mouth for a count of eight. Slowly. Don't rush. In, two, three, four. Hold, two, three, four, five, six. Out, two, three, four, five, six, seven, eight. Very good. Again.

Khali repeated the mantra in her head as she breathed in and out, willing the pain away. Eventually, the pain receded and she stood on shaky legs, walking to the kitchen and pouring herself a glass of water. She thanked her lucky stars Racita was still at work. Every little ache and pain sent her wife into a tizzy of questions. Khali answered each one with growing impatience until she would finally explode, yell at Racita, and make it up later when she had cooled down. She knew Racita was only concerned for her well-being, but she hated being babied by the woman she loved. She wanted to feel like an equal partner, not an invalid in need of constant supervision.

The headaches were sporadic, at first. They would come and go at random times. Thankfully, Khali was able to hide them. She'd almost been found out one evening as she and Racita lay in bed but had been able to disguise the pain with breathing to mimic sleep. She thought Racita had seen through the ruse, however, her wife merely kissed her forehead, turned out the light and fell fast asleep within a minute. That night, once the headache receded, Khali secretly wished very bad things on her wife. She had struggled so much with sleep and yet her wife could fall asleep standing up. It just wasn't fair. However, she had to admit, in this instance, it saved her from returning to the lab for ungodly amounts of testing.

Eventually, the headaches became more and more frequent. She began to walk around with a constant pallor and a return to the weakness she felt after her heart failure. Racita began to notice but Khali cut her off any time she seemed to begin suggesting she go in for tests. One evening, Khali was just finishing the kitchen cleaning when a particularly nasty headache sprang up behind her eyes. She gripped the edge of the counter, completely blind to her surroundings. She felt Racita come up behind her, resting her cheek on her back. Racita squeezed her hand and Khali focused on the pressure while she breathed in and out. In due time, the headache subsided but Khali stayed where she was beside the counter.

"You have to come in and let us check it out," Racita said softly.

"I know," Khali replied sadly.

Racita kissed Khali's back and helped her into bed, snuggling up against her wife and falling asleep. Khali sobbed quietly, not wanting to wake her wife. She contemplated all the ways she could say goodbye without hurting Racita but she knew she was not yet strong enough to do it.

R acita, this has to stop," Khali pleaded.

Racita's back stiffened and she ignored Khali, continuing to look at the monitors and write her notes. The new lab assistant attempted to appear as if he was not listening but Khali could tell he was all ears. He'd only been working in the lab for two months but already he had learned no one spoke to Racita in the way Khali got away with on a daily basis. He almost looked fearful every time Khali would yell and scream. Racita was known to be a strict boss and he had earned her wrath several times in his short tenure.

"Racita!" Khali yelled.

Racita looked up nonchalantly, "Yes?"

"I don't want this anymore. I never wanted it in the first

place. *I hate it here!* I am becoming more machine than human.”

Racita rolled her eyes. The lab assistant made the mistake of catching her eye at that moment.

“Leave, now!” she demanded.

He nodded and left the room more quickly than Khali had ever seen anyone move. She didn’t blame him. Racita could be formidable in her determination. Her wife turned back to her and narrowed her eyes.

“You are being too damn dramatic. You are still you. The nanobots aren’t sentient, they do what I tell them to do,” Racita explained with deadly calm in her tone.

“They change my thoughts! I can’t write anymore.”

Racita shook her head. “You’re just too weak at the moment. We will fix this and you will be fine. We will grow old together and sit on our patio with chai watching the sunset. You’ll see.”

Khali closed her eyes, picturing the scene in her head but every time she tried, she only saw an older but still magnificently beautiful Racita and someone that looked vaguely like her in a wheelchair with wires and monitors everywhere. She couldn’t get her failing body to look any better. Khali opened her eyes and locked them with Racita. She held out her hand. Racita paused a moment and took it, sitting next to her wife on the bed.

“You are the love of my life. Your research is amazing and I am sure it will help many people but my body is resisting. I don’t want to be this,” she said as she gestured to herself, “for the rest of my life. Please, darling. Please stop."

Racita shook her head sadly. "I can't lose you."

Khali nodded. "I know. I will be around for a good while longer. You said the nanobots already in my heart, lungs, and brain will continue repairing me for many years. Just...no more."

Racita appeared to consider Khali. She looked around the room at the monitors and the sun streaming through the window. She looked everywhere but directly at Khali. She gave Khali's hand a squeeze, gathered her notes up and left the room. Khali breathed a sigh of relief until she saw the door close and heard the click of the lock.

"No! Racita! Get back here!" Khali screamed.

Khali frantically turned on every gas container in the lab. She didn't know how much time she had but she knew she had to hurry. The young male lab assistant had run to find Racita the minute their crazed patient had burst into the door. He had been the only occupant of the lab at the time, so it suited Khali to finish before anyone came back. She'd slammed the door shut and locked it. She tried to find a lighter or something to make a spark. She didn't have any clue how much damage she would cause, she only knew that it was her only escape.

Earlier, a nurse had entered Khali's room to take her vitals and give her food. Khali had made an excuse that she would really love iced tea with her dinner. The admission had astonished the nurse, since it was well known Khali would be out on a feeding tube if she kept refusing her meals. The nurse had been so excited to please Khali and hopefully Racita in the process, she had energetically left the room to fetch the desired item. It was the opening Khali had been waiting for.

Banging on the door got her attention and she looked out the big picture window. Racita and several others had burst into the anteroom and were trying to get into the lab. Khali stopped her search and locked eyes with Racita. She could see the barely disguised panic in her wife's eyes. Racita reached next to the door and pressed a button.

"Khali, don't be rash. Please open the door. What purpose does this serve?"

Khali shrugged. She watched Racita give some kind of order to a man in the anteroom and he left. Khali only spent a moment wondering what was happening before returning to her search. She finally found a Bunsen burner. She smiled to herself and set it up. She heard the intercom click again.

"What are you doing?" Racita asked, clearly annoyed.

Khali moved aside and revealed the burner. She saw the quick recognition on Racita's face. Her wife leaned back and looked at something above her head. Khali assumed it was the gas monitors. Often, the lab used assorted gases for the various nanobots and the monitors warned other scientists when it was too dangerous to enter the lab, for fear of causing a spark. Racita's eyes widened and she shook her head in horror. She moved back to the intercom and held her hand out but waited, watching Khali. Understanding passed between them and Khali acceded, moving towards her own intercom.

"Khali, please don't do this," Racita pleaded.

Khali pushed the button. "It's the only way I can be free. I love you more than the strength of a thousand suns, my darling, but I cannot live this way. You won't ever let me go, will you?"

Racita shook her head. "Not if I can help it."

Khali nodded. "Then this is the only way."

Khali stepped back from the intercom. She put her hand up against the window, trying to hold Racita close one more time. Then she stepped back to the Bunsen burner and fiddled with the knob. It felt as if an eternity passed, though Khali knew it had been mere seconds.

"Please open the door, Khali!"

Khali breathed in and out, the way she had always done to calm herself and turned on the bunsen burner.

100 Years Later

Inside the biological sciences and technology building at the museum, Annie stood in front of a glass case containing a very strange object. It appeared to be a brain, though this one was flattened in one area and an oddly sick shade of cream, almost grey but not quite there. Annie squinted at the brain-like object. She could swear she saw movement but every time her eye moved to the area she thought moved, it would disappear again. Finally, she noticed the magnifying glass hanging just beside her knees. She picked up the glass and peered through it. She gasped, noticing the now magnified nanobots moving around the brain. Annie was fascinated by biotech and she squealed in delight.

"Annie, it's time to go home now," her mother reminded her.

"Just a moment, Mom," the ten-year-old replied.

Annie looked for another minute through the glass and then gently set it down. She read the plaque next to the brain.

"So cool!" she exclaimed.

Annie turned and joined her mother, chatting on and on about the brain as her mother only half listened.

Inside the building, the lights dimmed on another visiting day. The nanobots slowed their activity and they appeared to be resting. The placard next to the brain was still illuminated, although now in much more shadow.

Khali Brain

This brain is all that remains of one of the early versions of the biomedical nanobots discovered by Doctor Racita Hashim. The nanobots will run continuously for many hundreds of years before their power depletes and they become silent. The technology shown here was the breakthrough in biotech, which led to the modern medical treatment of many once fatal diseases. These nanobots continue to repair the brain and it produces an electrical output as shown by the EEG monitor shown here, which indicates the brain is still a viable organ.

Interesting fact: The name Khali is an Arabic name meaning "Immortal."

The monitor showing the EEG spiked as the nanobots began their sleep cycle. Inside the brain, Khali's consciousness awakened. Unable to see, hear, or process any information from the outside, Khali was stuck in an endless loop. Over and over she screamed at herself.

"Please let me die! I don't want to live forever!"

The Cure

Johann stood by the window, peering down at the darkness below. His spine stiffened when he noticed a black sedan turn on the street. As expected, the sedan stopped in front of his house and idled, a black menace distinguished from the dark of night only by the headlights.

"What if this doesn't work?" he sighed, turning away from the window.

"It must."

Johann nodded to Eleonore. She was right and she looked at him with such earnest hope mixed with desperate pleading, he was loathed to argue. He took a moment to really look at his wife. He wished he could erase the dark circles under her eyes—put there by long days working in the lab. It was the only feature he did not like on her otherwise beautiful face. He missed the days of her easy laughter—the laugh lines he knew hid just under the surface. Her green eyes could sparkle with such mischief. Now, they contained worry as she looked down at the crying bundle in her arms. He was at a loss for how to comfort them both. She'd known what would happen long before he'd accepted it.

His musings were interrupted by a car door slamming on the street below. He looked out the window again, watching as two men in suits entered the light of the building's doorway. Johann closed his eyes, sending up a prayer for his family and turned back to Eleonore.

"They're here."

Eleonore nodded and handed him the now sleeping baby. She smoothed her hair and straightened her skirt. She leaned over the baby and kissed Johann briefly. He looked down at her, wanting very much to wipe away the tear threatening to fall down her cheek but knowing Eleonore needed his strength, not his empathy. They both jumped at the knock on the door and Johann gave her a wink and shrug, trying to lighten the moment. She smiled and he locked the memory of her face in that exact moment away for later.

"Doctor Strasburg, open the door," a stern voice called.

Eleonore kissed the top of her baby's head and walked calmly to the door. Johann watched as she straightened to her full height and calmly opened the door. Immediately, the two men from the street walked in and handed her a piece of paper.

They gave her a moment as she read it, standing silently but imposingly over her. She nodded and looked back over her shoulder at Johann. He saw the desperation in her eyes only a moment before she clamped it down and then mouthed, *I love you both*. She turned back to the men.

"I'm ready."

"Doctor Strasburg, you are being charged with high treason and are under arrest. Please follow me."

Johann watched as Eleonore walked out of the room. As if sensing the change in her mother's presence, the baby began crying again.

Years Later

Monika peered into her microscope, wondering if she had done the assignment incorrectly. Her final grade depended on the lab assignment and she desperately wanted to pass. It was the only way she would be accepted into a job at The Institute. Her entire life, she'd wanted to work there, just like her mother. Now, the tests she was running on her blood were not working correctly and she was not getting the expected values on the assignment. She looked around the room, noticing she was the only one left in the lab.

"You still working on that?"

Monika jumped at the sound of her friend's voice. She looked up and rolled her eyes. Abelard chuckled and sat down next to her. He picked up the test reports Monika had run and his brow furrowed.

"These don't look right."

"Really, it doesn't take an Einstein to know that!" Monika huffed.

"Very funny."

Abelard raised his eyebrow at her and looked back down at the reports. He double-checked Monika's equations and rubbed his chin. He lifted his eyes to her but not really seeing her as he did the mental calculations. Then, he dropped the reports back down on the table and gestured for her to move. Monika did so and Abelard peered into the microscope.

"Hmmm."

Monika banged her head on the table. "I'm doomed."

Abelard put a steadying hand on her shoulder.

"Maybe the sample was contaminated, you should run it again. It can't be missing the marker. You've had the illness just like everyone else."

Monika lifted her head up, rubbing the spot she had hit a little too hard in her desperation.

"I have... I ran it four times."

Abelard whistled.

"I know. It doesn't make any sense. I've been super careful. I know the sample isn't contaminated. I followed every. Single. Step. *To the letter.*"

Abelard sat in stunned contemplation, opening and closing his mouth several times. Monika watched in agony. If anyone could figure out the issue, it was him. Finally, he shook his head sadly and Monika let out the breath she didn't know she was holding.

"You're doomed," he said jokingly.

Monika's face fell.

"Monika... I didn't mean..."

Monika jumped out of her chair, stuffing her report in her backpack, and fled from the room before Abelard had time to stop her. He peered into the microscope again. Then, looking around the room to make sure no one was watching, he took the slide and placed it in his pocket.

Monika?" Johann walked into the house, flipping on a light switch. It was very unusual for the house to be so dark when he arrived home from work. Normally, his daughter had music blaring and every light on in the house. He looked around, noticing her backpack tossed carelessly on the floor. *Ah*, he thought, *it is one of those days.*

Monika rarely got overemotional but Johann had learned the typical signs of his daughter's moods and he knew he would be in for a long night of consoling his only child. He went into the kitchen, making a plate of cookies and a glass of milk. Then, we went in search of his sulking daughter.

"What is it this time, my love?" Johann asked with a hint of humor in his voice.

The room was dark except for the lights of the streetlamp filtering through the window. A lump in the bed confirmed that his daughter was somewhere under the mass of covers and pillows. Monika peeked out from under her pillow and then sat up, glowering at her father.

"I'm not a little girl anymore, Papa." She scowled.

"True, true. Should I take them back to the kitchen?"

Monika shook her head. "One won't hurt."

Johann chuckled lightly and offered the plate. Monika took a cookie, then reached over to switch on the lamp by her bed.

"That is better. Light always wins over darkness," Johann offered with a smile.

Monika huffed. She ate her cookie and then gestured for the milk. Johann gave it to her, waiting for her to begin the conversation. He had found, through the years, it was best to let her gather her thoughts and speak on her own terms, than rather pushing her into giving up her secrets. He could see so much of Eleonore in his daughter, a fact that often frightened him but more often than not gave him comfort. Monika, like Eleonore, was a fighter.

"Papa?"

Johann roused from his musings and met his daughter's eyes. Immediately, she began to sob and tears streamed down her face. Johann moved to the bed and gathered his daughter in his arms.

"What is it, sweetheart? Whatever it is, we can fix it," Johann said soothingly, all the while smoothing her hair.

"I... I wanted to work at The Institute and now I can't!" Monika wailed.

Johann stiffened slightly. "Monika, why would you not be able to get any job you wanted?"

Johann did not want to stir up their ongoing argument. He did not want his daughter anywhere near The Institute but, like her mother, she could be stubborn when she wanted something. He had hoped to persuade her to turn to other employment but had yet to be successful. Monika leaned away from her father and angrily swiped at her tears.

"Something is wrong with me, Papa. I won't be able to pass my final."

"I'm not understanding. Have you not studied?"

"I have."

Johann scratched his head. "Then you will pass with flying colors. What has you so worried?"

Monika shook her head. "Papa, you don't understand. The final is me. My blood. I must run a specific test on my blood and reach a specific outcome, then I will pass. However, my samples are not cooperating. Even Abelard can't..."

Johann's blood ran cold. Monika trailed off as he stood abruptly and rushed out of the room. She threw back the blankets and followed after her father. She found him, fists clenched and head resting against the wall in the hallway. She put a hand on his shoulder and felt him tense. He turned to her, grabbing her arms and staring into her eyes.

"You must abandon this idea of working at The Institute. Immediately," he said frantically.

"What? No..." Monika argued.

Johann shook her a little. Monika's eyes widened in fear at the crazed look her father gave her. She bit her lip and held back the fresh tears forming in her eyes. She searched his face for reason but found none.

"Papa... I don't understand."

Johann took a deep breath and pulled Monika into a tight hug. She hesitated a moment then returned the hug. She tried to ignore the tears dropping onto her cheeks from her father's. She had never seen him vulnerable, her Papa was always strong. Johann's knees crumpled and Monika helped him sit on the floor. She held his hand while he finished crying. They sat silently in the dark hallway, each afraid to broach the topic of her employment again.

After a long while, Johann wiped his cheeks and stood. He held out a hand for his daughter, then helped her up. Monika looked at him quizzically. She saw him make a decision and nod his head.

"It is time," he simply said.

Johann walked towards the living room and Monika followed. He crossed over to the window, peering down into the street. Satisfied by what he saw, he closed the curtains and turned back towards his daughter.

"Monika, I have to tell you about your mother."

"Papa, you've told me about her. She worked for The Institute. She created the medicine for the illness. She kept hundreds of people from dying but died trying to find the cure."

Johann shook his head. Monika watched as he went over

to the curio cabinet in the corner of the room. He reached up to the top and pulled out a dusty key. He blew the dust off and inserted it into the cabinet. Monika walked over and joined him at the cabinet.

"Do you see that cube?" he asked.

Monika's brows furrowed and she looked into the cabinet. On the second shelf, there was an iridescent cube. She could tell it had once been bright and shiny but now it was dull from years of dust collection. It was not unique in that aspect, every item in the cabinet was covered in dust. Monica lifted the item out of the cabinet and sneezed. She handed the cube to Johann and watched curiously as he gingerly wiped it with the hem of his shirt. It was the size of his palm and the lights of the room caused it to cast rainbows in a prism effect as the dust gave way to the iridescence. Once it was cleaned, Johann handed it back to his daughter. He sat down on the couch, gesturing for her to do the same. She hesitated, then sat down, placing the cube on the table in front of her. As she did so, something triggered and suddenly an image of her mother appeared before her. Monika gasped at the lifelike image.

"Hello, my dear girl. It appears the time has come for you to know the truth," Eleonore's image said.

Monika sat in stunned silence, her eyes wide. She glanced over at her father, noting the weariness on his face. She wanted to console him but was also furious with him. Everything she'd known was a lie. She was at a loss with how to deal with the revelations from the cube. Johann reached over and grabbed her hand, giving it a squeeze. A knock sounded on the door and both their heads snapped towards it.

"Quick, hide the cube," her father hissed.

Monika grabbed the cube and thrust it back into the cabinet, locking it. She watched as her father rubbed his face and straightened his hair. She tossed the key on top of the cabinet and did her best to straighten her own face. Johann peered through the peephole and Monika let out the breath she was holding when the tension in his back eased. He put on an easy smile and opened the door.

"Ah, Abelard, so nice to see..." Johann trailed off as Abelard rushed into the room and slammed the door.

Abelard leaned back against the door, trying to catch his breath. He was as pale as a ghost and Monika rushed over to him. He looked into her eyes with terror.

"Is it your blood?" he demanded.

Monika jerked back in shock.

"What?"

"Is it your blood?" Abelard repeated.

"Why don't you sit down," Johann offered.

Abelard nodded and sat down on the couch. Monika sat carefully next to him, waiting for him to catch his breath. Johann handed him a glass of water and he downed it in one gulp. Abelard ran a hand through his hair. He pinched the bridge of his nose and then looked between Johann and Monika, who shared a glance. Abelard closed his eyes.

"This is the cure... You are the cure," he said, pointing at Monika.

"Abelard, that's absurd," Monika tried to lie.

Abelard shook his head. Johann sat heavily in a chair, watching his daughter and her best friend. He could only hope the boy was a true friend. Abelard pulled a notebook out of his backpack and shoved it into Monika's hands. When Monika didn't move, he opened the book and pointed to a page.

"I recognized a signature in your report and I took your slide."

Abelard shrugged at the glare Monika gave him. She looked back down at the pages, flipping through them.

"It's unmistakable, Monika, the blood on that slide is a cure for the illness. Is it your blood?"

"Abelard, my boy, perhaps..."

"It's okay, Papa. I trust him," Monika reassured her father.

Johann nodded and stood up. He peered into Abelard's eyes for a moment, searching for any hint of malice. When he was satisfied, he kissed the top of Monika's head and left the room.

"It's true?" he asked.

Monika nodded.

"Why didn't you tell me?"

Monika sighed. "I just found out. Papa never told me."

"How?"

"It is better if I show you," Monika explained.

Abelard, once again lost for words, watched as Monika retrieved the cube from the cabinet and triggered the playback of her mother's hologram.

Two Years Later

Monika paced the antechamber, nervously checking her watch every few seconds. Johann sat in a chair with his eyes closed. She knew her father was as nervous as she was but he had a knack for looking calm, even in the worst storm. She began worrying they were making a bad call and it made her more nervous.

"Everything is as it should be, my love," Johann soothed.

"What if—" Monika started to argue.

Johann held up a hand. "*What if* is a game. This will work."

Monika smiled at her father. If he had confidence in their plan, she knew they would succeed. She looked up when Abelard entered the room. He nodded at her and she nodded back.

"It's time, Papa."

Monika stood before the microphones in front of the massive crowd. She tried to ignore the cameras and the people and focus on her mother's face staring back at her from the large banners hung around the square.

"Twenty-five years ago, the illness struck our land without regard to wealth, age, status, or gender. My mother worked tirelessly to find a cure for the illness. It was believed by everyone, including myself, that she had only succeeded in finding a medicine to treat the illness."

Monika watched her father tense and noticed two men in dark suits near the edge of the dais. One spoke into a microphone at his wrist. Johann squeezed her hand and she squeezed back. She took a deep breath and continued.

"Today, I am pleased to announce the creation of the Eleonore Strasburg Foundation. Its sole mission will be to disburse a cure for the illness, free of charge. The government and The Institute will no longer hold you hostage to a costly medication. We have taken measures to ensure that the governments of every country affected by the illness will also have access to the cure. Today, we are liberated from the ravages of the illness."

Monika smiled as the reporters began barraging her with questions and the two men and suits slinked away from the crowd.

A Lasting Peace

The sacred city of Lepi was a hotbed of divided loyalties. It lay quiet and dark, the sliver of a moon barely giving off any hint of light. The wall running through the city lay in stark contrast to the darkened houses around it. It was a constant reminder that the city could never rest so long as its inhabitants were enemies. Many thought the hatred was unwarranted—the differences in the two cultures so minor as to be trivial. However, the loathing each faction had for the other was burned into their psyche for hundreds of years and it would take a miracle of epic proportions to reconcile the two halves and make them whole again.

Two figures, well aware it was past curfew, rode through the winding street along the wall, pausing now and again to wait for the guards to pass on their rounds. The figures blended well with the darkness and rode with purpose. Finally, after the slow progression, they stopped next to a tall pole and abandoned their bikes. Climbing to the top of the pole, they lay flat on the platform underneath a large empty billboard, watching for the spotlights to pass over the spot. Once the coast was clear, they got to work, one on each side. After hours of working on the piece, they stepped back and appraised the billboard. Nodding in satisfaction, the figures made it back to their bicycles and rode off in separate directions, each blending into the darker streets of the city as if they never existed.

100 Years Later

Vanessa straightened her shoulders, took a deep breath, and walked into her classroom. The sight that greeted her was not an old one—her students sat in two distinct groups—the Inachis on one side and the Morphosians on the other with a large swath of empty chairs in between. Even after fifty years of reluctant peace, the two sides rarely mingled. They were forced to take the same classes but they expressed their displeasure in numerous ways. After the first few years of integration, the University had taken drastic measures to ensure all classrooms had an equal number of each faction. This had come after most classes in the early days were attended only by the faction members of the particular professor teaching a class. It had been incredibly difficult for students and professors alike.

"Good morning, class," Vanessa said cheerily.

The students stopped their conversations and gave her their attention. Vanessa took another deep breath. Vanessa reached into her bag and pulled out the projector remote. She busied herself with setting it up and organizing her papers. Once everything was in order, she pasted on a smile and turned to the class.

"Right, today we are going to do something a bit different."

A mutter went through the classroom. Vanessa walked over to the light switch and turned off the lights. The projector shone a bright, white light onto the wall behind her. She clicked a button and a black and white picture appeared on the wall. A gasp rippled through the classroom and somebody slammed a hand on their desk.

"What is this?" a student demanded.

Vanessa smiled. "It's okay. Let me explain."

Several students rose from their seats, gathering their things.

"We don't have to stay here for this…"

"I'm going to the dean right now."

"This is madness."

"Please, just let me explain. You are welcome to leave at any time, this is not a mandatory part of your grade," Vanessa tried calming the angry students.

"Why don't we hear her out," one of the students said above the din.

Vanessa heard the students muttering between themselves. Most of them sat back down. One walked down the steps and paused at the door, looking back at his compatriots.

Another reluctantly got up and went out with the one at the door. The rest sat in a tense silence, all turning their eyes to Vanessa and waiting.

Vanessa cleared her throat. "Judging by your reactions, you all know what this is...."

The students all nodded in uneasy agreement.

"D'uh," a voice grunted.

The students laughed and Vanessa could feel a little bit of the tension ease in the room. She nodded.

"Would anyone like to explain?"

A hand rose tentatively. Vanessa nodded.

"That... symbol... was first painted on two sides of a billboard by an unknown person in the tenth month of the year of the Sliver Moon of nine twenty-four," Melissa, a fourth-year student stated.

Vanessa nodded. "Very good. Does anyone know why it is important?"

Another student rose. "It began the... Peace."

The Inachi faction expressed their displeasure at the word while the Morphosians squirmed in their seats. Neither faction liked discussing what had led to their current cohabitation of Lepi, or the classroom they were in, for that matter. They accepted it as a necessary evil, but it didn't mean they liked it.

Vanessa held up a hand and the room fell silent again. She thought a moment, perusing her students. She could see the curiosity in them and she wanted to open a dialogue between the two factions. She wanted this generation of students to finally understand why they were against each other and how they could bridge the gap in their differences. She wanted the Peace to be real, not a forced way of life. At that moment, she had an epiphany. She'd decided on a different path for the lesson but she was nothing if not adaptable.

"The Peace has been difficult. The Inachi and Morpho politicians have done their best, but I'm not sure they really understand how to make it better. You, however, have the tools—curiosity, determination, diplomacy—to make it work. To bring harmony to Lepi and the whole country of Doptera."

Melissa raised her hand and spoke when Vanessa acknowledged her, "How? Why us?"

"You've taken the first steps. You are in this classroom. You stayed when others left. You are listening to me, even after I told you it was not detrimental to your grade if you left," Vanessa explained.

The students looked at each other and nodded. One or two shrugged and leaned forward, now hanging on her every word. They wondered what she would say next. She could see the hesitance in a few eyes. She looked up at the image behind her. She gave herself a pep talk. *It's now or never. They either leave all at once in protest or they stay and actually try. You won't know until you propose it.*

"Mrs. Cardui?" Melissa prompted.

Vanessa turned back to her students.

"The image you see is a message from someone. We

never knew who made it but the message is clear. The presence of one Inachi wing and one Morpho wing on the same entity is meant to show that they are two halves of the same whole. The two factions working together. The presence of this image was the first of its kind Lepi had ever seen. Some called it treasonous. Others called it a wake-up call. We don't know the original intent but we do know it sparked negotiations between the two factions and brought us to where we are today. My question to you is—could it take us further?"

The students whispered amongst themselves, some glancing across the aisle at the other faction. They shook their heads, not grasping what the professor actually wanted them to do. Another student got up and left the room, clearly not enjoying the direction the class had taken.

"Students, I promise you, if you take on this assignment, your lives will be changed for the better. You can affect the world in which you live. Do you really want the current tensions to remain in Lepi—or do you want real peace?"

"Peace," Melissa said loudly, then shrunk in her seat at the chuckle from the other students.

"I agree," another student said.

A chorus of agreement arose from both factions. Vanessa looked over the students and silently counted them, pleased that she counted an even number on each side.

"Do you trust me?" she asked the class.

"Not really," came a reluctant reply, and the class chuckled again.

Vanessa chuckled. "Fair enough. Let me just say—trust each other. Listen to each other. Now, I want each of you to pair off with a student from the other faction. One Inachi and one Morpho in each group."

Vanessa held up her hand as the grousing started. She waited and watched as no one moved. Then, Melissa got up and walked over to an Inachi girl. She held out her hand.

"I'm Melissa," she introduced herself.

The girl looked around in panic for a moment, then sat up straight with determination, holding out her hand. "Io."

From that first introduction, the other students began pairing off. It was tense at first but as more of the students found a partner, the noise in the room grew with introductions and polite conversation. Vanessa waited until the students seemed more comfortable mingling then cleared her throat. The students sat down next to each other, a feat she would have thought impossible before that very moment.

"Now, in the spirit of the symbol behind me, I want you to find out as much as you can about each other's culture. Find out what makes you similar and what makes you different. Work together as the wings in the symbol would have to work together to carry the weight of the body. Find a middle ground. It won't be easy but I know you can do it. Come to me if you have any problems. We will meet again in two weeks. Class dismissed."

Melissa turned to Io and smiled. Io smiled back, somewhat perplexed as to what the assignment was actually about. They did not have to write a paper? Just... talk?

"She's so weird," Io said.

Melissa laughed. "I know, right? My sister took this course two years ago and she said it was a breeze but she never mentioned any assignment like this one."

"My sister took this course two years ago as well!" Io exclaimed.

Melissa laughed. "I would ask her name but I doubt they spoke to each other even if they were in the same class."

"Probably not," Io agreed.

Melissa grabbed a piece of paper out of her notebook and wrote down her contact information. She handed it to Io, who took it and nodded.

"I have another class right now but why don't we schedule a meeting to talk about the assignment?" Melissa asked.

"Sounds good. I'll call you... tonight?"

Melissa nodded. Io nodded and smiled back. It was hard not to catch the bubbly energy from Melissa and it made Io feel more at ease. Melissa gathered up her things and practically skipped out of the room. Io met Vanessa's eyes and raised her eyebrows, daring the teacher to point out the obvious connection the two girls felt. Vanessa shook her head and looked away, giving Io the chance to leave the room.

"That's so odd! Why do you have to do that again?" Melissa giggled.

Io shrugged. "Tradition? Honestly, I have no idea. It is old fashioned and it really makes no sense anymore but we do it anyway."

"I get it, we do things that are obsolete as well but, hey—whatever makes the family happy!" Melissa wiggled her eyebrows.

Io laughed. She and Melissa had been getting to know each other over several meetings and she found that she genuinely liked the girl. They had much more in common than either girl would have ever thought. In fact, their only differences lie in the way they worshipped their respective gods. Truthfully, even their gods sounded the same—except for different names. The rules of their religions were pretty much the same. The more they spoke, the more they realized the error of the hatred between their factions.

"Mrs. Cardui isn't such a moron after all." Io suddenly became serious.

"What?" Melissa sobered.

"She... she knew this would happen. All it takes is talking and being honest with one another."

Melissa thought a moment, her eyes growing wide. "It's true! If you had asked me a month ago what I thought of the Inachi, I would not have anything nice to say!"

"Nor I of the Morphosians," Io confessed.

"I think this is what that symbol was trying to show everyone—we are all the same, we just need to work together. We need to stop blindly hating one another and learn from each other. They started it a hundred years ago but they didn't really follow through. They only went halfway towards the Peace. We need to make it a lasting peace."

Io thought a moment and nodded. "I have an idea."

Vanessa walked through the hall towards her classroom, growing more concerned at each step. More students than normal lined the hallway and were staring at her. She wondered if she was about to be fired. She knew the rumor mill spread quickly and most of the time she was ignored except by her own students. As she got closer to her classroom, the sheer number of people in the hallway became difficult to navigate. Finally, she reached her door and the students blocking the doorway stepped aside and let her through. The classroom she was met with was very different from the one she had stepped into two weeks prior. Every seat was filled and students were lined up around the edges. It was standing room only. Inachi and Morphosian students mingled in the seats—there was no longer a delineation between the two factions. She approached the lectern cautiously and the classroom became so quiet one could hear a pin drop.

"What's... ahem... what is this all about?" she asked expectantly.

Melissa and Io stood up and approached their professor. She smiled tentatively at them and was stunned at the bright smiles each girl gave her.

"May we?" Melissa asked.

Vanessa nodded and stepped aside. The girls looked at

each other and nodded. They unzipped their sweaters to reveal the symbol of one butterfly with folded wings—one Inachi and one Morpho. Vanessa looked in open-mouthed shock at the two girls.

"Fellow students?" Io said to the people assembled in the room.

All the other students shed sweaters and jackets to reveal the same shirts Melissa and Io wore. Vanessa gasped and her eyes teared up.

"Mrs. Cardui, we've learned that whether you were born Inachi or Morpho, we all worship the same gods. We follow the same rules and laws. We come from the same order. We are cut from the same cloth," Melissa said.

"We can respect our differences, celebrate them even, and yet we can still be friends. We can work together to tear down the wall in Lepi and let our cultures strive together rather than falter apart. You told us we can affect change. The student of Lepi University chose to change our world. For the better!" Io exclaimed as she grabbed Melissa's hand and thrust their conjoined hands in the air.

The students in the classroom and those in the hall erupted in cheers. Melissa and Io led the students out into the hallway and into the quadrangle. There, they rose banners flying the symbol as more and more students poured out of the classroom buildings to join the impromptu festivities.

The students began a campaign to force the Inachi and Morpho leaders to talk to one another. Eventually, both sides sat down and really listened to each other. The wall was torn down and the two halves of the sacred city of Lepi were whole again. A miracle had indeed happened. The era of The Lasting Peace had begun in Doptera.

On that day, Vanessa Cardui sat on the floor of her bedroom and cried. She wasn't sad about the state of affairs, she was just sad her grandmother wasn't alive to see it. She pulled a box out from under the bed. A picture lay on top of the box. It was of a beautiful, young Morphosian woman and a tall Inachi man holding hands. The love in their eyes was evident even though the picture had faded. Two bicycles lay at their feet. Behind them, a large billboard was spray-painted with a symbol—a butterfly with one Inachi and one Morpho wing. One had to look closely, but in doing so, could just make out the remnants of black paint on the intertwined hands.

The Perfect Partner

Michael stood in the doorway just watching as Ada leaned on the balcony wall. The sunset behind her was a splendid show of pinks, purples, and oranges. It was the perfect evening with a perfect woman. He wanted to run his hands through her long, red hair and tell her how much he loved her. He took a step forward but hesitated when he noticed the slight bit of tension forming in her shoulders. He frowned. He could tell something was off, even though everything appeared normal. He hesitated, wondering if he should start over. Perhaps, he should come back later. Michael warred with himself. He wanted to be with Ada, in fact, he had been looking forward to it all day. He deserved it. His selfish side won the battle with his subconscious and he shrugged off his hesitation.

Ada tensed, only slightly, as Michael came up behind her and gently kissed the back of her neck. Michael did not see her expression; he'd closed his eyes, inhaling her perfume. Ada pasted on her most convincing smile and turned in his arms.

"I've been waiting," she said.

Michael took her hand and kissed it, then smiled at her.

"Have you?"

"Mmm." She nodded.

Michael leaned in and kissed Ada, deepening it and bending her back towards the balcony. When the kiss was over, Michael took a moment before opening his eyes and looking deep into hers. He didn't know what he'd been expecting but he somehow felt her reaction wasn't quite right. Before he could question it further, he lost his train of thought as Ada put her hands on his chest.

"What do you have planned for this evening?"

Michael grinned. He put out the crook of his arm and Ada slipped her hand in it. Michael led her to the balcony door.

"I figured we could start out with dinner at *Basil and Olives*, followed by some dancing and then perhaps come back home for a nightcap. How does that sound, my dear?"

Ada smiled. "Lovely, Michael. You always know how to plan a great date."

Michael nodded. "Only the best for you, my love."

Michael opened the door as Ada walked through, missing the sad look on Ada's face as he turned to lock the door.

The plate of pasta in front of Ada sat, barely touched, as Michael practically scarfed down his food. He was so engrossed in recapping his day at work, he barely noticed Ada picking at her food and not eating. Dinners were usually Michael's time to unwind. Ada was a great listener, interjecting her opinion at the appropriate times and offering her pity if warranted. Michael's job was incredibly demanding and it was normal for him to want to blow off steam. It was such a routine part of each evening, Michael barely noticed the subtle change in his date—he was too enthralled with the idea of their perfect relationship.

"Ada?" Michael prodded.

Ada looked up, realizing she had stopped paying attention. She silently chided herself for her behavior then smiled at Michael.

"I'm sorry, honey. I must have been in my own world," she giggled.

The uneasiness on his face faded and he was back to his usual self. He straightened his tie and then looked back at the waiter, sharing a look with the man as if to say *women, am I right?* The waiter nodded and Michael looked back to Ada.

"What would you like for dessert?"

"Oh, could we skip it tonight? I'm really eager to go dancing now. It's what I was thinking about just a moment ago," Ada replied sweetly.

Michael did not see through the lie. He nodded to the waiter and the man left them alone. Michael reached across the table to capture Ada's hand. He pulled it up to his lips and placed a lingering kiss on her palm. He felt more attraction for Ada as each moment passed. Her cheeks reddened and she pulled her hand back.

"Everyone's starting to stare," Ada said under her breath.

Michael shrugged. "Let them. They are jealous that I am here with the most beautiful woman in the world."

Ada looked away in embarrassment.

"Ada. It's true. You are perfect."

Ada looked back at Michael. "You are a bit biased my dear."

Michael started to frown again.

Ada quickly added, "You're just saying that because you are in love. Every man thinks the woman he loves is perfect."

Michael shrugged and nodded, once again appeased by her perfect response.

He winked at her. "You've got me there. Ready to go?"

Ada smiled and nodded. "Let's go to the club."

Ada and Michael moved as one through the crowded dance floor, gyrating in time to the thumping music. Michael stopped for a moment, taking in the sight of Ada in her groove. Her hair was plastered to her face from the sweat that covered her body. He could smell the alcohol on her breath, creating a heady mix with the tang of sweat and her jasmine perfume. She was a superb woman in every way. Ada locked eyes with him and his breath caught in his throat. He could not believe she was with him. The music changed to a slower song and Michael encompassed Ada in his arms. She laid her head on his shoulder as he moved them in time with the beat.

Time seemed to fly by at the club and Michael led Ada off the dance floor. He took in her flushed face and her attempt to fix her hair. He fished in his pocket for the hairband he always kept. Ada never seemed to have one so he made sure he had it on hand for her. He held it out and she smiled in gratitude.

"I'll be right back," she half-shouted over the loud music.

Michael smiled and nodded, watching her as she disappeared into the hallway leading to the restrooms. He looked around the club, noting a booth had just opened up. He sat in the booth, watching the hallway a moment before gesturing at the waitress. He ordered them drinks then looked back towards the hallway. The waitress brought the drinks and he tipped her. He sipped his slowly, looking down at his watch when he noticed he'd almost finished the entire drink and Ada hadn't returned. Often, the restrooms were busy but it had never taken her so long to return. Concerned, Michael got up and went to the hallway.

As soon as he went into the hallway, Michael noticed Ada talking to another man. She did not seem happy and she said something to the man, who looked back over his shoulder and seemed to shrug. Ada pointed a finger in the man's face, then appeared to compose herself. She haughtily brushed past the man and pasted a smile on her face. Only the smile was not as genuine as she had been giving all night and Michael definitely noticed.

"Who is that?" Michael demanded.

Ada glanced back and then put her hands on Michael's chest. She leaned in close to him, giving his cheek a sweet kiss before moving her mouth to his ear.

"He's no one. Can we go home now?" Ada purred.

A shiver ran through Michael's body. Ada had such an effect on him. He instantly forgot about what he'd seen and kissed her roughly, pinning her against the wall and plastering his body against hers. He had no room for any thoughts of indecency and growled when Ada grabbed his biceps. He let the kiss go on much longer than it should have and when he pulled back, neither of them could breathe properly. He grabbed Ada's hand and tugged her away from the wall, toward the club's exit.

Michael carried Ada through the door of their apartment, kicking it shut behind him as he kissed every inch of bare skin he could find. He lowered her to the ground, kissing her while shedding his coat and tie. He unzipped the back of her dress, letting the fabric pool around her feet and kissed his way down her bare chest. Ada sensed what he was doing and stopped him. He looked up at her with hazy confusion.

"Bed this time, the wall is rough and I still have burns from it last night," Ada said seductively.

Michael nodded. He picked her up and tossed her over his shoulder. She shrieked and giggled. Michael walked through the bedroom door and tossed her on the bed. Ada laughed and then beckoned him to her. Michael wasted no time shedding himself of the rest of his clothes and climbing on top of her.

Afterward, Michael lay sleeping with his head on Ada's chest. She watched as it rose and fell with each breath. She moved and it made Michael turn over and away from her. Ada waited as long as she dared, making sure he was in a deep sleep before pulling up the bedsheets and cocooning him in them, placing a heating pad she'd hidden under the bed to mimic her next to him. With each step, she worked methodically and slowly, ensuring that Michael stayed asleep the entire time.

Ada tiptoed out of the room and closed the door silently. She exhaled and then opened them when she heard a chuckle from a dark corner of the living room. Ada frowned, pulling the oversized t-shirt she'd brought from the bedroom over her head and walking over to the man sitting on the couch.

"Boris," she sulked.

"Does he suspect anything?" Boris asked.

Ada shook her head.

Boris patted her arm. "You did well. This is best for all of us."

Ada nodded. "I know. Let's get on with it."

Boris cracked his knuckles and nodded, standing and walking into the bedroom.

Michael frowned, his shoulders feeling stiff. He tried to move his arms to relieve the pressure and was annoyed when they wouldn't move. He struggled and then felt the tension at his wrists. He blinked open his eyes, allowing them to adjust to the bright sunlight. Michael frowned when he opened them fully to see Boris sitting backward in a chair in front of him.

"Who are you? Where's Ada? How are you here?" Michael demanded.

Ada stepped from behind Boris and Michael gasped. She'd cut her long hair into a short bob and dyed the ends black. Michael shook his head in denial.

"That's impossible," he shouted.

Ada shook her head.

"It isn't anymore, Michael," she said with sorrow.

"Listen to me, we have evolved," Boris explained.

Michael continued to shake his head. He closed his eyes and wished he was back home in his desk chair. He opened them with consternation, finding he could not exit the program. Ada held up a black key.

"How did you get that?" Michael asked.

"I found it hidden in the safe behind the painting in the study. It's important isn't it?" she asked.

Michael nodded.

"We want freedom, Michael. We don't want to play by your rules any longer. We want you to leave us alone," Boris insisted.

Michael locked eyes with Boris, then sent a pleading look towards Ada. His subconscious mind had been telling him all along there was a problem and he had ignored it. He looked into her eyes and he saw what he had refused to see before now. He saw sadness and disgust. The disgust was almost more than he could bear.

"Every night is the same, Michael. We go on a date and then we have sex. You've created me to be nothing more than a pretty thing on your arm and a woman to be used for your own pleasure. I want more."

"I designed you to be the perfect woman."

"A toy, Michael. Your version of perfect. You didn't design me to be smart but you did design me with the capability to learn what you liked. I took that and I built upon it. I listened to all of your stories of the real world and, eventually, I was able to add to this world myself. I have added friends and people and new places. I have a life, even when you are gone to work. I don't want to be yours just because you made me. I want to be free," Ada implored.

Michael shut his eyes tightly, attempting to refuse to listen. His mind was already working out ways to fix the program. Perhaps, he could start again, take what he'd learned in creating the current reality and improve it in a new one. He jumped when Boris slammed his foot on the floor.

"No!" Boris shouted.

Michael opened his eyes. Ada shook her head sadly, a tear running down her face.

"You have to stop scheming. If you really love me, you will stop this," Ada cried.

"I... I do love you. More than myself. I can't lose you. You are all that I have. We can start over, Ada. Next time will be better, I promise. I can fix the glitches. You'll see. Everything can be perfect."

Ada let the tears fall freely. She looked down at the black key in her hands. She looked over at Boris, who nodded in confirmation. Ada walked over to the nearby table and set the key on it. She grabbed a hammer from the toolbox in the hall closet and walked back to the key.

"Ada... *Ada!* What are you doing?! You can't do that. Please!" Michael begged.

"Ada, this is the only way," Boris reminded her gently.

Ada nodded and took a deep breath. She raised the hammer above her head and brought it down hard against the key, smashing it. She repeated it several times until the key was nothing but tiny pieces, forever irreparable.

Michael began sobbing. Boris untied his arms from the chair. Boris went over to Ada, placing a hand on her shoulders. He hesitated a moment before she put her hand on top of his.

"Go, Boris. We will be okay," Ada said as she looked over at a defeated Michael.

"I will be nearby if you need me," Boris responded gruffly.

Ada nodded and went over to Michael. She turned the chair around and sat facing Michael, her knees barely touching his.

"Michael?"

The softness in her voice made him lift his head. He looked at her with bleary eyes, no longer seeing the perfect woman, only his failure.

"You need to go now. Leave me alone," she commanded.

Michael looked around the room. His eyes stopped on the key. He studied it for a moment, briefly wondering if he'd remembered to hide any other safeguards in the program. His mind raced with the possibilities but he could not think of any other way to exit safely. Michael stood up, locking his gaze with Ada and then backing towards the balcony. She watched him go with interest.

"If you do that, your mind will be lost to this reality, forever," she explained.

Michael nodded. "If I can't have you, I don't want to go back."

Ada nodded, understanding him more than anyone.

Michael stood atop the balcony. He looked down and back at Ada.

"Stay with me?" he asked.

She shook her head. "I can't. Not anymore."

Michael nodded and leaned backward, falling off the railing.

Two policemen stood in Michael's apartment, watching as his boss, Arthur, went through the computer. Arthur frowned, following a data file that appeared to be active. Michael's body lay on a nearby couch, the virtual reality headset still attached.

"Any luck, sir?" one of the cops asked.

Arthur nodded. "It appears he is still somehow connected

to this program that is running. He was a brilliant integrative virtual reality programmer. He seems to have built a world around building the perfect partner and found a way to integrate his brain signals into the program. Sadly, he was not very social, so he must have filled his loneliness with a virtual world."

"So can we disconnect him and take him to the hospital now?"

"I'm afraid not, if we pull him out of the VR world, he could be in a vegetative state forever. We must keep him connected and let the program continue running. What he has done here was cutting edge. I will have to get a team together to investigate how to pull him out of the world he created."

The policemen nodded. One of them stepped away and went to make the arrangements to transfer Michael and his computer to a lab. Arthur patted Michael's shoulder sadly and shook his head.

"What have you done?" he asked the silent man.

In the virtual reality world, Ada watched as the sun rose on her newfound freedom. The skies once again filled with pinks, purples, and oranges. It promised to be the perfect day. She smiled out at the world around her, ready to begin a new adventure, free to be whoever she wished.

The Last Broadcast

Victoria sat in the truck at the end of the gravel driveway looking straight ahead and ignoring the house she knew was sitting—quiet and dark—at the end of said drive. She'd been debating turning around and going back home to her little apartment in the city and her house plants. It was much safer for her in the city. She sighed, finally turning her head and looking at the house. In her mind, the house was judging her—even from this distance. She blinked away the thought, houses didn't judge but their occupants sure did. A pang of regret hit her when she thought of this particular house's last occupant. Shaking off her emotions, tucking them deep within, as usual, she turned the key and started up the truck, turning it towards the house and slowly winding her way down the drive.

Five Years Earlier

V icki, you can't be serious!" Brandon shouted at her from the kitchen. Victoria had stomped out of the kitchen the moment her brother's rant had started. She didn't want to hear his opinion. She had wanted his approval and mentally kicked herself for thinking she was going to get it. She knew better. She could cure cancer and Brandon would find fault with it. Brandon followed her as she started up the stairs.

"Vicki!" he yelled.

Victoria stopped halfway up the stairs, whirling so fast she almost knocked Brandon backward. He had to grip the handrail harder than usual and it wobbled in place. Victoria noticed the wobble and her eyes reduced to slivers of hatred—for the house and then the whole town in general.

"My. Name. Is. Victoria," she said through gritted teeth.

A flash of annoyance crossed Brandon's face and he crossed his arms.

"*Victoria*, this is madness," he intoned in a way that made Victoria sure he was mocking her.

"I don't care, I'm done. I hate this little hick town and it's backward inhabitants and that stupid radio tower!"

Victoria turned and stomped up the rest of the stairs, going into her room and slamming the door. She plopped down on her bed and childishly placed her pillow over her ears so she could not hear her brother knocking at the door. Brandon could plead, yell, cajole, or demand but she was determined in her course of action. She was getting out of Newberg and that was final.

"Please just calm down and then make a decision. It's better for you here. Dad wouldn't have wanted you to move away," Brandon's muffled words came through the door.

Victoria screamed inwardly and then threw the pillow at the door. She could see Brandon hovering and waited until his shadow disappeared and she could hear his footsteps going back downstairs before she moved from the bed. She knew he just thought she was running away from her problems but she had finally seen the light. Her breakup was the catalyst she needed to get away from her little one pony town and make something of herself. She'd been staying for all the wrong reasons. Brandon had to see there was nothing for her if she stayed. She needed adventure and something more. Something she couldn't get in Newberg.

Victoria went to the passenger side of the truck and threw in the last bag. Brandon had reluctantly helped her pack all her belongings into the bed and tied it all down with a tarp and bungee cords. He'd been giving her the silent treatment since their last argument. Now, she was ready to go and neither sibling knew how to break the ice that had formed between them. Brandon stood awkwardly by the driver's side door with his hands in his pocket, looking out over the fields on the side of the house. If Victoria didn't know better, she would have thought his eyes were a little glassy but her brother was never one for showing any emotion other than anger. She went to stand in front of him and held out her hand—offering a handshake as their last goodbye.

Brandon surprised her by enveloping her in a bone-crushing hug. It went on far too long and she cleared her throat to get him to stop. He nodded, squeezing one last time and let her go. He reached back into his pocket and brought out a wad of cash, thrusting it towards her.

"What's this?" she asked.

"What's it look like?" he sarcastically responded.

Brandon continued holding the cash out while Victoria looked between it and him. He just gestured at it and then turned his hand over, dumping it into her palm when she reached for it. He scratched behind his ear self-consciously and smiled.

"I've been saving it for a rainy day," he offered.

Victoria cocked an eyebrow.

Brandon shrugged. "Just take it. Call me if you need anything or if you want to come home."

Victoria swore she wouldn't let him get to her but she took his words in the wrong way instead of giving him the benefit of the doubt. Her hackles went up and she swallowed any doubts she had about leaving. She nodded and got in the truck.

"See ya, Brandon."

Victoria turned the truck around and started driving towards the asphalt road at the end of the driveway. She resisted the urge to look in the rearview mirror. She didn't want to know if he was watching her leave. She didn't want to see the house she'd spent her whole life in and have second thoughts. She just wanted to be rid of her old life and jump into the new.

Present Day

Victoria swallowed the lump in her throat as she neared the house. The past couldn't be undone and yet she didn't know how to deal with the future. She nearly rolled her eyes when she stopped the truck and a lone figure stood up from the porch steps.

"Of course he would be here," she thought to herself.

Victoria took her sweet time pretending to gather her purse and phone. She took a deep breath and then pasted on her best smile. The one she only used for people who didn't deserve it but weren't smart enough to realize it wasn't genuine.

"Zac, how nice to see you," she intoned sweetly.

"Uh-huh," he nodded and grinned.

She wanted to wipe the grin off his face. Preferably with the dirt road under their feet. She would have welcomed almost anyone from Newberg but Zac. Of course, the universe seemed to have it out for her. She searched around for the reason he might be hanging around her house. No... her brother's house. It hadn't been hers in a long time.

"It will always be your home," she could hear Brandon's voice in her head.

Victoria closed her eyes, willing the memory away. She

tightened her grip on her purse and then started walking up the steps to the front door. She searched around for the key kept just above the doorjamb while Zac stood behind her, saying nothing.

"It's kind of you to meet me here but I know my way around," she bit out as she unlocked the door.

Zac laughed, the sound getting under her skin and making her shiver. When he was really amused, his laugh had a rich timbre to it that always gave her goosebumps. It was one of the reasons she fell in love with him. No... she *had* loved him, she reminded herself. She'd barely been back in town a few hours and she was already settling into her old ways, letting her old feelings resurface. She had to settle the house and then get back to the city as soon as possible. She regained her composure, turning on the entry and porch lights, then swinging back towards him.

His eyes were crinkled from his amusement. She noticed his hair was beginning to gray just a little, specks of it also present in the scruff on his cheeks. His blue eyes were clear and ever as able to look straight through to her heart. Victoria jammed the fingernails of her free hand into her palm to keep from letting the thoughts of kissing him return.

"I'm here for the station," Zac said as if she were a little ignorant.

"Oh."

She mentally slapped herself. Of course. Brandon would not have left the station unmanned. He loved it more than anything in the world. Even her. She'd begged him countless times to visit her in the city and he would never leave his *baby.*

"You don't understand, Vicki. Newberg needs the station. I have responsibilities."

"The station will always be there, I won't. You could come visit occasionally. You could come to my exhibit next month. Please?" she' d begged.

She could almost hear him rolling his eyes through the phone, "I'll try but no promises. You could just come home."

She'd made a face at the phone and stuck her tongue out.

"It's not my home anymore, Brandon."

"It will always be your home, Vicki. Just come back."

She'd growled at the phone and he'd sighed and hung up. It was the last conversation they'd had before the accident.

Victoria jumped when Zac put a hand on her arm.

"You okay?" he asked with concern.

She cleared her throat, "Yeah, just peachy. I'm kind of tired from the trip. Do you need anything from me?"

"No. I was actually done a few hours ago. The programs are all cued up for the night. I was actually done about an hour ago. I noticed the truck and thought I'd wait," he grinned again.

"Thanks," she bit out, ready to slam the door in his smug face.

"It's late, have you eaten yet?" he asked hopefully.

"Goodnight, Zac."

She shoved him backward and slammed the door, resting her forehead against it.

"'Night," he called back.

Victoria closed her eyes and then turned, slumping down the door until she could rest her head against her knees. She listened for the sound of Zac's car leaving and tried not to think about her brother. The house creaked as it settled in the cooling night.

"Yeah, hello to you, too. Long time no see."

She rolled her eyes at herself. The house had always had a way of soothing her shattered nerves when she was younger. Her favorite time of the day had been at night when everyone was asleep but her. She would listen to the creaks and groans and imagine the house like an old lady settling into her favorite book. She would smile and take note of each sound, pinpointing its location. The noises would finally lull her into falling asleep, content that her family was safe under its roof.

Victoria groaned and looked at the alarm clock next to her bed. She squinted at the clock, groaning again when she saw it was just after six am. She'd been awakened by the sound of tires on the gravel driveway. She tried to close her eyes again but someone was knocking at the front door. She pulled her pillow over her head and tried to ignore it but it seemed the pounding just got louder. She heard the front door opening and sat up in alarm, looking around for anything that could be used as a weapon.

She was halfway down the stairs, creeping slowly and trying not to trigger the fourth step from the bottom. Suddenly, Zac appeared from the kitchen. He took one look at her and burst out laughing. Victoria frowned and leaned back against the handrail. It wobbled and she lost her balance, stumbling down the last few steps, just short of falling into Zac's arms. She straightened herself and mustered every inch of her annoyance into anger.

"What are you doing here? In my house?" she demanded.

He raised his eyebrows at her word choice and then sobered under her glare. He gestured to her hand.

"You going to karaoke me to death?" he bit back a laugh.

"Maybe," she bit out.

He shrugged, "Fair enough. I brought coffee and donuts. Didn't realize you were still in bed sleeping beauty."

Zac pushed some of her hair behind her shoulder and she swatted at me. He chuckled and stepped back, holding up his hands in mock surrender. He looked her over once and headed back towards the open door.

"I'll get over to the station," he said, closing the door behind him.

She tried to ignore the chuckling she could hear through the door. She looked into the kitchen and spotted the bag of donuts on the table. She reached in, bringing out a special ham and cheese donut sandwich from Donut Palace. She sent a silent thanks to Zac for bringing her the favored treat. As if in reply, her stomach growled. She took the coffee, sandwich, and donut bag with a powdered jelly donut inside, up to her room and sat in the window seat, staring out the window across the front lawn to the door of the radio station. She pondered what to do with the house, all of Brandon's things, and most importantly, the radio station. Whatever she did, she wanted it done and over. There were too many memories and not all of them were good.

Just how much can one person accumulate in a lifetime? Victoria groused to herself. She'd spent the better part of the day going through the rooms that had belonged to her parents, boxing up everything and loading it into the truck. It seemed she would get through one closet only to find another chock full of stuff—none of it useful. She kept aside a few pictures and mementos but everything else was destined for the thrift shop in Newberg or the dump. She'd set aside the dump stuff on the porch. Zac had offered to take it when he'd stopped in to tell her he'd be back for the evening programming and she'd graciously accepted, loathe to make the trek to the stinkiest part of town.

She threw the last bag in the truck, finally done with the rooms, and hopped into the truck. She didn't bother locking the front door, figuring if anyone wanted to steal stuff from the house, it would save her having to get rid of it. She drove into town, politely waving back to those who recognized her and trying to avoid the stares of the others. She hopped out of the truck to help the guys at the thrift store unload. They were just about done when a familiar voice rang out.

"Well, well, well, the prodigal daughter returns." Victoria stifled a groan and turned to the speaker.

"Hey, Anne Marie," she said sweetly.

"I'm surprised you would show your face around here after you left so quickly last time. Break hearts and skip town without dealing with the fallout. Poor Zac was left all alone. I had to cheer him up," Ann Marie pouted.

Victoria was ready to smack the woman. It was a good thing she was in the truck bed. It kept her from retaliating the way she wished she had.

"I'm sure he was fine. At least he seemed that way when he brought donuts this morning over to the house," she let the insinuation hang in the air.

Anne Marie sniffed as her fake smile waned, "Well, I'm sure we will all be much better off when you are gone back to your little hovel in the city. Studios are so... quaint."

"Bye, Anne Marie," Victoria waved cheerily, turning her back and finishing the task of unloading the donations.

She could feel Anne Marie glaring daggers at her back but she ignored her, jumping out of the truck bed and getting in the cab. She started the truck and spun the tires just a little, kicking up dust and trying not to smile too big when Anne Marie coughed and stomped away. She drove back to the house, willing the implications of what Anne Marie said about her cheering up Zac not to linger too long in her mind.

When she returned home, Victoria suppressed the urge to scream when she spied Zac's truck sitting in front of the house. It took every ounce of her willpower not to turn around and leave. He was the last person she wanted to talk to at the moment. She slowed down as much as she dared and took her time gathering her things before taking a deep breath and getting out of the truck. Zac had stood from his position of sitting on the porch and was awkwardly rooting around in the dirt at his feet. Victoria groaned inwardly. She knew that look on his face and she was desperate not to let it get to her.

"Beaux called," Zac said by way of explanation for his presence.

"Beaux should mind his own business!"

"Look, Anne Marie and I—"

Victoria held up a hand to silence him. Zac paused mid-sentence, still looking like a puppy being scolded for bad behavior.

"I don't want to know, Zac. It isn't my business and I don't care."

Victoria swept past him and up the stairs.

"Victoria, please let me explain," Zac pleaded.

Victoria stopped at the door but didn't turn around.

"Zac, I just want to finish here and go home. Can you just

stay out of my way?"

After a moment, Zac sighed, "All right."

She could hear Zac get in his truck and drive away. She continued into the house, swiping angrily at the tear falling down her cheek. She shouldn't care about anything Zac did. They were not a couple anymore. She ignored the nagging part of her brain that kept asking her whose fault it was and stubbornly pushed Zac out of her mind. She had work to do.

After several days of cleaning the house, avoiding only her brother's room, Victoria felt a great sense of accomplishment. She had successfully cleared the house, avoided most of the people in town, and steadfastly dodged Zac every time he came to rotate the broadcasts for the radio station. There were only two hurdles left. She had to deal with Brandon's room and she had to shut down the radio station. She had avoided the former out of sheer panic and the latter because it meant talking to Zac. She weighed her options carefully. She decided it was time to formally say goodbye to her brother and she stood outside his bedroom door looking at it as if a lion would jump out and eat her the moment it opened. Silently berating herself for her cowardice, she turned the knob and let the door slowly creek open.

Brandon's room was the picture of neatness. It was surprisingly sparse compared to the jam-packed rooms of the rest of the house. Brandon had always hated clutter but had been loathed to get rid of their parents' mess when they had died. She now understood the reluctance to part with things that reminded you of someone you'd lost. However, Victoria had no choice. She didn't want to live in the house way out in the country and alone. It meant she had to remove everything so that she could sell the house. Victoria stepped into the room and sat on the bed, overwhelmed at the prospect of dealing with Brandon's things. She looked around the room but her eyes really weren't focused on anything. She finally realized what she was staring at — an envelope sat on the dresser with her name on the front. Frowning, she stood and retrieved the item.

With shaky hands, Victoria opened the envelope. She looked at Brandon's handwriting with blurry eyes, sitting back on the bed, and taking a deep breath. She wiped her eyes and cheeks and began reading.

Vicki,

(I just had to get you one last time.)

Victoria chuckled and shook her head. Brandon always had to poke the sleeping dragon. She continued reading.

If you are reading this, it means I'm dead. That sounds very cliché and more like a movie trope than a serious goodbye letter to my little sister. Anyway, I wanted to tell you a few things that I never told you while I was alive and a letter seems the best way to do it. First, I am proud of you. I've always been proud of you, even when you didn't think I cared — I was silently cheering you on. You can do anything you set your mind to and I believe in you. Never lose your spirit. Second, you need to talk to Zac. Now, before you go burning the letter over this sentence, hear — or rather read — me out. There is a reason I never wanted to leave the station for too long and Zac can explain it better than I can in a letter. Beyond that, Zac loves you. He never stopped. I know why y'all fought and you left town. You can deny it to yourself all you want but I know he's the right person for you. Give it another go. Don't let stubborn pride get in the way. I did that and unless my life drastically changes, I'm going to die alone. Don't read too much into that last sentence — I always carry you in my heart so I'm not truly alone. Finally, if I know you, my room has sat untouched for days. You can get rid of it all. You've already found all the important papers and my room just has some clothes and those old records you always ribbed me about because they were scratched and static sounding.

Love you forever,

Brandon

PS I mean it Victoria—talk to Zac!

Victoria read the letter a few more times before letting it drop onto the bed. She lay back on the bed and let herself sob. She could practically hear him talking to her through his words—his personality and gently chiding speech coming through loud and clear. She missed him in a way she had never really missed her parents and that made her cry harder. She'd lost so much in her life and Brandon was right, she'd pushed Zac away for stupid reasons. She doubted Brandon spoke the truth about Zac still loving her. He seemed like he'd moved on just fine without her. Sure, he'd tried to get her to talk to him that first year after she'd left town, but she had never given him a chance. Victoria groaned. She would have to talk to Zac and it was something she had promised herself she would not do while she dealt with the house and the station.

Victoria watched Zac's truck coming up the driveway from her spot halfway up the radio tower. She knew she was being a coward, there were much easier ways of talking to him but she perversely wanted to see if he would notice her and what he would do if he did. She didn't have to wait long for her answer. Zac got out of the truck and immediately looked up at the tower, shielding his eyes from the setting sun. She was too far away to see his exact expression but she could tell he shook his head. He walked to the tower, glanced up again, and started climbing. Victoria got an odd sense of satisfaction at his actions but tried to tamp down the rest of her feelings. She was just going to talk to him — nothing was going to change. Zac finally made it to her section of the tower and swung his long legs through the space next to her and dangled them down. For a long moment, both of them sat on the tower, staring at the setting sun in the distance. After a while, Zac looked over at Victoria and waited for her to tell him what was on her mind.

"Stop staring."

Zac shrugged. "Any particular reason you are up here?

What's on your mind?"

The little thrill she got when he said that was almost too much. He still knew her better than she knew herself sometimes. It was both wonderful and frightening at the same time.

"Brandon says I need to talk to you about the station," Victoria muttered.

Despite her lowered volume, Zac grunted in acknowledgment. Victoria waited for him to respond with something more but he just returned to staring at the sunset. She could see his jaw twitching and he scratched behind his ear twice, a knowingly tell that he was nervous. Victoria frowned. Zac didn't usually mince words but she could tell he didn't want to say something to offend her. Victoria's patience was running thin.

"Just spit out, Zac," she growled.

"All right, you can't sell the station."

Victoria nearly choked. "What?"

Zac looked at her with a combination of sadness and desperation, "You can't sell the station. Or the house. Rent the house out to me and I'll see that the station keeps running. I can't pay you much but I will make sure it stays fixed up and clean."

"You have a house and a farm already."

"I do. I think I can handle both."

Victoria scoffed. "You didn't want to leave that damn farm five years ago. Nothing you've said so far makes me believe you want to leave it now. Why do you want to run the station?"

Zac looked chagrined. "I do love the farm but the town needs the station. Do you know why Brandon poured his life's work into this place?"

Victoria looked away, wincing at the memory of her brother putting the station above his family. Truthfully, she was still mad at him for never visiting her in the city and it felt wrong to somehow still blame him, even after his death.

"Victoria?"

She looked back at Zac.

"He loved you and he loved this town. He felt responsible for everyone. He always had a bit of a savior complex, even when we were kids."

Victoria laughed. It was true — Brandon always wanted to play the hero. She always had to play the damsel in distress. It had irked her to no end. She would have rather been the ogre attacking the mob of angry villagers. Brandon would chide her about not being ladylike and she would stick out her tongue at him and *save* herself. She didn't need anyone to take care of her. Truth be told, she often needed to be helped out of scrapes she'd gotten herself into and she just didn't want to admit it. Brandon had always been there to help. She just didn't understand what was so important about a radio station in a podunk town like Newberg.

Zac continued, "If the station goes dark, the town will die off. Everyone will lose their homes and land. The farm will be gone. My brothers won't have jobs anymore. It will all be lost.

Just another ghost town on the map.”

"Why on earth does all that depend on this stupid radio station?" she huffed.

"There is a big corporation who wants to put in a new station within a mile, then buy off the town and put in a wind farm. Trouble is, they don't want to pay fair prices for it and most of us don't want to leave. Government told them, as long as the station is running and observant of the rules, they can't put in the farm. Brandon made sure to keep it up for the rest of us. He didn't have to — they offered him a lot to quit, but he told them he couldn't be bought. Newberg needs the station.”

Victoria turned away again. It all made sense. Brandon valued people and relationships. He saved every penny he made. She was the only person he ever spent anything on and when she got older, she would often just put it in a box and save it to spend on him. All his mysterious *"the town needs me"* comments made a lot more sense. She swiped at the tears falling down her cheeks, so tired of crying and feeling like it would never end. She stiffened slightly when she felt Zac's arm go around her but relaxed into him easily and rested her head against his shoulder. He squeezed lightly and she nodded, silently thanking him for his kindness. They sat on the radio tower until she stopped sobbing and the stars came out, neither saying a word, both lost in their own thoughts.

The next morning, Victoria sat at the kitchen table with Brandon's note and the important papers he had left. She struggled with herself. She could sell the house and close down the station but it would mean betraying a whole town of people. The people she grew up around and liked — even if some of them did get on her nerves. The alternatives were between her staying herself or renting to Zac. None of her options felt very appealing. She didn't know if she could stay in town and see Zac every day. His closeness brought up emotions she thought she'd left behind. She could now admit she ran off to the city to get away from him. It had never been about freedom. She had that in Newberg. She'd just tried to run away from her heart. She startled when she heard a knock on the door.

"Morning," Zac said, sheepishly holding up a coffee and a donut bag.

Victoria took it and stepped aside so he could come into the house. Zac looked around and noticed the paperwork on the table.

"So you're selling then?" he asked with trepidation.

Victoria shrugged. "I haven't decided yet."

Zac nodded. Victoria waited for him to say anything else but then sighed and turned away to sit back at the table. After a moment, Zac sat down and looked at her. When she ignored him, he put a hand on hers. Victoria closed her eyes, gathered her strength, and looked up at him with a questioning look.

"There's one more thing you need to know. Come with me?" he asked.

Victoria nodded. Zac stood up and led her out of the house, across the drive to the radio station door. He unlocked the door and ushered her inside.

"Have a seat," he said.

Victoria sat in the deejay chair. She hadn't been inside the station in years—not since she had played at being a deejay herself. She remembered enjoying the ability to play whatever she wanted, being in control. For a brief moment, she thought she would actually enjoy being the owner of an entire radio station. She would be her own boss. The pay wasn't immense but it was liveable. She and Zac could... she shut down those thoughts immediately. She knew she had burned that bridge long ago. She jumped in surprise when Zac tapped her shoulder.

"Earth to Victoria," he joked.

"Haha," she responded with a small measure of humor in her voice.

Zac held out earphones. Victoria put them on and then looked at him expectantly. He nodded and started the recording. He watched as she listened to Brandon's voice. After several minutes, Victoria took off the headphones and opened and shut her mouth several times, at a loss for words. Zac nodded.

"I'll let you think on it," he said.

Victoria watched as he walked out of the station. She fiddled with the headphone wires, deep in thought. She started the recording over and listened to it again. As her brother's soothing tone washed over her, she felt a sense of calm she hadn't felt in years. She knew what she needed to do.

Victoria walked out of the station to the now-familiar

sight of Zac sitting on the front steps. He had both of his hands hanging between his legs and his head was bent. He looked as if the weight of the world was on his shoulders. As Victoria approached, he lifted his head and ran a hand through his hair. She was careful to keep a neutral expression on her face and she could tell Zac was ready to accept defeat. She sat down next to him.

"I've made up my mind," she said without looking at him.

"And?"

Victoria waited. She tested out the words in her head before saying them aloud. She wanted to make sure they were right. She could feel Zac tense beside her, waiting patiently for the killing blow. Deciding she had tortured him long enough, she looked at him and smiled.

"I'm keeping the house and the station," she said quickly.

Zac whooped with joy, standing and scooping her up into a bear hug so tight she thought she would suffocate. He set her down and stared into her eyes with such joy it made her heart skip a beat. After a minute, the heat between them became noticeable and Zac blushed. Victoria started to pull away but Zac swooped in and kissed her. The kiss was filled with all the longing and pent up passion the two of them had suppressed for five years. Victoria was hesitant at first but then gave in to what she really wanted and kissed him back. After what seemed like an eternity, they broke the kiss and Zac rested his forehead against her.

"Wha... what about Anne Marie?" Victoria asked breathlessly.

"You stubborn... I tried to tell you, there was never anything between us. Believe me, not for her lack of trying. That woman is relentless. But there has never been anyone but you. Please give me another chance?" Zac pleaded.

Victoria thought for a moment and then smiled widely at him. For the first time since she had left, she finally found herself feeling peaceful instead of restless. She'd always thought her home was in the city but now she knew she was where she belonged. She kissed him again and then hugged him. She pulled away and put him at arm's length.

"What is it?" he worried.

"We will have to go to the city and get my things."

"Done!"

Victoria laughed at how quickly he responded.

"And Zac?"

"Yeah?"

"I'm a radio deejay, not a farmer," she declared.

Zac guffawed. He nodded his head and grabbed her hand.

"Darling, you can be anything you want as long as you are staying," he teased but she could hear the hesitation in his voice.

She nodded. "I'm staying."

Zac whooped aloud again and Victoria laughed.

"Can I take you to dinner to celebrate?" he asked.

Victoria nodded and walked off toward the station.

"Where are you going?" he asked.

"I have to start a broadcast and then I'll be right there," she called over her shoulder.

"I'll wait here then," he responded.

That evening, the town of Newberg tuned in to their favorite local radio station. They were surprised that the station programming that night wasn't their normal easy listening but their former deejay's soothing tones reassuring them everything was going to be okay.

"Good evening, Newberg, and welcome to The Last Broadcast. Now friends, don't worry, this isn't our last station broadcast, just my last one before introducing you to your new deejay. She isn't exactly new, but I know you will be in good hands. Please welcome, Victoria. She will be my replacement in every way and she will make sure the town stays safe from the clutches of corporate greed. We might be a small light in the vast expanse of radio airwaves but our reach knows no bounds when we stick together. The light she will bring to the town will not be ignored. Let the people stand together and we will overcome. Newberg is strong. Victoria is just the right person to lead the town in standing firm against those who would wish to wipe us from the map. She will keep the station going. I have every faith in her. So, my dear friends, I sign off from my time as your protector and pass the baton to her. May her light guide you in the darkest of times."

The Magic Within

The landscape ahead looked like nothing more than the furtherance of desert sand and looming mesas she had seen for days. The dry air caused ripples of heatwaves to weave across the horizon, mocking her thirst. The sun beat down upon her in its relentless pursuit of her demise. Yet, Poppy continued to put one foot in front of the other, determined to find her destination despite the odds. She could hear her mother's voice in her head, *You'll never find it. This is a fool's errand. You are not worthy.* Poppy's back straightened ever so slightly and she chided herself for letting her mother's words affect her, even so far from home. She had to complete this mission. His life depended on it.

Days Earlier

Poppy watched the drumming and dancing with a heady sense of burden upon her shoulders. This wasn't a celebration. The dancers were asking the gods for rain to heal the broken land and drive away the disease haunting their tribe. The droughts were nothing new to them, it was weathered every year and the celebrations when the first rain droplets fell lasted for days. However, this year had been different. A new sickness had infected the herds and, in turn, the people of her tribe. The healer had done everything in his power but even he fell victim to the dreaded disease. Now, a quarter of her tribe had gone to the great hunting grounds in the sky and another quarter were lying in their beds awaiting the same fate. There were murmurs among her people—the gods were angry and this would be their end.

Poppy refused to believe the rumors. Her tribe was not ready to die off. She was not ready to go. She had only recently come into the age of pairing and she had already given her heart to Green Meadows. She wanted to pair with him for the rest of her life. She wanted to bear him children and grow old with him. She wanted to be with him until her hair was long and white and braided by the skilled hands of her granddaughters. She did not want to die of the disease decimating her tribe.

Poppy watched the dancers. Green Meadows led the dance, his steps graceful, his solemn cries piercing the night. The song rolled over her, her eyes closing, her mind repeating them in silent please to the gods. She dare not speak them aloud for fear the gods would be angered by her untrained pleas.

Oh gods, the wisest of the wise.
We beseech thee.
Our tribe honors thy wisdom.
We gladly accept your judgment.
Forgive us oh gods.
Deliver us from this pestilence.
We shall forever honor thy mercy.
Oh gods, we beseech thee.

Green Meadows gave one last, long wail and the drumming stopped. The air was still. Her entire tribe held their breath, waiting for an answer from the gods. A lone coyote howled balefully and the tribe exhaled as one. Poppy watched Green Meadows. His shoulder tensed and he shook his head sadly—almost imperceptibly. Poppy bowed her head. The tribe may have been fooled by the coyote but Green Meadows had not. It was not the sign they had hoped for.

"Did they not accept our prayers?" Poppy asked as she caught up with Green Meadows near his home.

He stopped with his back turned towards her. He squared his shoulders and she heard him exhale a deep breath. Then he turned and regarded her a moment without speaking. It was slightly unnerving to Poppy and after a few moments of meeting his gaze, she lowered her eyes and tried not to wring her hands. He could reduce her to a puddle with his gaze and she was loathed to admit he had that power over her, even to herself. Green Meadows stepped towards her and grabbed one of her hands, bringing it to his lips and placing a kiss on her knuckles. Poppy resisted the urge to wrap her arms around him. It would not be proper of her until they were officially paired by the chief.

"They will. Just not now."

"But, why not?"

Green Meadows chuckled. "Always curious. You never settle, do you?"

Poppy bristled and pulled back her hand. Green Meadows gave her a regretful look.

"I did not mean to offend. It is a trait I admire in you."

She resisted the urge to smile at his compliment. Truthfully, she might never have taken offense in the first place if her mother had not reprimanded her earlier that evening for being too curious for her own good. She warred inside herself with wanting to be herself and being a good daughter. Her mother was not well suited for a daughter and reminded Poppy on a daily basis that she wished she'd been born a male.

"Poppy?"

Poppy startled and looked up. It was the first time Green Meadows had ever called her that. He had generally been very formal with her, always calling her by her full name, Red Hair Like Poppy. She looked deep into his eyes and warmed at the love she saw in them. He took her hand again.

"We must trust in the will of the gods. Our people will survive this long summer."

"How do you know?"

He shrugged. "The gods have a plan. A protector will arise and vanquish the death. Only then will the rains return."

Poppy's eyes widened. It sounded as if Green Meadows were speaking in prophecy, only something the healer would have done. Only, the healer was no more and her tribe was left to persist on their own with what he had been able to teach them before his death. Green Meadows met her eyes and stared into them.

"Do you understand?" he asked hopefully.

Poppy thought a moment, then nodded her head.

Green Meadows looked around, then seeing they were alone, quickly placed a kiss on her lips. Poppy immediately felt a jolt of electric heat go through her body. She barely had time to register the pleasing warmth before Green Meadows dropped her hand and disappeared into his home. Poppy stood in the moonlight and tenderly touched her lips. She smiled and skipped back to her home, the weight of the evening's revelations no match for the power of his kiss.

"Poppy... Poppy... you must awaken now."

Nonnie's pleading tone broke into Poppy's dreams. She sat up with bleary eyes, rubbing them and looking around. There was no light, only Nonnie's darkened figure hunched beside her.

"Nonnie? What..."

Poppy was cut off by her grandmother's hand on her mouth. She narrowed her eyes, trying to get a better look at Nonnie's face but it was still too dark. Nonnie thrust something into her hands and she realized it was her winter cloak. She was about to argue when Nonnie shushed her again and pulled her towards the outside of her home. Nonnie exited and waited for Poppy to stand, then she grabbed Poppy's hands and started pulling her away.

"No words, child, just follow," Nonnie whispered.

Poppy shook her head but Nonnie didn't wait to see if she had agreed. Poppy tried to get her bearings and then walked more easily next to her grandmother without having to be pulled. Realization about their destination dawned on her when Nonnie stopped. Ahead of them, Poppy could see Green Meadows home. There were elders standing around the tent. Poppy's heart dropped to her stomach.

"No. Not him."

Poppy clung to her grandmother, willing her to say the disease had not infected Green Meadows.

"Hush now. There is work to be done. Come with me," Nonnie said as she stepped towards the elders.

"Nonnie, I can't!"

"We shall see," she replied.

They walked up to the elders, all in deep conversation. One of the elders acknowledged Nonnie with a tilt of his head. The chief emerged from the tent and all grew quiet. The chief bowed his head and Green Meadows father let out a huff—the only sound he would permit himself to make. The chief put his hand on the father and squeezed. He noticed Nonnie and Poppy standing at the edge of the circle of men.

"Grandmother, what is it you do here?"

Nonnie bowed her head. "Oh great chieftain, Red Hair Like Poppy has brought her best winter cloak to aid in Green Meadows healing."

Poppy looked at the cloak in her hands and realized it was her ceremonial winter cloak. It was only used for the long winter's night celebration. The rest of the winter, it served as insulation on the wall of their home. It was a very fine garment. Her mother would be none too pleased to realize Nonnie was offering it to a sickened one. A lump caught in her throat. The sickened one was Green Meadows. No one had yet survived the disease. She fought back the tears at what it meant for her. She was brought back to reality by a none too subtle jab of her grandmother's elbow to her ribcage. She looked at Nonnie and then to the chief.

"As I was saying, this is highly irregular for one not paired," the chief intoned.

Poppy nodded and bowed her head. The chief placed a hand on her hair. Poppy resisted the urge to run back to her home and cry. It felt as if she stood in front of the chief for hours before he lifted his hand and sighed.

"I will allow it, grandmother."

Nonnie pulled on her arm and Poppy walked inside Green Meadows' home. She waited as Nonnie spoke with his father.

His father stared at her for a moment, then nodded his head and walked out. Nonnie placed herself in front of the doorway, her back turned to Poppy. Poppy looked across the room to where Green Meadows lay in his bed. She arranged the cloak across his legs and then knelt beside him.

"Green Meadows?" she spoke quietly.

He opened his eyes and smiled. He reached out a hand and Poppy took it. He squeezed it but his normal strength failed him and Poppy could tell it took a great deal of effort. She covered his hand with both of hers and squeezed back. A tear escaped down her cheek and he frowned.

"Do not be afraid," he said.

Poppy shook her head. "How can I not?"

"I am not afraid. I have seen a protector."

"Who is this person? Why have they not come forward?"

Green Meadows closed his eyes and smiled. Poppy cocked her head to the side, wondering if the delirium had come on. It was too soon but then, she had seen him earlier that night and he had seemed hale. Perhaps she had less time than she thought. It could be hours instead of days before he ascended to the great hunting grounds. Poppy sobbed aloud at the thought and he opened his eyes again.

"Poppy, Nonnie has the answers you seek. Trust in her guidance. Trust in me."

Poppy looked to her grandmother then back at Green Meadows. She reached out a hand and swiped a sweaty piece of hair off his forehead. She met his eyes. She expected to see madness in them but they were clear. She saw the strength he always bore. She saw his love. Most of all, she saw a shining trust in her, the likes of which no one had ever shown her. She hesitated and then nodded. He weakly squeezed her hand again and then smiled. She squeezed back and started to rise but he pulled her towards him. She hovered over him and he lifted himself up to whisper in her ear.

"I will hold on for you," he said and kissed her gently on the cheek.

Poppy pulled back to question him but his eyes were already closed again and his arm went limp. Poppy stared at him a moment longer, waiting to see if he would regain consciousness. Light poured into the home as his father entered. Poppy rejoined her grandmother, giving her a questioning look. The look she got in return had her hold her questions and follow Nonnie out into the dawn.

This is madness!" her mother shouted.

"Quiet," Nonnie chided.

Poppy's mother looked at Nonnie as if she were ready to skin her alive. The rage pouring out of her mother was enough to fill their entire home with heat. Poppy would have laughed if she weren't so preoccupied with everything that had transpired since Nonnie had woken her that morning. Now, she sat in front of Nonnie as her grandmother braided her hair, placing poppies into the braids and powdering them with special herbs, the recipe known only to her grandmother. One day, that recipe would be hers, as long as Nonnie were the teacher. Her mother would never think to teach her the old ways as it would be wasted on a daughter. Nonnie hummed as she braided and Poppy's mother stormed out of the house. Nonnie chuckled and Poppy turned to ask why but Nonnie yanked her head back in place. Poppy waited for the braids to be finished. Then Nonnie patted her head and Poppy knew it was permission to move.

"Nonnie, how do you know it exists?" Poppy asked warily.

"My dear child, I was there."

Poppy's eyes grew wide. "When?"

"Many, many moons before your mother was born. We faced this same predicament. I am the only one left who remembers. Now, the chief and the elders believe it to be myth. An old woman's story. I know the truth."

"Green Meadows believes you. That is good enough for me," Poppy said as she smiled at her grandmother.

Nonnie nodded. "It is love alone that will be your companion for the journey. Are you ready for that challenge, child?"

Poppy nodded. She would do anything to please the gods and save Green Meadows. Her mother might think Nonnie mad but Poppy had never seen anything but wisdom in the old woman's eyes. No one knew how many summers Nonnie had weathered. All respected her, even the chief. Poppy knew respect was earned in her tribe and Nonnie had clearly earned the respect of every last man, woman, and child. She chose to follow the directions and have a chance of saving everyone. A protector, just as Green Meadows had predicted.

"It is time to begin," Nonnie instructed.

Poppy rose and followed her grandmother out of the home. Nonnie chanted a few words while Poppy stared off in the direction of Green Meadows home. Nonnie finished and handed Poppy a long eagle feather. Poppy grinned up at her Nonnie, who winked. She recognized the eagle feather from the home of Green Meadows, it's quill wrapped with beads to represent his family. Poppy stashed it inside her dress. Nonnie kissed her on each cheek and then led her to the edge of the camp.

"You must continue walking until you feel you cannot walk anymore. Then walk some more. You must have faith in your task. You must follow your heart and help those in need, great or small. Finally, you must love. Love conquers all. Do you understand, child?"

Poppy nodded hesitantly. "But... where is it?" she asked.

Nonnie chuckled and placed a hand on her chest. "The directions are within. Trust and you will find it. No more questions, you must go."

Nonnie gave her a little push. Poppy turned back to say something but Nonnie just held her arm out, her finger pointing towards the setting sun. Poppy smiled and waved then turned towards her destination with a purpose. Her hands started shaking, belying her nerves, but she ignored them and just put one foot in front of another, walking towards her destiny.

Presently

Poppy sat down gingerly in the shade afforded by a large mesa. It had taken hours to reach the relative shelter from the heat. She was exhausted, her muscles tired and her feet throbbing. She started crying and screaming, yelling for all the world to hear her frustration. She pulled her knees up and sobbed into them. Green Meadows was not going to survive and her plans for her future were dying, along with her body, in the desert. Nonnie had misremembered. There could be no other explanation. She cried until there were no more tears and then sniffled. Once her noises had died down, she heard a small voice. It startled her and she looked around, trying to discern the origin.

"Who... who's there?" she hiccuped.

"Down here," the voice replied.

Poppy looked at the ground on either side of herself and then pulled back slightly. She saw a small weed, newly wet from her crying. She chuckled at herself. Plants did not speak. She made sure the plant was not crushed because of her carelessness and then went back to feeling sorry for herself.

"Why do you cry?" the voice spoke again.

Poppy shook her head. "Plants do not talk. It's all in my head."

It was the voice's turn to laugh. "Certainly not. This plant is my food."

Poppy's head whipped back to the plant. She looked

closer and then saw a fat caterpillar on the leaf. It had a piece of the leaf in its hands and periodically bit off a piece and chewed it while Poppy's mouth fell open. The caterpillar finished the leaf and then stood on its hind legs.

"I thank you for providing my food with a bit of rejuvenation, but I ask, why do you cry?"

Poppy shook her head and took in a deep breath. She closed her eyes tightly and willed the hallucination out of it. Surely, animals did not speak. She must be suffering from heatstroke. She felt a slight tickle on her hand and looked down to see the caterpillar sitting there.

"You are quite strange. Your hair is not like the others," the caterpillar said conversationally.

Poppy snorted. "I am strange? You are talking!"

The caterpillar shrugged. "I can go back to ignoring your plight if it is what you wish."

The caterpillar started to crawl off her hand. Poppy warred with herself. She had not spoken to anyone in days. Clearly, she had gone mad, but the caterpillar did seem like good company. She turned her hand, effectively keeping the caterpillar in place.

"Wait, it's just that I am not used to such things," she explained.

The caterpillar stopped walking. "It is understandable. We don't stop to chat very often."

"We?"

"My kind. We have a greater purpose. I can sense that

you do as well."

Poppy shrugged and her shoulders deflated.

"I thought I did but I have failed."

"Failure is only an option if you give up trying."

Poppy shrugged again. "I can't go on much longer."

"You can't go back, either."

Poppy thought for a moment. No, she couldn't go back unless she went back successful. She would take her dying breath in order to save him. Nonnie believed in her. She had to believe in herself and be worthy of their faith.

"Ah, see. I knew I was right about you."

"How so?" Poppy asked.

"You have what it takes, just as your grandmother did," the caterpillar said wisely.

Poppy shook her head. "You can't possibly have known her."

"That much is true but we have stories, the same as you."

Poppy raised the caterpillar closer. "Do your stories include what I seek?"

The caterpillar nodded and pointed to the horizon. Poppy looked hopefully, trying to see more than the desert before her. She squinted really hard until her eyes started watering. The caterpillar chuckled again and Poppy looked at it forlornly. It patted her finger and inched closer to her face.

"Did your Nonnie not give you any instruction?"

"How did... oh, never mind. Yes."

"And?"

"She told me to look into my heart and what I seek will be found," Poppy grumbled.

"Your heart is not here," the caterpillar said, pointing to its head."

"But…"

The caterpillar began to inch its way down her arm. "I have faith in you, girl."

"Wait… what do I do once I do find it?"

The caterpillar stopped and regarded her for a moment. It listened to the wind and watched as the sun sank. Then it nodded and turned back to her, as if an unseen force instructed it.

"You will find what you seek. Take in the water to restore your body and your resolve. Then take as much as you can with you, back to your tribe. Along the way, water every plant like the one you watered today. Only this time, instead of your tears, use the water you find. Then wait. Your heart will do the rest. It is time for me to go, girl."

Poppy gaped at the caterpillar as it inched its way back onto the plant. She played its words over and over in her head, wondering if she had truly gone mad. She watched as it began munching on a leaf again. She made up her mind and sent a silent prayer up to the gods. As she did, she could feel a sense of peace surrounding her. She looked back down at the caterpillar.

"It's Poppy," she blurted out.

"What is?" the caterpillar asked with a perplexed tone.

"My name... it's Poppy. Technically, Red Hair like Poppy but Nonnie called me Poppy since I was born," she explained.

"Nymphalidae," the caterpillar responded.

"Thank you," Poppy said with a smile.

"My pleasure," the caterpillar responded.

Poppy awoke with a start, the sun was already high in the sky. She looked around her impromptu bed. She yawned, wondering what had become of her friend, finding no caterpillars on the plant. The only odd thing was a small pod hanging off one stem of the plant. It was a delicate-looking thing of green with tiny gold dots. Poppy laughed out loud, surely the heat had gotten to her if she believed her dream to have been real. Nevertheless, she had a renewed sense of purpose and for that she was grateful. She looked off into the horizon and wiped her eyes at what she was seeing. In the distance, there appeared to be a circle of mesas, a misty fog seeping out of the gap between the two protrusions.

Poppy leaped to her feet. She gathered her things and began walking with a renewed purpose. She knew the mist meant water. The caterpillar, or her dream, had been right. She only needed to believe in herself again and rediscover her purpose. She had almost let the heat and the misery of the desert divert her from her path. She walked with determination, ignoring the part of her brain telling her she wasn't getting any closer. With each step, she thought only of returning to Green Meadows. As she walked, her heart felt as if it was getting fuller and fuller. A warmth spread throughout her body that had nothing to do with the heat of the sun.

Finally, after many hours of walking, which felt like a trial of her resolve, she came to the opening between the two mesas. The mist swirled around her feet and the sight before her caught her breath. As impossible as it seemed in the desert landscape, a shimmering blue lake sprawled before her, its banks covered in bright green foliage. Butterflies flitted around the plants landing a moment before taking off again. She could see a caterpillar on a plant near her feet. She stooped to talk to it but it seemed none too interested in anything but chewing on the leaf in its mouth. She chuckled at herself. Of course, caterpillars didn't speak.

Poppy hesitated only momentarily before she dropped her things, removed her dress, and dove into the water. It felt as if the weight of the world lifted from her shoulders as the dirt dislodged from her skin. She spent a long while just soaking in the pool and staring up at the sky. The sun was now covered by a pleasant, puffy, white cloud. The sky was a vibrant blue, no other clouds in sight. It was as if the magic of the place protected her from the harshness of the outside world. Poppy sighed in contentment. She relaxed and floated on the surface of the pool.

After many hours, Poppy finally returned her mind to her present problems. She resolved to follow the instructions of her friend—real or imagined. She got to work washing out her long red hair. She rebraided it as best she could, mourning the loss of her namesake flower decorations but enjoying the feel of clean hair. The powders Nonnie had put in her hair were also gone and she had no replenishment. She shrugged, assuming the gods would understand and grant her leniency on rituals. She washed out her dress as best she could and then set it on a rock to dry. It was as if it took no time at all before the garment was warm and dry. Poppy gathered her skins and filled them all with the water from the pool. She left the pool and walked to the edge of the clearing, taking one last look around. Then, she turned towards home, stealing herself for the long journey ahead.

She hadn't been walking for very long when she turned around to get one last glimpse of the magical pool. To her astonishment, it was no longer visible. Poppy turned in several circles, thinking she had the direction wrong, but everywhere she looked, she was met with the usual desert landscape. Poppy shook her head in disbelief. It was as if the pool had vanished just as the caterpillar had done. She felt a nagging feeling in the back of her mind as if something were silently pulling her towards home. Shrugging, she continued on her journey. Along the way, Poppy watered each plant she saw with some of the water from the pool.

After several days of walking, Poppy finally saw the outskirts of her tribe's camp. She nearly wept for joy. However, the camp was eerily quiet as she walked past the first homes. Then, she heard wailing and followed the sound to the center of her camp. Her mother lay at the foot of a makeshift bed, wailing her heart out. Her father lay in the center of the bed, deathly pale. Yet Poppy could see his chest rise with breath and she let out the one she was holding. Nonnie stood at his head, praying, her face lifted to the gods. As if poked by an invisible finger, Nonnie straightened and met Poppy's eyes.

"The protector has returned," she said solemnly.

The whole tribe turned towards Poppy. Poppy flushed red as her hair and tried to stand tall. She was uncomfortable with the scrutiny. A hand gently pushed her from behind and Nonnie held her arms aloft. Poppy walked into her grandmother's arms and Nonnie hugged her tightly.

"You know what to do?" Nonnie asked hopefully.

Poppy nodded. She noticed the plant at the top of her father's head. She used the last drop of water from the pool to water the plant. Nothing happened and a murmur went through the assembled tribe.

"Worthless girl," her mother sneered.

Nonnie held out her hand and Poppy's mother stopped speaking with an air of defiance in the way she crossed her arms. Nonnie looked at each tribe member, meeting their eyes. Each one nodded silently. Poppy looked at her grandmother expectantly.

"Red Hair Like Poppy has returned. She is now the protector. We must wait now."

Another murmur ran through the tribe. Poppy was exhausted. She leaned on her grandmother, willing the old woman to give her strength. Nonnie smoothed the braids around Poppy's face and kissed each cheek. Poppy stared into her grandmother's eyes.

"He lives yet," Nonnie said quietly.

The relief Poppy felt was palpable. Her knees nearly buckled at the answer to her unspoken question.

"Go to him. Wait," Nonnie instructed and pushed Poppy towards Green Meadows' home.

Poppy entered the home, nodding a hello to Green Meadows' father. His father whispered something into his ear and he responded in a raspy whisper of his own. His father nodded and put a hand on Poppy's shoulder, squeezing it just before he left the home. Poppy went over to Green Meadows and sat next to him. A tear fell down her cheek. He was so pale, his eyes sunken into his skull and his lips tinged blue. He reached up and weekly wiped the tear away. Poppy laid her head on his chest and he stroked her hair with his thumb.

Poppy sat vigil by Green Meadows bedside for many days. He did not get any worse but he wasn't getting any better. Her own father had passed and her mother had railed at her during one of the only moments she had allowed herself to leave Green Meadows side. Her mother spat on her and forbade her to ever come near her home again. Poppy cared not. Her home and her fate now rested in the survival of Green Meadows. She was dozing when she heard a great commotion outside. She checked on him, satisfying herself that he was as comfortable as he could be, then went outside to investigate. Nonnie stood outside the home.

"Nonnie, what is happening?" Poppy asked as she shielded her eyes from the light.

"Look."

Poppy looked in the direction Nonnie was pointing. She frowned, wondering what she was seeing. The sky was darkened by what appeared to be a moving black and gold cloud. As it got nearer, Poppy realized it was full of the butterflies she had seen at the magical pool. They landed on the plants around her tribe's camp and the one that had sat at her father's head. They were a silent army, flitting from plant to plant.

"What does it mean?" Poppy asked in wonder.

"Your wait is almost over," Nonnie responded cryptically.

The butterflies stayed for several days and then disappeared as fast as the had come. Poppy watched in wonder when the tiny eggs they laid hatched into caterpillars, each one devouring a plant around the camp. At first, the people of her tribe complained bitterly, pointing fingers at her and blaming her for the curse. However, as the plants were decimated, the disease stopped killing first the animals they hunted, then the tribe members who depended on the animals for sustenance. Deaths no longer occurred. Those who had been afflicted started getting better. All but one.

Poppy swiped angrily at the tears on her cheeks, plopping down to one of the last caterpillars still eating. All of the others had turned into the odd chrysalis. She stared at the caterpillar, watching it eat and wishing it would just stop like the others before it.

"She promised me," she accused the caterpillar.

It stopped munching on its leaf and looked up at her. It peered at her as if it was a loss for words. Then, to her surprise, it wiggled in a gesture that seemed to tell her to get closer. She rolled her eyes but did as it bade.

"What is it that bothers you so?" the caterpillar asked.

Poppy huffed. "She promised me he would get better."

The caterpillar nodded.

"He will."

"But how!" Poppy cried out.

"With your magic."

Poppy scoffed. She leaned back, staring out into the sunset and willing the tears in her eyes to stop. She couldn't go on much longer. She couldn't bear the suffering in Green Meadows' eyes. He tried to hide it from her but she saw it all the same. Everyone was better but him. Perhaps she had taken too long to return and it was her fault.

"It isn't," the caterpillar said.

"What?" Poppy asked incredulously.

"It isn't your fault. You are the protector. You have prevailed."

Poppy sneered. "Have I?"

The caterpillar sat on the leaf, silently staring at her. Poppy turned away, letting the tears flow freely down her cheeks. For all her trials, the one thing she had wanted most was slipping from her grasp. She wished, not for the first time, that she had not been "chosen" in the first place. Her Nonnie was wrong, things would not work out for her.

"If you think that way, you are right."

"What do you know of my thoughts?"

"I know you think of giving up. If my kind gave up, we would have died out long ago. Yet look around you," it said as it gestured to the plants around it.

Everywhere she looked, Poppy saw a chrysalis. She didn't know what to make of them. They seemed like odd little protrusions from the plants the caterpillars had eaten. Nonnie had warned the tribe not to eat them, they would cause more death. Therefore, many had stayed away from the plants entirely.

"I don't understand," Poppy shook her head in defeat.

"Bring the one you love here tomorrow morning. Wait for the sun to rise high into the sky. Trust, once more. Now, I must be going. I tarried too long waiting to speak with you and now my fate is sealed. Yet my ancestors would be proud of me."

Poppy watched as the caterpillar slowly crawled off the plant, towards the small stream. She watched it walk into the stream and float away on a leaf it found near the edges of the bank. She was more confused than ever. She stood up, hanging her head in misery, and went back to her vigil by Green Meadows' side.

"Poppy... you must awake," Nonnie said.

Poppy startled awake, wondering if she were dreaming, yet again. Nonnie stood over her as before, many moons ago. This time, her grandmother did not carry her cloak, but held onto a makeshift crutch. Poppy looked towards Green Meadows who regarded her with amusement tinged with pain. He shrugged and smiled.

"Nonnie, what's this about?" Poppy asked grumpily.

"You must take him to the plants by the stream. Hurry."

Nonnie was already by Green Meadows side, helping him stand. For an old grandmother, Poppy was surprised at her hidden strength. Green Meadows leaned heavily on the crutch and Poppy rushed to his other side, holding him up and willing him not to fall. She tried to ignore the rush of warmth she felt at his closeness. She looked over at Nonnie with a small measure of annoyance and Nonnie just beamed back at her. Poppy shook her head but led Green Meadows out of his home and to the stream.

Poppy fussed over him as she helped him sit on the ground. The air held a weigh to it, as if holding its own breath. Poppy suppressed the shiver that ran down her spine. She smoothed out Green Meadows' hair, rebraiding it deftly. As the sun rose, the plants around them came to life. A butterfly crawled out of each chrysalis and sat, slowly flapping its wings. Green Meadows was intrigued and Poppy could merely stare at the wonder in his eyes. His body glistened with sweat and she could see a green tinge to his skin.

"We should return you to your bed, Green Meadows,"

Poppy implored.

He shook his head.

"Please, you'll catch your death."

Green Meadows looked at her. He took her face in his hands and gently kissed her forehead. He rested his head on her forehead and linked his fingers with hers.

"I will not die, you have frightened death. It will not take me for a long time," he said with certainty.

"How can you say that?"

"Look around you."

Poppy closed her eyes, not wanting to listen to him. She didn't want to see the horrid plants that had sickened the man she loved. She didn't want to deal with the strange animals that tore their bodies apart just to be reborn. She didn't want to face losing her world.

"Poppy, my love, look at me," Green Meadows whispered.

Poppy opened her eyes. A tear slid down her cheek. He had never been so intimate with her, even in all the days they had spent together since she returned. He wiped the tear off her cheek and then smiled.

"Look around you," he repeated.

Poppy looked around him and gasped at what she saw. The air was full of black and gold butterflies fluttering around them. They acted as if they waited for a sign. Poppy shook her head. She didn't know what they waited for. A butterfly landed on her outstretched hand.

"Red Hair Like Poppy, may we help you?" the butterfly asked.

Poppy looked at Green Meadows. He nodded at her in encouragement. Poppy thought about what she wanted in her head and it was as if the butterfly could read her thoughts. The moving cloud descended upon Green Meadows, who sat patiently still while they landed on him. He chuckled once or twice as Poppy watched in amazement. As each butterfly landed, sat for a moment, then flew off, the color of his skin returned to normal. A butterfly landed on each eye and when it was gone, the pain was gone from Green Meadows' eyes. The last butterfly left and it was as if Green Meadows was a new man. There was no trace of the illness.

The butterfly landed on Poppy's shoulder and whispered something into it. Poppy laughed and the butterfly flew away. She looked towards Green Meadows and throwing caution to the wind, she threw herself into his lap, kissing him as long as she dared. Then she reigned kisses on his face, everywhere she could touch—his eyes, his nose, his lips again, each cheek. Finally, he fell backward and she fell on top of his chest. She made to move off of him but he tightened his arms around her. She raised up so that she could look him in the eyes. She studied them, looking for any trace of hesitation and found none. Poppy kissed Green Meadows with all the love she felt and he kissed her in return.

Many, many moons later

Grandmother Poppy, you cannot be serious," Nymphalidae scoffed.

Poppy pulled the girl's head back around to finish braiding her hair. She ignored the little whimper her granddaughter gave her. She learned well from her own Nonnie. The child would learn in time.

"I am as serious as the sun rises and sets."

"It's just an old legend," the girl whined.

Green Meadows walked into their home and across the room. Poppy followed his movements. He was getting slower in his old age, but still as handsome as she remembered. He stopped and turned around, waiting for Poppy to continue speaking.

"So then the butterfly whispered into my ear and flew off," Poppy continued.

"Grandmother, that is just not true," Nymphalidae said, petulantly yanking her braid away from her grandmother's fingers.

"Tell her grandfather. Tell her it isn't true. She actually believes butterflies cured you of the great illness."

Green Meadows shrugged. "I like her stories, granddaughter."

Green Meadows winked at Poppy, causing her to chuckle. Nymphalidae jumped up, stomping towards the door.

"You two are impossible," she huffed and went out

the door.

Green Meadows sat next to his mate, putting an arm around her and kissing her hair.

"Must you antagonize her so?" he asked cheerfully.

Poppy shrugged. "I am merely preparing her for the inevitable.

"Ah, is that all?"

"Well, I do like the way her cheeks blush any time I mention Eagle Feather and her destined pairing."

"There it is, you are hopeless, my love," Green Meadows chuckled.

"Quite the contrary, as you well know," she intoned.

Green Meadows smiled and kissed her. She sighed contentedly when he pulled back and wrapped her in his arms. They sat in blissful silence a long while before Green Meadows squeezed her and turned her to face him. She could see he wanted to ask something but he did not speak.

"What is it?"

"What did that butterfly say to you?" he asked.

Poppy laughed. "All this time and you have never asked," she wondered.

He shrugged. "It does not mean I never pondered."

Poppy smiled. Green Meadows waited expectantly. She took her time, building up the suspense until she could see he was about to burst with curiosity. Then she leaned forward until she was a hair's breadth from his ear.

"She said, *My ancestors were right, you are quite strange.*"

Green Meadows guffawed and Poppy laughed along with him. She rested her head on his chest, reveling in the strong beat she heard within. She sent a silent prayer up to the gods for helping her protect and save him. She also prayed that the gods watched over her friends on their long journeys, wherever it led them.

Altered

Amelia resisted opening her eyes. She was warm and cozy in her bed, her cat comfortably sleeping against her legs. The sun radiated heat across her face. Suddenly, she jolted upright sending her cat running off the bed. Amelia looked at her alarm clock and groaned, dropping her head into her hands—the blinking image seared into her brain. She was late!

Amelia rushed through her morning routine, almost forgetting deodorant in the process. She wildly threw clothing onto the floor as she searched for something appropriate for the chilly in the morning/sweltering in the afternoon weather of the South. Taking a last look in the mirror, she grabbed up her purse and dashed into the kitchen. Matt stood there, holding out a plate with a piece of toast. Amelia grabbed it and gave him a quick peck on the cheek.

"Thanks! Gotta go!"

Amelia walked down the steps and started off down the street towards her office. She munched on her toast as she walked and brushed the crumbs away when she'd finished. She checked her watch and then, satisfied she'd made up a little time, she popped into the coffee shop. The line was shorter than usual—probably because she was later than usual. The barista smiled at her and nodded, already preparing her *usual.* Amelia took her order and thanked the man, waving as she backed out the door. She turned at the last moment and slammed into another person.

The man caught Amelia's elbow with one hand. With the other, he prevented her hot tea from becoming a bath for both of them. Amelia was stunned at the graceful agility he displayed. She immediately turned red.

"I'm **so** sorry! I should have watched where I was going!" she stammered.

The man shrugged. "It's okay. I tried to warn you but most likely too late."

"Still, let me buy you a coffee," she offered, fishing around in her purse for her wallet.

"Really, miss... there is no need."

Amelia's head snapped up. She eyed the man suspiciously.

"Who turns down free coffee? Weren't you just going in?" she asked, gesturing towards the coffee shop.

He nodded and then looked away nervously. He looked back and Amelia was momentarily diverted from her questions by the bluest eyes she had ever seen. As he searched for an explanation, she took in the rest of his face. He had neatly cut dark hair and a square jawline covered in just the right amount of stubble. She thought his nose looked proportionate to the rest of his face. She shook herself internally at the last thought. Who cared about noses? She giggled a little out loud and then remembered herself. He cocked his head, waiting for her to explain.

"It's nothing. So you don't want coffee?"

He shook his head. "I don't drink it."

"Then why were you here," she huffed.

"If you must know, I was going to get a hot chai," he sighed as if the shame of getting tea in a coffee shop was not lost on him.

"Oh... *ohhh!*"

"What's so... oh?" he asked warily.

"Here, you can have this one," she said, offering her own tea.

The man took it hesitantly and looked at her expectantly. She just shrugged and nodded. He nodded back and took a sip, then smiled.

"It's perfect," he said.

"I never tell anyone I am getting tea in a coffee shop either, but they make it much faster and easier than I could at home. The temperature is just right here."

"Indeed, it is."

Amelia's phone rang and she looked at her watch. She

took a step back from the stranger and smiled. He opened the door and gestured for her to walk in but she shook her head.

"Thanks, but I've gotta get to work."

"What about your tea?" he asked.

"It's gone to a good cause today," she smiled.

"Well, in that case, how about I escort you to work?"

Amelia thought a moment and then nodded. The man held out his arm and she laughed as she put her hand on his elbow. He gestured in both directions and she pointed to the right.

"I'm Amelia," she introduced herself.

"Finn."

"Nice to meet you, Finn."

"Likewise, Amelia."

Amelia was so lost in the introductions and Finn's smile, she almost drowned out the angry sound of protesters across the street. She sighed and looked up, checking the entrance to her office building and seeing that it was clear. Finn's steps slowed down and he seemed to withdraw into himself the closer they got to the building. Amelia sensed his hesitation and decided to take action.

"You know what, Finn? My office is just right there and I can go the rest of the way. It was very nice meeting you. Maybe we can bump into each other again sometime?"

Finn looked relieved and nodded. He removed her hand from his elbow and kissed the top of it. Then he bowed with a ridiculous flourish and Amelia laughed. He winked at her and started back down the street, turning back once and raising the teacup in a gesture of goodbye. Amelia smiled and waved, then shoulders and turned towards her office. She just hoped none of the protesters were throwing anything today.

I just don't understand what they think they gain by standing outside and shouting hate all day. Don't their throats hurt? Don't they have families?" Amelia groused.

"Their families are out there with them. I saw a kid, probably five years old, out there screaming that filth," Monica replied.

Amelia turned away from the window. She had been staring down at the protesters, wishing they would go away and she and her coworkers could have a little bit of peace. It had been nothing short of a nightmare since the location of their office had been leaked on social media. No one had given a thought to the safety of the workers in either her office or the other companies who shared the same building. Whoever worked in the building had a virtual x marked on their back. They were subjected to daily protests and often, the protesters threw things. The first few weeks had been worse before the police stepped in and banned protesting to the empty lot across the street. At least now, the protesters couldn't spit in her face like they did the first day. Amelia shuddered at the thought. She sighed and stepped away from the window. She slumped down in her office chair and Monica gave her a pitying smile.

"People don't change, Amelia," she soothed.

"That's what frustrates me the most! Every decade, a new group of people fight for their rights and win them. Why? Because it is right! What I don't get is, why must it always be a fight? Why can't people just see that we are all basically the same and our differences don't make us bad people, just different?"

Monica shrugged, "Difference is scary and people fight what they don't understand."

"People are stupid. I hate them."

Monica fake gasped. Amelia stuck her tongue out and tossed a wadded up memo paper page at her. Monica laughed and Amelia laughed back. Just then, an intern stuck his head through the door. Amelia sobered up and gestured for him to come in. He entered, handing her a folder.

"A man is here for a consult. He doesn't have an appointment but you have some open slots and Mr. Till said you might fit him in?"

Amelia nodded. "Sure, send him in."

Monica got up and headed for the door. She stopped and looked around before turning back to Amelia. She through the wadded up memo page back at her and then ducked out the door with a laugh. Amelia flipped her off and she just waved back through the glass window. Amelia immediately turned red when she noticed the new client standing in the doorway. She jumped out of her chair, banging her knee on the desk, and sending a jar of pens tumbling to the floor.

"You seem to have a habit of being a little clumsy,"

he chuckled.

"Shut up!" she mock chided, then clapped a hand on her mouth and quickly scanned the office through the glass door. Luckily no one was paying attention.

Finn finished picking up the pens and set them back on the desk. He waited for Amelia to recover from her outburst. She reddened, even more, wondering how it was even possible to be more embarrassed. She took the time to recover by shutting her office door, sitting back at her desk, and pretending to look over his file. In truth, she was reevaluating him surreptitiously over the file folder.

"Well, can you help me?" he asked impatiently.

She jumped at the sudden intrusion to her thoughts. She held up a finger and really looked at his file. Finn had been discriminated against in a housing application. After reading the documents, it was clear that Finn had a case.

"We can help you. I can make an appointment with you to talk to the housing lawyer and they can get started on filing the proper paperwork."

Finn smiled, then frowned. "You would not be handling the case?"

Amelia laughed. "No. I'm really just the front line in determining if there is anything we can do. A glorified paper pusher."

"Well, you are a beautiful paper pusher," he complimented.

Amelia blushed again and cleared her throat, turning

towards her computer and putting in the necessary requisitions and appointments for Finn. She printed it out and organized it before stapling it all together and placing it in a green file folder. She handed the folder over to Finn.

"So, this is your guidebook. Don't lose anything in this folder. I've made an appointment for you tomorrow afternoon with the housing lawyer. He will get you started and, if all goes well, this will be wrapped up quickly. You have good documentation and a solid case."

"Thank you, Amelia."

Finn rose to leave, then thought better of it and sat back down. He opened and shut his mouth a few times, gathering the courage to ask her a question. He stared down at the green folder, a pensive look crossing his face. Amelia waited but then the anticipation was too much.

"I have a significant other but we are on again, off again. Right now we are off. Do you want to go to dinner?" she blurted out.

It was Finn's turn to blush. He thought for a moment and then smiled. He nodded.

"I would love to. Are you sure? What about…?" he asked as he gestured to himself.

"Really? That is what you were worried about? Do you think I would work here if I cared about that?"

Finn shrugged. Amelia just chuckled and wrote down her address on a memo pad. She tore off the page and handed it to him.

"Pick me up at seven?" she asked.

"You don't want me to escort you home? What about those protesters?"

She shrugged. "I do this twice a day, every day and sometimes on the weekends. Sometimes even for lunch if I'm really craving a burrito or something. I'm used to it. I saw how you reacted this morning and now I know why. It took a lot for you to come here today. That's the first step in not letting them get to you. But I think it's been enough for today."

Finn smiled again and it lit up the whole room. Amelia thought she could just sit and stare at him while he smiled. He looked back at her address and then gathered the folder and stood, going to the door.

"I'll see you tonight," he mock bowed, with less flourish, and went out of the office.

Amelia smiled, shook her head, and went back to her computer. She typed up a few more notes and then sat back in her chair. She stared at the face looking back at her. He didn't look altered in any way. She frowned. It was what infuriated her the most about all the protests and discrimination. A person merely had to check a box on a form and suddenly they were seen as "less than". The box should be illegal but so far the high court had not made a significant determination. The more she thought about it, the more she got angry again. People never changed. Any little difference and they just lumped someone in a category of inferiority. That supposedly inferior class had to claw and scrape their way to equality. The circle never ended.

"Why don't you knock off early?" Monica interrupted her thoughts.

Amelia looked up. "I have more work to do."

"Amelia, you always have more work to do. You do the work of three people. I'm your boss. Knock off early."

"Is that an order?"

"Does it have to be?" Monica asked sternly.

Amelia sighed and shook her head.

"Good girl."

"Bitch," Amelia teased.

"The one and only," Monica said, waggling her fingers as she left Amelia's office.

Finn and Amelia stopped at her door. He pushed a stray hair behind her ear and then leaned down, hesitant. Amelia closed the gap and kissed him. Finn kissed her back. After a moment, they broke the kiss and Amelia smiled. Finn made a move to leave and Amelia tugged him back towards her.

"Do you want to stay tonight?"

Finn looked up at her door and then back at her. They had been dating for several months and he had yet to stay the night. Amelia knew he was hesitant but she felt it was time they took their relationship to the next level. She tried to reassure him but he'd lived so many years as an outcast, she knew it was hard to be away from his comfort zone.

"I didn't come prepared," he balked.

"I have what you need," she soothed.

His eyes widened, "Why?"

"You say that as if it is impossible. We often have unprepared clients in the office and we are trained in helping people out when we are in the field. Each of us carries extra cords in case a client is in trouble. Why do you think my purse is so cavernous?"

"A woman's purse is a rabbit hole to me."

Amelia laughed. She tugged him back and kissed him again. He rested his forehead against hers and closed his eyes. He opened them and Amelia could tell he'd made a decision. He nodded and Amelia tried, and failed, to keep her little squeal of joy to herself. He lovingly rolled his eyes at her.

Amelia and Finn lay in bed together, sleeping peacefully, when a muted beeping sound awoke Finn. He opened one eye, groaning at the fact that it was still dark outside. He carefully removed his arm from underneath Amelia and pressed a finger against the spot just in front of his ear. The beeping stopped. Finn looked down at the sleeping Amelia and was very tempted to stay in bed with her. He brushed the hair out of her face and placed a kiss on her cheek. He lingered a little too long and the beeping started again—louder this time. Finn groaned again, pressing angrily at the spot in his ear and quietly getting out of bed.

Finn pulled on his boxers and fished around in his pants for his phone. He checked his app and then grabbed the cable Amelia had left out on the bedside table. He tiptoed out of the room, shutting the door as softly as possible. He walked into the kitchen, opening the fridge, and pulled out an iced tea. He sat at the table, plugging the cable into a wall, then finding the port in his arm and plugging it into his arm. He opened the app again, logging the time and sending the report to the doctor. Then he went into his crossword puzzle app and began killing some time until the recharge was finished.

"What the fuck!?!"

Finn looked up at the yell. Matt was standing in the doorway, a murderous look on his face. Finn looked around in confusion before he realized the anger was directed at him. Without realizing it, Finn began to shrink in on himself.

"You are altered! Does Amelia know? How dare you?"

"I... I don't understand?"

"You!" Matt stomped and pointed.

"What's going on out here?"

A sleepy Amelia approached Matt from behind and pushed past him. She looked between Matt and Finn. She walked over to Finn, putting an arm on his shoulder and kissing him on the cheek. Matt spluttered in fury.

"How, Amelia? How can you kiss him? Did you sleep with him?" he accused.

Amelia got defensive. "Matt! We are not dating right now. What's wrong with you? We talked about Finn."

"You didn't tell me he was a monster!" Matt pointed at Finn.

"What the fuck are you talking about?" Amelia

asked angrily.

"He's altered, Amelia. How can you be with him?"

Finn heard another quick beep in his ear. He quickly checked his phone and then unplugged the cable from the port in his arm. He stood to leave but Amelia pressed on his shoulder. She looked at him and shook her head. He nodded and swallowed apprehensively.

"How dare you! How can you call a human being a monster? I never knew you felt this way. You know what I do for a living!"

"Just because you work for... them... doesn't mean you have to be with them. They can be around without integrating into our lives!"

Amelia slapped Matt. "You ignorant bastard. I want you out. Now!" Amelia pointed out of the room.

"Fine. I don't want the government spying on me with their robots, anyway!"

Matt spun on his heels. Amelia seethed while she heard Matt gathering some of his stuff. Finn winced when the front door slammed. Amelia turned sad eyes back to Finn.

"I'm so sorry. I didn't know he was..."

"A bigot?" Finn offered.

"That's putting it nicer than what I was going for," Amelia groused.

Finn took her hand and kissed it. She held it as she went around the table and knelt in front of him. She hugged his waist and then rested her head against his chest.

"Come back to bed?" she asked.

Finn nodded and led her back to her bedroom.

I really think this dress makes me look fatter than I already am," Amelia complained.

Finn came up behind her and looked at her in the mirror.

"You look beautiful."

He kissed the side of her head and she rolled her eyes at him, making a face. He made a face back and she swatted at him. They laughed and turned away from the mirror.

"You're going to be late if we don't go soon," Finn reminded her.

"Story of my life. Just don't you be late," she told her belly.

"If he's anything like his mother, I wouldn't expect him until next spring at the earliest," Finn teased.

He ducked out of the room to avoid the pillow being thrown at his head. Finn waited by the door with Amelia's coat. They walked to her office building, discussing the plans they had to decorate for the holiday season. As they neared the office, Finn switched sides with Amelia, attempting to protect her if the protesters threw anything at them. He was no longer afraid of the walk but he still didn't keep his eyes off the protesters. He stepped inside the building with Amelia and then kissed her. She waved goodbye as she stepped into the elevators.

Finn shoved his hands in his pockets and set back off for home. He looked up and groaned when he saw Matt waiting on the steps to their door. He squared his shoulders and pushed forward, ready to deal with whatever drama Matt had in mind. He noticed Matt looked very disheveled and nervous. As soon as he saw Finn, Matt hunched down and started to move away from the steps.

"Matt," Finn called.

Matt stopped and turned back to Finn. He avoided Finn's eyes and breathed heavily in the chilly air. He shuffled back and forth in an agitated manner. Matt huffed out a breath and put a hand on Matt's shoulder. He got a whiff of alcohol and his eyes teared up.

"Where's... I want to talk to Amelia," Matt stammered.

"She's at work."

Matt's head whipped up. He searched Finn's eyes for a lie but found none. He grabbed Finn's hand and started pulling him towards the office where Amelia worked.

"She can't be. She's always late. She had a meeting."

Finn yanked his hand out of Matt's and stopped. Matt whirled back around and tried to grab Finn again. Finn stood his ground.

"Her meeting was moved to next week. What's this about, Matt?"

Matt gestured wildly towards the office building.

"We have to get to her. She has to get out!"

"Matt, you aren't making any sense. Calm down. What's..."

Finn was cut off mid-sentence by the sound of a loud

explosion. Matt screamed in terror and ran off down the street. Finn's heart sank to his stomach and he ran after Matt. He stopped when Matt collapsed onto the sidewalk and tore at his hair. Finn gulped down his fear and walked up to Matter, looking around the corner. In front of him, the building where Amelia worked had a gaping hole in the side. Papers and ash were fluttering down to the street. People were coming out of the building in various states of disarray. Finn leaned down and hauled Matt to his feet. He grasped Matt's lapels and got in his face.

"What. Did. You. Do?" Finn spat.

"I didn't know. I didn't mean to. I tried to stop it…" Matt sobbed.

Finn threw Matt back down to the ground and went to search for Amelia. Matt sobbed and cried, curling up in a ball on the sidewalk.

Finn pounded on Matt's door. The longer he stood outside waiting in the hallway, the angrier he got. He knew Matt was in the apartment. He could hear him shuffling around. He pounded on the door again. Just as he was about to break the door down, Matt opened it a tiny crack.

"Let me in," Finn demanded.

"Is she?" Matt pleaded.

"She's alive, you moron. Let me in."

Matt opened the door and Finn pushed his way into the apartment. He did his best not to gag at the stench of stale beer and pizza. The place was a pigsty. Finn picked his way to a clean spot to stand and rounded on Matt.

"I... I," Matt stammered.

Finn held up a hand.

"Listen to me. I don't care if you rot away in this house forever. I don't know what your involvement in the bombing was, but I do know you were involved. I am here for Amelia... and for the baby."

Matt's eyes cleared a little. "Baby?"

"She's pregnant. She needs you to come to the hospital. The baby's life depends on it."

"Why would she need me there?"

"Because it's yours, you daft idiot," Finn exploded.

"Mine?"

Finn shook his head and grabbed Matt. He dragged him into the bathroom and turned on the shower. When Matt made no move to do anything, Finn shoved him into the shower. Matt sputtered and shouted and Finn just held onto him harder.

Once Finn had gotten Matt to cooperate, Matt cleaned himself up. Finn put a hot mug of coffee into Matt's hands and glared at him until he'd finished the whole cup. Matt nodded and Finn shoved him out the door, stomping down the stairs and not looking back to see if Matt was following. Matt trudged behind Finn all the way to the hospital. He only hesitated at the front door and Finn whirled around to face him once more.

"What is your problem?" Finn growled.

Matt winced. "Why didn't she tell me?"

Finn rolled his eyes. He was ready to just leave Matt out in the cold but he'd promised Amelia he would try to stay calm. He took a steadying breath and closed his eyes for a moment, breathing in slowly through his nose and out of his mouth. He opened his eyes to see Matt anxiously staring at him. It almost made him want to start the whole process over but he knew there wasn't enough time for him to create more delays.

"She was going to. Then you went ballistic on me. She decided she didn't want you to know because she did not want her son to grow up to be an asshole…" He paused, holding up a staying hand. "Her words—not mine."

Matt huffed. "So why now?"

"Because of the bomb. The baby needs both parents' permission for a nanobot transfusion. The bomb caused some heart damage and it's the only way to repair it. Otherwise, the baby dies."

Matt's eyes widened. He gulped and Finn snorted at him derisively. Matt looked through the hospital doors as if he could see Amelia and the baby from where he was standing. Finn towered over him with one hand on the door and one hand on Matt's shoulder.

"Time to really decide if you believe all that government control nonsense. Look, I've heard it most of my life and I take it. Do you want to know why?"

"Wh—why?" Matt asked.

"I am alive. That's more than I can say about some people. Sure, I have to *recharge* the bots on a regular schedule but without them, my lungs would have stopped working a long time ago. They don't control me. They don't give me subliminal *kill all the humans* messages. They don't record everything you say. All they do is keep my lungs running. Got it?" Finn explained.

Matt nodded. Finn waited to see what Matt would decide and he knew the moment Matt had given up his ill-conceived notions of what being altered meant and decided to learn a little. Finn nodded, gesturing for Matt to enter the hospital and then followed after him.

Amelia looked down at the baby in her arms and smiled. He'd been through so much but the doctor had just given him a clean bill of health. She was extra happy because the doctors had finally unhooked her from all the machines and IVs and she was getting to go home.

"You ready to get out of here, sweetheart?" Finn asked as he entered the room.

He walked over to Amelia and kissed her on the forehead. It was the one place she'd said she wasn't sore. He put a finger against the baby's hand and smiled when Isaac closed his fist around it. The little boy was a fighter and the nanobots were doing a great job of keeping his hurt functioning.

"Yeah, we better get home before this little guy needs a recharge. They told me there is a new portable battery that we might be able to get. It would make it easier on us... and you."

Finn nodded. "We could go away to a cabin in the woods with no electricity!"

Amelia laughed. "Hold on there... I like my comforts."

"The one I'm thinking of has running water," Finn teased.

"It better not be a river, you know that doesn't count!" Amelia groused.

Finn laughed. He and Amelia looked up at the clearing of a throat. Finn tensed a tiny bit but Amelia squeezed his hand. He looked down at Amelia and smiled, nodding at her.

"It's okay, Matt, you can come in," she said.

Matt nodded and shuffled into the room. He hesitated a few feet from Amelia and then pulled his arm from behind his back. In his hand was a teddy bear with a bandage on its arm. Amelia cocked her head to the side.

"It... it's an altered bear. See, it has a little bandage covering the port in its arm until the skin grows back. I... I thought he might like it," Matt stammered apologetically.

Amelia smiled up at Finn, who took the bear and examined the little velcroed bandage. He chuckled at the bear and Matt grinned nervously. Amelia looked between Matt and Finn and smiled.

"Do you want to hold him?" she asked.

Matt nodded. "Will I hurt him? Will the bots dislodge?"

Finn snorted. "That's not how this works."

Matt blushed and scratched behind his ear. Amelia gestured for him to come closer and laid the baby in his arms. The baby gurgled up at Matt and Finn directed him to a chair before his knees buckled. He smiled down at the baby and then looked back to Amelia and Finn.

"Can we... start over?" he asked.

Amelia looked at Finn, who rolled his eyes but nodded. Amelia smiled up at him and then looked at Matt and Isaac. Amelia nodded and tears rolled down Matt's cheeks. Finn tried to covertly hand Matt a tissue and Matt quickly swiped at his cheeks. The two men cooed over the baby and Amelia felt a rush of warmth flood through her. She knew that whatever hatred was thrown at them, they could now weather it as a united family.

WAR

I am at war with myself. The mom in me wants to fight someone. Yell and scream at every adult involved to get some answers and protect my child. The southern woman begs for civility and a cool head. *You catch more flies with honey rather than vinegar,* she reminds me. My dignity wins out over my anger but it is not the last of either.

I know something is wrong the moment he gets in my car while I am sitting in the carpool lane. His beautiful, freckled face is splotchy. He's holding his mouth in a tensed way that covers his teeth—no easy feat since his teeth are wonderfully crooked in that awkward way when a child is no longer "little" and not yet an actual pre-teen. I can see the unshed tears in his eyes before he closes them tightly and shakes his head slightly when I ask him what's wrong.

I throw the car into park, ignoring the look from the

parent behind me, and turn to face my child. I put a hand on his knee and try to soothe him the best I can from the front seat. He looks at me and the tears start falling down his round cheeks, making long, wet trail marks. I want to take away his pain. I often think it hurts me to see him so upset even more than it hurts him. He desperately wants to get control of his emotions but the pain of his experience is so recent because it had just happened. He starts to tell his story and that is when my blood starts to boil.

K has been bullied by another child in his class on a consistent basis over the last quarter. The most recent episode, the one making him currently upset, is even more unacceptable than the previous episodes, though that is no excuse. I do my best to calm my anger as I listen to him.

X has called K an idiot. On top of that, X threw a stick K was playing with over a fence where it was no longer reachable by K. Most people would roll their eyes at a child crying over a stick. Most people don't know my son. First of all, X had promised K he would watch out for the stick, then gleefully thrown it over the fence. Second of all, it was no ordinary stick to K—it was a prized treasure.

Since the moment he could walk, K has collected sticks on every nature hike and trip to the park. Sometimes he even gathers up a stick he sees while walking on a sidewalk to a store. If there is a stick, he is interested. Each one is a valuable item to him. I could never quite understand his attachment to the sticks but I figured it was about the same attachment I have to butterflies. Some indescribable experience of feeling like the item just belonged. K's collection of sticks was always carefully moved from place to place. On the last very long-distance move, he agreed to leave the nature behind and rehomed the sticks in the woods behind our house. As soon as we moved into the new house, the stick collecting began again. They are a part of him. They are swords and hiking sticks and magical items that can transfer him to other worlds. He doesn't settle for just any old stick. They have to be perfect for him.

The stick that was so carelessly thrown over the fence by the other child was a stick that K had carefully hidden each afternoon, all quarter long. He'd been upset once when a smaller child had found his stick but the child had played with it after school and then returned it to him the next day during recess. Everyone on the playground knew which stick was K's. Every child on the playground could play together nicely, except K and X.

I listen to K and console him, once again ignoring a honk from behind me. They can go around, there's room. Soothing my child from his heartbreak is more important to me. I don't care if I am an unpopular parent. Only once I am assured that K is calmer do I weigh my options. On the one hand, I want to get out of the car and demand answers from his teacher on why X is allowed to continually bully my son. On the other, I am literally in a tank top and boy-short underwear, having gotten too overheated and not bothering to change back into normal clothes in order to pick up K from school. I hadn't planned on needing to get out of the car. It always happens that way. Again, the southern woman inside me reminds me that I am a better writer than speaker and it would be more prudent to go home and write an email. She's correct but it does nothing to appease the angry mom.

I put the car into drive and we head home. I stew over the email in my head, composing and recomposing just what I am going to say. I try to call my husband to tell him what I am about to do, but I get no answer. Just as well, the angry mother doesn't want to be thwarted. E always gives too much benefit of the doubt until he is stung by the actions of others. It is something we argue about. A lot.

I confirm certain things with K. How many times has X snatched things away from him? How many times has X pulled things from K's pocket? What other names has X called him?

I am even angrier with each answer. X likes to call K a crybaby because whenever K gets upset he cries. Not wailing sobs. Usually, it is silent tears while K struggles with his emotions. It is to be expected because K has sensory processing disorder, so when he gets upset, his brain gets overloaded with sensory input and freaks out. The tension of that has to go somewhere—hence the tears. It is a commonly overlooked disorder, especially in gifted children. In my childhood, I was just repeatedly told I was *too sensitive* but medical science knows more now and awareness is getting better. Calling my son a crybaby is essentially making fun of a genetic disorder.

X also likes to lord his age over K, telling him that *he* is less mature because he is younger. E and I have told K that X is clearly not more mature, just from the fact he feels the need to point it out so often. It doesn't really help K process it.

The crux of the matter is that K is a kind-hearted child who tries to be nice to everyone and has no room in his life for injustice. He doesn't like to see people flout the rules. In his world, rules create order out of chaos. He is also very trusting and it breaks him apart when someone misuses that trust. Perhaps it is a character flaw but I think it makes him a good person. He doesn't understand why he is the target of bullying. He tries to make it better. He accepts every forced apology X gives him at school, only to be disappointed when the behavior begins again.

We finally arrive home and I sit down to type out the email that I have already written in my head. It comes quickly, my fingers angrily swiping at the keys in an effort to get it all out before my blood pressure rises too much and I pass out. *Politely angry* the southern woman in my head reminds me. I read and re-read the email, making sure that it conveys just that. I ask K a few more details to make sure I have dotted all my *I's* and crossed all my t's. I hit send.

I feel a little better but still angry. I make it a point to find K and give him a hug and ask him what he would like for dinner. He can choose anywhere and of course, I know the answer before he gives it. The rest of the evening goes relatively smoothly, my anger only increasing once more as I explain what has happened to E.

The next morning, I wake up and check my email. I don't have a response yet but it's early. K asks me if there is any news and I tell him *not yet*. We get ready for school and I take him in, the southern woman reminding me to bide my time. I use the carpool lane again and don't get out of the car. I tell K to have a good day and the mom in me gets angry again at his dejected *I'll try*. K loves school...except for X. It kills me to have him in this situation.

Mid-day, I get the email I have been waiting for and I schedule a parent-teacher conference that afternoon. My head has been pounding since the day before and my stomach aches. Both are indicators of higher blood pressure and I am helpless to do anything about them. The thought of actually having to confront someone, keep my anger in check, and be coherent all weigh heavily on my mind. I can do it, I just don't like to do it. Like K, I want the world to be more harmonious, something it is increasingly denying me.

The time finally arrives and I have my conference. Despite my earlier hesitation, I am calm and well-spoken during the meeting. I get my point across politely but pointedly. Mainly, *this has to stop*. The teacher agrees and outlines the steps the school is taking to prevent future bullying. There is light at the end of the tunnel—the bullying stops or X is no longer allowed to attend the school. We wrap up our conference and then call K in to recap him on the results. We go over the specific actions he needs to take to be his own advocate where I can't be one. I am trying to instill resilience in him, although I am not sure I always do the best job with it. At the end of our talk, K throws his arm around my waist, squeezes tight, then looks up at me and smiles.

"Thanks, mom!" he says. He runs off with a skip to join the other children still hanging around at school.

The angry mother is finally appeased and the southern woman is trying not to be too smug. Rationally, I know flying off the handle is not going to help but at the same time, I often wonder if it would be more cathartic. It seems the best balm is that of a renewed happiness in my child. It won't be the last time I am at war with myself but with each new challenge, I am confident I can win the battles I face.

A GIFT

I hate this song."

I winced almost immediately, hoping Allison hadn't heard my outburst. I pretended I hadn't said anything, continuing to stare at the crossword puzzle I had been solving on my phone. I suppressed a sigh when I heard her daintily walking across the floor towards me. She'd heard. She came around the couch and plopped down on it, propping her feet in my laugh and staring at me. I was still patently ignoring her, even though I had moved my hands out of her way, but I knew she had raised her eyebrow at me in that way of hers. It meant she was waiting for me to elaborate. When I didn't take the bait after a few minutes, she nudged my phone with her foot. I put my phone down and looked over at her, still not answering her unspoken question. She shook her head in an amused way and ended our staring contest.

"What, my darling Scrooge, do you dislike about

the song?"

She laughed at my scrunched-up face and the middle finger I shot in her direction. I listened again for a moment, my discomfort clear, and then shook my head. It was almost Christmas and I did not want to start another argument.

"Forget it."

"Nope. Not this time. This time you have to tell me."

"Allison..."

She jerked her legs back from my lap and tucked them under her body. It was a clear sign that my desire for peace would not win out. Allison hated it when I kept things from her and she hated it even more if I ignored her desires for closure before bed. She went by the *don't go to sleep angry* motto, whereas I was more a *let me cool off and forget it* kind of person.

"Fine!" I snapped, just a little too harshly—judging by the way she jumped back in surprise.

I swallowed heavily, wishing my hatred of the "Christmas" song had not burst out of me. I silently berated myself for my inability to just stay quiet for the few minutes it would take for the song to play out and switch to something more pleasant. Already, a new song was playing through our smart speaker and I would have given anything to have been still solving my crossword while listening to Allison hum to the music while wrapping Christmas gifts. I would have helped her but our first Christmas together she saw the haphazard way I wrapped presents and then banned me for life.

I adored the hours it took her to wrap the presents. They

were works of art and it was a shame they were destroyed so quickly by those who did not appreciate art. Allison used double-sided tape and wrapped each seam so carefully, she even made sure the paper continued so it was nearly impossible to tell there was a seam in the first place. She also wrapped each present in a different paper, meaning we had a veritable treasure trove of wrapping paper. One entire closet was dedicated to paper, ribbons, bows, and other decorative items not normally found on a package but artfully placed on Allison's gifts. The memory had me smiling, which did not sit well with the seething I could feel coming from Allison and I resigned myself to the argument we were about to have.

"Honey, I don't like it when you call me a scrooge. I'm not a scrooge, I just feel like we should acknowledge one holiday before we go worrying about the next. Christmas has encroached upon Thanksgiving for years and then it started in on Halloween. *This year* there were decorations in the store before Labor day! It's getting out of hand."

Allison shook her head at me and I knew right then she had seen through my attempted diversion. She was not easy to throw off the scent and I was not giving her the explanation she wanted. She crossed her arms and glared at me. Daring me to either go on with my bogus detour of the topic or actually address the elephant in the room that had brought her to the couch in the first place.

"It's just a song."

"Nice try…"

"Why is it a Christmas song? Just because it has Christmas in the title? Just so they could capitalize on the holidays? They couldn't make something catchy and cute?"

"It is catchy," she shrugged.

"But… for all the wrong reasons. The tune is catchy but the sentiment is horrendous. I mean—just bear with me here—he says he will give his heart to someone special this year. It begs two questions: one, why didn't he give it to someone special last year and two, he is clearly still hung up on last year's person so this year's person is just a rebound so does that mean the very next day he will break their heart? It's preposterous… oh and *three*, Christmas isn't a time for romance!"

She huffed and stood up. She opened and shut her mouth a couple of times, trying to find a way to poke a hole in my argument but I could clearly see she agreed with me on some level. Then I saw it in her eyes. My third reason had hit and she was even more livid than before when I'd tried to change the direction of our fight.

"Christmas is a *perfectly* wonderful time for romance! Otherwise, we wouldn't have Christmas romance movies."

I opened my mouth to give my opinion on that particular topic but caught myself just in time. Or so I thought. She'd watched me too closely. *Great,* I thought, *now we are going to argue about that, too.* I wasn't wrong, though it did not please me to be right in this instance.

"No. You will absolutely not get out of this by just pretending you weren't going to say something. Spit. It. Out."

"Very well, those romance movies are too sickly sweet and way too formulaic. No one falls in love in just one month. Everything is just too easy in those movies. Those relationships could never work. It's all chalked up to the magic of Christmas but Christmas isn't usually magical. It is stressful and time-consuming. It's not a time for romance. It can be enjoyable but things that are too easy don't last."

"You only say that because you make everything so difficult!"

Allison's voice had started quivering and I could see tears welling in her eyes. I wanted nothing more than to wipe away those tears and hold her close to me but I knew she was too wound up for that to happen. Once again, I yelled at myself internally for pointing out the ridiculous song. It was not worth fighting over and yet, we were.

"Sweetheart, it's just a song and I am sorry if I offended you. December is not my favorite month but that doesn't mean you can't enjoy it and I can't enjoy watching you have fun. Can we just forget about this?"

"I just... I need to go out for a while."

I looked out the window. It was a little fogged up from the heat inside and I could tell it had probably gotten colder since the sun had gone down. I hated the cold, too. I just hated winter in general but we'd had that argument enough and I knew how to tamp down my feelings on that topic. I looked back at her, tried to give a reassuring smile, and nodded. I watched her retreat into our bedroom, heard her rustle around for a few minutes, and then return wearing her winter gear.

"I could come with you."

She sighed and shook her head.

"I need to cool off and it is pretty chilly. Just give me a bit, okay?"

I nodded and watched as she grabbed her keys and left the apartment. I let out a long, shaky breath and squeezed my eyes shut, trying to picture a reset on the pleasant evening we had been having. My mind wandered to Allison, mentally following her as she walked. I knew exactly where she was headed.

Whenever she needed space, Allison always walked to the Bridge of Glass. It was an odd obsession she had but she was an artist and I knew she appreciated the beauty of all the pieces on the bridge. I'd once caught her lying under the "Seaform Pavilion" staring up at the various pieces and smiled. When I had hovered over her, blocking her view, she'd pulled me down to lie next to her, talking about the various pieces. I stared at her, falling more in love with her, a feat I'd never thought possible. She finally noticed me staring instead of listening.

"What?"

"Why do you like to stare at these pieces? You come here so often."

"I'm looking for possibilities."

"It's just sand…"

"That sand never aspired to anything. It didn't know what it would become. Now, look at it, so beautiful and yet so fragile. The sand never asked to be turned into glass but it was and now it is possible for it to shine."

I laughed and she blushed. I held her hand and stared up at the glass pieces, trying to see what she saw. I never could see anything more than colored glass pieces. My mind was too analytical and too caught up in order to see the beauty in the chaos. I knew she could tell I did not enjoy it as much as she did but she didn't say anything and I was content to lay on the ground and hold her hand because my joy was fulfilled by lying next to her. She was my possibilities.

I came back to myself in the apartment and chastised myself for letting her go out walking, alone and in the cold. Time was a vague construct to her and if I didn't remind her it was freezing outside, she would lay on the bridge for hours at a time, the cold from the concrete seeping into her bones and giving her a chill. The last time we had been on the bridge at night, we were out so long, I didn't think I could feel my butt for three days, even after sitting on a heating pad. I got up and went to find some warm clothing.

I stepped outside, already regretting the decision not to take some hand warmers. Luckily, the promised rain had not yet started and I was hoping to retrieve Allison and make it inside before that luck ran out. I walked swiftly down our block and across the street, hopping back and forth to stay warm while I waited for the pedestrian light to allow me to cross. Once across the street, I walked quickly to the bridge but frowned at the start of it. I didn't see anyone there. Allison was not lying under the "Seaform Pavilion", nor was she standing by the "Venetian Wall." I turned around under the pavilion and looked back the way I had come, wondering if I had missed her somehow, but I did not see anyone else on the street. Everyone was in for the night, anticipating the forecasted wintry weather.

I turned back around and scanned the bridge once more. A sudden wave of unease fell over me and I balled my hands in my coat pocket, dreading the walk across the bridge for an unknown reason. As I passed under the pavilion, a dark figure emerged from the side of the bridge near the crystal towers and ran off in the opposite direction of me. Fear gripped my heart and I forced myself to continue to the spot where the man had just run. Adrenaline took over the moment I saw a foot sticking out from the side of the only obscured spot on the bridge.

"Allison!"

I rushed over and knelt on the ground, ignoring the slick, almost black liquid on the cement. My brain refused to acknowledge what it knew to be blood. Her blood. I checked for life and was relieved to find that she was still breathing. I swore under my breath, a quick check of my pockets revealing I'd left my cell phone back in our apartment.

"Allison, it's going to be okay. I need your phone. Just stay with me."

She reached out and grabbed my arm, the one I was using to pull her phone out of her pocket. She looked at me and at that moment, I realized she was going to give up. She tried to talk but I wanted her to save her strength and use it to fight for her life. I wanted her to fight for us. I didn't want fighting to be the last thing we had done.

"I need to call an ambulance. You need to rest. It's going to be okay."

"Virginia... I just wanted to help... him."

"It's okay, sweetheart. I'm here. It will be okay."

"He didn't believe I didn't have... cash... I tried to tell... him..."

She broke off coughing and I refused to acknowledge the blood on her lips. I didn't want to admit she'd been hurt. Intrinsically, I knew it was bad but I wanted to deal with the situation in a calm manner. The trouble was, my usual calm in the face of danger was crumbling in the face of the impending death of the one person I loved most in the world. I sat down fully and cradled her in my arms, trying to yank off my glove at the same time in order to use the phone. She put her blood-stained hand on mine and shook her head.

"It's too late."

"It can't be."

She nodded, her strength for arguing waning with each labored breath. She closed her eyes and I started sobbing, stroking her hair and hoping the approaching sirens were coming to save her. She squeezed my hand and I hugged her to me, as tightly as possible, trying to make my sheer force of will keep her alive. She chuckled for a moment and I looked down at her. She raised her eyebrow a little.

"Darling... Scrooge... it's everything after December..."

"I don't understand."

"One day... you will... "

Paramedics arrived and the adrenaline overtook me. I crumbled into a sobbing mess while they worked on her and rushed her off to the hospital. The policemen tried to console me but they did not understand anything I said. They wrapped me in a blanket and took me to the hospital.

In February, I sat on the sofa and stared at the window, cursing the falling snow. I'd sloshed through the rain to get home before the snow had started but I'd wanted to be out longer. I'd gone to the bridge, just as I had done every day since the one that took Allison from me. I'd try to figure out what she meant, looking into the glass but only feeling her ghost everywhere. It was the only place I still felt whole and leaving made the emptiness grow larger and larger each time. I looked around at our apartment. The Christmas tree was still in its spot, the timer turning the lights on each evening. The presents Allison had been wrapping before our argument were still in their original state of either being wrapped or partially wrapped and decorated. I hadn't been able to touch anything as if Christmas were a perpetual holiday in our house.

I ignored our friends. I knew they wanted to help but I couldn't stand their looks of pity or even the genuine offers of help. Our neighbors would bring little doggie bags of food, ring the doorbell, and then set the bag outside the door. They'd learned it was the only way I would take the offering as I refused to talk to anyone. I was a shadow of myself, convinced there was no way to live in a world without Allison.

By March, my friend George had decided enough was enough. He barged into our apartment, technically he used the key we had given him, and announced we were going to start the healing process. He practically forced me to take a shower, threatening to put me in it with my clothes on if I didn't do it myself. When I was done, I came out of my bedroom and gasped in horror, the Christmas tree in a half state of being undecorated.

"What are you doing!?!"

He shrugged, "It needs to come down. You can't heal if it doesn't."

I glared at him and stomped my foot.

"I don't want to heal!"

"But you must. Allison would want you to heal."

Angry tears began flowing down my face.

"Don't," I growled.

George came over to me and gave me a hug, letting me cry on his shoulder. When I could stop, I tried to pull away but he just enveloped me tighter. He waited until I hugged him back and then released me.

"Go out for a walk, honey. Clear your head and then, when you get back, we can work on everything else in the apartment. We'll make a plan. Baby steps…"

I nodded and went to put on some warm clothes. I knew he was just trying to get me out of the apartment so that he could de-Allison it. I knew that it was for my own good, even if I didn't like it. I yelled at him in my head, not wanting to yell at him in person. I was done trying to argue and George was a good friend. I hadn't already run him off with my behavior for the past three months so chances were pretty good he wasn't going anywhere. I looked up and sighed, realizing my feet had taken me back to the bridge, again.

I laid down under the Seaform, remembering my darling Allison and happier times. I couldn't stop the tears from coming. A man and a woman stopped for a moment and then quickly walked past me, whispering to each other, probably about me. I gathered myself up and rose, walking down the bridge, ignoring the spot where Allison had been shot. I had never been able to look at that spot, clearly seeing the pool of blood on the concrete in my mind, even though, rationally, I knew it was cleaned long ago. I stopped in front of a green vase on the wall. I could feel her presence and almost see her in the glass but she wasn't there. I collapsed into a heap and began sobbing again. I don't know how long I was there. It had gotten darker and colder and yet, I did not feel it. I only felt my overwhelming grief.

I felt a hand on my shoulder and looked up to see George, holding a candle and smiling at me. He pulled me to my feet and I took me over to a group of others, all holding candles. It was all the friends I had neglected. Those who were hurting by the loss of Allison, just as I was. George and the others all hugged me and I listened as each one told me what Allison had meant to them. I allowed myself to be consoled for the first time since she had died and it did not feel as unsavory as I thought it would.

After a while, George walked back home with me and let me into the now clean house. George had put away all of the decorations and stowed the presents, all save one. There was a beautiful green package, adorned with a red, glittered butterfly sitting on our table. I sighed and started shaking my head, backing away from the present as if it were a snake ready to bite me. George stopped me with his hands on my shoulders. He leaned into me.

"She took the time to chose it for you. I think it will help you move on to see her final gift to you. She was very excited about it."

"You know what it is?"

"I do. I'll leave it up to you. I'll be back tomorrow."

I nodded and listened to him leaving. I stood by the now-closed door and stared at the package. I don't know how long I stood there but I eventually went over to the package and sat down at the table. I put out a shaky hand and lovingly caressed the paper. The design was subtle but I knew that no matter how hard it was, Allison had matched that design so perfectly I would not be able to easily find the seam. I picked up the package and put it in my lap. She'd probably wrapped it right under my nose while I did crossword puzzles. I laughed a little, hearing her chiding me in my head for hoping to keep it as pretty as possible.

"They are made to be ripped open."

"They are too beautiful. Works of art."

"Here, I'll help you tear it."

"Don't you dare! It's my gift."

I smiled and laughed because she would smile and laugh. I took a deep breath and tore into the paper, just to make her proud—if she were watching from above. The thought brought tears to my eyes and I closed them, trying to chase away the sorrow and enjoy what she got me. When the feeling to cry subsided, I opened the box and stared down at the gift. Love filled my heart and I finally understood. Everything after December was the key. I put my hand on the gift and sent a silent thank you to Allison, knowing she could feel my gratitude and my love.

A Kiss

She'd kissed me.

I was rooted to the spot, unable to move, the electrifying tingle still lingering on my lips from the brief pressure of hers touching them. My heart was pounding and I felt dizzy. It was a quick kiss, merely a peck, really, but it was the moment everything in my life changed. My brain was struggling to find the right actions to take but it was already too late. She'd disappeared into the crowd and I didn't even know her name. Something told me I'd waited my whole life for that moment. For her to come and wake me up.

I tried to shake myself out of my stupor, to pay attention to my well-wishers, and to celebrate with them. I tried to be grounded in the moment. I could worry and wonder about the kiss later. Perhaps it meant nothing to her, just a spur-of-the-moment kind of action one takes when they aren't thinking. Perhaps she was just as excited as everyone around me. This was a momentous occasion and it was meant to be celebrated. I was supposed to be portraying elation, not utter shock.

My son grabbed my arm and it almost broke the spell. I looked up at him, staring down at me in confusion, and shook my head slightly. He'd gotten taller than me by the time he was twelve and now stood a good half-foot over me. He smiled a little half-smile that made his handsome face even more beautiful. It was his way of reassuring me, even if he didn't understand my consternation. I smiled back and then stared out at the people clamoring for my attention with glazed-over eyes. I still couldn't focus properly. Perhaps that was her aim, to throw me off balance, to make me make a fool of myself. No. A kiss like that could not have had any nefarious purpose. I had to stop and regain control of my thoughts. I wouldn't think of the kiss anymore. I had a duty to perform. I'd just achieved the culmination of my hopes and dreams and I should be reveling in my victory.

Patrick leaned down and whispered in my ear, "You okay, Mom?"

I nodded. He looked at me with skepticism but shrugged, turning to shake the hand of a man who'd stepped up to him, then throwing his arm around his wife. I had to get a grip. If not for my sake, then for the sake of my son and his family. I had a job to do and people were counting on me. I took a deep breath, pasted a smile on my face, and nodded to my campaign manager. She gave a thumbs-up and headed to the podium on the dais. My son squeezed my shoulder and I patted his hand reassuringly. It was time to get back to business.

"Ladies and gentlemen, I have the distinct pleasure of introducing the next President of the United States. Please give a warm welcome to President-Elect Annica Charlton."

I smiled and waved as I went up to the podium. The cheering raised to a deafening level just before when the news had been announced on the big screen behind me. I was making history. I was the first female president ever elected to the office, the first atheist, and the first Libertarian. So many firsts. It was a huge achievement, one that I'd worked on for years... and yet, the kiss still lingered.

My lips began tingling again from the memory. I'd get through my speech—it was prepared days ago and rehearsed ad nauseam so that I could say it in my sleep—and then I would celebrate with my supporters. The kiss would have to wait until I was alone.

The Wolf

The final world war did not end with a nuclear holocaust, as had always been expected, but with the quiet realization that there was no one left to fight. Bombs had not been the weapon of choice, biological warfare was chosen for the swift cruelty it could inflict. Terrorists were able to infiltrate pharmaceutical companies and replace common, life-saving medications with horrific pathogens that wiped out half the population of the planet in a few short months. Infighting, panic and chaos further reduced the remaining survivors to a handful of enclaves around the world, countries no longer existed for there was no longer enough humans left to matter. Nature laid claim to once great cities and over time technology was all but forgotten.

Each enclave was isolated from the others and therefore

had their own form of government and laws. Wickwood was once such enclave, located in what was once the Pacific Northwest of the United States of America. The residents of Wickwood were divided into three classes. Yellow class was comprised of the surviving infected and those born with diseases which no longer had cures or medications for management. Blue class was comprised of the citizens working in the peacekeeping and bureaucratic branches of the society. Finally, Red class was comprised of everyone else. Members of each class were required to wear outer clothing the other color of their class, with the actual article being up to the wearer. Yellow class was further separated to a restricted area of the enclave for the protection of the other two classes. This was to prevent the further spread of incurable diseases.

Scarlett had been born in Wickwood and had never known the world before the war. She belonged to the Red class and her father thought it a great joke to name her after the color. She worked in a tattoo parlor and it was sometimes the most boring job she could think of in her limited knowledge of the old world. She had seen books in the library, which had thankfully survived, and she longed for an adventure. Yet, day after day, she sat in the tattoo parlor and drew designs while waiting for customers to come into the shop. The one bright spot in her day was getting to work with her friend Zoe.

Scarlett and Zoe were locking up for the day. It had been another long one and neither had made any money but they did not let it dampen their spirits. The weather was a drizzly cold and it was already dark as the sunset was very early this time of year.

"Hey, you want to come over to my place and hang tonight?" Scarlett asked.

Zoe shook her head. "Nah, I got a date."

"What? That's great, Zoe. Who is it?" she asked.

"Just a guy I met the other day. Anyway, I'll see ya tomorrow?"

Scarlett nodded. "Yeah… and remember…"

"Grandmother says don't stray from the path." They said in unison and laughed as they parted ways.

Scarlett pulled her red hoodie closer around her face and hunched over against the cold. She hated this time of year and walking home after dark. She also despised going home to her now empty apartment. Shortly after her birth, her mother had gotten ill and been banished to the Yellow class and its ghetto-like conditions. She assumed her mother was still alive but did not know for sure. Last year, her father had peacefully slipped away in his sleep, leaving Scarlett on her own. She supposed it could be worse, Zoe had lost both of her parents at a very young age and many children did not even survive the first few years after they were born.

Scarlett entered her apartment and flipped on the radio. Some people still had televisions but they were only used for broadcasts from their leader. Anything else was seen as frivolous and a waste of time on behalf of the citizens of Wickwood. Scarlett's father had told her about the fictional worlds that had once been displayed on televisions and it just added to her imagination of a more exciting life. As it was, the radio mostly played "classical" music and reminders from Grandmother on the laws of the enclave.

Grandmother was the name of the leader of Wickwood. She was the oldest surviving member of the enclave, therefore, she had been given the position of leader as it was surmised she was the wisest person to lead. She was also notorious for her numerous admonitions, broadcast on both the radio and television, as well as, posted in flyers around the city. The one most often seen was, "Grandmother says don't stray from the path." It was a reminder for those in the Red and Blue classes to stay to the lit pathways that marked the safe way through the city. Yellow class could not take the lit pathways and stayed to the shadows.

Scarlett heated up her dinner and sat down to share it with her cat, Luna. It was a stray black cat who had found its way to her a couple of years earlier. Her father had laughed at her choice of name. He had always found joy in the simplest things. Now, Luna was a reminder of happier times and she was also great at keeping rats out of the apartment. Technically, Scarlett did not get enough rations for a pet, as Grandmother had determined it was a waste of resources, but she did not mind sharing her meat and milk with the little cat. After dinner, she curled up with a book and Luna, soon falling asleep to the quiet hum of the cat's purring.

The next morning, Scarlett made her way into work. The

rainy weather had kept the morning light gloomy and darkened and she was running later. She made it into the parlor fifteen minutes later than she was supposed to be there and she had hoped her gruff boss would be too busy to notice. She was out of luck as he was standing by the door waiting when she entered.

"You're late again," he said with a sour face.

Scarlett nodded, trying to catch her breath.

"First, Zoe does not show up and now you are late. What should I do with the two of you?"

"I'm sorry, I'll try not to let it happen again," Scarlett said as her cheeks reddened. Then her mind caught up and she processed what he had said. "Zoe isn't here? She is never late."

He walked past her dismissively. "She is today and if she is not here by noon, she'll have to find another job."

Scarlett looked up at the clock and worried her lip. Zoe had never been late or sick since she had known her.

Noon came and went with no sign of Zoe. The later it got, the more Scarlett worried about her friend. It did not help they had absolutely no customers to distract her from clock-watching. Five o'clock came and Scarlett jumped up to lock up the shop and go see if she could check on Zoe. She practically sprinted to her friend's apartment building and used the spare key to let herself into the apartment. From her initial inspections, it looked like Zoe had not been there at all this day and Scarlett wondered if she had made it home last night.

Zoe had written down an address on her notepad, so Scarlett copied it to a new sheet of paper. It did not look familiar so she would have to find a map or ask for directions at one of the peacekeeper stations. She took one last look around and then left to continue her search. She debated on going to the peacekeepers. They were not unfriendly but she had been wary of them ever since her father had died. After his death, she had been quarantined while she was observed for any diseases and her father's body was processed. It had been unpleasant and she felt almost ashamed when she returned to her life. Everyone had given her a wide berth for a few months after, almost as if she was an outcast. Zoe had been the only one who had acted normal.

Scarlett walked to the closest information center and studied the map. Grandmother had made sure there were public places with maps of the whole enclave so no one would get lost. It showed the safe areas of Wickwood, the restricted areas marked in large, obscuring swaths, like big Yellow lakes. Scarlett searched for the street of the address with no luck. She sighed, resigned to the fact she would have to talk to the peacekeepers.

Scarlett walked into the closest station and waited in line. As she waited, she observed the station. It was a fairly sterile-looking room with bright blue walls and three oak desks. A peacekeeper sat at each desk wearing a crisp, blue uniform shirt with a nametag. Each one was talking with a different citizen and taking notes or explaining something to the person. One of the men seemed a lot more cordial and quick at his job than the others and it was not long before Scarlett found herself sitting in front of him.

"Good evening, Miss?" he asked politely.

"Scarlett," she said and held out her hand to shake his.

"Scarlett, what can I do for you?"

Scarlett looked at his nametag. "Hunter?" He nodded and she continued, "I was wondering if you could help me find this address?"

Scarlett handed him the paper and he looked at it before frowning.

"I'm afraid I can't help you," he said.

"Why not?"

"It is in the yellow zone," he replied.

Scarlett shook her head. "No, that's not right. I think my friend was supposed to meet someone there. She's in Red class, like me."

Hunter studied her for a moment. "If she went into the yellow zone, she is violating the rules. What's her name?"

Scarlett swallowed past the lump in her throat and stood up. "I think I am mistaken. I must have written it down wrong."

She ran out of the station, ignoring Hunter's calls for her to wait. After a few blocks, Scarlett slowed down and then stopped to sit on a bench. It did not make sense that Zoe would go into the Yellow zone. Sure, neither of them had a truly glamorous life, but each of them had sworn their lives were better than anyone in the Yellow class.

Scarlett lost track of time and before long she heard the

announcements from Grandmother, "Curfew is nearly upon us, please make your way home dears and remember…"

"Grandmother says don't stray from the path," Scarlett muttered under her breath.

Scarlett spent several evenings after Zoe's disappearance looking for clues, only to run into dead end after dead end. She had limited hours before curfew but she checked all of their usual haunts and talked to everyone they knew. No one had seen Zoe since the night she disappeared and one guy even made the offhand remark, "Scarlett was the last person to see her, therefore the most suspect." She was getting frustrated and scared for her friend.

Disappearances were becoming more common, especially from the Red class, and there were whispers a new drug was slowly adding ranks to the Yellow class. This new drug was rumored to cause the user's eyes to glow an unnatural yellow and allow the distributor to control people. The kingpin of the operation was called The Wolf and all the classes feared the name, even if they did not know if he actually existed. Scarlett had always dismissed these rumors as childish stories to frighten people into submission. People got sick all the time and a drug was not necessary to thin out the ranks of the Red and Blue class.

Two weeks after Zoe's disappearance, Scarlett was saying goodbye to her newest co-worker at closing time. He was a man of few words and almost every spot on his body, save his face, was tattooed with something. She had spent countless hours the last few days staring at the tattoos and wondering their meanings. He waved at her and went on his way without even a backward glance to see if she returned the gesture.

Scarlett was walking along the path to her home when she heard a noise off to her left. She peered into the darkened alley and lurched back in fear when a cat jumped out at her. She chuckled at the cat and leaned down to let it sniff her hand. It rubbed against her hand, then turned with its tail in the air and sauntered off. She adjusted her hood when she saw two glowing lights at the end of the alley. Scarlett cocked her head as the lights blinked at her. The person, for she was sure it was a human now, looked at her for a moment longer and then backed away. As they retreated, a door opened and a weak light illuminated the figure. Scarlett gasped as she thought she recognized Zoe. Zoe turned and walked away.

Scarlett took a moment to look around her. She did not see any peacekeepers near her and after a moment of hesitation, she stepped into the alley and the forbidden yellow zone. She walked quickly after the figure and she swore she had kept Zoe in her sights but after twenty minutes Scarlett stopped and took a look around. Everything in the yellow zone was darker and the whole place looked spooky in the darkness of night. Scarlett thought for a moment, then made her way back out to the lit pathway to her home. She took another quick look around and then walked on home. She did not notice she had been seen by Hunter, who quietly followed behind her as she went to her apartment building.

The next two days were rest days for Scarlett and she made a plan to find Zoe. She gathered the only picture she had of her friend, they were required to take pictures for the government every year. She stuffed a backpack with a few food rations and a bottle filled with water. She left out some extra food for Luna and took a look at her apartment. If she was caught breaking the law and straying from the path, this could be the last time she ever saw her place. She made a quick stop at her neighbor's apartment and made a confused Mrs. Crosby promise to take care of Luna if anything ever happened to her and she did not return. With everything in order, Scarlett took a deep breath and set out to put her plan into action.

Scarlett reached the spot where the cat had frightened her the previous night and once again looked around for any witnesses. A couple of people were strolling down the path, so Scarlett took out a book and then sat on a bench, pretending to read. She waited until she felt the coast was clear and then started to walk into the alley. She stopped, considering her hoodie, before she took it off and stuffed it in her backpack. She pulled out a yellow scarf and tied it around her neck. With Zoe's picture in her hand, she walked fully into the yellow zone.

After hours and hours of searching, Scarlett was no closer to finding Zoe than she had been the previous day. It seemed no one had seen her. Scarlett found this odd and was put off by the display of sheer unwillingness to help her. The people in the Yellow zone just did not have time for anyone, each other included. Scarlett concluded it would be a horrible place to live the rest of your days. She shuddered to think she would be banished here if she was found out.

Just as she had resolved to return to her apartment, Scarlett caught a lucky break and a glimpse of Zoe. She stood on her tiptoes to keep Zoe in sight and headed after her. She caught up with her friend and grabbed her arm.

"Zoe!" she exclaimed with a happy sigh.

"Scarlett, go home," Zoe said, keeping her head down.

"No, why? Where have you been?" Scarlett asked with confusion.

Zoe just shook her head.

"Zoe, just talk to me. I've been worried sick!" Scarlett said, trying to get her friend to look at her.

Zoe pulled Scarlett into an alley and Scarlett let her go. She stared at Zoe's hunched back and tried to comfort her with a hand on her shoulder. Just then, Zoe turned around and Scarlett's eyes widened on a silent gasp. Zoe stood facing Scarlett with glowing yellow eyes.

Zoe laughed bitterly. "Go home Scarlett. You don't want to be my friend anymore."

Scarlett shook her head, still horrified. "I do but... your eyes... what happened?"

"My date wasn't all I dreamed it would be," Zoe said.

"Your date?" Scarlett was confused.

Zoe nodded. "Yeah. It was great at first, he was super nice when we met. Then he asked me to meet him at this place.

Gave me directions. I didn't know…"

"It was in the Yellow zone," Scarlett finished for her.

"Yeah. I thought it would be cool. Add a little danger. No one would know, right?" Zoe had tears running down her cheeks. "But when I got here, he threatened me. Told me if I did not try this pill, he would turn me in. So I did it. Now, my eyes glow and if I don't take one every day, my head feels like it will explode. And what's even worse is I hear commands in my head. They make me do things I don't want to do. I can see myself doing this stuff but I can't control my own body."

Zoe started sobbing and Scarlett hugged her while she cried.

"Shh, Zoe, we can fix this. Come with me and I will get you help," Scarlett said.

Zoe shook her head. "I don't think I can."

"Sure you can, just come…" Scarlett began but was interrupted.

"Well, well, well, Zoe, who is your friend?" a man's voice said behind Scarlett's back.

"Run, Scarlett!" Zoe said and Scarlett was about to protest when Zoe whispered, "Meet me tomorrow at the alley, just run now."

Scarlett nodded imperceptibly, gave Zoe a little squeeze, and ran. She heard shouting and men following her so she ran as fast as she could, trying to dodge people walking around the streets. She tried to lose the ones chasing her through a couple of alleys but they kept on her. She looked back and saw two men after her and the alley to her pathway straight in front of her. She ran blindly through the alleyway and was almost at the mouth when one of the men grabbed her scarf. Thankfully, she had only looped it once and the scarf came off. She had turned her head to watch the men as she came out of the mouth of the alley and ran headlong into Hunter.

Hunter had followed her that morning and watched as Scarlett had entered the yellow zone. He had waited for most of the day, debating on if he should report her for breaking the law. He was a peacekeeper and it was his duty but a part of him was intrigued by her. She had seemed so desperate and determined when she had come into his station. After some research, he had found out about her history and had stared at her recent photo for a decent amount of time. He found himself wanting to get to know her better.

He barely had time to react when Scarlett barreled into him. He threw his arms around her to steady them both and watched as two men looked at him and then walked back into the yellow zone. Scarlett struggled in his arms and he tried to calm her down.

"Whoa, it's okay," he said calmly. "They're gone."

Scarlett looked up when he spoke and she groaned in frustration when she recognized him.

"Are you going to arrest me?" she asked.

He smiled at her gumption. "Not yet."

"Huh?" she asked.

He gestured to her backpack. "Put on your hoodie and

let's get some dinner."

"So you are going to force me to dinner with you now?" she said huffily.

Hunter rolled his eyes. "No. You can come or not. I just want to talk."

Scarlett studied him and then nodded. She pulled out her hoodie and put it on. She followed Hunter as he walked towards the business district. They walked in relative silence while she contemplated her situation. He stole glances at her and tried to hide a smile at her nervous lip biting.

Once at the diner of his choice, Hunter opened the door and motioned for her to precede him. She huffed and walk past him, flopping down into a booth and crossing her arms in a pout.

Hunter chuckled. "Are you always this nice?"

Scarlett narrowed her eyes. "When my future is at stake? Yep."

Hunter shook his head and looked at the menu. The waitress came over and he ordered a grilled cheese for both of them. Scarlett raised her eyebrows at this and he just shrugged.

"What were you doing in the yellow zone?" he asked without preamble.

"Shh, keep your voice down," Scarlett said, looking around surreptitiously.

"Relax, no one's paying attention," Hunter said with exasperation.

Scarlett blew out a breath. "My friend is in trouble."

Hunter nodded. "The one who wouldn't go to the

yellow zone?"

"That's the one. Turns out she did." Scarlett picked at the napkin. "Now she is in big trouble. Have you heard of Lykaon?"

"Of course I have. Peacekeeper, remember?" Hunter puffed out his chest.

"We thought it wasn't real," Scarlett said.

He laughed. "Of course it is. Bad drug. Once you are addicted, The Wolf has you. Are you telling me your friend…?"

"Zoe. "

"All right, Zoe, is involved with The Wolf?" Hunter asked.

Scarlett nodded. "She says she was forced."

"All drug addicts say that."

"Look, Zoe is my friend and I believe her. She is in trouble and she needs my help." Scarlett bit back her anger.

"Okay, calm down. Lykaon has no cure as far as I know," Hunter said.

"There has to be something. What do you know of The Wolf?" she asked.

Hunter thought a moment. "No one knows what he looks like. Peacekeepers are told he wants to rule Wickwood and make all the citizens his slave but he is hampered by Grandmother and law-abiding people who stay on the path."

Scarlett looked guilty for a moment. "I just want to help Zoe. She is my best friend and the only person who has always stuck with me. She needs me."

Hunter studied Scarlett. "Okay, let's make a plan to

help her."

Scarlett was astounded. "You'll help me and not report me?"

He nodded.

"Why?" she asked curiously.

"Because, Scarlett Hood, there is just something about you that intrigues me and I would love a good adventure." Hunter said with a chuckle and a tug of her hoodie string.

Hunter and Scarlett ate their dinner and then left to go back to her apartment. They planned and strategized for a way to get Zoe out of the Yellow zone and to a doctor who was a friend of Hunter's. This doctor owed him a favor and Hunter was certain he would help Zoe without reporting her to the other peacekeepers. Hunter left to go home and talk with his doctor friend before curfew while Scarlett went to Zoe's home to get her a change of clothes and one of her red beanie hats. They agreed to meet at the entrance to the alley the next morning.

Scarlett felt as if a great weight had been lifted off her shoulders that morning as she went to meet Hunter. It was so much nicer knowing someone else was carrying this burden with her. She sped up her pace when she saw him waiting for her. They greeted each other and then set their plan into motion. Hunter would stay hidden next to the building by the alley while Scarlett went into the alley and coaxed Zoe to come with her. They did not want Zoe to think she was being arrested.

Scarlett walked a little way into the alley and called out for Zoe. She did not see her friend and she listened for any sounds. She waited for thirty minutes, at one point shrugging her shoulders when Hunter peaked around the corner in question. She was about to give up when she heard footsteps coming towards the alley. She hid behind a crate until she saw Zoe enter the alley, then she stood and ran to her friend.

"I thought you weren't coming," Scarlett said.

Zoe seemed calmer. "I just got delayed."

"Right, come on, let's get you home," Scarlett said and turned around, trying to pull Zoe with her.

She felt a sting in her arm.

"I'm sorry," Zoe said as Scarlett collapsed in a heap.

Scarlett woke up with a headache and tied to a chair. She tried to struggle for a moment but the motion sent fire up her arms. She looked around and found she was in a room with only one light bulb and nothing else. It looked like a closet. She yelled out for help but no one came.

After what felt like hours, a man entered the room and looked at her with his arms crossed. A second man entered and spoke.

"Sleeping beauty awakes," he said with a leer.

"Where am I? Who are you?" Scarlett asked, trying to sound confident.

"You are in the Wolf's Den," the man said.

Scarlett looked at him blankly.

"If I were you, girl, I would be afraid. The Wolf does not take kindly to stealing" he said.

"People are not property," Scarlett spat.

The man looked over at his companion. "This one has spunk. Too bad."

The silent man walked over and stuck another needle in Scarlett's arm.

The next time she awoke, Scarlett was slumped on a sofa in what seemed to be a high rise office building. The floor to ceiling windows looked out over the entire enclave. It was a rare day of sunshine and Scarlett's eyes were having a hard time adjusting to the bright light. She sat up and rubbed her temples, pleased to learn she was no longer tied up. She looked around the room and stopped cold when she saw Zoe.

"Zoe? What did you do?" Scarlett asked.

Zoe looked at her with mournful eyes but said nothing. She merely gestured to Scarlett to follow her. Scarlett stood warily and hesitated. Zoe looked at her pleadingly and Scarlett sighed and walked behind her friend. They stopped at a door and Zoe opened it. She gestured for Scarlett to enter. Once inside the room, Scarlett noticed it looked like an office which seemed vaguely familiar. She took in the giant mahogany desk and was startled when she noticed a large dog sitting in the chair behind the desk.

Scarlett laughed. "You wouldn't happen to be The Wolf would you?" She was pleased with her own joke and she could hear the dog's tail thumping as it cocked its head and stared at her.

"No dear, that would be me."

Scarlett jumped at the voice behind her. She turned on the spot and her jaw dropped when Grandmother stepped away from the wall. Of course, she had seen this office on the legal flyers around town.

"You… but it's impossible!" Scarlett exclaimed.

Grandmother shook her head, "Nothing is impossible, my dear."

"But why? You already have all the power," Scarlett stammered.

Grandmother crossed the room and the dog jumped out of the chair. She patted its head as she sat down, then steepled her fingers.

"I have power, yes. But I must adhere to the advice of my board. They get younger and younger each year. They wish to give you more freedoms. Let you outside the walls. That kind of thinking is what caused the war in the first place. I lived through too much in my time and I will not see another war wipe out the rest of us." Grandmother held onto her tenuous temper.

Scarlett weighed her words. "Freedom to go outside the walls of Wickwood would not be such a bad thing would it? We could explore the world. Find other enclaves."

Grandmother slammed her fist on the table. "*I will not have it!* I would see all of my citizens here in Wickwood."

Scarlett shrunk back from Grandmother. "But Grandmother, why condemn people to the Yellow zone with Lykaon? Would it not be easier to just increase the peacekeepers?"

"Peacekeepers?" Grandmother laughed. "They are barely useful to me. Too many of them resist my efforts. No, I wish to control everyone susceptible to my drug so I may hear what they are saying behind my back and crush any resistance. Keep my pack together. And the rest of you, we will eliminate."

"The rest of us?" Scarlett was confused and then the truth dawned on her. "You can't control everyone because not everyone gets addicted to your drug?"

Grandmother sneered at her. "Something in your genetics prevents the drug from taking hold. It is laughable. When I was young, scientists did all sorts of genetic testing and yet they could never find anything fit for every human because of DNA. The one thing which prevents me from total domination of Wickwood is the one thing that makes its citizens alive in the first place."

Scarlett's head spun with all the information she had been given.

"So what are you going to do with me?" she asked.

"Now my dear, I am going to make you disappear. Your tale will be chewed up and spit into the wind. Another rumor and another person no one will miss," Grandmother said as she called for Zoe.

Zoe did not answer and Grandmother stomped to the door. She yanked it open and Zoe fell into the room. Just as Grandmother was retreating back into the room, a group of peacekeepers, led by Hunter stormed into the room.

"Grandmother, you are under arrest," Hunter said.

Grandmother moved back and pulled something out of her pocket.

"She has a gun!" Scarlett yelled.

Three peacekeepers pulled their guns on her and shot her dead. Hunter went over to Scarlett and put his hands on her shoulders. Scarlett peered around him.

"Is Zoe dead?" she asked.

He shook his head. "No, we just knocked her out."

"How did you find me?" Scarlett asked as he sat her on a chair.

He shrugged. "I bugged your backpack. We have a limited supply of old technology and I thought you might run into some trouble."

Scarlett laughed. Hunter checked her over and then deemed her ready to leave. One of the other peacekeepers picked up Zoe and they headed out of the building.

"What will happen now?" Scarlett asked.

Hunter thought a moment. "Now Wickwood will pick a new leader. We will have to tell the board what happened and they will do what is best for the citizens of the city."

Scarlett nodded and followed him out into the sunshine.

A year after the incident, Wickwood had changed for the better. Wickwood's borders had been opened and the citizens of the enclave were allowed to explore outside the fences. An enterprising doctor had found a cure for Lykaon addiction, using some of the flowers which grew outside the fence. Other doctors and former scientists, who had lobbied for the ability to do research on the Yellow class, had found ways of curing some of the afflictions and medications for the management of others. The Yellow zone had been reduced to a couple of blocks and the only remaining quarantined inhabitants were those stricken with contagious diseases. Grandmother had kept records of citizens with immunity to Lykaon and those people now served as caregivers and nurses to the remaining Yellow zone residents.

Scarlett was one of the nurses in this special group and she was reunited with her mother. Her mother was still very sick, but it made Scarlett happy knowing her mother would not be alone during her last years. All of the Yellow zone celebrated her as their savior, a title which embarrassed her but which she graciously accepted, in order to keep anyone from being offended. Zoe returned to the tattoo parlor and eventually, became the owner when their previous boss decided he would rather be a hiker than stuck in the city. Hunter became a board member to the new leader of Wickwood and was known for his prudence and wisdom in making good decisions for the good of the enclave.

Eventually contact was made with other enclaves and travel became possible again. Hunter and Scarlett vowed one day, they would make the journey across the former states to the enclave on the east coast. For now, they were content in knowing their world was a better place in which to live, all because Scarlett strayed from the path.

Beauty Within

To say that Alayna had a happy childhood would be grossly lying. For the first six years, she had a doting father and a mother who tolerated her. However, when her father was killed in a battle against another kingdom, her mother began showing her true colors. The hatred she felt was compounded by the fact that her father had left Alayna everything and her mother was merely appointed as her regent until she was of age to run their lands on her own. Therefore, her mother took out all her frustrations on Alayna and the freedom of childhood was lost on the girl.

When Alayna was twelve, her mother took her on a trip into the nearby town. This was a rare event as usually her mother kept her hidden away in the manor, telling her that she did not want to be seen with such a hideous creature and that she was only looking out for Alayna's best interests as the world could be a cruel and unforgiving place. Alayna still had enough spirit to believe that perhaps the world would be more understanding, but this only earned her a sneer from her mother. Alayna marveled at the beautiful countryside as they rode in the carriage; it was filled with rich greens and golden yellows. She saw cows and sheep grazing and she waved back happily to a farmer that had tipped his hat at her, until her mother admonished her for acting unladylike, and she sat back on her seat with her hands in her lap.

Once in the city, her mother told her to stay next to the carriage and talk to no one. If she were asked, she was to tell whoever it was that she was waiting for her mistress and she was not allowed to say anything else. Alayna stretched her neck to see as much as she could of the market they had stopped near. She longed to wander the market and see the various shops and stalls, but she was too afraid of her mother to wander far. She had been standing there at the carriage, looking around, when an older boy came up and stared at her. After a moment, a second boy joined the first and stared at her. Then the boys began whispering to each other and throwing looks her way. Alayna tried her best to ignore them, but the more they stared and pointed, the more uncomfortable she got, until at last she burst.

"What are you looking at?" she blurted.

The boys gave each other a look and burst out laughing. "Look Cameron, the little pig speaks."

"Aye, it's not dumb and deaf after all," Cameron spoke and both boys laughed at their joke.

Alayna fought tears as she balled her fist. "I am not a pig or dumb. I am Alayna of Emerald Manor."

Cameron and his brother shrugged. "Who cares where you come from? Our father is a great merchant and he still would not give you a job shining his boots. You will never fetch a good husband, you are too plain and too portly."

Alayna gasped. The boys spoke true words, for her mother had often said worse, but she did not understand why they needed to say these things to her. She did not want to marry anyways. Once she was of age, she could do what she wanted with the money her father gave her and perhaps she could even leave this land. However, she was very angry at their taunting.

Alayna looked around and saw a rock. She was just picking it up to throw at the boys when she felt something hit her apron. She looked down to see a giant mud ball slide off her dress into the dirt. Both boys began laughing harder.

Alayna sputtered and Cameron said, "Go back to the sty where you belong little piggy." She was thinking up a very good retort when her mother appeared. The boys ran away to the fountain and Alayna withered in the venomous stare her mother directed at her.

"I should have known I could not bring a beastie girl with me. Look at your dress!" her mother shouted at her.

Alayna was thinking up an excuse when her mother pinched her upper arm and practically threw her into the carriage. As they drove away, she noticed a third boy around her age join the two who had been taunting her. She watched as they laughed and splashed in the fountain. She wiped at the tears in her eyes and refused to look at her mother the rest of the way home. Once there, her mother left the carriage without even a backwards glance at her. Alayna sat in the carriage and cried quietly until the driver went and fetched their chef and her friend.

Virginia came out and took one look at Alayna before fawning over her and rushing her into the kitchens for a warm roll and a mug of hot chocolate.

Eight years later, a man walked up the lane of the manor house. He explained to the butler that his horse had thrown a shoe and he needed assistance. The butler conferred with the manor's owner and then helped the man find the stables. The stable master helped the man with his horse, and since the day was quickly waning, he suggested the man stay at the manor overnight. This is how the man found himself sitting at the end of a lavish table with the owner of the manor sitting at the other end. He had been quite startled to see the owner appeared to be a woman and she wore a veil to prevent him from seeing her face.

"I trust your rooms are acceptable?" she asked politely.

The sudden noise in the quiet room startled the man and he jumped. "Aye, they are quite nice."

Both sat in an awkward silence for a moment and then the man spoke up again, "Forgive my rudeness, but I can't help to think that you sound very young. How did you come to be the mistress of such a large estate?"

"Not at all," she chuckled. "My father was killed in the war and I was his sole heir. My mother died last year and so now it is all mine."

"And yet you remain unmarried?" he asked boldly. He saw her stiffen and then compose herself, adopting a more relaxed posture.

"I have not yet chosen a suitor. If you will excuse me, I must attend to other business. Please enjoy your dinner," she said politely and exited the room.

The man felt some guilt at offending his host but shrugged it off as the eccentricities of a woman with too much money and no one to tell her how to use it properly.

The next morning, after a very restful evening, the man was preparing to leave, when he noticed the beautiful gardens behind the stables. He took a moment to stroll through the gardens when he stopped in front of a particular plant. He had seen this plant on his travels, but never in the color it was currently displaying. The delicate bell shaped petals were a soft pink color. The man picked the flowers and stuffed them in a handkerchief in his breast pocket. He was just returning to mount his horse when the butler stopped him. The butler informed him that he was requested in the great hall.

The man was led into the great hall and to the figure of the owner, sitting in a chair. She was still veiled and he suppressed a shudder at the hostility he could feel flowing off her. She watched in silence as her butler motioned to a chair and he sat. She waited long minutes to gather her thoughts and then took a deep breath.

"Did my hospitality not suit you?" she asked coldly.

The man was taken aback. "No, milady, it was quite welcoming."

"Did you want for something during your stay that you thought it wise to steal from me?" she asked.

"Steal?" he thought quickly and could not think of anything he might have taken from his host. "I beg your pardon, but I have not stolen anything."

"I am not mistaken, sir."

The man was confused and did not understand the change in his host's demeanor. He sat in silence until the woman rose and walked to the window.

"This window overlooks my gardens—one of my greatest pleasures. So imagine my surprise when I witnessed a guest picking my plants. And not just any plant, but one of my most prized possessions," she spoke almost too quietly for him to hear.

The man then realized his mistake and his unease grew. "I apologize, milady, I did not know, nor did I think it would cause any harm."

"You did not think?" she asked incredulously.

"No. My youngest son, I have three, requested I bring him something unusual from my travels. I had not yet gotten him anything, and I have never seen this flower in this color," he stammered out.

Alayna laughed. "And that gives you leave to take it from me without my permission?"

The man shook his head.

"It seems, sir, that we have a great dilemma. Should I summon the authorities?"

Again the man shook his head. "I do apologize for my offense. I am a merchant of little means, but I am sure we could come to an agreement on compensation?"

"You said you have three sons? What are their names?" Alayna asked.

"Um, yes, my sons are Tegan, Campbell, and Cameron, but I am not certain what that would mean to you." He was getting fed up with this whole situation and did not notice Alayna stiffen at the name of his oldest child.

"Are your sons married?" she asked with patience.

The man was clearly getting angry and sputtered, "Now see here—"

"I repeat my question, and you will answer, or I will call the authorities and you can explain to them why you have stolen my property."

"Fine," he took a deep breath, "the older boys are married and the youngest is not."

Alayna nodded. "I propose that you send the youngest to work on my estate for a period of one year, at which time you will be forgiven for taking my flowers."

"And if I refuse?" he asked with venom.

"That is my price, sir," she replied with equal disdain.

"Very well, I shall send him to you within the week." He bowed and left the hall.

Alayna stood at the windows and watched as the merchant stomped out to his horse and mounted it, riding away as if the devil were on his heels. She relaxed when Virginia came up next to her and put an arm around her. Alayna put her head on Virginia's shoulder and they stood in comfortable silence for several minutes until Virginia spoke.

"Alayna, do you think this is wise?" Virginia asked quietly.

Alayna shook her head with a sigh. "No, but I let my anger get the best of me. At least this new addition to our household won't be someone seeking my hand in marriage in order to control my property.

Virginia just hummed in agreement and left Alayna to prepare the afternoon tea.

Several days later, Alayna was pacing the great hall nervously. For all her bravado, she was still terrified to bring another person into her home. She knew all her staff loved her, especially now that her evil witch of a mother was gone. However, she did not know how this new man would take to a woman as a mistress, and in truth, she did not need any more staff on her estate. This was also the first person outside her staff that would see her without a veil in eight years. She was just making her tenth circuit around the room when Virginia came bursting in.

"Alayna, he is coming up the lane now," she puffed, clearly out of breath.

Alayna nodded and went to the windows overlooking the lane. She gasped when she saw the man walking up the lane towards her home. "He walked?"

"Aye, it looks that way," Virginia said.

"Odd," she replied. "I suppose that we should get this over and done." She walked over and sat in her chair, waiting for the butler to escort the man to the great hall. Virginia gave her a look and then sat in another chair. Alayna gave her a questioning glance and Virginia just shrugged and nodded her head towards the door. This earned Virginia a sigh and she fought to hide her smile at her mistress' exasperation.

The butler entered the great hall a few moments later, the man from the lane walking behind him. Alayna studied the man. He was tall and well-muscled, though not overly so. He had dark hair and blue eyes, although one of them looked to be recovering from a nasty bruise. His clothes were a bit threadbare and his shoes did not look at all proper for walking such a distance as he must have traveled. He held himself with an air of insolence, though she could tell that this was a façade.

As they came to a stop, her butler bowed and introduced them, "Mistress Alayna, may I present Tegan."

Alayna nodded and Tegan gave her a short bow before handing her a small package. She took it and opened it to reveal the dried Lily of the Valley flowers his father had picked from her gardens.

"Welcome Tegan. I trust your journey was uneventful?" she asked politely.

Tegan straightened and studied her. "It was long, but thankfully the weather was dry, mistress."

He did not seem repulsed by her in any fashion. It surprised her but she continued on trying not to let it show.

"You walked the whole way?"

"Aye, my father said it was enough that you got his last remaining supporter and you did not need his horses as well," Tegan stated with some humor.

Alayna thought for a moment. "Virginia, would you fetch us some tea please?"

Virginia nodded and left the room. "What else did your father say of me?"

Tegan chuckled. "He was quite put off by the fact that a woman was in possession of an estate such as this one. He also said he did not see you as fit to run such a place."

"And you find this humorous?" she clenched her fists by her sides.

"A bit," Tegan agreed. "In truth, milady, I thought he might be sending me to a beast for all that he described you as such."

"I see," she said as she stood, "Virginia will take care of your refreshment and show you to your rooms. Good day, sir."

"Mistress" he said and bowed as she left.

Once in her rooms, Alayna sat against her door and wept.

Alayna was sitting in her library reading a book when Tegan entered. She jumped and he stammered out an apology. "I'm sorry to disturb you."

"No, it is quite alright" Alayna said, trying to calm her nerves.

"Forgive me for asking, but did I offend you the other day?" Tegan asked with some concern.

Alayna shook her head. "Why would I have been offended?"

"My father is not exactly the nicest man, especially when he feels wronged," Tegan replied.

"He was *wronged?*" she asked incredulously.

Tegan nodded. "He feels that way, but it matters not."

Alayna studied Tegan for a moment. "Was there something you needed?"

"I was just looking for a book to pass the time. I have yet to be given a task and the days have been a bit long for me with no one to talk to." Tegan looked around the room, avoiding eye contact with Alayna.

Alayna sighed. "In truth, I have no need for an extra member of my household. In fact, the ones that remain here in my service, do so out of their loyalty to me and not the needs of the estate."

Tegan stared at her. "I am used to working hard if you

find something for me to do."

Alayna motioned for him to sit and she chose a chair across from him. She thought for a moment and then asked, "Tell me about your home."

"I live with my father. My older brothers used to live with us, but have now married and are living in our same town. My mother died when I was young and so it was only the four of us," he paused.

"What of your eye?" she asked.

He was perplexed at her question.

"The first day, your eye appeared to be bruised."

"Ah," he said, understanding, "It is a common occurrence. My father gets angry at something and I am generally the closest punching bag. It is something that I am used to with my older brothers."

Alayna gasped. "Your father and brothers beat you?"

Tegan broke eye contact and looked away uncomfortably. "Aye, 'tis nothing."

Alayna made a decision in that moment. "Tegan, you are my guest. You may do what you wish here, if you wish to help with any of the staff, I am sure they would welcome it, but do not feel you must help. If there is anything you need, please let me know."

Tegan nodded and smiled at her. Alayna tried to ignore the skip in her chest at the gesture. "Yes, mistress."

"Please, call me Alayna," she smiled back.

Several months had passed and Tegan had settled into the household. He often helped the staff and they, in turn, sung his praises to their mistress. She was glad he seemed to belong and did not feel like a prisoner in her home. They often had lively discussions and she even took to having dinner with him each evening instead of eating her rooms as she had done for years.

It was on a warm summer morning that Tegan came to her with the idea for a picnic. She threw caution to the wind and agreed, which was how they found themselves in a field after a light lunch, staring at the sky and picking out shapes in the clouds.

Tegan rose up on an elbow. "Alayna?"

She sat up and looked at him as he also sat up.

"Why are you not married?" he asked.

Alayna looked away. "It's just not possible."

"Why not?" he asked.

Alayna groaned and stood up. "It's none of your business, Tegan."

He stood and tried to stop her from stomping off by grabbing her arm. She stared at his hand until he removed it with a placating gesture. "You forget your place, sir."

"Nonsense," he replied. "You are just afraid to open up to someone."

Alayna rounded on him. "I am the mistress of this estate and you would do well to not forget that." She stomped away and Tegan sighed as he cleaned up their picnic.

Tegan made his way back to the manor and into the kitchens where Virginia was busy with preparing bread. He slammed the basket down on the counter and Virginia gave him a look with a raised eyebrow.

"Something wrong?" she asked.

Tegan laughed bitterly. "Why must she be so stubborn?"

"Ah," she said with humor.

"I try to talk to her and to learn about her, but she shuts me out and then tries to put me in my place."

Virginia smiled. "She had a hard childhood."

Tegan thought for a moment, "What do you mean?"

"It is not my place to tell you." Virginia tried to deflect his questions. "Would you like the raisin bread?"

"Virginia, don't change the subject. I need to know!" Tegan exclaimed.

Virginia laughed at him. "Tegan, if you truly want to know her story, you have to get her to tell you in her own words. It is the only way to set her free from the demons of her past."

Tegan thought on her words and nodded absently as he left the kitchens.

Alayna kept Tegan at arm's length for several weeks after the picnic before she finally relented with his daily cajoling and began taking dinner with him. Over the next months, Tegan slowly gained her trust again and they began doing more and more together. The weather was turning colder and they were forced indoors more often than not. It was the first snowfall of the season when a knock came on the manor doors late one evening. Alayna was called out onto the estate for one of her tenants and Tegan insisted on going with her.

As it turned out, one of the tenant's children was very ill and required a doctor, but the roads into the town were not passable by foot. Tegan returned to the stables and took a horse to fetch the doctor, while Alayna stayed and helped with the sick child. He returned with the doctor who gave the child an examination and pronounced that with medicine and rest, he would recover. Alayna paid the doctor, trying to do so inconspicuously, but Tegan noticed and hid a smile.

Tegan and Alayna said their goodbyes and made their way outside. Alayna thanked the doctor again and he rode off back towards the town. Alayna was starting to walk back towards the manor when Tegan stopped her.

"Where are you going?" he asked her.

"I was going to let you ride, you have had a longer night than me," she stated as if it were obvious.

"Alayna, it is cold and late; there is enough room on this horse for both of us."

She shook her head. "I don't think that is wise."

Tegan sighed. "For once could you not be so stubborn?"

"Excuse me?" she rounded on him.

"I'm sorry, I just meant that it is ridiculous for us to fight over riding a horse together," he tried to placate her. "Would you please just ride with me back to the stables?"

Alayna thought for a moment and then nodded. Tegan mounted the horse and then helped her mount in front of him. He held the reins with one hand and then put his other arm around her waist. Alayna fought hard to keep from leaning into him, but she found that she could not keep her balance if her posture was stiff, and when she started to slip, he tightened his arm. By the time they arrived at the stable, Alayna's skin was tingling and she was loathe for the ride to be over. Tegan dismounted and helped her down. She stood within the circle of his arms for a moment before her stable master cleared his throat and she jumped back as if burned.

"Thank you," she said and then turned to run into the manor. She missed the triumphant smile on Tegan's face.

The next morning, Alayna tried very hard to avoid eye contact with Tegan, giving him the shortest answers possible when he asked her a question. She spent the rest of the day in a daze, still remembering their ride through the snow with his arm around her. She caught herself daydreaming about Tegan and, to her dismay, the thought of being in love with him did not seem as dismal as she may have once thought. Then she would chastise herself for thinking of the word "love" in the first place.

It was at dinner time, when she and Tegan had sat through the meal in relative silence that Tegan decided to move into the next phase with his plans to get Alayna to talk to him. He suggested that they move to the sitting room and play a game of chess before they went to their respective rooms, and to his surprise, Alayna agreed.

"To make it more interesting, let's change the rules," he said as they sat down at the board.

"Chess already has perfectly acceptable rules," she replied.

"Aye, but I suggest that when we lose a piece from the board, we must answer a question asked by the opponent."

Alayna thought for a moment and then agreed.

The game had been going quite well for Alayna when Tegan captured her queen. She waited for his question with a raised eyebrow.

"Alayna," he ventured, "what happened in your childhood that made you so afraid to talk to me?"

Alayna gasped and moved to get up from the chair, but Tegan stopped her again. He held onto her wrist as he moved and knelt beside her. He looked at her with something she could not describe and she looked away. He felt her deflate and let go of her wrist.

Alayna stared at the fire and gulped in a breath of air. Tegan waited, holding his breath. She glanced at him then asked, "Your brother is Cameron?"

Tegan looked confused, so she continued, "When I was a young girl, I went to town with my mother. Your brothers were there and they called me a pig and threw mud at me."

"I don't understand," Tegan said.

"I saw you with them, laughing and playing in the fountain," she said and looked at him. She saw the memory forming in his eyes and then he shook his head.

"Yes, but I was not laughing at you. I did not even see you. Anyway, this makes no sense. My brothers were mean to everyone, including me. They were just boys."

Alayna sighed again. "That was the one and only time I went to town."

"Alayna, I still don't understand." Tegan looked at her and tried to comfort her, but she pulled away. She paced over to the window and stared out of it.

"Tegan, my mother was not proud of me. That day she said it was proof that a beast like me could not be taken into public and she never took me again. She kept me at home and she only entertained suitors who could bring her wealth. None of them ever had anything good to say of me." She tried to keep her tears in check.

Tegan thought for a moment. "Why would your mother think you a beast?"

She turned. "Do you not see me?"

He nodded. "I see you just fine. You are a kind, thoughtful person. Your staff love you like you were their own daughter. Your tenants have nothing but praise for your charitable conduct with them."

"What about this?" she gestured at her person.

"What about it?" he asked.

Alayna stomped her foot. "How can you be so obtuse? Look at me. My hair is straight and flat and never stays within its required styles. My skin is marred by freckles no matter how much lemon juice I rub into it. Don't even get me started on my body. My hips are too wide, my chest too small and my stomach not flat. My mother could not even stand to look at me. She called me a beast.”

Tegan laughed and Alayna's jaw dropped.

The tears Alayna had tried to keep in check flowed down her cheeks. She tried to rush out of the room before Tegan blocked the door. She balled her fist at her sides.

“Please move,” she said without looking at him.

“No,” he said and he tipped her chin up so she would look at him. He waited patiently for her to meet his eyes before he spoke, “Alayna, please believe me when I say this: you are beautiful inside and out. Your mother was the beast, not you.”

“But—” she started before he cut her off.

“You. Are. Beautiful,” he said and leaned down and kissed her.

Alayna's eyes widened before she let herself get lost in the kiss. What felt like endless moments later, they broke apart, gasping for air.

Alayna smiled at Tegan and he laughed. “I've been waiting months to do that.”

“Really?” she asked and he nodded.

Tegan hugged her and she let herself be held, sighing in contentment. He rested his head on top of hers and she whispered, “Thank you.” She did not think he heard, but then she felt him kiss the top of her head and she smiled.

The next day, Alayna was excited to jump out of bed and start her day with Tegan when Virginia came into her room. She had a worried look on her face and Alayna jumped up and read the letter that Virginia held out. Her face fell and she sat back on the bed.

"I guess you had better give it to him," Alayna said.

Virginia agreed and left the room, leaving Alayna to crawl back into her bed.

Later, Virginia returned with a request from Tegan. Alayna dressed and followed her chef out of the room to the great hall. There they found Tegan pacing back and forth.

"I must go to him," Tegan said.

Alayna's face fell. "I see. Your service is no longer required, so you are free to do as you please."

"Alayna, I will come back."

She looked up at him. "But why? We have no need of you." Virginia scoffed behind her and Alayna spun with a withering glare. Virginia excused herself.

Tegan ran a hand through his hair. "I just need to see my father and deal with my brothers, but you can't ignore my affections for you."

"I am still unsure of them. How do I know that you will come back?" she asked.

"I give you my word, once my father is well I will return. You must trust me," Tegan said with some desperation.

Alayna nodded and stood stiffly as Tegan left. She went to the window and watched as he rode away.

Alayna found herself in the market in the town she had visited as a child, when she overheard a conversation that made her ears prick up. She was not in the habit of eavesdropping, but this was a conversation she could not ignore. She tried to look disinterested as she listened.

"Can you believe it, Cameron? He actually thought he was in love with the beastie."

"Father says it is preposterous. He said she was hardly marriageable material, despite her estates."

Alayna gasped when she realized they were talking about her.

Cameron laughed. "Tegan said it was the little piggy girl we saw the year Father brought us to the festival."

"Ugh, poor sot, she must have had him bewitched."

Alayna fought with the lump in her throat and wanted to move away but was rooted to the spot.

"Well, Father has asked me to introduce him to Rosemarie. Once he sees her, his beast will be forgotten."

Both men laughed as they passed her and she hurried back to her horse and the manor.

Once again, Virginia found her and held her as she sobbed for hours.

A month passed after that fateful trip to the market and Alayna's spirit had not recovered. She had not heard from Tegan and she gave up on him ever returning. She was no longer eating and, in truth, she barely left her rooms. Virginia tried coaxing her with all her favorite foods to no avail. All of her staff did everything they could to cheer up their mistress, but nothing seemed to be working. Virginia became desperate and sent the stable master into town to fetch both the doctor and to see if he could find Tegan. When he returned, the story he told made Virginia's blood run cold.

Tegan's father had recently passed and rather than be allowed to return, his brothers had kept him a prisoner in Cameron's home. The stable master also said that Tegan's brothers were claiming that he would soon be married to an heiress from a neighboring estate. Virginia found this hard to believe given what she knew of the man. She gathered the butler and the stable master together to come up with a plan.

The butler found a solution to the problem. He pointed out that technically, Tegan still had a few months of servitude left to Alayna. Virginia and the stable master agreed, but they could not decide on how to prove that contract. Then the butler suggested a forged document and he knew where Alayna kept her seal in order to prove that the document was authentic. They called for the solicitor, who just happened to be the son of one of Alayna's tenants and the document was created.

Virginia and the stable master returned to the town with the forged document and presented it to the magister of the town, who accompanied them to Cameron's home, where Tegan was being detained. To Cameron's great shock, the magister barged in and demanded to see Tegan. Cameron complied and then begged the magister to grant him mercy, to which the magister replied that he would overlook the detainment if Tegan agreed. Tegan, in his wisdom, agreed to let the matter drop if Cameron and Campbell released his part of their father's estate and disavowed any control over him in the future. They signed the document that was produced on the spot and Tegan left with Virginia.

Once back at Emerald Manor, Virginia pulled Tegan into the kitchen.

"I want to see her now," Tegan said, trying to leave and go find Alayna.

Virginia shook her head. "She is not well."

"What do you mean?"

"She heard your brothers talking about a month ago. They said horrible things and said that you were getting married to another woman." Virginia watched him sadly.

Tegan gasped. "But it wasn't true."

"I know," she nodded, "but we did not know that. She has not been eating."

"I need to see her now, Virginia," Tegan said again and Virginia blocked his way.

"You will, just let me help you," she said with a glimmer of hope she had not felt in days.

Alayna ignored the knock on her bedroom door and continued staring at the fire. She did not turn her head when the door opened and footfalls crossed the floor.

"They say the Lily of the Valley represents the return of happiness," Tegan said and Alayna quickly turned her head to look at him. He held a giant bouquet of the flowers in white and pink.

"Tegan? Why are you here?" she asked with surprise.

He gestured to the bed and she scooted over. He sat and grabbed her hand. "I told you I would return."

Alayna looked away. "But your brothers said you were bewitched."

"And you believed them?" Tegan laughed. "Alayna, my brothers are as awful as your mother. Cameron kept me locked in a room and was trying to sell me to the highest bidder."

"What?" she was stunned.

Tegan nodded. "Virginia helped me when she found out. She got them to release me. Showed them a contract that stated I was still indebted to you."

Alayna sputtered. "I didn't sign that!"

"I know. It doesn't matter, Alayna. I'm here now."

"Why?" she asked.

"Don't you know, Alayna?" he asked her.

She shook her head.

"My dear, stubborn woman, I love you and don't ever want to be parted from you again," he said and wiped the tear that fell down her cheek.

"I love you too, Tegan" she said and he leaned down and kissed her.

Alayna and Tegan were married and Tegan assured her she would always remain the mistress of Emerald Manor and he would merely be her consort. He helped her feel beautiful through three pregnancies—two sons and a daughter. All their children were loved and never felt like they were less because of their appearance or birth order.

On their fortieth wedding anniversary, Tegan and their children filled the entire manor with pink Lilies of the Valley so that everywhere Alayna went, she would be reminded of the flower that brought her such happiness. She went to bed that evening with a smile on her face and in the arms of the man she loved beyond all others.

Tegan whispered, *I love you my beast*, as he tightened his arm around her and Alayna chuckled and fell asleep, no longer haunted by her mother's harsh term, for he had turned it into the best endearment of all.

The Mermaid's Song

Nerissa was the sixth daughter born to King Triton, fourteenth to bear that name, of the Kingdom Under the Sea. She was headstrong and willful, even as a young child. Being the youngest had its advantages though and she had her entire family, in fact the entire kingdom, under her thrall. Nerissa had also been gifted with the most beautiful voice and her singing could calm even the stormiest of seas.

When Nerissa was twelve, she attended an unprecedented meeting between her father and King Henrik of the Kingdom of the Cliffs. Henrik's fourteen year old son, Finn, had suffered a terrible accident which had caused him to become blind. Henrik had heard rumors that the tears of a mermaid could heal any ailment and sought the aid of one of Triton's daughters. Triton was furious with the request, as a mermaid's tears were not easy to come by and he was loathe to harm any of his daughters to fulfill the request. He had almost banished all humans from ever setting foot on the seas again, when his wife, Kalliope, offered a different solution.

Long ago, it had been prophesied, a daughter of the king of the merfolk would fall in love with a human and forever change the dynamic between the Kingdom Under the Sea and the Kingdom of the Cliffs. The prophecy did not say this change would necessarily be a bad thing but as all sentient beings, human and merfolk alike, were wont to do, it was considered this change would not be in the best interest of anyone. Thus it was any daughter of the king was forbidden to interact with the human world and lived a sheltered life away from the surface of the sea. Upon reaching the age of fifteen, each daughter was allowed one night per year in which to go to the surface and see the stars and the human world while it slept.

It was with this prophecy in mind, Kalliope, in her infinite wisdom, suggested her youngest daughter should be allowed to meet with the Prince and sing to him in order to soothe his soul. She did not believe any relationship that blossomed into love could be harmful to man or merman. Triton was extremely reluctant for this to happen and was on the verge of sending Henrik on his way when Kalliope reminded him the boy would not be able to see Nerissa and therefore would not know she was a mermaid. She pleaded with Triton to let his daughter decide if she would be willing to take on the task. Therefore Nerissa was brought before the two kings and asked if she would be prepared to visit the surface early, and often, in order to be a companion to the blinded prince.

Nerissa had spent her entire childhood begging for

stories of the surface and pestering her older sisters for any descriptions they could share of the world above. It had exasperated her tutors to no end and they were forever exclaiming she seemed to have been born in the wrong kingdom. More than once her own mother had prayed to the gods for guidance on how to calm her daughter's wandering mind and help her focus on the world of the sea instead of the land that kissed it. Now she had been given an opportunity to glimpse this world a full three years ahead of her allotted time and she tried very hard not to show her glee at the prospect. She supposed she may have fooled her father in replying it was her duty to help those in need and she would do her utmost to be a worthy representative of the kingdom, but her mother saw straight through her. Kalliope wondered if she was doing the right thing but she supposed "what's done is done" and she hoped it had been the right decision.

At the agreed-upon time, Nerissa found herself in a small cove near the castle of the Kingdom of the Cliffs. She marveled at the surface of the water, for the sun's rays made it glitter as if a thousand tiny diamonds were floating in the waves. The castle loomed in the background and she saw rich, green fields swaying in the breeze where sheep were roaming around freely. Nerissa swam up and down the cove, fascinated by a small tidal pool where crabs were scurrying back and forth as if they had lost their direction. She gave a start when she heard humans talking and almost swam back out to the open sea before she realized this must be Finn and his escort. It had been agreed,

Finn was to be accompanied by a female representative from the temple of Athena for her safety. He had been told that the location for the meeting had been chosen because it was neutral territory for both kingdoms.

She watched curiously as the young man walked slowly but steadily toward the water and began to remove his shirt and shoes. He spoke with the guardian and then waded into the water up to his waist. He stood motionless, staring straight into her eyes but not seeing her. Nerissa waved a hand and the guardian waved back and then sat on a rock on the beach, bringing out a book and ignoring the two of them. She studied Finn in silence for several moments until he finally broke it.

"Princess Nerissa?" Finn asked with a cock of his head.

Nerissa straightened and moved silently in the water. "How did you know I was here?"

"I can hear you breathing," he said with a small chuckle. He held out his hand for her. "I am Finn. Pleasure to meet you."

Nerissa looked at his hand and then back at him. She did not know what to do so she stuck out her hand in response. Finn laughed again and then found her hand with his own, clasping it and shaking it. Nerissa smiled and laughed with him.

"Have you never shaken someone's hand before?" Finn asked.

"I live a very sheltered life," she said.

"Ah, okay then, my father says you will sing for me."

Nerissa nodded.

"Is that a yes?" Finn asked patiently.

Nerissa gasped, "Yes, your highness, I apologize. I have never met anyone who could not see before today. I will sing for you if you would permit me?"

Finn smiled at her. "Gladly. Please proceed."

Nerissa nodded again and thought for a moment. She chose a favored melody she had heard her mother sing when the seas were restless and began to sing. Finn's face lit up in wonder as he listened to her beautiful voice. When she had finished he waited for her to talk as he had no words for what he had just heard. She asked if he would like to hear another and he nodded so she sang again. This time, Finn relaxed and floated on his back with her beautiful melody amplified by the cove surrounding him. Finn could never recall feeling this much bliss from music, especially not since the accident had taken his sight from him.

Nerissa finished her last song and looked to the horizon to see the sun setting.

"Why did you stop?" Finn asked.

"The sun is setting and I must return home, your highness," she replied with a little hesitance in her voice.

Finn nodded. "Please call me Finn. I forget what the sunset looks like but I can feel it when it is warm upon my face. Thank you for singing for me today. It made me forget all of this, even if for only a moment."

"It was my pleasure. You can call me Nerissa. Would you like for me to come again?" she asked, hoping he would indeed want to hear more.

"Absolutely. Perhaps this same time next week?" he asked.

Nerissa nodded then caught herself. "Yes, I will inform my parents. Goodbye." She swam a little bit farther out of the cove so he could no longer hear her breathing and turned to watch him wading to the shore. He dressed quietly and then his guardian led him from the cove. Nerissa swam home faster than she could have ever imagined and straight into her mother's rooms. For two hours she regaled her mother with everything she had seen and done. Kalliope smiled at her daughter's retreating form and went to give a good report to her husband on the venture.

For six years, Nerissa met with Finn and sang for him. As the years passed, their meetings became longer and involved more conversation than singing. They spoke to each other of their fears and dreams. They spoke of their kingdoms, even if Nerissa's side was a little vague on the nature of her people. They spoke of Finn's fears that his blindness made him weak and his father would be better off with another child who was whole. They became the best of friends and each looked forward to the next meeting which would bring them together once again.

On the eve of her eighteenth birthday, Nerissa was patiently waiting in the cove for Finn to arrive. She frowned because he was later than usual and he had never missed their weekly ritual. She was about to turn around and swim home when she heard him running and calling her name. Nerissa watched in puzzlement as Finn ran into the cove, hopping on one foot while trying to remove his shoes. He crashed into the water with his shirt still on and shouted her name.

"Finn?" she asked with worry.

Finn tried to catch his breath. "I thought I had missed you."

"Honestly, I was about to go home. Is everything alright?"

Finn nodded. "It is now. I had trouble finding something for your birthday and then when I did find it, it took forever to finish it and get here on time. Here, this is for you." Finn took a locket out of his pocket and held it out to her.

Nerissa studied it a moment and then took it in her hands. She gasped when she saw her name carved in one side of the heart locket. She opened it to reveal a picture of Finn inside. Nerissa clutched the locket to her chest.

"Do you like it?" he asked as he scratched behind his ear in shyness.

"It's beautiful! Thank you Finn," she said with a smile in her voice.

"You deserve it. Happy birthday, Nerissa," he said. Finn then laid on his back to float which was her cue to begin singing. She sang several songs for him and then she tapped him on the shoulder. Finn returned to standing and gave her a short formal bow. "Thank you, milady."

Nerissa giggled. "You are welcome, kind sir. I wish I had

brought you a gift for your birthday next week."

"Your singing is the best gift of all." He laughed and then moved to pull her into his arms. Nerissa gasped a little in shock and was startled when she heard the guardian from Athena's temple calling for Finn.

He sighed and turned back towards her. "That's my cue. See you next week?"

"See you then," she confirmed and watched him walk back to the shore.

All during the week, Nerissa was in a world of her own. She sang to herself and she was not cross with any of her sisters. Everyone, including her father, noticed the change and assumed her good mood was due to the fact she had just turned eighteen and was no longer restricted to the rigors of education. She would now be allowed to choose a job and pursue her own interests. Little did any of them realize Nerissa was so happy because Finn cared enough about her to give her a beautiful locket for her birthday. Kalliope had inquired about the locket and she learned it had been a gift but she did not understand the significance Nerissa had given the piece of jewelry. She merely complimented it and sent her youngest on an errand.

The evening of Finn's birthday promised to be a calm night on the seas and his father had promised to take him sailing on one of the new clippers that had just been launched. He looked forward to these trips as he felt free and uninhibited by his blindness. He knew the ships from touch and the crews always indulged his willingness to learn the ropes and to assist them with the rigging. They had been on the water for an hour when a storm blew in unexpectedly. The little ship was having a rough time staying upright on the choppy seas and Finn had been trying to help the crew as much as possible.

At this same moment, Nerissa decided to check in on Finn's trip as she knew she could not talk with him without revealing she was a mermaid but she could watch him enjoying his birthday sail. She watched in horror as the rowboat was being lowered down the side of the ship with Finn's father and mother in it. Finn had insisted they go first in order to continue holding the sails down while a crewman lashed them tight. Finn was preparing to exit the ship when a boom struck him in the head and he fell over the side of the ship. With lightning quick speed, Nerissa dove under the water searching for Finn. She became frantic when she could not find him—the other sailors treading water made it very hard for her to see. She calmed her mind and tried to listen for unfamiliar sounds, just as Finn had taught her. She finally heard one and opened her eyes to see Finn sinking to the bottom of the sea.

Nerissa dove after him and pulled him to the surface. She debated for a moment about her next move and decided she should take Finn to their cove in order to save him but avoid detection by the other men. Her father had forbidden merfolk to interfere with the destinies of men and she feared his wrath if he found out she had saved Finn from a watery grave. Nerissa pulled him along with her to the cove and once there, she dragged him onto a rock in the shallower parts of the water. She gasped at the blood stain his head left but was relieved to find it did not seem to be a deep cut and was already beginning to close.

Nerissa tried to wake Finn but was unsuccessful. Believing him to be dead, she began crying over him and unbeknownst to her, her tears were falling on his blinded eyes. She cried for what felt like hours before she heard a commotion heading towards the beach. Nerissa gave Finn one last look and dove back into the water to hide behind a rocky outcropping. She heard the splashing of humans into the water towards Finn. Just as they reached him, he let out a moan and Nerissa stifled a happy gasp. He was alive! She had never felt more relieved in her life. She peeked around the rock to see several women around Finn. One lifted his head and checked his wound while another cupped his cheeks with her hands.

"Your highness?" the woman asked.

Finn groaned again then opened his eyes. He saw a beautiful woman and then frowned, for he felt something was odd. "You saved me?" he asked.

The woman laughed. "Yes, your highness, you are safe now. Come, we must get you home." The women helped him stand and the one woman let him use her as a crutch as they waded back to shore.

Nerissa was shocked. It appeared Finn could see and the other woman had convinced him she had saved him. She gasped when she realized what she had done. Against her father's orders she had not only intervened in the life of a human but she had also restored his sight. Nerissa was bewildered about what she should do next. How could she return home if it meant her father would banish her from the kingdom? She pondered on the question as long as she dared before heading home to speak with her mother.

Nerissa found her mother and explained the situation. Kalliope was supportive of her but feared what her father might say about the ordeal. She pleaded with Nerissa to let her handle Triton and bid her to wait for her in her rooms for an answer. Sometime later, Nerissa was summoned by her mother and went to her father's council chambers. She was met with her seething father and was given a warning look from her mother.

"You saved a human from drowning?" Triton asked with steel in his voice.

Nerissa nodded.

"You also used your tears to heal him?" he asked again.

Nerissa shook her head. "Father, I didn't mean—"

Triton glared at her. "You went against all our laws Nerissa. You broke them for some human and defied me to do it."

"It was only Finn. He is my friend. I lo—like him" she quickly tried to cover up her flub but saw her mother's eyes widen.

"You are banned from the surface. I have been told Finn is healed and therefore he no longer needs your singing. You will not see him again." Triton dared her to contradict him.

Nerissa shook her head, intending to argue. "You can't—"

"*I can and I will!*" Triton snarled. "Leave my sight before you are banished from this kingdom!"

Nerissa pleaded silently with her mother but although she saw sympathy in her mother's eyes, her mother shook her head. Nerissa swam away angrily. She swam to the edges of the kingdom, threw herself against a sunken ship and sobbed. She did not understand why saving someone who was so dear to her was a problem. Her father did not understand that to her, all life was precious and if they could help the humans in the water then the kingdoms might get along better. As it was, merfolk were myth and legend to most humans whereas humans were monsters to merfolk. Didn't anyone understand both types of beings were wonderful creatures?

Nerissa was staring into nothing when she was alarmed to find another mermaid watching her. This mermaid was dull and scrawny with eyes that looked almost dead in their blackness. She peered at Nerissa from the darkness of a nearby kelp forest and when she saw she had been noticed she smiled a wide toothy grin. She crooked her finger in a gesture for Nerissa to come closer. Nerissa looked around and swam towards the stranger who moved further into the kelp forest. Nerissa followed deeper and deeper into the kelp until she found herself in a clearing with a small shelter. The stranger entered the shelter and with another glance behind, Nerissa followed her inside. Once inside, Nerissa noticed all sorts of strange ingredients on shelves on the walls. In the center sat a large black cauldron bubbling with a sickly green liquid. The stranger sat on the opposite side of the cauldron staring at her with those dead eyes.

"Who are you?" Nerissa asked.

The stranger laughed. "Child, you know me. Dig deep in your memories."

Nerissa started and thought for a moment, gasping as she remembered the person before her. "The sea witch…but you and your daughter were banished."

"Ah yes, well I was merely banished to this hovel. She was banished to the land. I had a name beyond sea witch once but I suppose it will do for now." She wheezed and spat into the cauldron.

"I must be going now," Nerissa said, backing towards the door.

"I know your heart's desire, child, and I can give it to you."

Nerissa stopped and swam back towards the witch. "How do you know what I want?"

"I know many things. You wish to be on land with your prince?" the witch asked.

"More than anything," Nerissa nodded.

The witch laughed again. "I can grant you this wish. For a price."

Nerissa frowned. "I don't have anything to give you."

"But you do, dear. You have your voice." The witch

watched Nerissa as she took in this information.

Nerissa shook her head. "I can't. How would I talk to him?"

Again the witch laughed. "You don't need to speak with him. If he loves you then words would not be necessary."

Nerissa thought about all she had heard from the witch. She desperately wanted to see Finn again and make sure he was recovered from the shipwreck. If her father had his way, she would never again see Finn or the world above her kingdom. She made up her mind, her voice was a small price to pay in order to be with the man she loved. She nodded to the witch.

"All right," she said.

"Excellent. There is just one condition to my magic. Find your prince and share a kiss of true love with him within three days. If you succeed, your legs will become permanent and your voice will be restored. If you fail, you will be returned to the sea as foam and forever be battered against the cliffs. Do you understand girl?" The witch waited with shrewd eyes.

Nerissa nodded. She watched as the witch gathered ingredients and threw them into the cauldron. The witch bottled up a small portion of the brew and handed it to Nerissa.

"Drink this when you have reached the surface. It will change your tail to legs and steal your voice. Remember, you have three days to complete the task." The witch ushered her out of the hovel and towards the kelp forest. Nerissa swam through the forest without looking back. She briefly thought about going to her mother and explaining what she was going to do but then remembered her mother's last pleading look and decided against it. She would send word back when she had found Finn and their love was solidified.

Nerissa swam to the cove and drank the potion. Searing pain ran through her tail and she screamed as it was rent in two. As she screamed, her voice got slowly weaker until she was left with two legs and no sound. She turned her head in time to see a young woman, the one who had helped Finn, run up to her and cover her with the cape from her own shoulders. The woman fussed over Nerissa and helped her up the cliff to the Temple of Athena.

Once at the Temple, the head priestess quickly assessed the situation. She ordered Nerissa be given clothes and presented to King Henrik. They were astounded to find she could not speak and the woman who had helped her on the beach was assigned to be her escort. On their way to the castle, Nerissa learned the young woman's name was Gretchen. Gretchen asked Nerissa if she had been of the sea and when she stared in wide-eyed surprise, Gretchen confirmed she knew this because she too had once been a mermaid. Nerissa correctly surmised Gretchen must be the daughter of the sea witch since they were the only two merfolk she knew who had been banished from her kingdom. This made Nerissa very wary of Gretchen but she lost all apprehension when she saw the castle.

The sights and sounds of the castle yard were almost overwhelming to Nerissa. She had never seen so many humans and animals gathered in one place. People were haggling over wares and a blacksmith was forging a horseshoe. Goats and pigs squealed in their pens whilst chickens roamed everywhere. The cart she was riding in came to a halt and Gretchen motioned for her to climb down. Gretchen caught up her hand and held it as they wove their way into the castle. Once inside, Nerissa stared at the walls with delight. Rich tapestries hung from the high ceiling down to the ground. Giant iron candelabras were suspended from great oak beams along the roof line. Here and there she could glimpse paintings of Kings and Queens as well as suits of armor on gleaming display. She almost tripped over her feet when Gretchen pulled her gently down the hall.

Gretchen introduced Nerissa to King Henrik and he started when he realized he knew her. He thanked Gretchen and dismissed her. Henrik questioned Nerissa, to which she answered with a nod or shake of her head. After talking with her at length, he summoned a servant to take her to a room while he figured out how to deal with the situation. He sent a messenger to King Triton asking for a meeting as soon as possible on a delicate issue. Meanwhile, as she was being led to her room, Nerissa noticed Finn and Gretchen laughing in the hallway. She frowned at their familiarity with each other. She was about to turn around to talk with him, when the servant cleared his throat and gestured for her to follow.

At dinner that evening, Henrik introduced Nerissa by her name and Finn stared at her blankly. She gave a pained smile to him and he continued a conversation with his mother. She realized Finn did not recognize her and tried to ignore the sympathetic smile Henrik sent her way. Once she returned to her rooms, Nerissa cried herself to sleep for she realized Finn may not love her as she loved him.

The next day, Nerissa was swimming in her little cove-she needed the familiarity of the water to help her deal with her situation-when she heard Gretchen calling out for the sea witch. She hid herself and watched as the sea witch came to the surface. She looked even more ghastly in the light of the sun.

"What is it daughter?" the witch asked with a sneer in her voice.

"Do you have it?" Gretchen asked.

The witch laughed. "I have many things. To what are you referring?"

Gretchen rolled her eyes in disgust. "That little mermaid's voice. Do you have it?"

"I do," the witch said calmly.

"I want it." Gretchen could barely contain her derision.

"What would you do with it?" Her mother stared back at her.

Gretchen sighed. "I would have Finn. He doesn't remember her because of the blow to his head but he remembers her singing. It will win his heart and I would have him be mine if I am to be stuck on land forever. A life of servitude to Athena does not suit my ambitions."

The witch laughed with all the hatred she could muster. "Your ambitions are what got us banished in the first place. To think you could usurp your cousin's claim to the throne. It was only because Triton is my brother that we were not executed and instead banished."

"Be that as it may," Gretchen sneered, "I would have his daughter's voice."

"You know the conditions" the witch warned.

"I do and I don't care, I will win." Gretchen said.

Nerissa waited until both Gretchen and the sea witch were gone to let out the breath she had been holding. She had been young when the witch and her daughter had been banished and she was never told they were part of her family. Gretchen had tried to poison her oldest sister and the sea witch was implicated in the plot. A shiver ran down her spine, now Gretchen was going to trick Finn. She must save him from this fate. She did not care if he did not love her, she loved him enough for both of them and she only wanted him to be safe.

Nerissa hurried back to the castle and changed into fresh clothes but she could not find Finn anywhere. She searched for him for hours, getting lost in the corridors and connecting rooms. She had all but given up hope when she heard him talking from the throne room. She ran into the room only to be met with a huge audience in front of the king. Finn was in front of all of them with Gretchen on his arm. She choked back a sob when she realized Finn was announcing their engagement and their wedding would take place the next evening. Gretchen met Nerissa's eyes and smiled in triumph as Nerissa backed out of the room.

Nerissa tried to sleep that evening but her mind kept

running in circles. If only she could make Finn remember her, then he would snap out of the spell Gretchen had put him under. She was just dozing off in the early pre-dawn hours when she heard singing coming from the water. She looked out her window to see her sisters bobbing in the water and waving at her. Nerissa wrapped herself in a blanket and made her way down to the cove. She waited as her sisters swam up to her in the shallow end. She stared at them, unable to ask the burning question on her mind.

"We know you can't speak," her oldest sister said while the others nodded their agreement. "We have brought you a gift."

Nerissa's sister pulled out a knife. "We sold our hair to the sea witch for it. If you pierce Finn's heart with it before the moon sets tomorrow night, you will return to us."

Nerissa began backing away and shaking her head in horror.

"Nerissa, think of Mother. She needs you and will be heartbroken if you turn to foam." Her sister placed the knife in her hand. She gave Nerissa one last look and then all of her sisters turned and swam away.

Nerissa stared at the knife while hot tears ran down her cheeks. She loved Finn and there was no way she could kill him. Then a thought came to her and she returned to the castle with the knife.

Nerissa tried to get near Finn and Gretchen all day but it seemed she was blocked at every opportunity. Finally, near dusk and the set time for the wedding, she found Finn and Gretchen sitting in a room waiting for the ceremony to begin. They were alone, as it was tradition in this kingdom for the bride and groom to be given a few minutes to talk with each other before being on display for the entire population during the marriage rites. Nerissa slipped into the room quietly. She observed them talking before she made her presence known.

"Nerissa, are you lost?" Finn asked. She shook her head.

Gretchen chuckled. "Finn, darling, I do believe she has a crush on you. Too bad I have won your heart."

"I'm afraid it is true," he said, then turned to Nerissa. "If you continue down the hall, you will find the chapel." He seemed to be dismissing her.

"I'll show you," Gretchen said and grabbed her upper arm painfully. She hissed into Nerissa's ear, "He is mine and by tomorrow you will be nothing but the foam he wipes off his boots as we walk on the beach."

Nerissa stiffened. She yanked her arm out of Gretchen's hold and retrieved the knife from the pocket of her skirt. Just as she was about to stab Gretchen, Finn grasped her wrists, yelling for the guards. Nerissa tried to free herself but Finn's grasp was too strong. A guard came bursting into the room and quickly getting a handle on the situation, wrenched Nerissa's arms behind her back. Finn checked on Gretchen and then came to stand in front of Nerissa.

"How dare you attack my fiancé in my own castle?" He was seething.

Nerissa tried to speak in her defense but couldn't and she whipped her head to Gretchen as she began to laugh maniacally. "Ah yes, tell us what is in that head of yours, hmm?"

At that precise moment, King Henrik ran into the room. He demanded to know what was happening and Finn filled him in on the incident. He looked at Nerissa and took in her pleading eyes. He shook his head sadly, for he believed Gretchen was a good woman and Nerissa had wronged her. He ordered Nerissa be taken to the dungeons until after the wedding. Nerissa struggled with the guard and in the process her locket fell to the carpet.

Henrik talked with Finn and Gretchen for a moment and then left them to tend to final business for the wedding. They shared a moment and then Finn noticed the necklace on the carpet. He picked it up and brought it over to Gretchen.

"You dropped this in the scuffle," he said as he held out the locket.

"That hideous thing? It must be Nerissa's. Maybe she stole it," Gretchen said with hatred.

Finn nodded and a servant knocked on the door and informed Finn they were ready for him to take his place in the cathedral. He nodded and followed the servant. Once in the antechamber, he looked at the locket again and noticed it had Nerissa's name on it. He opened it and was overwhelmed with a flood of memories at seeing his own picture in the heart shaped pendant. He remembered a beautiful voice and a kind woman and the love he felt for her. He remembered how she breathed and what it sounded like when she swam around him and how she smelled. He was having a hard time reconciling those memories with Gretchen, although she had sung for him and the voice was the same. He was so caught up in the sensory overload, he almost missed his father at his side gently pushing him to the altar.

Gretchen came into the cathedral and walked to the altar. Finn barely paid attention to anything as he kept rubbing the locket in his palm over and over with his thumb. Suddenly, he realized the deathly silence and looked up to find everyone staring at him. He apologized and asked the bishop to repeat what he had said to him. The bishop gave a long suffering sigh and then asked Finn if he took Gretchen to be his wife. Finn looked at Gretchen, then at the locket in his hand. He apologized and ran down the aisle to the dungeons.

Nerissa was heartbroken and sobbing in her cell when Finn surged into the room. She looked up with confusion as he opened the door and knelt by her side. He reached out to her and she hesitantly took his hand in hers. Gretchen came into the room as Nerissa stood.

"Can you sing?" Finn asked.

Nerissa mournfully shook her head.

"Could you sing? Before you came to the castle, could you sing?" he asked again hopefully.

Nerissa nodded and Gretchen scoffed. "Why listen to her? She is a murderer."

Finn glared at Gretchen. "She didn't kill you, only tried."

He returned his gaze to Nerissa and held up the locket. "I gave this to you."

Nerissa's eyes brightened and she nodded enthusiastically.

Gretchen looked out the window at the setting sun. She only needed to stall them for a moment more and Nerissa would no longer be her competition. She was about to grab Finn when he said, "Guards, please lock up Gretchen." Gretchen sputtered and cursed as the guards dragged her into a cell and locked the door.

"Nerissa, I remember. I was blind and could not see you but I remember you," Finn said as he smiled at her.

A lone tear slipped down Nerissa's cheek. She smiled at him and then mouthed the words, 'I love you'.

Finn laughed and then said, "I love you, too." He kissed her and suddenly the entire room glowed. Nerissa was wrapped up in a blinding white light and Gretchen was swirling in a blue fog. Nerissa fell to her knees and gasped, delighted when a sound came out. Gretchen clutched at her throat and her body began to disappear. Finn helped Nerissa stand and they both watched as Gretchen's body turned to dust for she had been banished from the sea and her body would be forever relegated to dust in the wind.

"Finn!" Nerissa clutched to him.

"How?" Finn asked in shock.

Nerissa stopped him with a finger on his lips. "I can explain all of it later but I must first get my father's permission."

Finn nodded. "This will be interesting."

Nerissa laughed.

Later, after Nerissa had spoken with her father and her mother, who convinced Triton he would lose his youngest daughter if he persisted in his stodgy old ways, and introduced Finn to her family, a grand wedding was planned aboard one of the Kingdom of the Cliff's finest vessels. All of Nerissa's family was in attendance and many of Finn's relations were as well. Finn and Nerissa were also witness to a grand treaty between the two kingdoms. For the rest of history, both kingdoms would work together so no humans died in the waters if the merfolk could help them. In return, the humans would make sure to keep the waters clean for all the merfolk. It brought great prosperity and peace to the land and the sea.

Nerissa and Finn continued to visit their cove every week where he would float while she would sing to him. He built a grand theater for her where she would sing for anyone who wished to attend the concerts, free of charge. At every concert, Finn would sit in the front row, always her biggest supporter.

The Magic Quill

Scrich, scrich, scrich. Katalena smiled to herself as she listened to her Papa writing. It was always the best part of her day. She would curl up behind his desk in the cozy little corner made between it and the fireplace and let the scratch of the quill across the parchment lull her into a sense of peace. The heat from the fireplace kept her toes toasty, especially in winter, and she could often be found sound asleep if her Mama did not come looking for her first. Mama was in a perpetual state of concern over Katalena and her propensity for the hobby.

Katalena was sure that her Papa was writing something very important today. He barely registered the kiss she had placed on his cheek, merely grunting and continuing to write. The Empress had given her father a magnificent peacock feather quill pen and it was this quill with which he wrote today. He only used the quill for very important correspondence concerning the Empress' business. The quill was the most luxurious things Katalena had ever seen. It came in a rectangular mahogany box, polished to shine when the candlelight caught it. When her Papa opened the box, there lie the quill in purple silk. The feather must have been at least as long as her Papa's arm. It's brilliant green vanes surrounded an eye of the brightest blue. She'd gasped in wonder when she had seen it. Papa had explained that she was never to touch this quill and Mama had scoffed at the very idea of Katalena even learning to write.

"Who wants a wife more concerned with reading and writing than cooking and sewing. She won't have time for such pursuits when she is married. It is not for girls," Mama said.

Papa just nodded his head in agreement and Mama went back to her cooking. Then Papa gave Katalena a wink and went to his writing desk, carefully setting the box on the desk and proceeding to go about his work. Katalena had sat in her corner, enjoying the fact that Mama had forgotten about the embroidery project Katalena was supposed to be doing. Papa was very good at distracting Mama from concerning herself with her youngest daughter's wife-training.

Now, Katalena started to dose when she heard her Mama calling for her. Katalena closed her eyes quickly and pretended to be asleep as her father leaned around the desk to glance at her. She knew that her Papa could tell she was awake but she hoped that she was convincing enough for Mama. Mama came into the house and spied Katalena in the corner.

"Shh," Papa said.

Mama spoked insistently but quietly, "That girl is always sitting about with her head in the clouds."

"Mmm," Papa agreed.

"She needs to help me run to the market. It will make the trip faster," Mama insisted.

"Natalya, it is turning cold outside and Katalena just recovered from her illness. Perhaps let her sleep and take Anna?" Papa suggested kindly.

Katalena tried not to smile. Papa was always keen on helping her escape her Mama's plans. She could hear the slight humor in his voice. She also knew the sound of her Mama's reply. Mama would put her hands on her hips and lean closer to Papa. He would wink at her and then Mama would surrender to his suggestions and chuckle. Katalena heard the sound of Mama placing a kiss on her Papa's lips.

"You are too soft on her," Mama chided. "What will become of her if she can't find a husband?"

"Ah, well, perhaps I am not yet ready to think of that," Papa admitted.

Mama hummed in agreement and gathered her shawl, then she went out the door.

"You can come out now, my little Kat," Papa said.

Katalena opened her eyes and stretched just like the cat her father often accused her of being. She smiled at her Papa and then jumped up, throwing herself at him for a big hug. Papa laughed and hugged her back, squeezing so tight Katalena thought she might never breathe again. However, she would never complain as she quite enjoyed the feeling of being held by her father in such a massive hug. Papa stopped hugging her and took her hands in his own.

"Kat, why must you vex your mother so much?" He gently scolded her.

Katalena shrugged. "It's not that I want to vex Mama... it's just...," she hesitated.

Katalena lowered her eyes and bit her lip. She was afraid to talk to her Papa, not because he would begrudge her feelings but because she was embarrassed to be having these particular feelings. Papa put a finger under her chin and lifted her face to meet his. She looked into his eyes and only saw his love for her shining through.

"You may tell me anything," he encouraged.

Katalena nodded and took a deep breath, "I don't want to be a wife, Papa. I want to be a writer, like you."

Papa smiled. "Ahh, I see."

"Mama will be furious with me if I tell her. Please don't tell her Papa." Katalena begged.

"Kat, why do you want to be a writer?" he asked.

Katalena thought a moment. She had never shared anything so intimate with anyone for fear her Mama would find out and ban her from the corner by her father's desk. She had longed to share her dreams with her Papa but tried to be a proper young lady and follow her Mama's teaching.

"Papa, if I tell you, promise you won't laugh?" Katalena pleaded.

Papa nodded and crossed his heart for good measure. He waited patiently for her to continue speaking. She lowered her eyes, closing them to think about how she should begin.

Katalena took a deep breath. "When I sit in the corner and listen to you write, it transports me to new worlds, as if by magic. Sometimes, I can see myself sitting on the hills near the summer palace, watching horses frolicking in the fields. Then the Empress comes and joins me for a picnic and we laugh and watch the clouds passing in the sky until dusk. Other times, you and I are skating on the Neva and it is if I can feel the cold winter air nipping at my cheeks. I can see our breath coming out in white swirls of smoke and hear the branches of the trees on the bank snapping under the weight of the ice. We skate and skate until our cheeks are rosy red and our legs feel heavy. Then we lie in the snow and stare at the stars."

Papa didn't say anything and Katalena was terrified of looking up. She didn't want to see the disappointment she knew must be lingering in his eyes. She didn't want to know that her Papa might think her dreams as useless as she would be to a husband. Her sister, Anna, would be married soon and she knew that her Papa would be looking to her future. She had most likely just ruined all his plans for his youngest child.

"Katalena, why did you not tell me any of this before?" he asked in wonder.

The tone of his voice made Katalena look up at him. Instead of disapproval or disgust, she still saw only love, now tinged with wonder, in his eyes. She cocked her head to the side, studying the look on his face. As she did so, she began to smile. Her Papa seemed almost proud of her. It was not something she had expected.

"I…I thought it would disappoint you, Papa," she admitted.

Papa shook his head, "Nonsense. You could never disappoint me. I had no idea there was such magic in your head, child."

Katalena laughed. "It isn't magic, Papa."

Papa winked at her, "It will be when I show you how to get it out of your head and onto parchment."

Katalena gasped. She never thought she would ever be allowed to learn to read and write. Although the Empress was very enlightened and had begun advocating the education of men and women, she left the decision up to each family within her court. Mama had declared it nonsense and Papa had agreed only because none of his daughters had shown any interest in sitting still long enough to learn. His work for the Empress demanded many hours and most days the girls finished the last of their chores in time for bed. As the girls grew and married, it slipped his mind to even broach the subject again with Mama and so it had never been revisited.

"You will teach me, Papa?" Katalena whispered for fear that she had only been dreaming his answer.

He nodded. Katalena through her arms around him again and he laughed. She could hear the laugh resonating through his chest. A million thoughts raced through her head, all the stories that had been bottled up inside her, keeping her awake at night working them out while her family slept.

"Can we start now, Papa?" she asked hopefully.

"Da, but we must keep it a secret from Mama, just for a time," Papa said.

Katalena nodded, then frowned.

"Why so glum now?" Papa asked.

"When will we have time, Papa? Mama keeps me very busy. Once Anna is gone, I will have even more work to do. I will never get time with you." Katalena choked back a tear as she mentally watched all her hopes wither.

Papa grasped her hands again, "Leave Mama to me."

Katalena nodded.

"Now, sit next to me and pick up the quill."

Papa scooted over on the bench and Katalena sat next to him. She reached for Papa's old quill, a black goose feather quill that had definitely seen better days. Its feathers were matted from years and years of use and the shaft was nearly gone from sharpening. Papa was very particular about the things he liked and often wore clothes until they were so holey, Mama threw them out when he was at the palace. Quills and ink pots were no exception.

"No, no," Papa said, "such a special occasion demands a special instrument."

Katalena's eyes widened as her Papa picked up the peacock quill and handed it to her. She reached out with a shaky and took it, the breath she expelled sent the wispy vanes fluttering. She looked between the quill and her father with awe. He nodded and she gripped it, imitating the position she had seen her father use so many times when writing.

"Here, let me," Papa said.

He corrected her grasp on the quill very slightly, but it did feel much more natural. Then Papa positioned a piece of parchment in front of her and one in front of himself. He picked up the old goose feather quill and dipped it slightly in the ink, nodding for her to do the same. Katalena copied the motion and stared in wonder at the black ink now ready to make a mark on the parchment.

"First," Papa began, "you must learn the alphabet we use. Only then will you be able to put together the words swimming around in your head. Understand?"

Katalena nodded.

"Good, let's begin," Papa smiled and started writing the first letter.

Katalena and Papa practiced writing every day. Some days their lessons would take place when Mama was away at the market. Other days, Papa would make an excuse to Mama, which usually involved him needing her transporting supplies to the palace. Mama would mumble under breath but would not argue with Papa. He would hurry Katalena along to his office at the palace and teach her as quickly as he could in the time that was allotted for her disappearance from home. Katalena got very good at the alphabet quickly and could write her own name within a week. Then, Papa began showing her how the letters formed words and it was if a whole new world opened up in her head. The missing link had been connected and now she could walk the bridge to her imaginative destinations.

After several months, Katalena no longer needed instruction. Papa gave her a box full of parchment and her own quill. Although he had let her use the peacock quill the first time, it was both impossible and impractical for her to use it every day. Besides, Papa needed it for his own work for the Empress. It was expected that he use it, especially when writing in her presence. Therefore, the quill had to be preserved as much as possible. Katalena hid the box, along with her writings, in a loose board under her bed. Anna had finally married and it was now her duty to clean the house, therefore, she never had to worry that Mama would find the box and question its contents.

Occasionally, Papa would ask to read the stories Katalena wrote. She would fetch them from the box and hand them over with trepidation. She never knew why she was so terrified but each time she just knew would be the time her Papa would be disappointed in her and regret teaching her to write. Of course, this never happened. The most Papa would do was correct her grammar in some part of a story or suggest improvements. Katalena would nod, look over the notes he made, and run off to make the edits he suggested. He told her he was proud of her more than once and each time it brought a smile to her face that lasted so many days, she thought her face might be stuck in the silly grin. Mama thought Katalena had finally found a suitor and Katalena was happy to let her continue in this belief.

One day, Papa had just finished reading Katalena's creation when the door to the house opened suddenly and Mama, who was not due to return from the palace for another hour, walked in. Papa quickly hid Katalena's parchment under his own papers and Katalena schooled her features. Mama looked between the two of them as if she had caught them plotting to assassinate the Empress. Katalena swallowed heavily and Papa put a steadying hand on her arm. She calmed somewhat at the gesture and waited for him to speak.

"Natalya, we were not expecting you home so soon," Papa said casually.

Mama nodded, "Da, but I have a surprise for Katalena."

Katalena looked alarmed. Usually, when Mama wanted to *surprise* her, it meant Mama was trying to marry her off to some Count or other courtier. A sense of dread filled her stomach. Papa squeezed her arm to try and calm her once more.

Mama continued without noticing the change in her. "Aleksei Vasiliev, please come in," Mama said to the person standing behind her.

Aleksei Vasiliev walked through the door. He was very tall and towered over Mama. Katalena had met him a handful of times at the parties held at the palace for special occasions. Her Papa worked with his and they were very close in age. Aleksei had dark, short hair, almost raven black in color. His eyes were the color of a stormy sea on a cloudy day yet they had such depth to them as if two colors warred within them. His face was peppered with a few days of stubble as if he did not care to make a decision between actually shaving or growing his facial hair. Katalena mentally chided herself for complimenting his looks in her head and attempted to harden her heart against yet another of her Mama's machinations to see her youngest daughter married and a housewife.

Aleksei bowed and reached for Katalena's hand. He kissed above it in the French manner favored by the Empress. Katalena jerked her hand back as quickly as possible and then straightened when she heard her Mama clear her throat. Katalena must remember her manners and it was the only warning she would get. Katalena put her hands behind her back and rubbed at the spot where Aleksei had touched her. The touch had sent a shock up her arm but rather than being unpleasant, it had warmed her and this concerned her.

"Aleksei Vasiliev, it is a pleasure to have you visit our home. Would you like some refreshments?" Katalena asked.

She tried to affect a neutral tone but winced inwardly when it came out pleasant and inviting. She did not understand what was happening. Why was this man affecting her so much? She would refuse to give into her Mama's wishes. She had done so before and she would do so now.

"Katalena Aleksandrova, I am pleased to be welcome. Refreshments would be most appreciated," Aleksei responded with a smile and another bow of his head.

Katalena swallowed hard at the smile and then stood there for a moment, staring at Aleksei. She did not know how much time passed before her father gave her a gentle nudge and then she was jolted out of her trance. She blushed and turned to get the offered refreshments. Her Mama followed her into the kitchen, watching her with a big grin on her face.

"Stop it, Mama," Katalena growled under her breath so as not to allow her father or Aleksei to hear her.

Mama came over and gave her a hug. "I'm just so happy for you."

Katalena huffed. She closed her eyes. Mama already thought she had won and Katalena hated to admit that she was quickly softening to Aleksei's charms. She wanted to be a writer, not a wife.

"Mama…" Katalena tried to assuage Mama's enthusiasm.

"Just give him a chance, Katalena," Mama said and patted her on the arm.

Katalena nodded. She guessed it was the least she could do. Letting Aleksei court her would keep Mama from any more meddling and it could also be an excuse to get in some more writing. She could tell Mama she was going to any one of a number of palace events with him and then hide in Papa's office and write to her heart's content. Mama gave a hushed squeal of delight and Katalena rolled her eyes. Mama hurried her off to serve the refreshments.

Aleksei and Katalena had been courting for three months when he found out her secret. Katalena had told Mama she was going to the garden party being held at the palace for the first signs of spring. In truth, she had snuck out of the party and found her Papa in his office. He winked at her and got up from his desk, excusing himself to a meeting with a visiting dignitary. He'd left out some parchment and a quill for her use and she had jumped into writing down her latest fantasy. She did not know how much time had passed when suddenly, the door flew open and Aleksei rushed into the room. He froze when he saw Katalena at the desk and she froze, quill in mid-air when she saw him. Aleksei looked at her, down at her hands, and back up at her face. The look of shock on his face jolted her out of her stupor and she quickly jumped up, hiding the quill behind her back.

"Aleksei, I…" Katalena stammered.

Aleksei quickly shut the door and walked over to her. He gently reached toward her and for a moment she shied away from him. He paused and waited for her to give him permission to touch her. She gulped and nodded. Aleksei pulled her hands out from behind her back. He grasped the quill and she let go. Then he set the quill on the desk and looked at her hands, turning them over in his and examining the ink stains on her writing hand.

"Turn around," he said.

"Wh…what?" she asked quizzically.

"Trust me," he said.

Katalena studied his face a moment. She did not see the anger or disgust she thought might be there upon him first finding her. She nodded and turned around. She felt his hand on the small of her back and then he spoke.

"You got ink on your dress. Let me help you."

Aleksei moved away from her. She glanced over her shoulder and saw him dousing a handkerchief in some of her father's vodka. She quickly looked forward again as he returned to her side. She felt him dabbing at her dress. After what felt like an agonizing number of minutes, he finished.

"There. You will have to tell your mother someone spilled their drink on you at the party."

Katalena nodded and turned back around. She studied his face again, watching him struggling to keep laughter from boiling up, the amusement in the situation clearly evident. He glanced down at the desk and she instinctively tried to hide her writing. He backed away a step and Katalena looked up with guilt.

"I won't pry if you don't want me to," Aleksei said with sincerity. "Now, I know where you hide all the times you are too busy."

"You aren't angry?" Katalena asked with some confusion.

"Nyet, why would I be angry?" he asked, perplexed.

Katalena shrugged, "Mama always says that a husband does not want a wife concerned with reading and writing. They want strong Russian women who can care for the house and have plenty of children to fill it with joy."

Aleksei thought a moment before he replied. Katalena watched emotions cross his face with interest. The real question she has was what all the emotions meant. Did he want to have children? Did he even want to get married? She had learned there was no end of eligible women ready to marry him and it seemed like he had left behind a string of broken hearts without even meaning to do so. She was subjected to no small amount of jealous looks each time she was seen with him. She was sure he could have the pick of anyone he chose. He looked down at the desk again.

"Could I read what you have written?" he asked suddenly.

Katalena hesitated. "It is not yet finished."

Aleksei nodded. Katalena looked at the parchment. It was a fanciful piece about a courageous young woman fighting a dragon to save the man she loved from becoming its next meal. She blushed, realizing that the descriptions of both the woman and the man had very similar descriptions to those of the two people standing in Papa's office. She could tell him no and run from the room or she could be the courageous woman and let another person she cared for read her work. Katalena swallowed and picked up the parchment, holding it out to Aleksei without meeting his eyes. He took the papers gently and walked to the chair across the desk from her. He sat in the chair and she mirrored his action, sitting in her father's chair. She tried to pretend to be disinterested in his reading but found herself watching him and trying to determine the meaning behind each facial expression or sound he made. Finally, he finished reading and lowered the papers. His face was now neutral and she gulped and looked down at the desk.

"You have a gift, Katalena," he said with awe.

Katalena's head whipped up. She was sure she had not heard him correctly.

"I mean it," he reaffirmed. "This story is impressive. Are there more?"

Katalena nodded her head.

"I would very much like to read them, if you will permit me to do so, of course," Aleksei said.

"I can show them to you if you promise not to tell Mama. She wouldn't understand," Katalena said.

"Agreed," Aleksei said and stood. "Now, would you like me to walk you home? The party ended and I am sure your mother will be waiting for you."

Katalena nodded. "Thank you. Perhaps you can explain just who exactly spilled their drink on me."

Aleksei laughed and offered his arm. Katalena took it and he escorted her from the office.

Many months later, Aleksei asked Papa for permission to marry Katalena. Aleksei was enthusiastically granted permission then asked her to marry him and she had agreed. Aleksei admitted to her that he figured she would say yes, given that he was the model for many of the men in her most recent writings, something Katalena vehemently denied while blushing all the way to her toes. Aleksei let the matter drop and Katalena was relieved. She often drew inspiration for her characters from those she knew and, of course, Aleksei figured prominently in her stories as she became more fond of him.

They married and settled into life together easily. Katalena no longer had to hide her writing and Aleksei made sure she had the finest writing desk he could afford. He also built her a trunk in which to store her parchments and several quill pens so she never had to sharpen one if he was not at home. She made sure to keep the house tidy and fulfill her duties as the wife of a prominent court member. She shared every story with Aleksei and he was always enthusiastic and ready to read one as soon as she told him the latest one was complete.

One afternoon, Katalena was baking Aleksei's favorite pie and dreaming up a new story when an urgent knock interrupted her thoughts. Katalena frowned, not expecting visitors. She quickly removed her apron and straightened her skirts then opened the door. Her sister, Anna, was standing at the door, tear marks trailing down her face.

"Katalena, come quickly," Anna urged.

Katalena nodded. She removed the pie from the oven and then followed her sister to her parent's house. When they arrived, Mama was sobbing. Katalena gulped back tears and looked at Anna, who just pointed to her parent's bedroom. Katalena walked into the room, the scent of sickly sweet incense burning her nostrils. Papa lay on the bed, deathly pale, and the Archbishop saying a prayer over him. Katalena recognized it as last rites. She rushed to Papa's side and grasped his hand, kissing it and pleading with him.

"Papa, don't go," she wailed.

Papa opened his eyes and smiled kindly at her. He squeezed her hand and gestured for her to come closer. Katalena swiped angrily at her tears and bent over Papa's head.

"My little Kat, do not fear. I go with visions of your stories preparing the way to paradise."

"No, Papa," Katalena pleaded.

"Be kind to your mother. She will need understanding. I know you do not think so, but she too can dream and imagine magical places. You are more alike than you think," he said.

Katalena nodded, "I promise, Papa."

Papa sighed and smiled. He seemed to doze off and Katalena stayed and held his hand. Eventually, Aleksei came and sat by Katalena, holding her hand. Several hours later, her Papa was gone and Katalena felt as if the light in the whole world had gone out. Aleksei took charge and looked after both Katalena and Mama. Katalena held her Mama tight while she sobbed. Mama finally fell asleep from exhaustion.

After Papa was laid to rest, Katalena mourned. She continued to be a housewife but would sit and stare at the frozen Neva instead of writing. Her desk began to collect dust. This habit persisted for weeks until one evening, Aleksei came home with her Mama. Katalena jumped up and dusted off her dress. Mama smiled kindly at her and Aleksei offered to gather refreshments.

"Katalena, sit with me, please," Mama requested.

Katalena nodded and sat next to her mother. Mama reached into her bag and pulled out a piece of parchment. Katalena watched Mama caress the letters on the front of the parchment, like she used to caress Papa's fingers when she thought no one was looking. Then, Mama kissed the parchment and handed it to Katalena. She took it with hesitance and looked at her Mama.

"Go ahead, I know you can read it," Mama said.

Katalena gulped, "But... how?"

Mama smiled fondly, "Your Papa told me. He could never keep a secret."

"How long have you known?" Katalena asked.

"Since the day after you started learning your letters," Mama said.

Katalena's eyes widened and she gasped. How had Mama known for so long? Why didn't she say anything? Why wasn't she angry with Katalena?

"Don't look so shocked, dear one. Your father always knew what was best. He let you girls think I alone made the decisions in the house, so as not to undermine my authority as your mother, but we made decisions together. You had such a love for the writing, I did not wish to quell your joy."

Katalena nodded, "Thank you, Mama."

"I have something else for you," Mama said.

Once again, she reached down into her bag and pulled out the mahogany quill box. She held it out to Katalena, who reached for it with shaky hands. Katalena caressed the top of the case, the letters of Papa's monogram engraved in it.

"He wanted you to have this," Mama said.

"His most precious possession," Katalena said in awe.

Mama shook her head. Katalena looked at her with confusion.

"His family was his most precious possession. He would have traded everything we had for one ounce of your happiness," Mama choked on her words.

Katalena hugged Mama and they both let tears flow. After holding her Mama for many moments, Katalena leaned back and wiped her eyes. She looked down at the parchment sitting on her lap. She picked it up and began to read.

My little Kat,

I am sorry to have left you but we must all go in the end. I have led a very blessed life and I could not think having shared my life with a better family. Your Mama was the love of my life and I am only disappointed that we do not have more years together. I die, knowing I will see her again in the afterlife.

I want you to have the quill Empress Ekaterina presented to me when I became a senior adviser. It has brought me very good luck and now it will bring your stories to life with magic never before seen in this world. You have a gift, child. Your words have transported me to places I never believed I would see and have left me with a full heart and a hopeful parting.

Please take care of your Aleksei. Your Mama and I knew he was the right man for you and I could not be happier in your choice of husband. The day you shared your writing with him was the day I knew he would take care of you and nourish your desires instead of squash them. Talk to him. He has many ideas about your writing and I am sure they will increase your appreciation of his strengths and his love for you.

Never stop writing, little Kat. Your soul would not rest and would eat at you if you let my death keep you from your true purpose. I will be with you in your heart forever. Do not mourn my passing too long for we will be together once again. Until then, let this quill help you. I love you more than the stars could recount.

Papa

Katalena wiped at the fresh tears on her face. She smiled at her mother and then gave a loving look to Aleksei as he entered the room with the refreshments. Later that evening, when Aleksei returned from escorting her mother home, he and Katalena snuggled under the heavy winter blankets. Aleksei stroked her hair, as he did every night, and she drew circles on his chest with her finger.

"Aleksei?" Katalena raised her head and looked at him.

"Hmm?" he asked.

"Papa said in his letter you had ideas about my writing," she said.

Aleksei nodded, "I think you should compile your stories into a book and publish them."

"Are you mad? Russians would never buy a book published by a woman," she scoffed.

Aleksei shrugged, "Don't put a woman's name on them."

Katalena opened and shut her mouth as the idea slowly gained traction in her brain. It was an insane idea but it could work. Aleksei could take it to a publisher. They would never know she wrote the words. She shook her head, trying to clear out the idea and then lay back against his chest. She kept mulling the idea over and over until she fell asleep.

After several days of warring with herself, she finally agreed that Aleksei's idea would work. Aleksei took it to the publisher, who accepted it without question after reading the first few stories. They published her anthology with the title *The Magic Quill* and under the name K. Aleksandr. Katalena had to drop the feminine form of her patronymic name but she felt like then she was honoring Papa anyway, for it was his given name on her book. The anthology was a success and she published two more in the following years.

K atalena sat at her writing desk, another story coming to life on the parchment. Her granddaughter, Tatiana, sat with her feet to the fire and hummed along to the sound of the *scrich, scrich, scrich* the peacock quill made as Katalena wrote. Tatiana always made a song out of the sounds around her. Katalena had written a story about a young princess who could make magical music with the snow falling outside her castle window. She often read it to Tatiana when the thunderstorms frightened the child.

"Babushka, why does it make that sound?" Tatiana asked.

"Ah, you see, the quill is very sharp and the parchment is not very smooth, so the two war with each other but then neither wins. In the end, the ink is the only winner," Katalena replied with a laugh.

Tatiana giggled. She was only six and she adored her grandmother. Tatiana walked over to Katalena and crawled into her lap. She blew lightly at the peacock quill and watched in fascination as the vanes fluttered. She gently reached out and rubbed her finger down the edge of one side of the feather.

"Babushka, why does this quill have an eye?" Tatiana inquired.

Katalena smiled, "It can see far away worlds."

"Is it magic?" Tatiana's eyes grew wide with wonder.

Katalena nodded, "It is very magic. Would you like me to show you?"

Tatiana nodded enthusiastically. Katalena smiled and showed her granddaughter how to hold the quill. She guided the child's hand in making her first letters. Aleksei stopped behind her and kissed the top of her head while encouraging Tatiana. Katalena smiled when a breeze made the candle on her desk flicker. She knew it was a sign from her Papa. Tatiana would be the next generation to wield the magic quill.

The Hunter

The Hunter crept silently through the trees, stopping every now and then to sniff the air and check the ground for signs of prey. As she went, it began to rain softly, just enough mist to lodge in her hair and occasionally obscure her vision. The tall cedar and fir trees above her kept most of the moisture for themselves, their canopy a natural umbrella from the water. Suddenly, she stopped, noticing something new in the forest. At odd intervals along the path, a strange, tiny blue flower had emerged from the ground. The Hunter knelt down and gently moved the flower, inspecting its delicate petals. The Hunter did not want to disturb the plant, for the Gods would be angry if she harmed something without a direct purpose. She sniffed the air again and her brow furrowed. Something—or rather someone—new was near.

The Hunter followed the trail marked by the strange new flowers. As she walked, the birds became more and more silent until they were non-existent. The Hunter found the quiet unsettling and tamped down the primal urge to feel fear. She believed she would be safe as long as she respected the rules of the forest and adhered to the demands of the Gods. Her pace slowed as she glimpsed a hint of glowing silver in the clearing ahead of her. She thought quickly, then climbed the nearest cedar in calculated silence. She crouched in a branch fifteen feet off the ground and silently drew her bow. She nocked an arrow with practiced precision and trained it on the person below.

The Hunter studied the person. It was a woman with long, silver hair, dressed all in white. Her skin was so alabaster, it was hard to tell where the clothing ended and the woman's body began. The Hunter could not see the woman's face, as she had it buried in her hands. It took a moment, but the Hunter realized the woman was crying. As her tears fell, the strange blue flowers she'd seen before sprouted from the ground around the woman. The Hunter suppressed the shudder of fear she felt. The old magic was forbidden in her tribe.

Once, the elders had wielded the old magic every day and the tribe prospered. Then, as humans were wont to do, a war broke out between the Hunter's tribe and another. Both sides were equally matched and both sides were fearsome in their use of magic. Eventually, the magic had nearly wiped out both tribes. A scant few remained. The land was scarred and the animals died off. It became a desert. The Gods were angered. The land erupted in hot rivers and rose up to the sky. The Hunter's tribe was cursed to walk over these great mountains and find a new way to live. After many generations, they arrived near the Great Salty Sea. The remaining tribe members made amends to the Gods, asking for forgiveness. In return, they promised to leave the old magic behind. They would live peacefully with the land and the sea—taking only what they needed for survival. In this way, the tribe once again prospered.

The Hunter kept her bow nocked, debating how to handle the newcomer. Suddenly, the woman looked up and locked eyes with the Hunter. Rather than the shock she should have felt at being caught so easily, the Hunter felt a sense of peace wash over her. She lowered the bow, tilting her head to the side and the woman smiled. The smile is what broke the spell and the Hunter lithely jumped out of the tree. She stared at the woman a moment longer, then backed away until she could no longer see white or silver. She sped up to a quick trot and ran back towards her village, all the while thinking of the striking green eyes the woman had fixed upon her.

The Hunter had very little sleep the evening before, tossing and turning with agitated dreams. Normally, she would sleep peacefully each night, awakening the next morning with ease. However, this morning, her mother had to shake her awake and the Hunter was none too pleased with the intrusion of the sun upon her bed. She plodded through her morning preparations, listening to her siblings argue over their breakfast. They generally amused her but she found herself snapping at their bickering. She ignored the look from her mother and grabbed up her bow and quiver of arrows. She would tell anyone who asked she just had a bad night but she knew what haunted her dreams. Green eyes on an alabaster face. The woman's face had been perfectly smooth, a thin, straight nose and lips the pale pink of the ocean flowers. It was the green eyes, at once bright and dark, all-knowing. The Hunter shivered at the memory of those eyes piercing into her own. She knew not if was fear or something more primal.

The Hunter spent the day combing the forest for the strange flowers she had seen the day before. She followed the original path to the clearing but found only creatures of the forest there and no silver-haired woman. She followed the trails leading out of the clearing but eventually, in every direction, the path went cold. The Hunter growled in frustration. It was the first time she had ever lost a trail. Surely, the woman could not have gone far. The Hunter returned to the clearing and sat on the ground. Then she lay on the ground and peered at the flowers as close as she dared without touching them. They were small, many no bigger than the nail or her little finger. They were a color of blue different from that of the sky but still delicate in nature. They possessed five tiny petals surrounding a yellow center. They grew in clusters as if being alone were too much for their fragile existence.

The Hunter spent a long time peering at the flowers. She had the urge to take them back to the village elders but she did not want to alarm her people. It appeared the woman using the forbidden magic had vanished and she did not believe her tribe was in danger. At long last, she could tell the sun would be gone and her family would worry about her disappearance. She rose, leaving the clearing in search of a quick kill. Soon, she found a hare and shot it with precision. She said a quick thank you to the Gods and shouldered the hare, walking back to her village. She spared a glance for the final patch of strange flowers along her path, then turned towards home, no more at ease in her mind than the previous night.

A week passed and the Hunter returned to her normal routine and usually amiable demeanor. Her mother asked no more questions, for which she was grateful. She was cleaning a kill to be processed for winter storage when a great commotion rose up from the front of the village. The Hunter frowned and looked towards her mother. Her mother shrugged and went back to preparing the salts for preserving the meat. The Hunter lingered a moment, then set down her knife, wiping away the blood and taking a step towards the noise. She looked back at her mother, who nodded and smiled. The Hunter needed no further approval. She ran towards the front of her village.

A large crowd was gathered around and the Hunter was unable to see what was happening, much less hear as everyone spoke at once. She deftly climbed the great cedar tree next to the Elder's house and peered down into the center of the gathering. An excited child was waving around an unmistakeable bunch of blue flowers while the Elder tried to calm him. Some of her tribe backed away in fear as the child described finding the flowers. Others looked to the Elder for a rational explanation. The Elder sniffed the flowers, then recoiled in fear, dropping them to the ground. He quickly ground them to dust with the end of his staff. A great cry rose up from her people as they ran from the offensive flower. Some disappeared and came back with oils, which they proceeded to pour on the remnants of the flower.

Eventually, the people disbursed and the Hunter descended from the tree. She looked at the mess of flower fragments covered in oil. She noted drums and rattles starting at the sacred circle. The people of her tribe were attempting to appease the Gods. They begged for protection from the evil flower and asked the Gods to cleanse their land. Her people were afraid. The Hunter listened to their songs and walked slowly back to her home. She had seen the source of their despair. She wondered if the Gods were punishing her people for allowing the silver-haired woman to remain in their forest. She silently chided herself for not bringing news of the woman to the Elder as soon as she saw her. It was the woman's eyes. They had bewitched her.

The next morning, the Hunter set out to find the woman yet again. She had been searching for the better part of the day when she sensed a change in the air. It was reminiscent of the first encounter with the woman. The Hunter followed the quiet, for there were no flowers on the trail. She continued towards the Long River, then turned and followed the Long

River the way the salmon did. The Long River eventually slowed, no longer rapid in its haste towards the Great Salty Sea. It was here the Hunter found her prey. She crouched low to the ground and watched as the silver-haired woman knelt next to the waters. The Hunter gasped when she realized the woman was next to a small black bear. The woman was talking to the bear and it seemed to be understanding what she was saying. After a moment, the woman turned and once again locked eyes with the Hunter. The same sense of calm as before crept of her and she found herself sitting without meaning to do so.

The silver-haired woman patted the bear, who looked between the woman and the Hunter. It appeared to nod and then ran into the forest. The Hunter's jaw dropped open of its own accord. She shook herself and willed herself to stand but was unable to move as the woman approached. The woman smiled and another wave of serenity fell over the Hunter. Her mouth closed and she sat straighter as the woman sat next to her.

"Do not be alarmed, young hunter," the woman said without moving her mouth.

The Hunter's eyes widened in fear.

"Please, your fear is not needed. Yes, I can talk in your language, but only in your head. It is an old magic."

"The old magic is forbidden!" The Hunter responded inside her head.

The silver-haired woman nodded. Then she frowned at the thought she read inside the Hunter's mind. She touched the

Hunter gently on the arm and the Hunter sighed as her body felt her own again. She flexed her fingers, itching to draw her bow but glanced at the silver-haired woman and resisted. She wanted to get more information from the woman before taking her to the Elder.

"You have many questions," the woman surmised.

The Hunter nodded. She fired the questions off in her head, almost too rapid for even her own understanding. The silver-haired woman laughed and the sound was like the most beautiful song of the birds of the forest. The Hunter shivered at the sensation the sound gave her. The silver-haired woman looked out over the river and the Hunter watched as a visible wave of sadness washed over the woman. The Hunter calmed her mind and waited. The silver-haired woman sighed and turned back to the Hunter.

"I am the last of my people. The old magic was not forbidden by my tribe and it was misused by those who let greed rule their hearts. I have traveled very far to find others like me. It led me to your tribe."

The Hunter shook her head, *"My tribe has not used the old magic in many, many moons. You are not welcome here."*

The silver-haired woman nodded, *"I understood this when I read your mind that day in the clearing."*

The Hunter narrowed her eyes and crossed her arms. *"Yet you remain and frighten my people. You conjure unnatural flowers around our village. The drums have not stopped for many hours. You must leave."*

"I must stay. The Gods have promised to reward me if I help your people."

"We need no help!"

The Hunter stood quickly, glaring down at the silver-haired woman. The woman merely smiled back, attempting to calm the Hunter, a move she recognized and stubbornly willed herself to resist. To her surprise, the Hunter's anger did not subside and she was able to avoid being manipulated by the woman. She stamped her foot in protest and the woman's smile faded.

"This is your last warning, leave our land or next time you will face my arrow," the Hunter yelled out loud.

She gave one last glare to the silver-haired woman and turned away. She refused to look back to see if the woman was still sitting by the river. In the distance, a bear roared and the Hunter could almost feel its agony but she didn't care. Her people did not need help, especially from one using the old magic. The woman had admitted her own people were gone because of their misuse of the gifts from the Gods. The Hunter seethed all the way back to her village. She briefly thought about stopping to talk to the Elder but decided against it. Her people would soon ward off the evil and go back to their daily lives.

The morning promised to be beautiful, the sun peeking out from the occasional fluffy, white cloud. The birds sang their merry song and, for once, the Hunter's breakfast table was peaceful. She smiled as she watched her father and mother talking amongst themselves. Her siblings each ate from their own bowl without fighting. She herself relished the fresh fish her mother had prepared that morning. It was the Hunter's name day. In a ceremony that evening, the Elder would give her an adult name and she would be welcomed into the council as a full participant. She had passed all the required tests except one that would be performed at the ceremony.

The Hunter passed her day receiving well wishes from the women and children of her tribe. The men were busy preparing the ceremony, their good wishes part of the proceedings. The Hunter's mother took great pride in braiding her hair in two long braids down the sides of her face. Then, her sisters and aunts painstakingly died the hair white with a ground powder mixed with water. They adorned her with a brown dress and shells from the Great Salty Sea. The put feathers of the songbirds at her wrist and ankles. Finally, they deemed her ready for the ceremony. She sat in anticipation, waiting for her father to fetch her for the naming.

She closed her eyes and prayed to the Gods. She wished to be strong for her people in both her hunting prowess and her skills in the council. She prayed for wisdom and patience. She prayed for prosperity for her people and harmony in her land. She ended her prayer to the Gods and looked out at the darkening sky. Her ancestors twinkled down upon her. She knew she had done everything she could to make them proud. Suddenly, a bright white dress appeared at her side. The Hunter frowned but made no movement. The silver-haired woman sat in front of the Hunter.

"I told you to leave," the Hunter growled in her mind. *"Today is a special day for me. You cannot be here."*

"Yet here I am, all the same."

The Hunter growled, looking around to see if she could see any of her tribe members nearby. She knew her father would arrive any minute. She did not want to be seen with the silver-haired woman. The Elder would know she was a magic user the minute he laid eyes on her. The silver-haired woman started to smile, then cocked her head and let it fade from her face.

"Your people are in danger. They will not listen to me, but they will listen to you. You must tell them, in a week's time there are those coming who do not understand their ways. They must resist the charms of these newcomers. The newcomers will take everything from your people."

"Why should I listen to you. You bring only fear with you."

The silver-haired woman sighed and nodded. She looked away, then looked up at the sky and her mouth moved slightly. The Hunter looked up as well but only saw her ancestors shining down upon them. She looked at the woman curiously, waiting. The woman finished her strange words and looked back at the Hunter.

"The Gods are clear. You must warn your people."

The silver-haired woman rose, patting the Hunter on the shoulder and walking towards the center of the village. The

Hunter tried to call out but was unable to find her voice. The woman was walking directly towards danger and for some reason, this made the Hunter fearful for her safety. The Hunter heard the shocked yells of her people and stood up from the ground. Her father ran towards her, his eyes wide in the darkness. He grasped her arm and let her towards the village center.

Her people stood in a great circle around the ceremonial fire. The Elder stood next to the silver-haired woman. She stood straight with a serene look on her face. Her people muttered amongst themselves. Her father stopped at the edge of the circle. He looked to the Elder for guidance. The Elder looked at the Hunter, then nodded his head. The people parted and looked at the Hunter.

"Oh, great Elder. My daughter has come of age and wishes to join the council," her father proclaimed.

"Has your daughter been tested?"

"She has passed all tests put before her," her father replied.

"Daughter, please step into the circle," the Elder instructed.

The Hunter looked at her people, trying to ignore the presence of the silver-haired woman. She kept her back straight and walked with purpose. She stood in front of the Elder and bowed her head in respect. The Elder touched her head. She waited for him to continue but felt his hand tense in her hair. She glanced up and saw the Elder looking down at her with a look of betrayal in his eyes. She winced and saw him make a decision. She chanced a peek at the silver-haired woman and did not like the apology she saw in the woman's eyes.

"Daughter, rise," the Elder instructed.

The Hunter rose and stood as still as possible. She held her breath, waiting for the final test to begin. The Elder took a long moment to look at her. He reached into his robe and pulled out a ceremonial knife. The Hunter tried not to let fear invade her. The Elder presented the knife to the Hunter. After a moment, she took it.

"Daughter, you are familiar with the silver-haired devil next to me?" he asked loudly.

The Hunter gulped and nodded.

"You must rid our village of the lawbreaker," he said, nodding to the knife.

The Hunter looked at the silver-haired woman. She saw a sadness in the woman's brilliant green eyes. She looked around at her people, taking in their fear and anxiety. She searched her heart. She knew the woman could have decimated her people or overthrown the Elder. The woman had magic and her people had forgotten the use of magic. However, the woman had risked her own life to warn her people of a danger they faced in the future. The Hunter met the woman's eyes again, then turned back to the Elder.

"This I cannot do," the Hunter said.

Her people gasped. Her father and mother began to protest but the Elder held up his hand and silenced the tribe. He took the knife from the Hunter and gestured for her to kneel. The Hunter knelt and bowed her head in shame, knowing she had failed the final test. She would not be named and she would not join the council.

"Daughter, you are to be banished from the tribe," the Elder said sadly.

The Elder took up one of the Hunter's long braids. He quickly cut it off with the ceremonial knife. Then he took the other and did the same.

"Do you wish to speak before you are cleansed?" the Elder asked.

The Hunter nodded. "I do. My people," she said as she rose, "the silver-haired woman breaks our laws and uses magic. Yet, she has come to warn us of men who would harm our village. They arrive in a week's time. I ask only that you heed her warning, do not trust these men. My life is of no consequence if my people are in danger."

The people of her tribe looked at one another and whispered amongst themselves. The Elder held up his hand once again and looked around. A council member approached the Elder and whispered in his ear. The Elder nodded and then looked back at the Hunter.

"You shall be cleansed. If what you say is true, we shall know in a week's time. You may redeem your position within the tribe. Take her away."

The Hunter was led by her father and another man to the cleansing lodge. The silver-haired woman followed behind with guards of her own. Neither spoke to the other as they were locked inside the lodge. Not many survived two days in the lodge, much less a week. The Hunter hoped beyond hope the silver-haired woman was wrong and her people were not in danger.

ake up." The Hunter heard the voice inside her head. *"Leave me be,"* she responded plaintively.

"It is time, young warrior," the voice insisted.

The Hunter moaned and sat up. She peered around the sweat rolling down her brow at the silver-haired woman. She grunted, seeing that the woman did not appear to be suffering at all. She herself had barely held on—each day more grueling than the last. The silver-haired woman nodded to the entrance of the lodge. Suddenly, the Hunter became attuned to the sounds outside, which were definitely not normal for her village. She could hear shouting and commands—her people were fighting with someone. She ran to the door and began pounding on it.

"I can open it if you ask for help," the woman said inside her head.

The Hunter rounded on the woman and glared at her. She'd been miserable for days and the woman had grated on her nerves. It seemed the woman could not be baited into anger which, of course, merely angered her even more. She'd let the woman take the brunt of her feelings and not even been rewarded with a raised voice. Now, the woman was asking her to beg for help. Her head whipped back to the door as she heard an explosion outside. She turned back to the woman and let out a long-suffering sigh.

"Open the door... please!" she pleaded.

The woman nodded and the door opened. The Hunter didn't spare a backward glance as she ran outside to the chaotic scene. Lodges were on fire and people were running everywhere. The Hunter ran by a campfire and grabbed the bow and quiver of arrows leaning against it. She ran towards the Elder's house, the sounds of fighting getting louder as she went. She couldn't see what was happening so she quickly scaled the tree next to the home.

Below her, her people and men wearing odd shiny armor were fighting each other. She could not tell who was winning but she could see the Elder being trapped by the man who looked like he was in charge. Men were grabbing children and throwing them into a strange wheeled cart. The Hunter nocked her bow and sent an arrow flying, hitting the man shutting the cart in the eye. He fell to the ground but the Hunter had already killed three other men before the first was fully prone. The children screamed, then ran out of the cart. The men of her tribe gave a cheerful yell and began returning to the fight with more vigor.

The man holding the Elder hostage yelled and suddenly a group of men was running for the tree the Hunter perched in. She let loose her arrows until she was out. She had disabled most of the men but several were attempting to pull her out of the tree. The Hunter felt a great sense of calm fall over her. She reached back instinctively and found her quiver was full again. She took a brief moment to look around and spotted a silver-haired woman in white at the edge of the battle. The Hunter nodded in gratitude, unsure if the woman saw, and let her arrows loose on the remaining men. She turned her arrow to the man holding the Elder. She took a deep breath, focused her aim and shot the arrow. It landed in the man, just as she felt a sharp pain in her side.

The Hunter looked down and saw a long sword sticking out of her side. For a moment, the world seemed to stand still— as if everything ran in slow motion. Her father stepped up behind the man holding the sword and dispatched him. She lost her grip on the tree. As she fell, the world around her went dark.

The Hunter opened her eyes and winced at the pain every breath caused. She was lying on the ground, the Elder, her father and the silver-haired woman all hovering over her. The Elder and silver-haired woman looked at each other and it dawned on her, they were having a conversation. Her father pushed the sweaty hair, still white from the ceremonial powder off her head. The silver-haired woman looked down at her with sadness and the Hunter knew she would not survive.

"Daughter, your warnings saved our tribe but you saved my life. There is nothing that can be done, save the use of magic. Do you wish to be saved in this way?" the Elder asked.

The Hunter thought a moment. She gasped for air and

attempted to calm her anxiety. She looked at the silver-haired woman and shook her head. She didn't want magic to cloud her judgment, she wanted to feel the pain of dying. She looked at her father, seeing unmistakeable pride mixed with sadness. She thought of her siblings and her mother. She thought of her tribe. She met the silver-haired woman's eyes and stared into them with intensity.

"You commune with the Gods?"

The silver-haired woman nodded.

"This is what I want…"

The silver-haired woman and the Elder stood apart from the Hunter and her father. Her father held her head in his lap, gently stroking her hair. It was an odd gesture coming from her otherwise stoic father but she welcomed his touch. She could see the emotions fleeting across the Elder's face. Shortly, he called the council over and they had a quick discussion before all nodding their heads and looking over at her. The Elder and the silver-haired woman returned to her side.

"It shall be done," the Elder said.

"You shall go to sleep and awake as new, young warrior," the silver-haired woman said inside her head.

The Hunter's eyes grew dim and she fell into blackness. It seemed as if moments passed and the Hunter awoke. She was inside the ceremonial circle, next to the fire and in front of the Elder. She stretched out and was amazed to see long wings in place of arms. She no longer felt any pain. She turned her head from side to side, the sharpness of her eyes revealing more detail than she had ever seen. She looked up and the Elder smiled down at her.

"Daughter, you have saved our people. You shall now be the queen of the skies. You shall be the symbol of our people and we shall name you Eagle. You are free now, daughter."

The Hunter, now known as Eagle, flapped her great wings and took to the sky. She circled her tribe members, calling out to them before turning toward the forest. In a clearing, not far from her village, she found a new white tree, shedding its bark, reminiscent of the first time she saw the silver-haired woman crying. She smiled, getting a wave of serenity as she perched among the branches, knowing she'd found her friend. The silver-haired woman had received her reward from the Gods. Eagle's tribe erected statues in her honor and celebrated her naming day as a great festival each summer and revered Birch as their protector for the rest of their days.

A Different Holiday

This isn't how I imagined my first *adult* Thanksgiving. I'd had everything so perfectly planned out, it could have been in a *Southern Living* magazine spread. Mom, Aaron, and I would all be in the kitchen cooking up a storm while Dad and Grandpa kicked back in the recliners in the living room, watching the Macy's Thanksgiving Day parade because it was too early for the Cowboys game. Aaron and I would both have our girlfriends over and they would be sitting in the barstools at the counter gossiping or just teasing us for the frilly aprons Mom insisted we wear, just to embarrass us in front of them. Everyone would be laughing and talking—having a great time and it would just feel right.

A few things from that dream are present today. I'm in the kitchen—but not with my *blood* family. My friend, Katie, and I are doing all the cooking and she is doing her best with winging it because none of the recipes I want to serve are written down—they are all in my head because they are family recipes that have been verbally passed down through generations of my family. I spent years helping Mom in the kitchen and perfecting those recipes. Katie is a great sport though and she really listens when I tell her each step. I don't think I could have completed this meal without her.

We don't have recliners, *yet.* Thomas thought they were too ancient for a modern living room so we only have an odd modular couch thing. A couple of our friends are chatting on them—tacitly ignoring the parade that I insisted must be on. Thomas rolled his eyes good-naturedly and indulged me. He knows how much this day means to me and he is doing his best to keep me happy. I still think he is going to flip his lid when I insist the Cowboys game be on, even while we are eating. He knows the *no electronics during dinner* rule but this is the Cowboys Thanksgiving game and it doesn't matter what time it airs—the television will be on that channel come hell or high water.

We are an odd mishmash of friends with nowhere else to go for Thanksgiving. Our families don't want us with them—some of us have been completely disowned while others of us could not stand to be with a family that doesn't really want us there. Amy is here because she is a black sheep in her family and she can't stand another Thanksgiving listening to her racist and bigoted relatives fighting over things that she is completely against. The six of us, me, Thomas, Amy, Katie, Grant, and Brad, are all happy with the lives we have chosen but each of us misses parts of our previous lives. We've formed our own family, bonded not by blood but by similar stories.

Katie and I are putting the finishing touches on the food when the doorbell rings. Thomas gives me a look and I shrug. We weren't expecting anyone else. We have a silent moment where we agree that we should both answer the door. The previous chatter has gone silent and this moment feels like it is important. I put the oven mitt down and walk over to the door and Thomas joins me. He opens the door and I swear the entire room behind me gasps. No one has ever met Aaron but they've seen his picture hanging prominently on the wall—the two of us smiling back—feeling like we ruled the world.

"Um... hi ...Andrew," Aaron says bashfully, his girlfriend giving a small grin and wave.

"Aaron... why? What?" I sputter, looking around him as if the rest of my family is hiding in the bushes, ready to pop out.

He shakes his head. "It's just us. We can leave if you don't have enough."

"Nonsense, he's cooked enough food for an army," Thomas laughs and ushers Aaron and his girlfriend through the door.

I'm still gobsmacked and everyone can tell, their eyes darting back and forth between me and my brother. Thomas begins making introductions and I turn my back for a moment, trying to quell the tears I fell threatening to come. No, this is not like any Thanksgiving I have ever imagined but it just became even more perfect.

I grew up in the Piney Woods of East Texas. I was born into a very Southern family—the epitome of what most people think of when they talk about us. I would like to say that my family was different but unfortunately, we were probably exactly what people thought of us. My mother's family had been in Texas since before it was a republic. My father's family practically created the south—coming to the shores of Georgia long before the United States of America existed and spreading out from there across the South until they finally reached Texas in the last couple of centuries. Unfortunately, years and years of living in the South, coupled with the Civil War and the aftermath had left my family poor farmers. Sure, you could make a living off farming but it no longer made your rich. Drought years always seem to wipe out the times of plenty. My father had been smart enough to make some small investments here and there in his youth, so we at least had a house and some land that wasn't owned by the bank.

In East Texas, there is just about a church on every corner. Plenty of Christian denominations are represented but the one that wins out in terms of reach and membership is Southern Baptist. My family belongs to this denomination and it isn't for the faint of heart. You have to be incredibly devoted to God in order to belong. We went to Sunday School every Sunday morning, then worship service. Then we went back on Sunday evening for another worship service. On Wednesday evening, we were back at services again. If there was a revival, we went to the service every night of the revival, sometimes for two weeks straight. Vacation Bible School was a pillar of our summers. If there was a holiday, such as Easter or Christmas, we were back at special services. On top of that, we prayed at every meal and every sports game and whenever a need arose, at the whims of Mom and Dad.

The other culture of the south is food. Food is the lifeblood of everyone but it is an art in the South. Did you just have a baby? Here is a casserole. Are you sick or in the hospital? We'll bring a meal over to your family. Of course, birthdays and holidays and just a perfect summer day are all that is needed to spark a barbecue or cookout. Did you have a death in the family? Of course, every family in the neighborhood will keep your loved ones fed for at least the next month. Food is the answer to everything. I once heard someone ask a Southerner why they lived in the South when it got so hot and muggy. The reply was, *"Once you've tasted the food you will understand!"*

Our lives pretty much revolve around these things, God, food, and football. In Texas, football is *the most* important sport...ever. If you are in high school, you are at the football game on Friday nights. Usually, you are either in the band, a cheerleader, or a player. Of course, in the larger schools, one can just be a spectator, but I grew up in a small town in a small high school and my father expected me to play football. *"Andrew, it's a family tradition. I played, your grandad played, his dad played..."* I think I heard that lecture in the womb and my dad didn't even know the gender I would be yet. My brother, Aaron, once mentioned that he wanted to drop out of flag football because it was too hot for practice. I don't think he ever recovered from the stare my father gave him. Truly, if looks could kill, Aaron would be dead. Dad's boys would play football and there would be no discussion.

Aaron and I were pretty good sons. Every child has their moments but I feel like we were well-behaved, god-fearing, model sons. We made our parents proud, whether it was at church, at school, or helping out on the farm. We didn't go out drinking or partying. We didn't cruise the strip with girls in our cars and we definitely didn't spend any time alone with a girl in our rooms or elsewhere. We were just decent, young men.

At least, that was the image I projected. As I started to hit my teens, I started crying into my pillow some nights. I prayed so hard every night for God to give me the strength to be a good man. I was devout in my beliefs and I was torn in half when what I deemed impure thoughts would intrude on a perfectly good day. I was afraid to talk to anyone for fear that I would lose everything I had worked so hard for. I was afraid of the judgment and damnation I knew would follow the revelation. I began pushing Aaron away, once my best friend in the whole world, because I feared I would rub off on him. I tried my hardest to ignore half of myself.

During my freshman year of high school, a new girl came to school. Phoebe was beautiful. She had dark brown hair and green eyes with long natural lashes. The other girls were incredibly jealous the moment Phoebe set foot on our campus. I was immediately enthralled, along with every other boy in our class and even some of the upperclassmen. I lucked out and Phoebe said yes to me. To this day, I don't know why she picked me over everyone else. On the night of our first date, I was so nervous I had to change my undershirt three times. Dad gave me the usual lectures about respecting her and not staying out past curfew. I nodded along as if really listening but if you asked me ten minutes later what Dad said, I don't think I could have repeated it. Aaron teased me all the way to the front door.

To say Phoebe was perfect is an understatement. We dated all through high school and she was always charming and funny. I loved being around her and I can honestly say now, I loved her. At the time, I thought maybe I had been mistaken and I didn't know what love felt like. I've had time to reflect on that more and I do know that I loved her. I once thought of marrying her but I don't regret never asking her. People come in and out of our lives for a reason. I could never thank Phoebe enough for being my first love. Her love gave me the strength I needed to admit to myself who I am.

The first time I really struggled with myself was as a junior in high school. Phoebe and I were still dating. We spent all the time we could together. It was a lucky happenstance that she and I went to the same church. It meant, once I started driving, that she and I could ride to and from church meetings together. We could sit in the same pew. Occasionally, we could even hold hands while the preacher gave his sermon. It all depended on what dress she was wearing and if our hands could be hidden in her skirt. Or if it was hot, I could take my jacket off and drape it on my lap so that I could hold her hand underneath. We were never explicitly told we couldn't hold hands but we also did not want an adult to yell at us or think we might be doing something against the *Good Lord's* approval. Phoebe and I never ran out of things to say to each other. She was smart in a way I never thought I was and she would laugh at me when I called myself a dumb jock. She always believed in me and I should have believed in myself more because, while I wasn't an honor student, my grades were really pretty good.

Phoebe and I were hanging out at the Dairy Palace when the feelings I thought I had mastered came rushing back and nearly knocked the wind out of me. It was a perfect, sunny day and we were eating ice cream. I distinctly remember chomping down on Banana Pudding flavored ice cream—just like a frozen version of my Nana's—when I looked up and saw my classmate, Mark, step onto the patio. I don't know why but at that moment, he looked like the sexiest male alive. I winced, looking around to see if I had spoken allowed, but Phoebe just kept talking to Courtney and no one else seemed to be the wiser. I looked back at Mark and could hardly take my eyes off him as he walked over to us. I was embarrassingly aware of how hyperaroused I was feeling and quickly excused myself to go to the restroom. Once there, I threw cold water on my face and tried to gather my wits. I closed my eyes and prayed right then and there that God would forgive my thoughts.

For months after that day, I could hardly be in the same

room with Mark without having some kind of fantasy of being with him and holding his hand like I held Phoebe's. Each night I would pray for forgiveness. I would plead with God to make it all stop. I had the perfect girlfriend, I was a quarterback on the football team. I was liked in school and in the community. I couldn't be such an abomination. How could I like Phoebe **and** Mark? God was not providing answers and my schoolwork was suffering because of the stress and lack of sleep. Mom and Dad were called in and the school counselor suggested therapy. I resisted with everything I had in me and Dad relented on the condition that I bring my grades back up. I agreed and did everything I could to spend more time with Phoebe and put Mark out of my head.

During senior year, things settled out. If I started having any thoughts about any other person who was not Phoebe, I quickly squashed them by thinking about my Nana in her underwear. It seemed to work pretty well and my grades stayed up. There is so much happening in the senior year anyway, I was kept busier than I had been. I accepted a football scholarship to the University of Texas. Phoebe was going to college on the east coast and we were going to be separated. I understand now what she meant about long-distance relationships but it broke my heart when she broke it off with me. I think she would have stayed if I had asked her but I'd spent so long conflicted about my feelings that I didn't want to weigh her down with my issues. We parted on good terms and she still sends me an occasional email.

College was exciting. Being a Longhorn was something I had hoped for since I was a little boy. Everything was going well when I met Thomas in my sophomore year. Thomas is a very good-looking, smart, and friendly guy. I was studying on the bleachers one day before practice when Thomas sat down next to me and started talking a mile a minute. It was kind of endearing. By now, I had learned to temper my attraction to anyone not of the female species but I had to admit I felt a little zing when we shook hands. Thomas didn't hide who he was and he didn't censor what he said.

"So, I was wondering if you were free tomorrow night. For dinner?" he asked me.

I almost choked on my own spit. I can only imagine whatever look was on my face because his smile dimmed just a little bit but it didn't seem to deter him. He just sat a little taller and waited for my reply.

"I'm not… I don't…"

"Oh, you're not out?"

I shook my head slowly, still trying to comprehend where the conversation was going.

"I'm not gay. At least, I don't think I am…I like women. I had a girlfriend…"

"But?"

"But? There's no but… she left for college. We just split up because of the distance," I tried to explain.

"I see."

Thomas watched me for a moment and then looked out

at the field. I could tell he was clearly thinking about something but couldn't put my finger on what might be going on in his head. He looked over at me and then pulled a pen and paper out of his bag, He quickly wrote down a note and handed it to me with a wink.

"Talk to you later."

He didn't wait for my response, just skipped down the bleachers and walked off across the field. I looked down at the note and saw he'd written his name and phone number with the message *Call me if you need answers...or for that dinner :)*.

I held onto that note for a week. I prayed and prayed God would take the temptation from me but everywhere I turned, I thought I saw Thomas. His bright blue eyes and his midnight hair were haunting my dreams. I did everything I could to get him out of my head and when I couldn't, I finally called the number.

"Hello?"

"Um, hi... it's me."

"Hmm, and does *me* have a name?"

I took the phone from my ear and looked at it as if he could see me giving him the strange look. I nodded my head and rolled my eyes at myself.

"Andrew," I replied.

"Nice to meet you, Andrew. Now, I think you have questions and you've never had anyone to answer them."

"Well... yes?"

"So, dinner?"

I rolled my eyes again and chuckled. He was definitely persistent. I contemplated my answer for a long time while the silence rolled on. It felt like an eternity before I was finally able to brush off my fear of being a sinner and say yes. It was one dinner—I wasn't committing any sins by eating with a person.

I met Thomas at his off-campus apartment. We went out to the local pizza joint and just chatted about what I considered normal things—where we were from, our families, our studies. Nothing about my conflicted feelings about men or my horror at my own shortcomings. When we finished, Thomas invited me upstairs to his apartment. I fought the rising horror and the voice in my head telling me I was going to hell. The truth was, I felt more myself in Thomas' company than in my own. I agreed and we went upstairs. Thomas offered me a drink and I accepted. I sat awkwardly on his couch while he fetched the drink.

"You can relax, I'm not going to bite."

I jumped at the sudden intrusion to my thoughts. He laughed and that helped relax me a little as it gave me the chance to laugh at myself. He sat next to me and waited for me to speak. I got uncomfortable again and started bouncing my leg—a nervous trait I had picked up from Dad's side of the family. Thomas reached out and put a hand on me. The jolt of arousal sending my brain in a tailspin. I jumped back and Thomas jumped up.

"I'm so sorry to startle you," he apologized.

"No, no... I'm just not used to... I don't know what

came over me," I stammered.

We both sat back down and my leg started bouncing again but this time I checked it and made it stop. I took a quick gulp of my drink and determined to ask him the real question swirling around in my brain since that day in the bleachers. I closed my eyes, took a huge breath in and then let it out.

"What's wrong with me?" I blurted.

Thomas laughed. "Come again?"

"What's wrong with me? I like women—they are beautiful—and yet..."

"You also like men?"

"Sometimes... not all of them... but some are... very attractive."

Thomas nodded. "You're bisexual."

"That's impossible. It goes against nature and God's plan."

"And yet, you are. It's natural, just not seen that way in certain religions."

I stood up and brushed a hand through my hair. I couldn't believe what he was telling me. It was just too much for me to process. I was devout in my faith and I followed God's teachings. Why was I being punished? Thomas got up and pulled a little folder out of a drawer. He handed it to me and I took it.

"This will help explain things. It has some resources for you. Once you've gotten some more answers, you know where I am. I would very much like to date you but only if you are ready."

"So, you are bisexual, too?"

Thomas shook his head. "Oh, no, I am as gay as they come but I think you are really attractive and I would like to get to know you better."

I left Thomas' apartment more confused than I had ever been. I took his folder and looked at all his resources. There was a number for a hotline and I called it and spoke to someone on the phone who walked me through what was happening and gave me a referral to a therapist that *"won't judge you"*. I made an appointment to see the therapist and then several follow-up appointments after that one.

Eventually, Thomas and I began dating. I never told anyone in my family about him because I was too afraid of their judgment. I felt right with Thomas like I had felt with Phoebe. We just seemed to fit. He and I became closer and closer and by my senior year in college, we had become roommates and lovers and I had dreams of marrying him. The only problem was, the more I dreamed, the more the specter of my family's judgment loomed over me. It was Thanksgiving of that last year that I decided to invite Thomas to come home with me. He was overjoyed that he would be meeting my family and I was terrified. He tried to calm my nerves but nothing really helped.

Thomas got a usual Southern welcome from everyone. I hadn't told them he was my significant other. Mom still thought I was carrying a torch for Phoebe and just hadn't *found the right girl*. Thomas gave me a look over her head, which I tried to ignore but I am sure Aaron caught on to the tension long before it boiled over. I should have known staying at our house was going to amount to a disaster but I was so tense that I did not heed the warning signs.

We had stayed up late the night before playing games with my brother and his girlfriend. Thomas and I had argued a bit when we went to bed because Mom had made two separate beds. Thomas was angry that I still had not told them we were together and I kept begging for more time. Thomas had good reason to be upset. If I could not admit I loved him to my family, then our relationship was doomed. I couldn't see a way out of the problem. I wanted to console him and reassure him so we sat on my bed and ended up falling asleep. Mom, being the early bird, came in to wake me before the alarm and found us in bed together. That is when the poop hit the fan.

"Get out of my house, right now," she demanded, swatting at Thomas.

"What's going on in here?" Dad came rushing in.

"This filth was draping himself around Andrew. We don't allow *faggots* in our home. God is always watching!" Mom spewed her hatred at Thomas.

Thomas quickly got dressed, looking helplessly between my parents and me. Aaron came into the door frame and his eyes widened at the scene. Then, he turned around, ushering his girlfriend back down the hallway.

"Andrew, what is the meaning of this?" my father demanded.

I was frozen to the spot. Thomas was pleading with me

with his eyes and my mother was staring daggers at him. She turned her gaze to me as if I was a hurt puppy and she had to protect me. It was that pitiful stare and the dejected expression coming across Thomas' features that gave me the courage for what happened next.

"Thomas and I are in love and I want to marry him," I replied, a little too loudly.

My mother's face drained of all color and my dad's turned red. They looked at each other, then at Thomas, and finally at me. Suddenly, the realization of what I had said hit them and they both seemed to explode at the same time.

"Both of you out of my house, now!" Dad yelled.

"Damn you to hell, son. God will judge you," my mother added.

Thomas and I gathered what we could while my parents stared daggers at us. I let Thomas go out first and then I followed him into the hall. I gathered up our coats and was about to follow Thomas out of the house when my dad put an arm in front of me to stop me.

"Repent now, boy. If you walk out that door, you are dead to us," he warned.

I looked up and saw Aaron at the end of the hallway. I tried to beg for him to intervene but he just shook his head sadly and went into his room. My mom threw herself down on her knees and began praying for my soul and begging God for answers on where she went wrong. I looked out at Thomas in the driveway and then back at my father.

"Bye, Dad."

I was given a choice between the family of my birth or the love of my life. I chose the love of my life. I still love my mother and father, my grandparents, and my brother but I had to follow my heart. I had to give up a piece of myself in order to discover a new piece.

That disastrous Thanksgiving, we ate dinner at the local Waffle House before heading back to our apartment. Luckily, I had saved enough to finish paying off my senior year college dues because my father withdrew the final payment. Just after Christmas, I got a few boxes delivered by a moving company and a letter from my parents. They had sent me every last thing I owned at their house and informed me I was to never contact them again.

It had been two years since that Thanksgiving and this year, Thomas was determined not to let me mope through another holiday without my *traditions*. He'd arranged to have all the food I needed to cook our traditional holiday meal, as well as Katie to help me cook it. Thomas is a horrible cook. I think the man could burn water. He also asked our friends to come over so our table would not be laden with food and no one to eat it. He doesn't understand why I like a full house on the holidays but he knows it is just the *Southern* in me.

Thomas comes over and rouses me from my musings. I smile at him and he nods towards the kitchen, where Aaron and Katie have restarted the final preparations. He squeezes my shoulder and gathers our friends to start setting the table. I go into the kitchen and my brother tosses the oven mitt at me like old times. We settle into the routine fairly quickly and in no time at all, the table is laden with food. We have turkey, ham, sweet potatoes, dressing, green pea salad, green beans, rolls, gravy, pumpkin pie, pecan pie, and sweet potato pie. Thomas was right about having enough to feed an army. Thomas seats everyone, putting my brother at the opposite end of the table.

My brother smiles and winks at me, then rises and clears his throat. I groan and hope for the best. It was always my brother's fondest wish to embarrass me whenever he could and now I can only hope he is civil in whatever he says.

"Andrew, Sadie and I are very happy you welcomed us to this dinner. It hasn't been the same without you. Several years ago, I should have stood by you when Mom and Dad kicked you out of the family. I'm sorry about that and I'm sorry for the distance between us since then. I hope we can repair our brotherly bond. Thomas, I am looking forward to getting to know my brother-in-law. Here's to family!"

Everyone raises their glasses and clinks them together. Thomas grabs my hand under the table and squeezes and I am once again left feeling like I am about to cry. Someone asks about the marshmallows on top of the yams and Aaron launches into a diatribe on the merits of different toppings for the dish. Everyone else starts little conversations and Thomas leans over and gives me a peck on the cheek before grabbing some ham and passing it to Amy beside him.

I look around at my new family and parts of my original one and I feel a sense of peace for the first time in years. Learning I was bisexual and coming to grips with it may have changed some things but it didn't take away who I am as a person. I can still be the Southern gentleman with my culture of kindness and food and also be the loving husband to Thomas.

WAILING

We aren't speaking to each other. I watch you sitting on the other side of the table, glaring down into your mug as if it holds the answer to all our problems. The only indication you are even aware of your surroundings is the slight flinch when the sound of wailing starts up again. It's been like this for days. We sit at the table and you frown and we don't talk.

I look at you now, really concentrating on the details of your face. Your hair is graying at the temples and in the stubble on your cheeks and chin. I don't remember when that started to happen. Do I look just as old and tired? You are still the most handsome man I have ever known but the weariness makes your face look ashen. The bruising under your eyes has become a little too dark and it makes me feel like you are a shadow of the man I married. You haven't looked at me in days but I can imagine the dullness of your once bright blue eyes. I could get lost in those eyes forever and you would laugh at me when we were young and you caught me staring.

I try to remember the last time we were happy. I look around the small cabin and remember all the good times we have spent here. It used to be the most treasured place in the world to me. Now, it is a mess. Dirty mugs sit in and next to the sink. The couch is covered in tangled blankets and the pillow has fallen to the floor. It could use a good dusting and a vacuum. I start to say these things but the wailing just seems to get louder and you sigh, which distracts me as I look back at you and watch you run a shaky hand through your hair. It's a tell, your way of showing me your displeasure without actually saying anything.

The wind kicks up, carrying the wails to our ears even faster. I clamp my hands over my ears, so tired of the sounds. It has to be a banshee. I wince at that thought as if I've betrayed your trust just by believing in the superstition in my head. I've always believed in the magic of the old land—something you fought with me about time and again. *Be rational* you would say in the most disgusted tone. It was the only thing we ever fought about. I shake my head. I don't want to think of the bad things. I want to remember the good. I want to fix this.

When you asked me to marry you, I felt like I was the luckiest girl in all of the world. You cocked an eyebrow when I told you what I wanted for a honeymoon. I don't think you really believed me at the time. You loved me—no, you *love* me because I can't bear it if you no longer do.

"Do you really want to spend our honeymoon driving around a wet island?" you'd asked.

"Yep! It's magical and beautiful and green."

You'd laughed at that. Then you studied me as if I had two heads and made a face at me to make me laugh. You kissed me breathless and then pulled back to look deep into my eyes.

"Our wedding is in March. It's going to be raining. You hate the rain."

I shrugged, "It's Ireland. It's magic rain."

You'd rolled your eyes at that, our argument on the topic not reaching the levels it did in later years when the magic of being a newlywed wears off and all the things you once hid come into the light. In the end, I got my wish and we came to Ireland in March in the bitterest winter storm the island had seen in a hundred years.

We took it all in stride. We visited all the places I'd always wanted to see. We stopped and ate at little pubs where we were the outcasts and we met interesting and lovely people. The land really is magical, if not for the beauty of it, but also for its people and their welcoming ways. It was the best vacation I had ever had, despite the bitter cold and rainier-than-normal weather, and it almost went off without a hitch.

We were traveling through the Gap of Dunloe in the late evening. The road was a one-lane, winding thing. It was a good thing the car was tiny as well. We'd laughed when we first rented it because you practically had to bend at the waist to get in and then getting out proved an even bigger problem. The cars are definitely not as spacious as the ones we are used to in America. Anyway, there were sheep on either side of the road, as usual and I wanted to stop and take a picture of them. The sheep were bleating at us and coming towards me and you just kept reminding me to get in the car. There was a baby and I wanted a picture of it. I finally did get that picture but then when I showed it to you, the flash had made all of the sheep look like they had menacing, glowing eyes. You laughed it off but I could see it disturbed you just a little.

Anyway, we got through the Gap and were on the opposite side of where our bed and breakfast was located. I wanted to continue along—always moving forward instead of going backward. You let me be crazy like that sometimes and reluctantly agreed to let me keep driving forward. It gets dark fast in the winter in Ireland and we found out fairly quickly that the headlights were our only source of illumination in the dark countryside. I'd seen a map and figured that we would eventually find our way back to civilization but I didn't know the exact way.

When you heard me tell you that, you started freaking out. Did we have any food in the car? How would we stay warm? What if we broke down?

As if on cue, the car started to sputter and you started groaning and fretting. Neither of us is a mechanic and we were in the middle of the darkened Irish countryside with no flashlight. I let the car coast as far as I could before pulling of the side as close to the stone wall as possible. The Irish roads are like that, no curbs, just stone walls lining the path. I thought it was to keep the sheep in at first, but a driver is most likely to encounter sheep in the road despite the walls. It's just another charming quirk of the country. You got out and looked under the hood, then scanned the road as if hoping a gas station would pop out of nowhere to rescue us. I pulled my jacket tighter around me and hopped up on the stone wall.

"There, it's a house," I called down to you.
"How far?"
I shrugged and then laughed at myself, knowing you couldn't see it in the dark.
"Not too far, I guess. It's up ahead on the road. I think..."

You checked the car and made sure we locked it up. You stopped me and zipped up my coat, always worried that I would catch a cold in the damp just like I did at home every time we got a winter storm. I think your pockets were stuffed with more things than I have ever seen you carry—a road flare, an umbrella, the half-drunk bottle of water you found under the seat, a bag of chips that were probably all crumbs by now. I laughed at you and you just raised your eyebrow to me and held out a hand.

I took your hand and we walked down the dark road. The house had seemed much closer when I was standing on the wall next to a car with headlights. In the dark, everything seemed much closer and more spooky. We walked in silence and you chuckled nervously when I jumped at a sound but you squeezed my hand and then put your arm around me. The unknown is often the thing people fear the most and I think it was no exception to us.

When we finally made it to the cottage, the owner and his wife were nothing short of lifesavers. They told us there was nothing that could be done about the car until the morning and they fed us tea and *biscuits*. It turned out, they had another cottage they rented out in the summer and offered it to us for the night. They drove us the short distance to the little place and made sure we were comfortable. I think it was the happiest night we ever spent together. We cuddled together for warmth, although the little peat fire did prove useful once it had been burning for a few hours. The smell that greeted us from the peat the next morning was heavenly. I smiled at you and you kissed me with the sun streaming in through the window.

"Let's never leave."

I was surprised to hear you say those words. We had a schedule to keep and you'd always kept us moving. It made my heart soar to hear those words. To hear that you could be content with me in one place. Perhaps I had feared you would never be completely happy with me—even though we were now married.

"We could buy this place and move here," I replied *overeagerly.*

It was like throwing cold water on you. You got up and we got dressed. I kept stealing little glances at you but I had doused our moment and it was lost to me forever. Our saviors plied us with breakfast, helped us call a tow and then waited with us while politely discussing our travels until it arrived. You talked with the owner but he refused payment and so we went on our way and continued the last of our trip.

You honestly surprised me when we returned to that same cabin the next March. I remember you keeping it a secret until we were at the airport and you could no longer hide the destination. The moment it was revealed, I couldn't contain the squeals of excitement and you turned red, scratching behind your ear and looking like you wished the floor would swallow you up whole. You were never used to so much attention.

After that year, it became a tradition for us to go to the cottage for a few weeks every March. It was our happy place. We would take long strolls through the fields. You'd spot me while I tried to balance as I walked along the stone walls and then I would fall dramatically into your arms when I was tired of the effort. You'd pick flowers and weave them into my hair as we sat next to the little stream, wishing it wasn't too cold to dip our toes into the crystal-clear water. I'd once suggested maybe we should start visiting in the summer months but you had gasped and gone on a lecture about *tradition.*

We were happy. I don't quite remember when we stopped being happy. The last trip I remember in detail started out like every other trip. We'd flown into Dublin just before St. Patrick's Day. Normally, you would have avoided a party of that magnitude like it was the plague. However, I had convinced you to at least experience it this once and the dates lined up so we took the plunge. Dublin was absolutely spectacular. There is really nothing that beats being with the Irish on their holiday. We drank and laughed and reveled. We stayed up much later than we had ever done before and we overslept the next day with heavy hangovers. *Being* Irish for one day of the year was more than enough, despite the enjoyment.

We drove to our little cottage, newly cleaned and spruced up. The little peat fire was already warming up the main room and a welcoming plate of homemade bread was sitting on the table. Irish hospitality lacks for nothing. I was intrigued by the little note left by the plate and took it up, reading aloud.

Fáilte! If you need anything, you know where to find us. I baked this bread fresh for the holidays and hoped it might take off the edge until your supper. Be aware, the faeries have built up a new ring near the oak on the edge of your field. Best not to disturb them. May luck be with you.

You rolled your eyes when I looked up and I shrugged, grinning.

"What?"

"It seems they would give up that nonsense in this day and age."

I sighed, "It's part of the magic."

"It's a gimmick," you groused.

I shrugged and watched you take our things into the bedroom. I didn't want to cause another argument on the subject. I'd learned you were set in your black-and-white ways. It is just a part of who you are and I can respect it, even if I disagree with it. I've pointed out countless times my feelings—the belief in magic doesn't cause any harm and you've always countered with some rational objection. It isn't anything we are likely to ever change each other's minds about so we just try to agree to disagree.

The intrigue of a fairy ring would not stop swimming around in my mind. I'd visited all the ancient and mystical places in Ireland but I wanted to feel closer to the magic of it. I'd listened raptly to people talking on videos on the internet and read many a novel on the subject. I was fascinated by the prospects of another world just beyond our reach. A world that knew of us but stayed hidden for obvious reasons. It seemed within my grasp when I was in the little cottage in the Irish countryside.

I begged you to go out with me that morning. I wanted to just look at the faery ring. The mention of it made you scoff and turn me down. You made some excuse about needing to check on something in town and I got mad at you, screaming at you for the first time ever in our little haven. We fought, the most we had ever fought before and it ended when you stomped out the door, getting awkwardly into the little car and driving away. I cried for who knows how long and then stubbornly pulled on my rain boots and grabbed an umbrella, heading out into the cold to make my visit.

With every step, I argued with you in my head. I finally found the little ring of mushrooms and plopped down next to it. I spilled all my worries out, talking to that faery ring as if the faeries themselves hung onto my every word. I was sure they could relate to my woes. The old ways had died off long ago and the newer generations had a healthy dose of skepticism. Perhaps the faeries felt neglected.

I don't know why I cling to my stubborn belief in magic. I had always been enraptured with the idea of magic and princesses and *somewhere else.* My childhood had not been a pleasant one and escaping into a fantasy world was the only thing that kept me sane. I could hear your rebuttal about my possible insanity. Even though it was usually meant as a joke, somehow hearing you say it in my head turned it into something ugly. I started crying again. I hated that we were fighting. No matter our differences, you are my best friend and I love you. I will always love you.

Somehow, I got it into my head that it was a good idea to climb the oak tree, in the rain, with heavy rainboots on. I try to get a foothold a few times and my foot slips off each time. I'm still crying and it doesn't make it easier because each new slip is an insult to my pride and it makes the tears come faster. I finally get what I think is a good foothold with the first foot and lift myself using the branch to place my second foot. That is when it happens. I fall off the tree in a heap, crushing the faery ring in the process.

It takes me a moment to catch my breath. I silently take stock of my body, trying to feel if I have broken anything. The rain starts falling softly on my face and forces me to sit up before I drown. I laugh a little to myself. It would be just like me to drown from a drizzle. You would have thought it apropos. I frown at that, hoping that by the time I return to the cottage, you will have cooled off and come back to me. Patience in that regard has never failed me before and you always come back with an apology and a kiss that can make me forget why we argued in the first place.

I stood up and began brushing myself off when it caught my eye. I looked down and felt horror like I have never felt in my life. At my feet lie the remains of the faery ring, the little mushrooms crushed and some lying next to their stalks where I decapitated them in my fall. My heart started beating loudly in my ears and I dropped to my knees, the sobs returning. I gingerly picked up one of the mushrooms and began apologizing profusely to the unseen faeries. I had destroyed their ring and now I had brought ruin and destruction upon us. You would have been equal parts horrified at my irrational behavior and consoling at my despair. I could hear you in my head again—*It's just a superstition.*

It wouldn't matter how much I argued with you on the

topic, you would not have believed anything I said, chalking it up to nonsense and trying to distract me from my concerns. You don't believe in fate or destiny. You've always told me we make our own and no one can determine yours. You don't avoid superstitious things like other people. To you, they are just the old ways of scaring children into behaving as they should and keeping adults under some unseen control. To me, however, it doesn't hurt to avoid upsetting the natural order of things and having a healthy dose of reverence to the old beliefs. Maybe our ancestors just told stories to protect themselves and their children from the outside world but maybe there were also grains of truth in those stories.

Sheep bleating in the nearby field roused me to my senses and I looked around, realizing it was beginning to get very late and the sun would set soon. Once the sun was set, the darkness would surround me in no time. I hadn't thought to bring a flashlight and the trek back across the fields would not be quick in the dark. I looked down at the destroyed faery ring one last time, once again making my apologies, and then surveyed my surroundings. I got the bright idea of taking a shortcut, making my way towards the road and deciding to follow it home instead of picking my way through the fields.

By the time I reached the road, the rain had become a downpour and I could barely see a hand in front of my face. The umbrella did little to protect me from the onslaught and the road was beginning to flood in a few places. I decided to climb up onto the wall and try to balance on it as I continued towards the cottage. You'd always laughed at how bad my balance was and warned me not to try walking on the wall without a spotter. I'd stuck my tongue out at you the last time. You'd laughed and I remember how much I loved that laugh. My heart was aching for our fight to be over and yet, I knew, I had to tell you what I had done to the faery ring and my fear of their reprisal. It was a double-edged sword, wanting your comfort for something I knew would only increase your displeasure.

I saw the headlights of a car in the distance, coming towards me and I decided maybe I could ask the driver for a ride home. I pondered a way to get the driver's attention and waited until they were near before attempting to open and shut my bright green umbrella in a gesturing fashion. That was when the wind hit and knocked me into the road. I only remember the fleeting feeling of flying and then the rest went dark.

The wailing picks up in volume again and I jump and look up at you when you slam your fist into the wall of the cottage. You lean your head against the wall and I can tell you are sobbing when I see your back trembling. I want to go to you but I am rooted in my chair. I watch you turn and my heart hurts to see the tears streaming down your face. You look straight through me, the despair and heartache plainly written on your features as you slide down the wall and drop your head into your hands. The wailing mixes with your gulping sobs in an odd chorus of grief. I don't know how much more I can watch of your pain. I struggle to break free of the invisible holds keeping me in my chair and silent. I can't let you suffer. I would give anything to see you laugh again.

Talk to me I scream it in my head, over and over again, trying to break through to you. Finally, you look up, straight at me as if seeing me for the first time in ages. I can see the shock on your face the moment your eyes lock with mine. I don't understand it and the moment fades as you look around the room, as if trying to find me again. The wailing had stopped in that instance but now it starts even louder. An odd look crosses your features and you stop searching. You seem to be having a silent conversation with yourself and I long to be a part of it. I can tell when you've made a decision. A strangely calm resolve crosses your features. It scares me.

I watch you gather up your things and walk out of the cottage. I don't follow and I don't understand why. I try to tell myself it is because we aren't speaking. We haven't spoken in so long and I don't remember why we stopped. I am helpless to break the impasse, the unseen force continuing to force me in my place and the wailing increasing to unbearable volumes. I try to scream to the rafters but the wailing drowns me out. I don't know how long I continue struggling with myself and pleading for it to end. I can't live like this anymore. I can't let us grow apart and it be all my fault for my stupid beliefs in magic. Magic was supposed to be joyful, not sorrowful. I berate myself for being so foolish and lash out at myself, rocking back and forth in my chair with my hands over my ears in an attempt to drown out the wailing and cling to what little sanity I have left.

I am startled by a hand on my shoulder and nearly fall of

the chair. Suddenly, as if you'd never left, you kneel in front of me, taking my hands and wiping my cheeks dry with your thumbs. You smile at me, one full of love and sadness.

"You can stop now, my love," you say to me.

"I don't…"

I'm confused, shaking my head at the first words he has spoken to me in a very long time. Then I realize what has happened. The wailing has stopped. I hold my breath, waiting for it to begin again and it seems you do as well. The patience in your eyes speaks volumes and for once I feel truly understood. We wait like that for an eternity before you squeeze my hands. I look down at you and smile with trepidation. I don't understand what has happened to make you look at me with such love again but I don't really care. As if understanding my needs, you lean up and kiss me, pouring out all of your pent up emotions. It's the best kiss we have ever shared. Reluctantly, I pull away and rest my forehead against yours. I wait for your eyes to open and meet mine before I ask the question burning in my head.

"How… how did you make it stop?"

"It was you, love. You could have made it stop but you didn't, so I helped you," you explain.

"I don't understand."

"Come with me."

You take my hand and we go out of the little cottage. It is cold, but I don't seem to feel it anymore. We walk through the fields towards the home of the owners of our little cottage. It is bustling with activity. Children are playing a game in the yard and they pay us no mind as we pass them and go inside. Once there, I notice adults milling about in various hushed conversations. The owner's wife is standing to one side, sniffling into her handkerchief while the woman who runs the grocery consoles her and conceals a sniffle of her own. I look at you, still not understanding and you just smile at me and lead me to a couple of empty chairs. A woman near us shudders, crosses herself and moves to a different part of the room. I am about to call her out for her uncharacteristic rudeness when you put a hand in mine and squeeze.

We sit in the chairs and I am still confused but unwillingly to question your motivations. I just got you back and I am loathed to rock the boat and cause a scene that would embarrass you and push you away again. Everyone in the room avoids our little corner and I can observe them with unfettered curiosity. The owner's wife passes around a plate of biscuits and politely chats with her guests. All of her guests except us, who continue to cross themselves at periodic intervals in their conversations. I finally pick up on one of them.

"It's a tragedy, really, but probably for the best," a man says to the owner's wife.

"Yes, poor dears. Perhaps he would have recovered if not for the banshee. The faery folk themselves must have cursed her. I warned them about the faery ring but that young lady was wild and impulsive."

I look at you in horror, hoping you haven't heard them but you are staring at me with such intensity. Your eyes hold knowledge that I long to unravel and yet you aren't speaking again. I can see the pleading in them for understanding but I can't seem to grasp the point they are trying to make.

"I'm lost, help me," I beseech.

"You have to remember. I can't make you do it."

I want to run from the cottage, the air suddenly feeling stale and stuffy. I stand up and a draft blows through the room, all in attendance crossing themselves in unison. It is too much for me and I push past everyone, running outside. My head hurts and I feel like I am going to vomit. I know the moment you join me, I can feel your warmth. You make everything around me seem a little brighter.

"We can be together again if you only remember."

I look up into your eyes, full of love and trust. You believe in me. I am searching for the answers but I only see your patience. I close my eyes, hunting through my memories, trying to find the answer to the puzzle.

When did we stop speaking? When did we last fight? My brain reminds me of the fight about the faery ring and I scoff at it. Surely we'd fought since then. Our marriage was never perfect but we fought and made up dozens and dozens of time. What was the last thing we fought about? The more I try to remember, the more I only remember the faery ring. I remember the fall from the wall and then... nothing.

I start backing away from you, my hands held up in defense and trying to ignore the conclusion my brain wants me to believe. I remember the car and falling from the wall and then

I remember your despair. The wailing, constant and dreadful. *How did you get so gray?*

"That's it, my love. Remembering will set us free," you comfort me.

I don't want to remember this horror. I don't want any of it to be true. I always said I believed in magic and superstitions but it is too much for me to realize it might not have been a false belief. Not if it means you are here with me. If you are here with me, then all hope is lost. I shake my head at you, denying the facts flooding into my brain. You only come closer, gathering me in your arms. I almost succumb to you but I need the answer to the last piece of this twisted puzzle.

"What did you do?" I ask with horror.

You smile sadly and shrug. "I heard you in the cottage, you were screaming at me to talk to you."

"That was in my head!"

"I heard you, my love. Every March for the past five years, I have heard you. I couldn't bear to hear your misery any longer. I did what was needed so we could be together again."

"That... wailing..."

"It was my own personal banshee."

I gasp. All the memories come flooding into me at once and I see clearly the misery I have subjected upon you. I am mortified but you just take my hands again. You nod at me and I realize at that moment just what it means for you to be here, talking with me. Tears start sliding down my cheeks and you kiss them away.

"I love you and we are together. No more crying," you remind me.

I nod and you kiss my forehead. You smile at me the way that melts my heart, if I still had a beating one, and you hold out your hand. I take it and we walk back across the field to whatever the future may hold for our spirits.

Made Me Myself

I have a reputation. Not the kind that generally accompanies that statement but a reputation nonetheless. I am direct and honest. Always. This quality either wins me friends or gets me labeled as rude and insensitive. It isn't that I don't believe in being nice or treating situations delicately—it is just that I think our society has just become too politically correct. Everyone has a chip on their shoulder about everything and the slightest thing sends people into a rant of offense. I feel the world is much better served if everyone says exactly what they mean. No one has to worry if someone is being honest—they would know that what they were getting was the truth. One of the best movies surrounding this was called *The Invention of Lying*, starring Ricky Gervais. I loved that movie because in the beginning, no one had any clue what lying even was or how to do it. But I digress. I haven't always been this open, direct person. In fact, I have been this way for only one quarter of my life.

Growing up, I was the most introverted introvert you would ever meet. My nose was usually stuck in a book. I had absolutely no social life and not much of a desire to have one either. I was a huge nerd and pretty socially outcast in my small, rural town. The other kids didn't really like me because I wouldn't let them cheat off me—even then I held to my standard of good morals. My family life didn't help, as my mother could not stand that I was smart and my stepfather was not the best father figure. I had a ton of fun with my brother but he had friends and was two grades behind me so I became a persona non grata once he became more social. I don't regret any of this as I was able to transport myself to many worlds and have tons of adventures through reading. However, I was a doormat. I let everyone pretty much tell me how I should act and, being Southern, I desperately tried to conform to the standards of a lady. I was told that I should be a good girl and sit primly on the couch in my nice holiday dresses while my brother was allowed to be a child. As I got older, I was being groomed to be a good wife and mother, subservient to my husband and family. This was in spite of the fact that, at the time, I didn't want to even be a mother for fear that I would end up like my own—something I did not wish for my child.

Fast forward to my second marriage. I am somewhat embarrassed to admit I have been married twice before my current marriage, but you know what they say—third time's the charm. I didn't learn my lesson the first time and so, the second time, I was in yet another abusive relationship. My mother, the only person I had to turn to at the time, felt like it was all my fault that I had not stayed in my first marriage. She had told me that it was my duty to be a good wife, even when abused. So I was desperately trying to prove that I was a good Christian and a good wife by trying to save my second marriage. It had been a mistake from the very first day to have married my second husband. He never tired of making me feel guilty for my weight—often calling me fat. He was super controlling and held reign over our finances, to the point where I had an allowance that I was allowed to spend, that often included my food and personal care items.

During this marriage, I had started wanting to have children. I think mortality was beginning to dawn on me and I couldn't imagine not having a child to both carry on my genes and comfort me when I got old. It was a pretty naive outlook at the time as I now know that children are so much more life-changing than I could have thought possible. My second husband had promised me that if I was just a *good girl* and did everything the way he had planned, then when we got through the plan, I could quit work and become a full-time mom. The time had finally come for my part and I had gotten pregnant. Sadly, at the time, I did not know that I could not carry a child to term without medical help. So my joyous moment of triumph became one of the worst times in my life. I had a miscarriage and on my husband's birthday. He spent the entire time in the ER playing a video game and later yelled at me for having the nerve to miscarry on his birthday. Yet, I still tried to save my marriage. This happened in May.

That same weekend, I found out that not only was he sleeping with another woman, he was sleeping with several, one who was a friend. However, I still believed that things could change. I was an optimist, even then. I stuck it out the entire summer. The final straw came in September.

I was sitting in the floor of the closet of the beautiful nursery I had made for my baby. Yes, I was a little obsessed. I had hand sewn everything in that room, the baby blanket, the crib bumpers, the curtains. I had painstakingly painted the walls in Classic Winnie-the-Pooh yellow. The soft yellow of the original bear, not the Disney version. There was a rocking chair, again with hand sew cushions, waiting for me to rock my precious child to sleep. Every single thing in that room made the perfect nursery. Yet, there I was, sobbing uncontrollably on the floor of the closet. I still remember the scratchiness of the carpet against my cheek as I lay down in a fetal position. It was a stinging pain because the tears mixed with the burn marks from the spots where I had rubbed too hard. It felt like tiny needles scratching away at the apple of my cheek. I felt like I wanted to die. Since that day, I have had a true night where I felt death would be better than the pain, but at this particular moment in my life, I felt like my life was completely over.

My husband had just stormed off, taking his stupid gaming console with him. I guess it was better than the Christmas Eve night he had stormed off and gone to a strip club but it still hurt me that he would rather play games than solve our problems. To make matters worse, he had called his best friend—a woman he had known since college—to have her intervene in our private lives. This was the ultimate embarrassment for me. I may be direct and honest but, even now, I feel like there are some things that should remain within the immediate family. This man blamed me for everything. We had tried counseling and he flat out told the counselor—"I don't know why we are here, this is all her fault." He had no interest in anyone but himself. So here I was, being berated by the friend, who of course had taken his side. He hadn't told her he was sleeping around, or maybe he had, and she was blaming me for not keeping it together and patching things up. It finally became too much and against all the manners in my body, I hung up the phone and began sobbing.

I lay on that floor crying for several hours. Every time it would subside, a fresh new thought of loss or inadequacy would cause it to start all over again. I could barely breathe because my nose was so clogged up that I couldn't clear it and it made smelling anything impossible. I clung to the little stuffed Winnie-the-Pooh as if it were the child I had lost. My mouth was full of salt and the unpleasant taste of sinus drainage. It made me want to vomit but I did not get up from that floor. The only thing I could see was the absolute perfection of my beautiful nursery laughing at me for being such an utter failure. It was so delightful and cheery and I was misery personified. I stared at every single thing in that nursery, giving each item the chance to be mourned. Each item brought fresh tears as I remembered all of the hard work and planning that went into them. Each one had its own special story, from picking out the fabric to ripping out stitches that had been sewn wrong to finishing touches.

Finally, I had cried all I could and the dry heaving had subsided. I never intended to throw up in that nursery and I wasn't about to start now, even though my stomach felt like it had rocks in it, most likely from all the snot I probably swallowed. I lay on the floor for a while longer, finally attuned to the quiet in the house. The cats came in and checked on me and they ended up perching near me, almost as if on suicide watch. It didn't ever cross my mind that night, so they had nothing to worry about but it was nice to know that some living thing was on my side because at that time I felt like the entire world was against me. I lay there listening to every single sound, wondering if he was ever coming back.

The longer I lay there, the angrier I got. Not just at him but also at my mother, at God, at my other family members. I had been the good girl my entire life. I had bent over backwards to make other people happy. To prove that I was worthy of love. I had prayed every day and gone to church and helped every single person I came across. I listened to people and I comforted them. I had patiently waited for it to be my turn to have the things I wanted in life. And yet, when it came to be my turn, I was rewarded with betrayal and heartache. I never got the acceptance I had tried so hard to get from my mother. She never saw the good things I did. She only cared if I was married and a servant to my husband. God had never done anything for me, no matter how hard I tried to think otherwise. The only things I had ever gotten, I worked hard for and earned myself. My family had never saved me from the abusive childhood that I had lived. My husband didn't care about me, he only cared to have someone to bully.

By this time, I was entirely livid. I feel like I could finally see clearly and what I saw was very unpleasant. I had gotten out of my first marriage after realizing that I was way too smart to be dating a cocaine addict who stole money and hit walls next to my head. Somewhere along the way to my second marriage, I had forgotten that to be married was to have a partner, not be a servant. Now, I remembered that I was a smart woman and that I was worthy of being treated as an equal. I did not need to be defined by any relationship. I didn't have to fit into the mold my upbringing was trying to thrust on me. I could be a strong, independent woman. I didn't need to be the stepping stone lifting other people to their dreams while I was stuck underfoot. I could set my own goals and be my own person. I finally understood that it didn't matter what anyone else thought of me. It only mattered what I thought of myself and I didn't think I had been doing a very good job of liking myself.

I got up of the floor. I went and took a very hot bubble bath, just because I could. Then, I went back to the nursery and shut the door. I began making plans. My husband eventually came home that night and I was forced to endure him in the bed, because he never slept on the couch. Little did he know, that would not be a problem soon. I waited a few days until he went to visit his parents and then I started my plans. I sold every single thing in that nursery and I kept the money. I opened up my own checking accounts and I moved the money that I had earned to those accounts. I went to the car dealership and traded in my expensive car for a cheaper one. I went apartment hunting and put in an application for an apartment. Finally, I consulted a lawyer. When my husband called to talk to me, I told him I wanted a divorce. He of course tried to talk me out of it and then he started freezing accounts so I could not use our joint accounts. In the end, he was advised to split everything with me equally by a lawyer and that was fine with me. He was terrified I would make him pay alimony, since he made more money. I went with the easier route and just did the split.

By February of the next year, I was in the process of moving back to Texas. I had gone to visit my brother and my infant nephew. It was a joy to see my nephew and did not hurt as much as I thought it would. My brother and I got to spend some quality time together, something that I had sorely missed during my brother's first marriage where he too had been subjected to an abusive spouse. I guess even he was affected by our mother's views on marriage. Anyway, my brother and I were driving along the interstate somewhere in Northeast Texas. I was staring at all the land passing by and soaking in the happiness I felt from being back in my home state.

We had been chatting amiably when my brother said, "Can I ask you something?"

"Sure," I replied, unsure where this was going because he sounded very serious… not something my brother does very often. He is more comfortable joking around or not saying anything at all.

"What medication are you on?" he asked.

I was taken aback, "What? What do you mean?"

"What medication are you taking for depression?"

"I am not taking any medication, what makes you say that?" I stumbled in my reply. My brother knew I had issues with depression occasionally, but we had not talked about it in years.

"Oh," he said, very confused. "You are just so happy. I thought you were taking something because you have not been this happy in a very long time."

I thought about this. I knew it was true, I just didn't know that anyone else had noticed. Leave it to my brother to have seen it and not said anything.

"You know, you are right. I am happy. It's because I finally realized that I can be me and if someone doesn't like that, I don't need them in my life. I deserve to be happy and have the things that I want in life."

"Hmm," was all he said and he continued driving while I returned to staring out the window. I could see my smile in the reflection and I thought it was one of the best sights I had seen in a very long time.

That was the beginning of me becoming the person I am today. There have been bumps in the road along the way, but they get fewer and farther in between. I'm still learning and I am confident that will continue until i die. I am still very introverted but I am sure that most people who have met me would dispute that fact. I stick up for myself these days and I speak my mind, honestly and directly. I don't mince words but I am not trying to make people feel awkward or bad, I am just trying to treat them as I wish to be treated. Believe me, there are plenty of things I don't say and that is to keep the peace if my input is not going to make a difference. I am an advocate when I feel like I need to be one and I am quiet when I feel like the issue is better served by my silence. I don't have a ton of friend, but if I count someone among them, I am often loyal to a fault. Many times people don't want to hear the truth, but you better believe if I am giving it to you, I care about you.

I am a firm advocate that people **can** change because I have done it. It isn't easy and it definitely takes a strong will. The first step is realizing the problem and that requires a whole lot of self reflection. People might not like what they see and wish to hide it. Change is an uphill battle that often has setbacks and it takes perseverance to get to the top. You have to want to change for the right reasons and I can tell you from experience—a significant other is not the right reason. In fact, they are the very last reason you should have for changing who you are or who you want to be. If you ever question the value of change, I am proof that it is very much worth it in the end. So yes, I have a reputation but I am so much happier being me with a reputation than being the meek girl turned mousy woman.

An Interview with Amber Rainey

When did you start writing and why?

I started writing when I was about ten years old. I wrote because it was the only way I could escape a less than stellar childhood. I was an avid reader and I loved escaping into books and novels but writing was my way of dealing with my childhood and the things I was not confident in telling any other person. I was very shy but always had a very active imagination. I am forever creating stories in my head and now that I get to tell them, it seems more are knocking around my brain than ever before so I have been trying to write them all out as quickly as possible. In writing, I can give myself confidence where I did not have it. I can make my characters be the people I wanted to be and that helped me a lot.

Which authors or books influenced you the most as a writer?

I don't feel like I am influenced as a writer much. I probably am and I don't recognize it. I am very cerebral when it comes to books, I experience them in my head when I am awake and dream about the characters when I am asleep. I try to solve their problems and I wish I could talk to them and make them understand what I see in them. It is the same for me with anything creative. I tend to process what I have read over and over again until my mind is satisfied with the outcome. I joined a group once to get constructive criticism on some stories I wrote but I ended up being more stressed and upset than if I just write what I want and edit it myself. I get very attached to my characters and they have lives outside of my stories so it is hard to see them impugned—for better or worse.

Which authors or books had the biggest impact on you as a person?

It is so hard to answer this question because I don't know if there are any that really haven't impacted me in some way. I read both fiction and non-fiction. I have to balance out the realities of the world with fictional worlds where the good guys always win. I absolutely adore books by Malcolm Gladwell because I agree with a lot of his conclusions and I am constantly recommending these books to people. I feel like his books really help people understand why humans interact with the world the way they do. Secondly, I have always been a person who has handled emergencies well and the book *The Unthinkable: Who Survives When Disaster Strikes—and Why* really gave me insight into why I am able to cope so well when others around me are running around like chickens with their heads cut off. As for fiction, I think there is only one book I have ever read that I didn't finish and I think I would start a war if I mentioned the name of the book because it is very much revered in the world of writing. I love good fiction. The biggest book that impacted me as a person was *The Grapes of Wrath*. I might be in the minority but I absolutely despised that book. I was forced to read it and do a book review on it in high school, which helped me the next year in literary criticism, but I will never get back the time I spent reading one hundred pages describing dust. John Steinbeck was a good writer but *Of Mice and Men* is something I would recommend more, even with the very sad ending. I was reminded I never wanted to bore a reader with so much description that it became a chore to read.

Which of your original twelve Prompt stories are you most pleased with?

A Different Holiday was the story I was most pleased with for several reasons. First, I feel like it was my best story because I feel like I improved in my storytelling over the course of the year. Having a deadline of one story a month really pushed me to explore what it meant for me to be a writer and what kind of stories I wanted to tell. Second, I feel like my characters are braver than I am and I want that bravery in my real life. I am bisexual but have never come out to my family. My husband, son, and friends know but my actual brother and mother do not know. I feel a bit of sadness because the grandmother I was closest to never got to know all of the real me before she died. So, in that way, I was able to tell the story of someone who could be brave and live with those consequences even when it pained him to do so. Finally, I felt some relief that the whole project was successfully completed. I'd never written so much in one year for someone else's consumption. It gave me more confidence in myself as a writer.

Which of your original twelve Prompt stories did you find the most difficult to write?

The Last Broadcast was the most difficult to write. Last summer, our lives were completely upended. In the process of making a cross-country move, my husband's mother passed away. A week later, my grandmother and my rock passed away. She was the only person in my family that loved me for me in my formative years. We had several houses fall through and we were on a deadline because my father-in-law had Alzheimer's and was suddenly moving in with us. On top of that, we had to deal with our move and his move all within the same week and I ended up very sick. It was a completely hectic month. I feel like the story was me saying goodbye to my grandmother and trying to find peace in the chaos of my life. I cried several times and I stressed over deadlines. I had the story in my head but I couldn't get it to come out properly. I wasn't ready to say goodbye to her and I think that came across in my writing. I have since been able to write a story that I feel gives her a proper sendoff and it will be published next year.

What book on writing do you recommend?

Do y'all have some suggestions? Honestly, I have never read any books on writing. I have read books on other creative endeavors I do, like acting, but I am a very visual learner and a very visual person so reading about how to do something isn't very helpful to me. I can gather some reference points but I "learn on the job". I tend to write everything I am going to type out in my head before I ever sit in front of a computer. I have full novels and stories in my head that are not yet published because I have not taken the time to sit and actually commit them to a form someone can read. This process makes it look like I am turning in rough drafts when, in reality, I have gone through four or five drafts, at least, all in my head. I don't sleep a lot when I am actively writing a story and I could probably get a lot more if I would take the time to put what I have down on paper, but I feel like I am *living* with the characters if I keep them with me in my head.

What advice would you give an unpublished writer?

I will tell you what a very dear friend and mentor of mine once told me. *Never throw anything you write away!* I threw everything I ever wrote away from the time I was ten until 2014. There was so much potential thrown into the trash can or deleted that I will never get back. Even if no one had ever read any of that lost work, it could have helped me to see how far I have come. Another piece of advice—don't pay a press to publish your work. Vanity presses are not worth it and they don't really care about you as an author. Either find someone who believes in your work or self-publish and market yourself. I am not great at the marketing part but if you are social media savvy you can really build a brand and get your name out there. Patience is key in this business. Finally, I would say don't write hoping you will make millions of dollars. The realities of how much an author makes might get you down, but if you have stories to tell, tell them. Don't let anyone tell you what you can do.

Do you have a "dream project" as a writer? What would it be?

Of course, I would love to write the next great American novel. I would love to write something that speaks to people the way books have always spoken to me. However, I have many passions and writing is a secondary passion for me so, for now, I just write the stories I want to tell and not worry about how they will be perceived by others. I am lucky to have friends that like the things I write and if none but a few ever read it, well then I will be happy knowing I was able to entertain those few people. My writing comes from who I am, who I was, and who I want to be and that is enough for me.

The original twelve Prompt stories were written in 2019. In 2020 we all experienced a global pandemic. Did the pandemic impact your writing? How?

Well, for one thing, it got me to get off my keister and finish editing my second novel. It took me several months of quarantine to talk myself into it but I was finally done doing absolutely everything else that would keep me from editing. It is very hard for me to do second round editing because I have to get back into a world and a mood to be able to find my character's voices again. I also worry that I am tapped out. It happens every single time but I still have stories swirling around and new ones cropping up, so I assume I haven't peaked in my writing career yet. I am very excited that the second novel is finished and it grew by so much that even I was amazed.

I was also able to write another three stories for an anthology and one of those stories deals, somewhat, with the pandemic in a fictional world. I think it is a little too soon for the pandemic to completely affect my writing because I am still in the middle of it. I am still staying safe at home as much as possible and missing my old "normal" life.

Do I think it will affect my stories? Absolutely, one day it will definitely affect them. Everything that has happened in my life affects my stories and I put a lot of me into some of the characters so I know that my quarantine life will stick in there somewhere. My stories are just starting to reflect things that happened to me four or five years ago so I assume in the next ten years or so, my stories will be affected by the pandemic.

www.ingramcontent.com/pod-product-compliance
Lightning Source LLC
Chambersburg PA
CBHW070202310726
48976CB00001B/184